P9-ELQ-089

"A gorgeously frothy, romantic confection of a book, with a sprinkling of magic and charm. Sweet, tender, and huge fun."
—JANE GREEN, *New York Times* bestselling author of *Tempting Fate*

"Sweet and intense, with delightful magical accents, a delectable romance, and yummy recipes."
— *Kirkus Reviews*

"A tantalizing mix of romance, wit, and family secrets."
— *Booklist*

"A love letter to family and food. It is pure delight and will charm readers."
— *The Parkersburg News and Sentinel*

"An enchanting, witty, and wholly satisfying mix of food, magic, romance, and self-discovery."
— NPR.ORG

Praise for *The Glass Kitchen*

"Linda Francis Lee's *The Glass Kitchen* is a novel about sisters and second chances, in which the possibility of magic is in the air like the aroma of a home-cooked meal. Heartwarming and filled with unforgettable characters, *The Glass Kitchen* is a wonderful place to spend your time; a page-turning story that will leave you deeply satisfied."

—Jen Lancaster, *New York Times*
bestselling author of *Here I Go Again*

"*The Glass Kitchen* is an enchanting novel filled to the brim with irresistible characters, a stirring romance, and just a pinch of magic. Texas charm mixes beautifully with the New York City setting in this story about family, food, and moving on. Sweet and sexy, this captivating story will leave you with a smile on your face and a definite belief in the magic of possibilities."

—Karen White, *New York Times*
bestselling author of *A Long Time Gone*

"*The Glass Kitchen* is a captivating, original novel with characters so finely drawn and three-dimensional, you'll feel as if you've known them your whole life. I really loved this book."

—Sarah Pekkanen,
bestselling author of *The Best of Us*

"How I loved this enchanting novel about discovering—and accepting—who you truly are. One to share with friends, sisters, and book clubs."

—Melissa Senate, bestselling author of
The Love Goddess' Cooking School

"This is beautiful, heartfelt, and delicious storytelling at its best."

—Sarah Jio, *New York Times* bestselling author of
The Violets of March and *Morning Glory*

"A captivating tale of sisters who believe they can escape their past by moving to Manhattan, only to infuse the city with a perfect taste of Texas."   —Randy Susan Meyers, bestselling
author of *The Comfort of Lies*

"The ingredients are right for a pleasant read in *The Glass Kitchen*. Linda Francis Lee lightly mixes cooking, romance, family, and a little magic into a winning blend. . . . *The Glass Kitchen* is filled with light and love. It's a delicious novel about self-discovery and fulfilling destiny."
                                                                —Examiner.com

"This latest by the author of *Emily & Einstein* could be Lee's best, most magical book yet. There's nothing at all far-fetched about this sweet, charming novel in which a woman does her best to resist love by throwing herself into her true life passion, which is cooking. Romantics at heart will absolutely love the chemistry and sparks that fly between Portia and Gabriel, as well as appreciate the brilliant and realistic voice of twelve-year-old Ariel. Readers and foodies alike may be rushing to the grocery store after reading this one."   —*RT Book Reviews* (4 ½ stars)

The Glass Kitchen

❖

Also by Linda Francis Lee

⁘

Emily & Einstein

The Ex-Debutante

The Devil in the Junior League

Simply Sexy

Sinfully Sexy

Suddenly Sexy

The Wedding Diaries

Looking for Lacey

The Ways of Grace

Nightingale's Gate

Swan's Grace

Dove's Way

Crimson Lace

Emerald Rain

Blue Waltz

The Glass Kitchen

Linda Francis Lee

St. Martin's Griffin
New York

This is a work of fiction. All of the characters, organizations, and events portrayed in this novel are either products of the author's imagination or are used fictitiously.

THE GLASS KITCHEN. Copyright © 2014 by Linda Francis Lee. All rights reserved. Printed in the United States of America. For information, address St. Martin's Press, 175 Fifth Avenue, New York, N.Y. 10010.

www.stmartins.com

Designed by Kathryn Parise

THE LIBRARY OF CONGRESS HAS CATALOGED THE HARDCOVER
EDITION AS FOLLOWS:

Lee, Linda Francis.
   The Glass Kitchen / Linda Francis Lee. — First edition.
      p. cm.
   ISBN 978-0-312-38227-8 (hardcover)
   ISBN 978-1-4668-5061-3 (e-book)
   1. Divorced women—Fiction.   2. Women cooks—Fiction.
3. Clairvoyance—Fiction.   4. Cooking—Psychological aspects.
5. Widowers—Fiction.   6. Manhattan (New York, N.Y.)—Fiction.
7. Texas—Fiction.   I. Title.
   PS3612.E225G53 2014
   813'.6—dc23

                                            2014000125

ISBN 978-1-250-04963-6 (trade paperback)

St. Martin's Griffin books may be purchased for educational, business, or promotional use. For information on bulk purchases, please contact the Macmillan Corporate and Premium Sales Department at 1-800-221-7945, extension 5442, or write to specialmarkets@macmillan.com.

First St. Martin's Griffin Edition: May 2015

10 9 8 7 6 5 4

Acknowledgments

❖

W HAT WOULD I HAVE DONE without great friends and family who helped in so many ways while I wrote this book? To all of them, I raise a glass in thanks.

Amelia Grey, Lisa Kleypas, M. J. Rose, Sarah MacLean, Alana Sanko, Jill and Regi Brack, Julie Blattberg, Lisa Chambers, and Liz Brack—good friends who were always ready with book talk and/or impromptu dinners.

Stella Brack and Anna Vettori—for a peek into today's Manhattan school world.

Joseph Bell, Peter Longo, Kevin Lynch, and Ron Smith—for lovely, long meals filled with amazing food and laughter. To Peter, for The Explorers Club, and Kevin, who who should have been a knight. To Joe, for teaching me the magic of ices. And it's hard to quantify how many times Ron saved one of my recipes.

Alessandro Vettori and his beautiful wife, Mary—for family dinners and elegant parties.

Jennifer Enderlin—a writer's dream, editor extraordinaire—for believing in this book and going above and beyond to make it the best it could be.

The amazing team at St. Martin's Press, who cares a great deal about books, most especially Sally Richardson, the late and greatly missed Matthew Shear, Lisa Senz, Alison Lazarus, John Murphy, John Karle, Dori Weintraub, and Jeff Dodes.

Carilyn Francis Johnson—for being the best sister, amazing best friend, and, as much as it pains me to admit it, still the best cook in the family.

And to Michael, as always, who is there during my cooking triumphs, but more important—given my predilection for adventures in the kitchen—is there to step in during my cooking catastrophes, ready to roll up his sleeves and help, or . . . eat whatever I put in front of him, with a smile on his face. What is that if not true love?

Cheers!

First Course

❖

Appetizer

Chile Cheese and Bacon-Stuffed
Cherry Tomatoes

One

❖

On THE MORNING her sister went missing, Portia Cuthcart woke up to thoughts of blueberries and peaches.

The taste of fruit filled her mouth, so sweet, so real, as if she'd been eating in her dreams. With a groggy yawn, she scooted out of bed. She pulled on her favorite fluffy slippers and big-girl's robe, then shuffled into the tiny kitchen of the double-wide trailer on the outskirts of Willow Creek, Texas. Without thinking about what she was doing, she pulled blueberries from the icebox and peaches from the fruit bin.

She might have been only seven years old, but she was smart enough to know that her mother would have a fit if she pulled out knives, or did anything near the two-burner hot plate. Instead, Portia pulled the peaches apart, catching the sticky-sweet juice on her tongue as it ran down her fingers. She found a slice of angel food cake wrapped in plastic and plopped the fruit on top.

Just as she stood back, satisfied with what she had made, her parents tumbled into the trailer like apples poured out of a bushel basket, disorderly, frantic.

Portia's oldest sister, Cordelia, followed. "Olivia's missing," Cordelia stated with all the jaundiced arrogance of a thirteen-year-old convinced she had the answers to everyone's ills. "Disappeared," she clarified with a snap of her fingers, "just like that."

Portia knitted her brow, her hair a cloud of whipped-butter curls dancing around her face. Olivia was always in trouble, but she usually did bad stuff right in front of their eyes. "Nobody disappears just like that, Cordie. You're exaggerating."

Her mother didn't seem to hear. Mama stared at the fruit and cake.

"Don't be mad," Portia blurted. "I didn't use any knives."

Her mother dropped to her knees in front of Portia. "Peaches and blueberries. Olivia's favorites. Why did you make this?"

Portia blinked, pushing a curl out of her eye. "I don't know. I woke up thinking about them."

For a second, her mother looked stricken; then she pressed her lips together. "Earl," she said, turning to Daddy, "Olivia's down by the far horse pasture, near the peach tree and blueberry patch."

Her parents' eyes met before they glanced back at Portia. Then her mother stood and pushed Daddy out the door. Even though the emergency was over, Mama's face was still tense, her eyes dark.

Twenty minutes later, the missing eleven-year-old Olivia pranced up the three metal steps of the trailer in front of Daddy, her lips stained with blueberries, her dress splotched with peach juice, flowers tangled in her hair.

It was the first time food gave Portia an answer before a question had been asked.

Not an hour after Olivia was found, Portia and her mother were in the family's ancient pickup truck, bumping along the dirt roads of backwater Texas until they came to her grandmother's café, a place that had been handed down through generations of Gram's ancestors. The Glass Kitchen. Portia loved how its whitewashed clapboard walls and green tin roof, giant yawning windows, and lattice entwined with purple wisteria made her think of doll houses and thatch-roofed cottages.

Excited to see Gram, Portia jumped out of the old truck and followed her mother in through the front door. The melting-brown-sugar and buttery-cinnamon smells reminded her that The Glass Kitchen was not for play. It was real, a place where people came from miles around to eat and talk with Portia's grandmother.

Portia smiled at all the regulars, but her mother didn't seem to notice anyone, which was odd because Mama always used her best company manners wherever they went. But today she walked straight toward Gram, who sat at her usual table off to the side. Gram always sat in the same place, watching the goings-on, doling out advice, and making food recommendations for all those who asked. And everyone asked. Portia had a faint memory of a time when Gram actually did the cooking, but now she left it to others, to hired help who stayed hidden behind swinging doors.

"She has it," was all Mama said.

Gram sat back, the sun streaming through the windows, catching in the long gray hair she pulled back in a simple braid. "I suspected as much."

Portia didn't understand what was happening, then was surprised when Gram turned to her and beckoned her close. "You have a gift, Portia. A *knowing*, just like me, just like generations of your ancestors. Now it's my job to teach you how to use it."

Mama pressed her eyes closed, steepling her hands in front of her face.

Despite her mama's frown, Portia was excited about this knowing thing. It made her feel special, chosen, and as each day passed, she began to walk around with a new sense of purpose, pulling apart more peaches and making creations in a way that set her older sisters' teeth on edge. Cordelia and Olivia weren't nearly as happy about the special gift Portia supposedly had.

But four months later, the thick Texas air was sucked dry when the girls' daddy was shot dead in a hunting accident. Four months after that, their mama died, too. The official report cited cause of death as severe cardiac arrhythmia, but everyone in town said she'd died of a broken heart.

Stunned and silenced, Portia and her sisters moved in with Gram above the restaurant. Cordelia found comfort in books, Olivia in flowers. Portia found comfort when Gram started bringing her into the kitchen in earnest. But strangely, Gram didn't mention one thing about the knowing, much less teach her anything about it. Mostly Gram taught her the simple mechanics of cooking and baking.

Still, that worked. The Glass Kitchen was known to heal people with its slow-cooked meals and layered confections, and it healed Portia, too. Gradually, like sugar brought to a slow boil, Portia began to ease out of a brittle state and find a place for herself among the painted-wood tables and pitted silverware in a way Cordelia and Olivia never did.

And then it began to happen in earnest, like the dream of peaches and blueberries, but more real, more frequent.

Without a single one of those promised lessons from her grandmother, Portia began to see and taste food without having it in front of her, the images coming to her like instincts, automatic and without thought. She found that she knew things without having to be taught. Rich dark chocolate would calm a person who was hiding their anxiety. Hot red chili mixed with eggs first thing in the morning relieved symptoms of someone about to succumb to a terrible cold. Suddenly her world made sense, as if she had found a hidden switch, the meaning of what she was supposed to do blazing to life like a Christmas tree lighting up in a burst of color.

During that first school year, and the ones that followed, without her parents, Portia spent her days studying and her nights and weekends in the kitchen. During the summers, Portia and her sisters traveled to New York City to stay with Gram's sister. Great-aunt Evie had moved away forty years earlier, escaping a prescribed life that boxed her in. Once in New York, Evie became an actress on Broadway, famous enough to buy a town house on the Upper West Side.

"This place will be yours one day," Evie told the girls.

All three sisters loved the old town house that rose up from the city sidewalk like a five-layer wedding cake decorated with perfect fondant icing. Cordelia and Olivia promised each other that as soon as they could, they would move to New York City for good. Portia didn't believe for a second that either of them would do it.

But ten years after their parents' deaths, three years after Cordelia married, Portia woke up knowing she had to bake a five-layer cake with perfect fondant icing. Once the cake was finished, Portia stood back, her heart twisting, and knew Cordelia was leaving Texas. No one was surprised when Olivia followed her to New York six months later.

Portia missed her sisters, but her days were full. She became the main cook at The Glass Kitchen while Gram sat out front doling out advice and food choices. And still no lessons on the knowing.

One day Portia whipped up a mixed-up mess of sweet potatoes and asparagus, two items that never went together. But somehow, the way she made it, had people ordering more. Just as she served up the last portion, in walked the young lawyer and up-and-coming Texas state senator Robert Baleau, and her world shifted. Despite being born and raised in Willow Creek, he was as foreign to Portia as if he'd moved there from Greece. He was from the opposite side of town, from a world of debutante balls and heirloom pearls. With his sandy blond hair and laughing blue eyes, he charmed her, moved her with his devotion to serving the people, not to mention her.

Soon he began taking her with him as he traveled around the county to political functions. People all over the region loved Portia and said that she made a pretty boy more real. All she cared about was that she adored Robert.

The day he proposed, she threw her arms around him before she could think twice. "Yes, yes, yes!" she said as he laughed and twirled her around.

Surprisingly, Robert's wealthy parents approved. It was Gram who didn't.

"They'll hurt you," Gram said, scowling. "You're not part of their world, and you never will be."

But with every day that passed, more and more of Robert's world embraced Portia Cuthcart, the girl who grew up in a double-wide—even if the fancier people weren't particularly comfortable talking about The Glass Kitchen or the legendary Gram.

As the wedding grew near, another shift began, as slow as thyme breaking through the earth in spring. Robert began to notice that Portia knew things. At first, he laughed them off. But soon he began to tense every time she knew she needed to bake or cook something—like his mother's favorite lemon bars just before she invited Portia over for tea. Or tuna casserole in a tinfoil pan, the kind perfect for freezing and giving to someone in need—just before a neighbor's wife died.

One morning Portia woke knowing she had to make long, thick strands of pulled taffy that she wove into thin lengths of rope. Robert walked into the kitchen and came to a surprised stop when he saw the braided candy spread across the kitchen counter along with everything else she had known she needed. "This is unnatural," he said quietly.

Confused, Portia blinked. "What's unnatural about whipped cream, Saran Wrap, and ropes of taffy?"

She was almost certain Robert blushed and looked uncomfortable. "Portia, sweet, normal women don't know things that other people are thinking."

"My grandmother knows." Portia kept her hands moving, twisting the taffy before it could stiffen.

"I rest my case. If anyone isn't normal, it's your grandmother."

Her hands stilled. "Robert. There is nothing wrong with Gram. And there is nothing wrong with me."

He blinked, then blurted, "You're telling me that after I had sexual thoughts this afternoon, and you went out and put together the very things I fantasized about, that that's normal?"

As soon as the words were out of his mouth, his eyes widened. Portia was shocked, too, but then she laughed. "You were fantasizing about me? Me and ropes of taffy and whipped cream?"

She let her laughter turn into a sexy smile; then she wiped her hands and walked over to him. For half a second, the good Christian politician started to succumb, but then he took her hands and gave them a reassuring little squeeze, placing them against his heart. "I want to marry you, Portia. But I need you to be like other women. I need you to . . . not bake pies before the church announces a bake sale. I need you to be *normal*. Can you do that for me?"

Portia was stunned into silence.

Robert kissed her on the brow and refused to discuss it any further. She knew to his mind it was a simple yes-or-no question.

Since it was Monday, The Glass Kitchen was closed. As soon as Robert left, Portia went in search of her grandmother, needing to talk. Something had been off with Gram recently. Great-aunt Evie had died only a month before, leaving the town house to the girls. They all missed her, but with Gram it was as if a piece of her had died along with her sister.

Portia walked into the kitchen and realized that Gram wasn't there in the same second that another bout of knowing buckled her over at the waist.

Heart pounding, she started to prepare the meal that hit her so hard. Her famous cherry tomatoes stuffed with chile, cheese, and bacon, along with pulled pork, endive slaw, and potato pancakes with homemade catsup. She cooked, knowing she could do nothing else, though she was surprised when she realized she needed to set the table for only one.

Gram must have gone out for the day without telling her. But ten minutes after Portia sat down to eat, Gram walked into the kitchen from the back parking lot. At the sight of the meal and single place setting, Gram had to steady herself on the counter's edge.

Portia leaped up and started gathering another plate and silverware.

"No need," Gram said, setting her handbag down, then headed out of the kitchen.

Portia raced after her, but at the doorway to her grandmother's bed-room, Gram turned and pressed her dry hand to Portia's cheek. "It's time. I should have known you'd learn the knowing whether I taught you or not."

"What are you talking about?"

Gram smiled then, a resigned smile. But she didn't answer. She shut the bedroom door.

Portia returned to the kitchen and paced, hating that she didn't know what the meal meant. An eerie sense of dread rushed through her. She decided that if Gram wanted to go somewhere, she wouldn't let her take the car. She wouldn't allow her near the stove or the knives. She would keep her safe from whatever might be coming, anything that could have been predicted by the single place setting.

It was summer and hot, the painfully blue afternoon sky parched by heat and humidity. Gram didn't return to the kitchen until nearly four o'clock.

Portia jumped and ran across the hard-tile floor. "What's wrong?"

"It's time for you to take over The Glass Kitchen for good."

"What? No!"

Portia kept trying to solve whatever was wrong. But that ended when Gram stepped around her and headed for the back door of The Glass Kitchen.

"Where are you going?"

Gram didn't retrieve her handbag or keys. There was nothing Portia could take away to keep her from leaving.

"Gram, you can't leave!"

Gram didn't listen. She walked out the door, Portia following, plead-ing, "Gram, where are you going?"

But what Portia hadn't expected was that her grandmother would stop abruptly underneath the suddenly stormy Texas sky and raise her hands high. Lightning came down like the crack of God's hand, quick and reaching, striking Gram.

Shock, along with electricity, surged through Portia, knocking her off her feet like a rag doll thrown to the dirt by an angry child. Her blouse ripped at the shoulder, blood marking the white material like a brand.

The rest was a blur—people hurrying to them, the ambulance screaming into the yard. What stood out was that Portia knew she was responsible. If only she hadn't cooked the meal. If only she had set the table for two instead of one. If only she hadn't allowed her grandmother to walk out the door. If only she had never had even a glimpse of the knowing.

But *if onlys* didn't change anything. Gram was gone, all because of a meal Portia hadn't even begun to understand but had prepared.

Standing in the dirt lot, The Glass Kitchen behind her, Portia promised herself she wouldn't cook again.

A month later, she married Robert, then began shaping herself into the perfect Texas politician's wife, erasing everything she could of herself until she was a blank slate of polite smiles and innocuous conversation. She slammed the lid shut on the knowing.

And became normal.

Second Course

❖

Soup

Crab and Sweet Corn Chowder

Two

⋰⋱

T HE SOUND OF TRAFFIC woke Portia.

Minutes ticked by before she realized where she was. New York City, on the Upper West Side, in the garden apartment of Great-aunt Evie's old town house, three years after her wedding, a month after her divorce from Robert Baleau.

Portia rolled over, covering her head with the pillow.

For the last three years, she had closed the door on visions of food until she had practically forgotten her unnerving ability was there. She'd worked hard to be like everyone else.

To be normal.

She groaned into the pillow. The only way she could be called normal was if normal meant stupid, not to mention naive. Why hadn't she realized that her husband didn't want her anymore? Why hadn't she figured out that the only real reason he wanted her at all was to make him seem more appealing to voters? More than that, why hadn't she known he would be so callous in getting rid of her after he'd come home and told her he wanted a divorce?

Not long after Robert had secured his place in politics, the supposedly good Christian politican developed a wandering eye, or maybe just gave in to it. Naturally, she had been the last to hear the whispers. But what she definitely hadn't heard until after the divorce papers were set in front of her was that the real reason he needed a divorce was because he had gotten one of his aides pregnant.

When the surprisingly quick divorce came through, she had fled Texas in a storm of devastation and betrayal, finding herself shipwrecked on the island of Manhattan, with nothing more than the two hastily packed suitcases and her grandmother's cherished Glass Kitchen cookbooks— thrown in even though she didn't want them.

Rolling back over, she tossed the pillow aside. She had arrived in New York City a month ago, but she had been in Great-aunt Evie's town house only since late last night, using an old key she had kept on her key chain. Before Evie had died, she had divided the town house up into three apartments, two of which she had rented out for income. Upon her death, one apartment had gone to each of the sisters.

Cordelia and Olivia had sold their floors. Before the divorce, Robert had wanted to sell her floor, too, with the garden out back, but she had never signed the contract. Thank God. While she was having a hard time imagining herself living in New York City, she wasn't crazy. Staying in Texas, where Robert and his pregnant new wife had already started to rule her world, was an awful thought. Here in New York, she had some-thing of her own. Everything was going as well as could be expected, given that her bank account was nearly as bare as Great-aunt Evie's kitchen cupboards.

The early morning air in New York was far cooler than it would have been in Texas, especially in the ancient bathroom, where the windows barely shut out the chilly gusts. Portia braced her hands on the old-fashioned sink, looked at herself in the mirror. Her eyes were still a deep violet blue, but the circles beneath them hinted at the stress that kept her awake at night. A year ago, she'd had sensibly cut, shoulder-length blond hair—perfect for a Texas politician's wife—tamed by a blow-dryer, hair spray, and a velvet headband. She scoffed. She'd been a cliché of big hair, sure, but what was she now? An even bigger cliché of the wronged wife kicked out of her own bed by her husband and the ex–best friend whom she herself had convinced Robert to hire as an aide. As her life spiraled out of control, so had her hair, growing and curling as it had when she was a child.

She turned on the old-fashioned spigot, the pipes clanging before spitting out a gush of water that she splashed on her face. Then she froze when her head filled with images of cake, thick swirls of buttercream frosting between chocolate layers. Her breath caught, her fingers curling around the sink edge. It had been three whole years since she'd been hit by images of food. But she knew the images were real—or would be if she allowed the *knowing* to take over.

She shook her head hard. She was normal now. The knowing was in the past. She hadn't done so much as toast a slice of bread in the last three years.

But the feeling wouldn't leave her alone, and with a groan she realized that the knowing was back, as if her move to New York, to this town house, had chiseled away every inch of normalcy she had cobbled together.

The images swirled through her. She needed to bake. Cake. A layered chocolate cake. With vanilla buttercream frosting.

The images were as clear as four-color photos from a coffee table book on baking. She could taste the mix of vanilla, butter, and cream whipped into a sugar frosting as if she had spooned it into her mouth. The chocolate smelled so real that a chill of awareness ran along her skin, pooling in her fingertips. She itched to bake.

But the last thing she needed in her life right now was to contend with something else she couldn't control.

She fought harder, but another bit of knowing hit. It wasn't just baking. She needed to cook, too. A roast.

She pressed one of her great-aunt's threadbare white towels to her face, resisting the urge. She had devoted the last three years to being the perfect wife. She had let her grandmother's Glass Kitchen go, closing the doors for good and selling the property for next to nothing to a developer who only wanted the land, splitting the money with her sisters. Her job had been to be at her husband's side at any function. Given that she had signed a prenuptial agreement, and with the meager settlement Robert had yet to pay her, she barely had two pennies to rub together. The last thing she needed to do was to waste money preparing a big meal. But the need wouldn't let go, and with a shudder gasp she gave in completely, the last of her crumbling walls coming down. Flowers, she realized. She needed flowers, too.

The knowing was rusty, coming at her in fits and starts, much like the water sluicing unevenly out of the faucet. Groaning, Portia dressed in jeans instead of a conservative skirt, and a big sweater instead of a silk blouse. She found flowered Keds in her great-aunt's closet, which she dusted off to wear rather than sensible heels. She wasn't Mrs. Robert Baleau anymore. She was Portia Cuthcart again, having taken back her maiden name.

The goal, her grandmother always said in the few times she actually said anything about the knowing, was to give in to the simple act of doing and have faith that eventually everything would make sense.

"Great," Portia muttered.

Once dressed, she went to her still-packed suitcases. A tiny bead of sweat broke out on her forehead when her fingers brushed against the spine of a Glass Kitchen cookbook. The handmade books had been passed down just as the knowing had, though just as with lessons on the knowing, Gram had never shared the books, either. Portia never knew they existed until after her grandmother's death.

Now she cracked the spine on the first of three volumes, her pulse beating in her temples. She recognized Gram's writing, notes scribbled between the crudely typed lines, new details learned and added, old ingredients scratched out. She turned the pages, her breath high in her chest, short bursts. Each generation of Cuthcart women had written in the margins, filling in newly learned wisdom along with the recipes. But even the recipes held gems of magic.

For perfectly boiled water, let it jump with enthusiasm, but not so energetically that it becomes exhausted, tiring the food it will boil.

And:

Never prepare a meal in anger, for the end result will fill the recipients with bile.

An hour later, when she came to the end of the volume, Portia jerked up, the book falling to the ground. Enough!

She scrambled out of the apartment, the cool morning air hitting her like a gasp of relief. With the Keds dangling in her fingers, she just stood there for a second, breathing, in, out, before she finally sat down to pull on the flowered sneakers.

She had just finished tying the last shoelace when she saw him.

He was tall, lean, with broad shoulders, dark brown hair. He looked primal, with a firm jaw and hard brow, walking toward her with a fluidity that seemed physically impossible, given his size. He had none of Robert's pretty-boy good looks, and there didn't seem to be anything practiced or politically correct about him. From the look of him, she imagined he was one of those New York businessmen she had heard about who traded stocks like third-world countries trade rulers, easily and ruthlessly.

Of course he wasn't dressed like a businessman. He wore a black T-shirt, long athletic shorts, and sweat-slicked hair. He had the smooth, tight muscles of someone who was athletic but didn't spend his days as an athlete. It wasn't hard to imagine him showering and then heading out of this tree-lined neighborhood on his way to some glass-and-steel office building in the concrete jungle of Midtown Manhattan.

She knew the minute he saw her, the way his eyes narrowed as if trying to understand something. She felt the same thing, as if she knew him, or should.

Images of food rushed through her head, surprising her. Fried chicken. Sweet jalapeño mustard. Mashed potatoes. Biscuits. And a pie. Big and sweet, strawberries with whipped cream—so Texan, so opposite this fierce New Yorker.

Good news or bad? she wondered before she could stop herself.

"No, no, no," she whispered. The images of food meant nothing at all. She wanted nothing to do with him, with any guy, at this point in her life. And she definitely didn't want anything to do with the kind she felt certain wielded power like a club. Robert charmed his way into control, but she knew on sight that this man would take it by force.

When he reached the steps, he stopped, looking at her with an intensity that felt both assessing and oddly possessive. It might have been an hour, or a second; no smile, no awkwardness, and her breathing settled low. She became acutely aware of herself, and him. Everything about this man pulled her in, which was ridiculous. He could be a serial killer. He could be demented, insane. With a body like that, he probably didn't eat sugar. A deal killer, for sure.

His head cocked to the side. "Do I know you?"

Portia smiled—she was Texan, after all, and had learned manners at a young age, even if it was out of a library book her mother "accidentally" forgot to return—and his expression turned to something deeper, richer like a salted hot fudge.

"No," she answered, the word nearly sticking in her throat. "Should you?"

Desire had caused the storm that left her shipwrecked in Manhattan—the desire her husband felt for another woman. But there had been her own desire, too, the desire for intensity and excitement in her own life, which she had suppressed when she married Robert. Sitting there, she felt that desire stir inside her like the first bubble rising in a pot of caramelizing sugar.

"I guess not," he said. "But you seem familiar." He put his foot on the bottom step, his hand on the railing, bringing him into her space with a confidence likely born of always getting what he wanted. "Do you run in the park?"

She glanced down at her flowered sneakers and wrinkled her nose.

"Okay, so I haven't seen you running," he said, his voice still rich and creamy but sliding into humor. Peppermint, she thought, the corner of his mouth hitching at one corner.

Portia laughed outright with the sort of ease she hadn't felt in months. Somehow this man who looked like he knew his way around darkness had chased hers away. "You don't approve of my shoes?"

"Is that what those are?" His lips hitched higher, a curl of his slowly drying hair falling forward and making him look more approachable.

"What are you, the fashion police?"

That caught him off guard. "Me? Hardly."

Portia stood up, skipped down, and stopped. Two steps still separated them, but given the difference in height, they stood nearly face-to-face. His laughter fled, and his eyes narrowed as he looked at her mouth. Her breathing slowed, and everything around her disappeared. She could make out the sparks of cognac in what she had thought were solid brown eyes. His nose was large, but somehow went perfectly with his strong face and jaw. His mouth was full, sensual. No one would call this man pretty, but something about the way his features came together drew her in. She felt a need, an urge to reach out, touch him. Which was crazy.

A truck turned the corner, hitting a crack in the asphalt with a loud bang, and she blinked. The man straightened.

Portia glanced around, took in the back side of the Dakota apartment building with its Gothic façade, antiquated moat, and wrought-iron balustrade around the perimeter, as if everything in her world hadn't shifted at the sight of this man.

He straightened abruptly, that sense of control settling back around him. "Can I help you with something?"

"No. No. I was just tying my shoelaces."

"Ah, then, fine."

He started up the stairs. She went stiff.

He stopped and raised his hands. "I live here."

"You live here? As in, you live in this place? Right here?"

His brow furrowed. "Yes."

This was her upstairs neighbor. More specifically, this was Gabriel Kane, the owner of the rest of the town house, the man she—or rather, Robert—had agreed to sell her apartment to before she refused at the last minute.

"Then these are your steps. Wow! Great place," Portia managed inanely.

Initially, she had sent word that she wasn't prepared to sell, at least not yet. No contracts had been signed. She had needed time to get her thoughts together. That was a month ago. Then, the minute she made the final decision that she was keeping the property, she had left a message with Gabriel Kane's lawyer herself, explaining the unexpected changes in her life.

She had apologized up and down but hadn't heard back. Granted, she had only left the message the day before, but she had assumed she'd hear right away. She had slipped into the apartment late last night, using the old key in hopes of avoiding Kane for as long as possible.

She didn't doubt for a second that the man was furious with her for backing out of the contract after he'd already bought the rest of the building from her sisters. There was no question in her mind that he would try forcing her to sell. Chicken that she was, she was counting on his lawyer to convince him otherwise. Even she knew a deal wasn't a deal until documents were signed.

"Have a great day!"

She practically leaped to the sidewalk, catching sight of an old man who was sitting in the window next door, peering out at her as she dashed toward Columbus Avenue.

Three

⬦

"**S**OME THINGS ARE TRUE *whether you believe them or not.*"

Gram's favorite saying. She had repeated it to Portia and her sisters more times than any of the three cared to count.

The minute Portia turned onto Columbus she fell against the nearest wall. Her knees were weak, her breath coming out in uneven jerks. Whether she wanted to believe it or not, Gabriel Kane had made her think of food. A meal. A meal at odds with everything he appeared to be and made her acutely aware of being a stranger in a strange land.

Thankfully, once her breathing started to ease, so did images of fried chicken and sweet jalapeño mustard. She remained against the wall for a bit longer as the images faded even more until they were gone, and she pushed away on a ragged breath and spaghetti legs. Seeing the man mixed in with thoughts of a meal was a fluke, she reassured herself. The images of food had nothing to do with the man or her apartment. And she felt certain she was right when her thoughts and tingling fingertips circled back to chocolate cake.

Next thing she knew, Portia hurried into the Fairway Market on

Broadway. The grocery store was unlike anything she had seen in Texas. Bins of fruit and vegetables lined the sidewalk, forming narrow entrances into the market. Inside, the aisles were crowded, no inch of space wasted. In the fresh vegetables and fruit section she was surrounded by piles of romaine and red-leaf lettuce, velvety thick green kale that gave away to fuzzy kiwi and mounds of apples. Standing with her eyes closed, Portia waited a second, trying not to panic. Then, realizing there was no help for it, she gave in to the knowing, not to the fluke meal inspired by Gabriel Kane, but to the chocolate cake and roast that had hit her earlier.

She started picking out vegetables. Cauliflower that she would top with Gruyère and cheddar cheeses; spinach she would flash fry with garlic and olive oil.

In the meat department, she asked for a standing rib roast to serve eight. Then she stopped. "No," she said to the butcher, her eyes half-closed in concentration, "just give me enough for four."

Portia made it through the store in record time. Herbs, spices. Eggs, flour. Baking soda. A laundry list of staples. At the last second, she realized she needed to make a chowder. Crab and corn with a dash of cayenne pepper. Hot, spicy.

Within the hour, she was back at the apartment and had the vegetables cleaned and set aside, the roast ready to go into the old oven that thankfully worked. The chowder done. Now it was time to start the cake.

The lower cabinet creaked when she pulled it open. Inside, she found an old Dormeyer Mix-Well stand mixer, plus several mixing bowls that had been washed so many times, the once bold red was a splotchy pink. The simple act of sifting flour soothed her, like meeting up with a once-cherished old friend. She closed her eyes as she mixed in the salt and baking powder.

She had to rinse the scuffed Revere Ware pots and pans before she started melting the Baker's Chocolate in a makeshift double boiler. Once that was done she moved on to the sugar, butter, and eggs until the rich chocolate layers of cake were baked and cooled. When she finally swirled the last bit of vanilla buttercream into place, Portia stood back with a sense that all was as it should have been. But she still had no sense of why she'd made the meal.

Good news or bad?

Frustration flashed though her. But she pushed it aside and focused on placing tall wooden stools around the old kitchen island. Four place settings. Four seats.

With her sisters living in New York, it stood to reason they would come over. But including Portia, that made only three. Who was the fourth?

The man upstairs?

Portia instantly shook the thought away. A completely different meal had sprung into her head when she saw him.

She glanced at the table. She still needed flowers.

The small corner market had rows of fresh flowers in white plastic buckets. Standing, the early fall sun on her shoulders, she opened her mind. She assessed the fuchsia roses and violet freesias, vibrant orange and pink gerbera daisies. Willowy white snapdragons.

It took a second before she realized what she needed. Daisies. Bright yellow daisies.

Looking down at the bucket of cheerful flowers, Portia felt light-headed. If she had to create a meal to cheer people up, then whatever lay ahead had to be bad.

Anxiety rose through her like dough rising in a towel-covered bowl. The image of the pulled-pork meal and her grandmother stepping into the lightning flashed through her. She hated the anxiety involved with the knowing and food. She hated not understanding, hated waiting for something bad to happen.

Portia cursed herself for taking a glimpse inside the Pandora's box of knowing. For three years she had kept the lid shut. If nothing else, she'd had peace. She needed to keep it that way. End of story.

She wanted to chuck the roast and cake in the garbage. But at this point, whatever was coming couldn't be stopped.

Or could it? Had there been a way she could have stopped her grandmother from being struck down by lightning?

Portia still didn't know why the sight of the meal had sent her grandmother out into the lightning. She only knew that if she hadn't made that meal and set the table for one, Gram never would have gone out into that storm.

Nothing had changed.

"No, Gram," Portia whispered. "Nothing about the Cuthcart knowing is a gift. Not to you. Not to me."

Taking a deep breath, she pushed the memory away, pulled out her cell phone, and called Cordelia, then Olivia, to find out if they were okay. Anxiety circled in her stomach, trepidation tapping behind her eyes. She was forced to leave messages.

She raced through a mental list of what else it could be. Robert?

Portia felt a shiver of hope, but guilt quickly followed. If something had happened to Robert, the knowing would surely have had her buying champagne.

Back at the apartment, she put the flowers on the table and started to pace. Finally, hoping for a distraction, she turned on Evie's ancient television. It was tuned to a news program and still working.

"The investment firm Atlantica General has confirmed the loss of two billion dollars of investor money. It is being reported that the loss was due to fraudulent trades by the firm's Low Risk group. If allegations of malfeasance are true, no doubt people will go to jail over this."

Portia's heartbeat flared, slowed, and then flared again. Cordelia's husband, James, worked for Atlantica General. Worse, James worked in the Low Risk group. Since starting at Atlantica ten years earlier, he had been a rising star, becoming one of the most successful young bankers at the giant.

She sat down hard, only to jump up again when someone knocked at the door.

Portia raced over and yanked the door open to find her other sister, Olivia.

"Did you hear?" Olivia said.

"About James?"

"Yes," her middle sister said without so much as a hello or hug as she walked in the door.

Back in Texas, Portia knew that the three Cuthcart sisters had been considered three kinds of blondes. Cordelia, the oldest, was pretty with her straightened hair and patrician nose. If Cordelia had been born to resemble a queen, middle-sister Olivia had been born to be the nymph. With her Cupid's-bow mouth and violet eyes, she lured men in to the rocky shores of her world. Portia knew that while her sisters were queens and nymphs, she was considered cute, the girl next door. There were worse things to be, sure, but just once she would have liked to be the beautiful one or the exotic one.

Today, Olivia wore olive-colored cargo pants that hung low on her hips, a multicolored yoga top that showed off her beautifully sculpted arms, and some sort of shoe that looked equal parts comfort and fashion. Olivia was the wild child of the family, living in a walk-up apartment on the Lower East Side, a serial dater who had broken more than a few men's hearts. Why she refused to settle down was a mystery to her sisters, a mystery that Cordelia and Portia had dissected from every angle but still didn't understand. Though Portia was starting to think that Olivia was just smarter than they were. Than she was, anyway.

Olivia glanced at the table and raised a brow, but didn't say anything.

Portia knew that look. Olivia didn't particularly care one way or the other about the knowing. As far as she was concerned, it had nothing to do with her. But that didn't mean she liked it.

"God, I hope that fourth setting isn't for James," Olivia stated, turning from the table. "Though you'd have to think he's probably surrounded by lawyers. Or cops."

Portia shivered.

Despite the crispness of her words, Portia knew why her sister was there. Long ago their mother had made her daughters promise that no matter where they were or how angry they were at each other at the time, if one of them needed the other, they would be there. No questions asked.

Which meant Portia knew what would happen next.

Cordelia sailed into the apartment like a perfectly dressed mother duck, not a hair out of place on her head, her subtle hints of makeup perfectly done, her blue eyes alert, determined as she set her expensive handbag on a chair.

At thirteen, Cordelia had perfected the jaundiced arrogance of a girl who believed she had all the answers. At thirty-five, Cordelia still felt she had all the answers. Where Olivia had always been considered the passionate sister, the oldest Cuthcart girl never showed any sort of emotion at all.

"We saw the news," Portia said. "Is everything okay with James?"

Cordelia's always stiff upper lip trembled.

"Jesus, Cordie," Olivia stated with all the calm certainty that there was no problem too big to be solved. "Is James getting arrested?"

"Olivia," Portia barked, just as Cordelia blurted, "No!"

Portia sagged. "What a relief."

"Not a relief," Cordelia stated. "He wasn't a party to the bad deals, but part of the two billion dollars was every penny of our life savings."

Cordelia stood there in her cashmere and pearls, her standard uniform for all the charity work she did in the city, tears in her eyes.

Portia wrapped her arms around Cordelia. Olivia just stood there. Portia gave her a look, after which Olivia gave a silent sigh, then came over and joined the hug.

"I am not crying," Cordelia stated, even as tears rolled.

"Of course not," Portia said.

"Nope, not you," Olivia added.

They stood that way for a few seconds, their hearts beating nearly as one until Portia broke the spell. "Stop stepping on my toes, Olivia."

Olivia burst out laughing. "I knew you couldn't take more than a few seconds of hugging."

"I can take hugging, Olivia. You're the one who can't take it. That's why you stepped on my toes."

But then they turned back to Cordelia.

"You're going to be okay," Portia said.

"Absolutely," Olivia added.

Cordelia stepped away, smoothed her bob, straightened her blouse, and drew a deep breath. "I love you guys," she whispered, and quickly cleared her throat. "It really is okay. But I'm stressed and I can't show it in front of James."

If Olivia was like a decadent chocolate-covered strawberry, and Portia a pineapple-and-spice hummingbird cupcake, then Cordelia was peanut brittle, still sweet, though with something more substantial added by way of peanuts, but unbendable.

"James says it'll be fine. So it will be." She raised her chin. "I'm sure it's not every cent of our life's savings. I'm overreacting, which is childish." Tears welled once more; Cordelia drew a deep breath and shook them away. "I just needed to let it out, then see that it isn't so dire. I couldn't do that at home."

Portia shot Olivia a quick glance, but she didn't say what she was thinking—that Cordelia always put a good face on a bad situation.

Cordelia caught sight of the food in the little kitchen, then turned and stared at the wooden stools around the island, the plates, the flowers. But when Olivia caught Cordelia's eye and raised a brow, Cordelia looked away. Portia had asked her oldest sister once why she hated the knowing so much that she generally pretended it didn't exist. Cordelia had dismissed the question out of hand. But Portia still wondered.

The three of them pulled up around the makeshift table and served each other plates piled high with Portia's feast. No one mentioned the unspoken question hanging in the air. Who was the last seat for? Instead, Portia and Olivia caught up on every bit of Texas gossip until Cordelia was able to breathe again, quickly turning back into the oldest sister.

"It's time to talk. I'm not the only one with problems," Cordelia said, breaking in. "You've moved in here, Portia. But have you figured out how you're going to support yourself?"

Olivia shook her head and sat back. "Sheez, Cordie, give her a break. She's barely divorced."

"*Barely* doesn't have any influence on a bank balance."

"She's right, Olivia. But I'm working on it."

"Really?" Cordelia got one of her know-it-all looks. "What are you thinking about doing?"

"Okay, so I don't know yet, Cord. But something will come to me."

"Let's make a list of possibilities."

Olivia groaned. "You and your lists."

Portia agreed. More than that, she knew this wasn't headed anywhere good. "Maybe later."

"There's no time like the present," Cordelia stated, her cheer exaggerated and fake.

If Portia hadn't known that her sister mainly wanted to distract herself from her own problems, she would have fought harder. As it was, she didn't know how to say no when her sister said, "Let's brainstorm."

"Cordelia—"

"It'll be fun!" Even more fake. "Just us girls, letting dreams run wild."

Olivia all but rolled her eyes. "You know she's not letting this go."

"Fine. I could be an assistant," Portia stated.

"Assistant to whom?"

Only Cordelia, and grammar zealots, would use *whom* in a casual conversation. Portia considered. "To an executive."

"You don't type." This from Olivia.

Portia glared at her one supporter. "Fine." She glanced back at Cordelia. "Then maybe I could be an editor."

"As if they don't type? Besides, an editor of what?"

Portia shot Cordelia a look. "Books."

"You barely graduated from high school—"

"I graduated!"

"But the only class you liked was Home Economics. I can't believe any school still offers those classes. Definitely don't tell anyone in New York about it."

"Why not?"

Cordelia didn't bother to answer. "I know what you could do. If anyone asks, tell them you went to cooking school. They teach cooking in Home Ec, right? They'll eat that up. New Yorkers are all about food." Cordelia hesitated, then said, "You know that."

Portia eyed her. "I don't cook."

Her sisters glanced at the meal in front of them.

"This was an aberration," she said. "I do not cook. Not anymore. You know that."

Cordelia and Olivia exchanged a glance.

Portia knew they were going to say something, something she wouldn't want to discuss. "Stop. Really. Don't worry about me. I'll get a job. First thing tomorrow I'll start working on my résumé."

Finally Cordelia stood. "I take it the bathroom in this place works?"

"No, but there's a Porta-Potty in the garden."

Cordelia's eyes went wide.

"Just joking."

This time, everyone laughed, even Cordelia, the tension in the room easing.

Cordelia headed out of the kitchen, and Olivia cupped her hands around a mug of hot mint tea laced with honey. Portia started to clear the table. But when she reached for the unused place setting, she heard Cordelia in the tiny foyer.

"Who are you?" the oldest sister was asking.

Portia glanced out of the kitchen and saw a young girl, eleven, maybe twelve, standing just inside the front door. Her curly light brown hair puffed like a cloud around creamy white skin, making her big brown eyes look even bigger. Freckles stood out on her nose, perfect and contained, like crayon dots drawn by a child. While the dots were meticulous, the girl was not. She wore a navy blue sweater over a white blouse that was mostly untucked from a navy blue plaid skirt. Her headband was askew, one kneesock up, the other down, spilling into black flats, finishing off what was clearly one of the private school uniforms that children wore in Manhattan.

"I'm Ariel, from upstairs." She looked around. "I heard all the noise. The door was open." Her pursed mouth dared them to contradict her. "Are you squatters or something?"

Olivia laughed out loud.

"No," Portia said. "We're not squatters. I live here."

The girl studied them, as if trying to get her head around anyone living in this run-down apartment. "But you weren't here yesterday."

"I moved in last night."

Cordelia scowled. "I still can't believe you moved here. You should have kept staying with me."

When Portia first arrived in New York, she had gone straight to Cordelia, not sure what to do about the apartment. But as with so many things with Portia, she had woken up yesterday morning knowing what she had to do. Next thing she knew, she made the call to the lawyer, then moved in here.

"And the rest of you are, what . . . friends?" the girl asked.

"Sisters."

"You must be Gabriel Kane's child," Cordelia said.

"You know my dad?"

"Olivia and I sold our apartments to your father."

The girl wasn't paying attention. She eyed the food.

Cordelia shifted into mother mode. "Are you hungry?"

"Starving. The new housekeeper-slash-cook made dinner, but it was really weird, like scary weird, and seriously, who wants to eat scary food?"

"Have a seat." Cordelia retrieved a plate as if it were her own home and loaded it with food. Just before she set it down at the extra place setting, she froze.

Her eyes narrowed, and her mouth pinched. Portia hated the battle she sensed going on in her sister. But she didn't repeat Gram's words.

"Some things are true whether you believe them or not."

"Sit," Cordelia finally said, setting down the plate. "Eat, before it gets cold."

Four

⬧⬧⬧

T HEY SAT BACK DOWN on the stools while Ariel gobbled up her food and Portia, Cordelia, and Olivia stared at her.

"What?" Ariel said, glancing up through a curtain of wispy bangs, the fork halting halfway to her mouth. "You've never seen a girl eat before?"

Cordelia smiled in the condescendingly maternal way she had perfected by age ten. "Perhaps we've never seen a young girl eat so fast."

Ariel shrugged, unbothered by the implied reprimand. "Like I said, I'm starved."

Cordelia started to speak, but Portia cut her off. "Let her eat in peace, Cord."

Olivia laughed. "Yes, eat. Though tell us," she added, studying the girl, "who all lives in your apartment?"

Ariel looked confused. "*Who all?* What kind of word is that?"

"It's a Texas thing," Portia clarified. "You know, like *y'all* for *you all.*"

"I don't get it. Who adds *all* to *you?*"

"It doesn't matter," Olivia interjected, waving the words away. "I just wondered who lives with you upstairs."

Olivia said the words casually, but Portia knew better. She knew her sister. Olivia was always interested in the possibility of a new man.

"Just me, my dad, and Miranda."

Olivia scowled. "Miranda?"

"My sister."

"Oh, really." Olivia's smile returned, slow, delicious. "So, your dad's single?"

"Olivia," Portia and Cordelia both snapped.

Cordelia no doubt said that because Olivia was being rude. Portia wanted to think she did it for the same reason, but the truth was that at the mention of the man upstairs, she felt, well, possessive. The thought of Olivia's lack of inhibition and beautifully sculpted body in relation to Gabriel Kane didn't sit well—which was ridiculous, since Portia was barely divorced and certainly not interested in Gabriel herself. But there it was.

"What?" Olivia asked, her tone defensive. "What did I say?"

Cordelia sighed. "One, it's inappropriate to ask a man's child if he's single."

"And two," Portia picked up the thread, "you only like guys who are . . ." She hesitated, glanced at Ariel, and then leaned closer. "T-A-K-E-N."

Ariel narrowed her eyes.

Olivia scoffed. "Now who is being inappropriate in front of the K-I-D?"

"Hello," Ariel said. "I can S-P-E-L-L."

Olivia pushed more food in front of her. "Keep eating." She turned back to her sisters. "I do *not* like guys who are taken."

Portia and Cordelia rolled their eyes.

"I don't," Olivia persisted, reaching up to twist her mass of curls into a loose knot on her head. When she let go, her hair fell in a tumble around her shoulders. "Martin wasn't taken. Neither was Daniel. And what about George?"

"True. But let's see. Martin, you broke up with because he had a cat."

"Sue me. I'm a dog person."

"Well then, Daniel should have been perfect for you: He had a dog," Cordelia said. "I can't remember why you broke up with him, just that you did via text message."

"Does anyone under the age of fifty use the word *via?*" Olivia shot back. "How old are you really?"

"You know very well I am"—she glanced at Ariel—"twenty-eight."

"Not!" Olivia and Portia laughed. "Thirty-five if you're a day!"

"Don't change the subject," Cordelia snipped. "We're not finished. You mentioned George."

Olivia shrugged and looked away.

Cordelia tsked. "Poor George. He would have been better off with a text. He only found out about your change of heart when he came home to your all's apartment and saw you'd thrown his clothes out the window."

Ariel gaped, fork forgotten in her hand.

"He deserved it," Olivia stated with calm certainty. "Besides, the apartment was a fifth-floor walk-up. I wasn't going to spend hours walking up and down those stairs taking everything down to the street. That's a rite of passage. Every woman should throw a guy's clothes out a window once in her life."

Cordelia scoffed. "A rite of passage is a sorority hazing or a bat mitzvah."

"Maybe for you, Miss Marry-the-first-guy-you-date."

"I dated!"

Portia groaned. "Please stop."

Olivia and Cordelia ignored her.

"You only dated one other guy, Cordelia, and that didn't turn out so well."

"What happened?" Ariel asked.

Without Portia noticing, the girl had dumped everything out of her backpack and had retrieved a notebook. She sat now, poised with pen in hand over an empty page, like a reporter, or overeager detective. Next to her plate, a smorgasbord of paraphernalia littered the table. Several pens of assorted colors, a calculator covered in $E = mc^2$ stickers, a wild-haired rendering of Einstein painted in fluorescent-green nail polish on an inhaler, a half-eaten KitKat bar, a mini-bottle of antibacterial gel, and multicolored knit socks with separate coverings for each toe, like gloves for feet. Portia loved the socks.

"What happened to the only other guy you dated?" Ariel persisted, ready to write.

"Nothing," the three sisters said in unison, which brought them back together, the energy between them shifting.

Olivia touched Cordelia's hand. That was the way with Olivia. Wild and carefree, blazing through anything bad with a bold fearlessness, but underneath a caring that Portia sometimes thought her sister worked hard to hide.

"Dating practically only one guy has served you well," Olivia said. "You and James are great together, and you'll survive whatever is going on now."

Cordelia gave her a determined smile. "Thank you, sweetie."

They shared a comfortable moment, Portia just barely realizing that Ariel studied them like a scientist scrutinizing a foreign species.

Olivia didn't seem to notice at all, lost in her own thoughts, until she wrinkled her nose, then leaned closer. Portia could see the sparkle in her eyes that she knew meant trouble.

"So it goes without saying that you and James are perfect, yada yada," Olivia said with another wave of her hand. "But let's just pretend. If you *had* dated anyone else before you left Texas, who would it have been? Brody, right? You were madly in love with Brody. You would have slept with—"

"Olivia!" Portia barked, nodding toward Ariel. "Inappropriate. On so many levels."

Olivia just shrugged innocently, though she didn't look innocent at all, and squeezed Cordelia's hand.

were singing. Even Ariel got into the act. Until the music snapped off mid-verse.

"What's going on here?"

Portia nearly tripped at the sight of Gabriel Kane.

He appeared every bit as powerful as he had earlier in the day, though now there was no trace of a smile. If possible, everything dark about his eyes grew darker as he took her in, his gaze sliding over her in a heated sear. She could have sworn he seemed confused, as if he couldn't reconcile the woman on the steps with the woman standing in the apartment.

"Dad!" Ariel laughed. If she was aware of the darkness, she didn't show it. "Come dance it out with us!"

Dad didn't look amused.

"Ariel, go upstairs."

Ariel's smile turned to a gape. "What did I do?"

"Upstairs."

"Dad!"

"Up. Stairs."

Portia watched Ariel march to the kitchen, stuff all her belongings back into her backpack, then sulk off. Cordelia, she noticed, quickly smoothed her already smooth hair, looking surprisingly uncomfortable. Olivia, on the other hand, definitely wasn't put off by Gabriel's tone. She looked him up and down. "Hi, I'm Olivia," she said, stepping closer.

Portia felt an instant flash of irritation.

"Good God, Olivia," Cordelia groaned, walking forward and extending her hand. "I'm Cordelia Callahan. Olivia and I sold you our portions of the town house."

"Gabriel Kane." He shook her hand.

He nodded briefly to Olivia, polite, but that was all, before turning back to Portia. She felt that same sense of vertigo she had experienced on the front steps, the world reeling a bit at the sight of him.

"This is our sister Portia," Cordelia put in.

Gabriel didn't look away from Portia. "We met. This morning."

Cordelia gaped for one silent second before saying, "You've met?"

Olivia only considered her.

"Sort of," Portia conceded.

Gabriel's eyes narrowed. "I didn't realized she was the woman who—"

The words broke off, and Portia filled in the gap: *"who backed out of selling me the apartment."*

He brow creased, his voice growing hard. "Why didn't you tell me who you were earlier?"

She grimaced and shrugged; the best answer she could come up with without having to admit she had hoped to avoid him like a girl in grade school.

His frown deepened, but Cordelia stepped forward, wearing a determinedly cheerful Texas welcome. "Would you like something to eat, Mr. Kane? Portia made more than enough food."

He glanced back into the kitchen, looking at the four used place settings. Then he turned to Portia. "You fed my daughter?"

"I hope that's okay," she said, forcing a smile. "She was hungry. As Cordelia said, we had plenty. I can make you a plate, too." *Please say no,* she prayed.

He looked like he wanted to say something, though something that had nothing to do with food. But after what looked like a frustrated second, he shook his head. "No, but thank you. And thank you for feeding Ariel." He started to leave, then turned back. "We need to discuss the apartment."

Portia smiled big. "Of course! We'll discuss tomorrow."

Though she knew she would do everything in her power to avoid him like the plague. The last thing she wanted was to discuss anything with Gabriel Kane.

Five

⁘

ARIEL KANE WAS ALMOST entirely certain she was disappearing. Using every millimeter of her massively smart brain, she was trying to figure out if it was even possible for a person to disappear. So far she hadn't come up with any sort of quantifiable answer despite the fact that she wrote everything she could down in her journal. Anything that seemed important, she took notes on. The only thing that was definite, however, was that she was definitely starving, even though barely an hour ago the ladies downstairs had shoveled heaping piles of really good food onto her plate. But not even the roast or cake made her feel less hungry.

Hungry or not, Ariel had liked sitting there while they gabbed away. Portia, the one who seemed to live there, with her sandy blond hair and giant blue eyes, was pretty but tired looking, like a favorite doll who had been played with too much. Then there was Olivia, the middle sister, Ariel had learned, the same kind of pretty as Portia, those blue-blue eyes and long curly hair, only wilder, alive, like if you touched her you'd feel a zap. And last, Cordelia, the only one who seemed like an adult, again with the blue-blue eyes and really blond hair, only hers was straight, perfect, not one thing about her out of place. Ariel had seen tons of women like that, mothers of other girls, both in New Jersey and now here in New York.

Whatever. There had been something nice about the way the sisters yakked away, like everything in the world was normal, a world where people didn't disappear. Ariel liked that best. Then they started dancing, which was really embarrassing because they were so bad.

At first she had felt bad seeing the three sisters dancing together, leaving her out. Then they had turned to her, pulling her into their circle. They didn't even notice that her dancing was as bad as theirs. Even worse, maybe. Her throat swelled like a big baby's just thinking about it. Only then her dad had shown up and ruined it.

He was pretty good at that, given that he had pretty much ruined her life. If things were different, she'd be back in her old room in New Jersey instead of sitting on the fourth floor of this town house. Her dad just up and moved them here six months ago, never bothering to ask if she wanted a new room, or a new bed, or even a new life.

The only good news was that she knew for a fact that her dad hadn't sold their old house. It still had all their old furniture in it. With any luck, he'd give up this New York City nonsense and move them back where they belonged.

She pulled out her journal and started to write, this time because she was supposed to. More specifically, the Shrink her dad had hired said she had to write out her feelings about her mom.

Ariel hated this kind of journal writing. It made her think about Mom, which made her feel like a bee buzzing in a jar, banging around trying to get out. Sure, her mom had died. And sure, she could hardly breathe whenever she thought about it. But Ariel was not some below-average preteen who needed help, which was exactly what she had told her dad. He had carted her and her sister, Miranda, off to an idiot therapist anyway. So she mainly used her journal to write down her observations about the world.

During her first visit with the Shrink, Ariel had sat in the guy's office on a creepy black leather sofa. When he started by asking her how she was feeling, she refused to give in to the tears that burned in her throat, and responded by asking him what self-respecting medical professional had black leather anything, especially in his office. He had looked at her, didn't bother to answer, and scribbled something on his notepad.

After that, she had simply said "No Comment" to everything else he asked, interjecting observations about the weather every once in a while to shake things up, until finally the guy realized she wasn't going to start talking away all of a sudden. He said fine. Since she wouldn't talk to him, she should write down her feelings in a journal.

Next thing she knew, her dad had gone out and bought her a pink diary with a miniature key. Hello, she was almost thirteen, not eight. When she mentioned this, directly after asking her dad if he'd like to join her for a cocktail before dinner—which he either didn't hear or intentionally ignored—he brought home a fancy journal with a leather cover. Like she was some sort of self-help freak. Again, nearly thirteen. Not thirty.

On the bright side, it did give her an idea for a title for her journal. *Musings of a Freak.* Intelligent, a little off-center. In a word, her. Ariel Kane.

So, anyway, she was supposed to write down her feelings. Truthfully, if she managed to get beyond the sick feeling that she constantly had about her mom, what she felt was cramped. Her dad, who never used to be at home when her mom was alive, suddenly went all *I'm going to be the perfect father* on them, pulling up stakes in Montclair, New Jersey, moving Ariel and her sister to the Upper West Side, into a town house that was like a hundred years old.

Since they'd moved here, all her dad did was work on the place (or should she say, boss other people around while they worked on the place), sit at the big desk in the downstairs office, reading *The Financial Times*, studying computer screens—basically making sure his empire stayed, well, empirick—and meddle in her life. Correction: *ruin* her life.

But the fact was, there was something about her dad that made people do what he told them. When he walked into a room, people quieted. When he asked a question, people embarrassed themselves trying to come up with the answer. He wasn't handsome, not like her uncle Anthony, whom everyone said was totally beautiful. But still, her dad didn't have to say much to have people jumping through hoops to do his bidding. At least that was the case with everyone but her older sister, Miranda.

Miranda was sixteen and had been forced to leave her boyfriend behind when they moved into the city. Ariel had seen the guy once only even back in New Jersey, since Miranda did a really great job of keeping him out of their dad's sight. Dad would combust if he found out Miranda had a boyfriend. While Ariel couldn't say the guy was anything to write home about, clearly Miranda thought he was, since now she spent most of her time slamming doors and throwing herself across her bed, going on and on about how unfair life was.

No question Dad needed more to do with his time.

For a while after Mom died, all three of them had walked around like zombies in a movie. For six months they had barely put one foot in front of the other. Then, out of nowhere, just as the school year ended and summer was starting, Dad came home and told them it was time to move on.

Move on?

Like people could do that?

Though really, moving to New York had made it possible to turn the whole dead-mom thing into a secret. Ariel had learned the hard way that people completely freaked if they heard.

So, in June they had moved into the city. In July, she and her sister had started with the Shrink. In September, she and Miranda had started new schools. Now it was nearly October and there was no sign that her dad was going to stop being in charge of all of their day-to-day stuff. She had pretty much given up on him going back to his old ways of distractedly asking them how their day was while reading the newspaper.

Previous scenario before everything went to hell in a hand-basket went something like this. . . .

Father Reading *The Wall Street Journal*: "How was your day, Ariel?"

Extremely Intelligent and Witty Daughter: "Great, just finished watching a bunch of porn online and I need ten dollars for lunch."

FRWSJ: "Ten dollars for what?" Said while turning page.

EIAWD: "Lunch."

FRWSJ: "Fine."

Conversations like that were totally things of the past (she didn't think it appropriate to put in writing her dad's new, not-improved-as-far-as-she-was-concerned reaction to the most recent time she had used her Internet porn wit), and Ariel figured she had no choice but to take matters into her own hands and find her father a distraction.

Since Gabriel Kane was nothing if not a poster boy for perfect behavior, he couldn't be tempted with the normal things like partying, poker nights, strippers, or even taking massively smart classes in the quest to be the next Renaissance man. Never mind. Ariel had put together a plan, one that would produce something/someone to take his mind off her and Miranda. She had tried to run the idea by her sister, but Miranda just rolled her eyes, announced that the Stupid Shrink should give refunds, and left Ariel standing alone on the stairs.

Seriously, if it weren't for her snooping, Ariel wouldn't know anything at all about what Miranda was up to. Thank goodness the Shrink had made Miranda write in a journal, too. And Miranda wasn't as good at hiding hers as Ariel was.

It was after reading Miranda's latest lovesick entry about the left-behind boyfriend and wanting to get back at dad *"for ruining my life!!!"* that Ariel decided to find a new woman to keep their dad busy. Not a wife. No way would he ever marry again. He totally loved her mom. But a nice lady, someone to date, was the best Ariel had come up with.

Granted, for the last few months, Dad had dated plenty, but he hadn't met anyone who held his attention for more than a nanosecond. And it was going to take more than a nanosecond to get him out of their hair.

In her original plan, she had considered taking out an online dating ad.

Wanted: Girlfriend

Nice man seeks really nice lady. There's a kid involved (a little lanky, but cute in her own extremely intelligent way), though she won't be any trouble, and I swear you'll like her. Interested parties call: 212-555-0654.

Perfect wording, like a commercial for a made-for-TV movie, and that was bound to interest somebody. She figured there was zero reason to mention Miranda. At this point, a full-fledged high school–variety teenager would probably be a deal breaker for any sane woman.

But in the end, she couldn't go through with it. If she spent her lunch money on an ad, one, it would take more than a few lunches' worth to afford it; and two, what was she going to eat in the meantime? Contrary to popular belief, not all newly pubescent girls had dreams of anorexia. Beyond that, how did you screen out all the skanks, gold diggers, and weirdos when you ran an ad to the masses?

Of course, now there was Portia, from downstairs. She was interesting, if you could overlook the awful apartment. Was it possible to like living in a place with cracked windows and uneven floors? And what was up with the sink? Big and deep, with the pipes showing underneath. Ariel could have sworn she had seen pictures in her social studies book of places like that from New York City in the Dark Ages.

Not a big plus, but the lady seemed to be available, and she didn't have that gold digger look in her eye. No self-respecting gold digger would get anywhere near that run-down apartment.

But she was kind of cool, even though she was a horrible dancer. Her hair was a nice sort of curly, which Ariel liked. And boy, could she cook. Didn't they say that the way to a man's heart was through his stomach?

Whatever, Ariel had to get this taken care of.

Miranda's journal entries were getting weirder. She had gone from just drawing big teardrops all over a blank page to writing *Life Sucks!* And now she had moved on to *I Hate Dad.* No exclamation mark. Strangely, an exclamation mark would have made Ariel feel better about it. An exclamation mark meant emotion. Miranda's journal didn't seem to have an ounce of emotion in it anymore.

Ariel knew from experience that the clock was ticking before her sister did something stupid.

She wasn't sure how she would hold on if another bad thing happened.

She was done with bad things. Seriously done.

Now she just needed the universe to listen to her.

Six

❖

IF ANYONE HAD TOLD Portia a year ago that the only job she could get in New York City would be as a "hamburger," she would have laughed and rolled her eyes. Not that she was much of an eye roller. But really? A hamburger? Could anyone with half a brain believe that a woman as smart as her could go from highly regarded Texas political wife to, well, hamburger?

But after two weeks of unsuccessful job hunting, that was exactly what she had done. Or rather, what she had become.

"Shoo!" Portia hissed, waddling down West Seventy-third Street as fast as the hamburger suit allowed, attempting to outpace the pack of little dogs that had escaped their dog walker.

It wasn't as if she hadn't thrown her heart into looking for a job. She had. She'd made calls and sent out résumés, but not a single person had been willing to so much as interview her. Sure, two weeks wasn't that long in the scheme of things, but her bank account told a different tale. She needed money, sooner rather than later. Robert still hadn't deposited the settlement in her account, and her savings were evaporating like a reservoir in the middle of a Texas dry spell.

As a result, she had jumped for joy when she received the e-mail from Angus Industries offering her a job in public relations. In hindsight, she should have wondered why they offered her employment without so much as an interview or a phone call. It turned out that *Food Industries PR* for Angus Industries hadn't entailed any actual public relations work. Instead, when Portia arrived at the address provided, only a block away from her apartment, she found herself at Burger Boy, where she was handed a rubber hamburger suit and told to direct the public to the fast-food hellhole.

When Portia realized what the job entailed, she wanted to say no. A thousand different ways she *should* say no flashed through her mind. But her pride had to balance the staggering expense of living in New York. Was it possible that a two-dollar box of cereal in Texas cost five dollars in NYC?

End result?

She had pulled on the burger suit, though no sooner had the manager zipped her up than Portia thought it smelled strange. Mr. Burger Boy had assured her she was imagining things. But as she stood on Columbus Avenue trying to entice passersby with discount coupons, the unseasonably hot fall day beating down on her, the suit began to waft the aroma of charcoal-grilled burgers. Not long after that, the dogs that had been sitting clustered around their dog walker as he talked on his cell phone made a break for it and came after her, leashes flying in the wind, like buzzards sensing fresh kill.

The manager emerged from Burger Boy just long enough to threaten her miserable life if she let one of those dogs take a chunk out of his costume. She had tried to wiggle out of the suit, but the zipper was stuck. When the manager disappeared back inside the shop, she had fled.

Now she waddled down the long block toward home, going as fast as she could. Her hair had gotten loose, curls falling all over her face.

One thing was for sure: This was all her ex-husband's fault. Well, her husband and her ex-friend Sissy LePlante. Portia swung along as fast as she could, her mind full of revenge fantasies—all of them involving skewering, grilling, or butchering. Hamburger related.

She was only two town houses away from her apartment when she realized that one dog was still following her. "Damnation!" she yelped, swatting at the pesky Jack Russell terrier leaping at her side, vibrating with excitement as he tried to get a piece of one of the two faux meat patties circling her waist. The only thing that kept the terrier from true success was that it kept getting tangled in its trailing leash.

Her husband thought she was a pushover? *Right.* Portia swung around and met the dog's eye. "Go home!" she thundered.

He squeaked, tucked his leg between his legs, and tore off.

"Ha!" she chirped, swinging back around.

Straight ahead, she could see the thick green trees of Central Park at the end of the long tunnel formed by apartment buildings. Pedestrians, locals and tourists alike, got out of her way. No one, not even the hardcore New Yorkers who had given her nothing but grief since she'd moved to town, were going to mess with Portia Cuthcart in a burger suit, a murderous light in her eyes.

Finally, she made it to the town house. All she had to do was get inside her apartment, find a knife, and cut the burger right off her body before she suffocated or melted.

She barreled up the front steps and through the thankfully, if surprisingly, open front door into the building's small vestibule. Momentum and velocity squeezed her through the opening, the sound of thick rubber against the door seal like a beach ball being rubbed to a squeal.

But if bad things come in threes—one, the burger suit, two, the dogs—then number three had to be the cherry on top . . . or the garnish on the burger. The very neighbor she had been working to avoid was in the vestibule, now crowded into a corner, his daughter on the opposite side.

Even plastered against the wall, Gabriel Kane made awareness slide along her skin.

"Oh, hello, Ariel," she stated, her smile forced. "Mr. Kane." What wouldn't she have given to be dressed in a fabulous little dress rather than ten pounds of rubber.

"This is a surprise," he replied, not looking one bit happy. "Though it explains where you've been every time I've stopped by to meet with you."

Awareness, indeed. Sheez. How many times did she have to remind herself that he was an arrogant New Yorker who wanted something from her, though not anything that had to do with shivers of awareness. "That's me. A regular busy beaver."

His eyes widened fractionally. It didn't take a genius to guess he wasn't a man used to people snapping at him. But after a second, a smile tugged at the corner of his lips. "You mean, a busy *burger*."

Portia glared at him. "Ha-ha."

His reluctant half smile ticked up a notch. Heat rushed through her, the kind of heat that had nothing to do with the layers of the thick rubber suit, which just made her all the angrier.

The man wasn't good looking in any classical sense, and never mind his broad shoulders, dark hair, and darker eyes. His features were rough-hewn in contrast to the quality of the suit he wore.

Portia hated his perfect suit.

On the other hand . . . that imperfect face? Lust. Even wrapped in a hamburger suit, she couldn't miss the flash of non-rubber-induced heat rushing down her body. Yep, pure lust.

I'm attracted to men who are kind and quietly intelligent, she told herself. Men who had sandy blond hair and light blue eyes, who held doors for ladies, and made liberal use of words like *please* and *thank you.*

The type of men who were stupid enough to run off with their wife's best friend.

"Do you work for Five Guys?" Ariel asked. "That's my favorite. If I was going to be a burger, I'd totally work for them."

Gabriel raised one of those dark brows. "How is it in the competitive world of burgers?"

The book about courtesy her mother stole from the library was hard to set aside, even north of the Mason-Dixon Line. Portia drew a deep breath, fought for a polite smile, and said, "I was hired as a . . . representative of Burger Boy, not Five Guys. Now, if you'll excuse me, I'll just get out of your way."

But when she tried to move to the smaller door leading down to her apartment, she realized she wasn't going to fit. Momentum had gotten her through the wider door. Nothing short of a good hard shove was going to get her through the other one.

Gabriel's raised brow raised a little bit more.

Damn, damn, damn.

"Need some help?" he asked.

What Portia would have given to be able to say *"No need to bother your little ol' self,"* flip her hair, and sashay off. But just as she had never been much of an eye roller, she had never been good at hair flipping or sashaying either. That was Olivia's department.

"Bless your heart. Maybe a tiny push," she conceded.

" 'Bless your heart'?"

"Just give me a push," she practically growled at him.

It took more than a tiny push to get her levered down the stairs without pitching headfirst like an overlarge bowling ball. While Gabriel angled her down the steps, Ariel called out if he started to make a move that would have her tumbling. But then they came to a grinding halt with Portia only halfway down the steps.

"We're stuck," Gabriel ground out.

"Hold on!" Ariel said, shoving her shoulder into the burger suit and flailing around underneath, trying to get a better look. "Found it! The lettuce is caught on the banister."

It wasn't bad enough that her husband had come home and announced out of the blue that he was divorcing her. Or that her former friend Sissy was now living in the house Portia had worked so hard to make a home. No, she had to get stuck in a burger suit and be manhandled down a stairwell by the kind of man who made her want to forget she was a lady. She really was going to kill her ex-husband, right along with the Burger Boy manager.

Gabriel and Ariel managed to get Portia to her apartment door, but then she came to a halt again. She stood on her toes, trying to see over the burger suit, then didn't bother to swallow back a curse. Not even a good Texas woman should have to live through this humiliation.

"A problem?" Gabriel asked, his tone utterly even. But he was grinning. She could just imagine him having a wonderful time telling all his sophisticated New York friends about the hamburger who lived downstairs. Though it hit her with surprising certainty that this wasn't a man who told tales out of school. In fact, she felt equally certain he was a man who didn't surround himself with friends at all, or even confidants.

Never having imagined she'd be wearing a burger suit, she had forgotten all about how she planned to get back inside. "Thankfully, I keep a key under the mat."

His grin flatlined and his brows slammed together. "You keep a key under the mat? In New York City?"

Portia's eyes narrowed. She'd had it. With him. With life. With this whole damned employment disaster. "Last I heard, burgers don't carry handbags."

Ariel gave a snort of laughter, which earned her a glare as well. "Go upstairs," he snapped.

"What did I do this time?"

"Upstairs."

It took a second, but Ariel stamped her way back up the stairs into the vestibule, then slammed the door to their apartment.

When Gabriel finally got Portia through her door, she waddled with determination over to the kitchen and managed to pluck the sharpest knife out of the drawer. With the grace of a sumo wrestler, she lifted the blade high like a samurai on the verge of seppuku. But before Portia could plunge the knife deep into the rubber bun, Gabriel was on her, grabbing her wrist and twisting it so that the knife skittered across the cracked linoleum floor. "Are you insane?" he demanded.

Her mouth fell open, then closed, then open again as if mimicking the very pedestrians who had gaped at her when she barreled down the sidewalk, a pack of yapping minidogs behind her.

"I'm not trying to kill myself, you, you . . . you!"

Quick comebacks had never been her strong suit.

"I am not trying to hurt myself," she said, enunciating each syllable. "The zipper's stuck. I have to cut myself out of this thing."

Gabriel fell back a step, and started to say something.

"No more sarcastic comments or weird assumptions," she snapped icily. "Just get me the knife." She wasn't feeling icy, though. Gabriel's eyes had changed. He wasn't looking at her waist—or her lack of one, given the suit—he was looking at her mouth.

Portia's heart sped up.

He didn't retrieve the knife. He turned her around, his hands impersonal. But when he jerked the zipper, it wouldn't budge. "Bend over and hold on," he said, pointing to the counter.

Portia turned slightly to look at him over her shoulder and glowered.

"Please?" he added as an afterthought.

Murder, she decided, was too good for Robert after putting her in this situation.

With a low growl, she shook her hair back, trying to get her curls out of her face again. Then she bent over.

But nothing happened.

She tried to glance behind her again. "The zipper? You? Working it?" She gave a scoffing laugh.

"You know, Ms. Cuthcart," Gabriel said, surprising her because suddenly he was so close his lips nearly touched her ear. "Once I get you out of this contraption, if I ever lean you over anything again, you won't be laughing."

Even in this damned burger suit a pulse of awareness shot between them that could have set all that rubber on fire.

Portia swallowed, then forced herself to roll her eyes, not that he could see. It was that or beg him to throw her over whatever he pleased the minute he managed to get her burger-free.

"Men always think that women never laugh at their technique," she managed. "I can assure you that you're all wrong."

She felt him stiffen, and then he burst out laughing. "God, you're a piece of work."

Before she could come up with a fitting response, Gabriel gave a good hard yank and the zipper came free.

The ceiling fan whirled above, and as soon as the burger fell open into two parts, she drew in a ragged breath, turning around. "Oh, my Lord, that feels good," she breathed.

She tugged at the suit, but he had to help before her arms popped out. Her little white tank top was damp with sweat and clung to every curve she had.

Glancing up, she saw his eyes had darkened again, as if he wanted to peel the rest of the burger right off of her. And not in a helpful Boy Scout kind of way.

Portia had been divorced only a little over a month, but she couldn't remember the last time she'd had sex. Not that her ex-husband suffered a similar fate. He'd had plenty of sex, with Sissy. The only person not having sex in her marriage was her.

Everything around them evaporated. The sounds of traffic. The thoughts of outrageously expensive groceries she couldn't afford. Even her ex-husband and ex–best friend's betrayal seemed distant.

Gabriel reached out, but he dropped his hand just before touching her. "What kind of a woman goes around in a burger suit?" he asked, his tone quiet.

She told herself to step away, but couldn't. "The kind who's looking for gainful employment."

"So you'll stoop to anything tossed your way?"

She stiffened, the mood sharp again. "No, not just anything. I turned down the position of Hot Dog, complete with an 'Eat Me' sign."

His features hardened before suddenly he shook his head and the side of his mouth quirked up. "You're impossible." He reached for her again. "Come on, let's get you out of this."

"I can do it."

He stepped back and raised a brow.

She struggled with the rubber before he pushed her hands aside, gently this time. She looked at him for a second, the air around them charged; then she gave in. As he started tugging the suit away, his gaze held hers, until finally he focused. In seconds he had sprung her free.

Thankfully, she was wearing some of Evie's old leggings. She wilted back against the counter, his eyes traveling down her body and then back up to her face.

"You need water," he said finally.

"I'm fine."

He went to the cabinet anyway, found a glass, and filled it from the tap. "Drink."

She felt too exhausted to do anything. "I'm fine, really."

"Portia." Just that, his tone warning.

She didn't know if it was the way he said her name or the way his voice settled deep in his chest, but suddenly she felt emotional. Suddenly everything was too much. She took the water and sipped.

"All of it," he stated, but softly.

The words ran along her senses, and he didn't take his eyes off her until she did as she was told. As soon as she was done, he took the glass from her hands, his fingers brushing against hers, and put it on the counter. Then he looked at her as if searching for something, just as he had that first day she saw him when she was sitting on the front steps. After

Ariel shook her head and rose, wandering out of the kitchen, surprising them when music suddenly blared. "Oops," she called out from the living room. "Sorry."

"It's Evie's old radio," Olivia said.

The three of them pushed up from the stools and walked through the arch that led to the rest of the apartment. "Remember how Evie would turn it on and make us dance with her?" Portia said.

"Yeah, and not to classical music."

"Swing."

"And rock."

"Punk!" Olivia cried out with a laugh.

Portia couldn't help herself: She twirled the dial, and the minute an old eighties punk song came on, she started dancing. "Come on! Let's dance!"

The others stared at her. But then Portia pulled Olivia in. Once Olivia got going, they turned to Cordelia.

"Oh, no. I'm too old for this."

"You're never too old for dancing. Besides, just a minute ago you swore you were twenty-eight."

Portia dragged her onto the floor, and she felt her sister's stress start melting away. All three of them danced and flailed. They turned in hops and sweeps toward Ariel, who looked half-wistful, half-disdainful, and they extended their hands.

"No way. I don't know how to dance."

"Knowing how doesn't matter," Olivia bellowed.

Then suddenly Ariel was in their midst, gyrating and waving her arms, shouting out random words from the chorus.

"Dance, baby!"

At the end of the number, Olivia swirled the dial, then smiled. "I love this one." She turned it up louder, then sang along to a crooning Brad Paisley ballad. She hooked her arm through Cordelia's, and Portia saw their older sister shake her head, but she smiled. And soon they all a second, not seeming to find the answer, or maybe just not liking the one he found, he reached out and tucked an errant strand of hair behind her ear. "You should eat something, then take a cool shower."

He stood close, and with her back against the counter, there was nowhere for her to go. She realized she wanted to sink into this man, and probably would have. There were moments in life, she had heard about, when a person finds where they are meant to be. She had thought that was the case with the knowing. Then again with Robert. And both times the feeling had been proven wrong. But there was something about this man, in this place, that made her feel like a parched traveler stumbling out of the desert and finding a cool sea.

"Who are you really?" she asked without thinking.

But just then his cell phone buzzed and he glanced at the screen.

"I've got to take this." He ran his gaze over her, yet again assessing. "Then we need to talk."

He retucked that same errant curl behind her ear that had sprung free again, and smiled, seeming amused, then headed for the door.

"You with the talking," she managed, a bit of her old self returning. "Next you'll be asking to do facials and braid my hair."

He gave a surprised laugh before he shook his head and kept going.

"Just so you know, there's nothing to talk about!" she called after him. "Especially not the apartment. The only thing I'm prepared to sell is this burger suit, but it's seen better days."

His rumbling laughter was shut off by the closing door.

Seven

⬩⬩⬩

ARIEL'S SOCIAL STUDIES teacher droned on.

Mr. Wickman was old—ancient, really. Probably forty. He was tall, thin as a rail, and had one eye that drooped. The kids called him Wink. Ariel hated that, hated how mean the kids could be. But she hated Mr. Wickman's assignment even more.

A report on ancestry.

Ariel got it. No sense belaboring a topic that had been massively boring the first time around. The last thing she wanted to do, on top of writing in a journal, was poke around in her family history. Yeah, right, she could see that.

Hey, Dad, tell me about Mom and her family.

When pigs flew, maybe.

A better topic was Portia downstairs. Ariel still laughed every time she thought of her barreling into the building dressed as a hamburger and practically squeezing the life out of them. Even more amazing, it was the first time Ariel had seen her dad smile in, like, forever. Granted, he swallowed it back before it took hold. But she'd seen it.

Whatever. It was a good sign. The only way to tell for sure if Portia could distract Dad was to have her over for dinner. Ariel had read on the Internet that you could tell a lot about a person by the way they ate. Did they throw salt over their shoulder if they spilled something? Did they chew with their mouth open? Did they tuck their napkin under their chin instead of putting them in their lap?

She was pretty sure Portia would pass the test, because she was smart and funny. Plus there was the whole *she can cook* thing. If she invited Portia to dinner and asked her to bring a cake, even if the dinner turned out to be a train wreck, they'd at least get a dessert out of the deal.

The only problem was that Ariel knew if she mentioned dinner to her dad, he'd never say yes. So really, why ask? On top of that, she had to do something, and fast. That morning she'd found a new guy's name written all over Miranda's journal.

> Dustin
> Dustin Ferris
> Mrs. Dustin Ferris

Miranda was kind of young to be thinking Mrs. Anything. Hadn't she heard about being a feminist, breaking glass ceilings, and keeping her own name? But it didn't take a genius to figure out that Miranda liked some new guy named Dustin. Which explained why her mood was getting better. Though if their dad found out about it, things would get a whole lot worse.

That was an even better reason to haul Portia upstairs and make her join them for dinner. Miss Potentially Bonkers Burger couldn't be worse than another Family Night of Miranda ignoring Dad, and Dad pointedly *not* ignoring Miranda.

Ariel bolted out of class feeling better despite the fact that she had to find a way to dig around in her family tree without anyone in her family knowing. She had a plan to distract her dad.

As soon as Ariel got home, she wrote out the invitation.

Dear Portia,
  You are totally invited to dinner.
  Tomorrow night with the Kane Family.
  7 P.M.
  Don't be late.

                        Your upstairs neighbor,
                        Ariel Kane

P.S. Feel free to bring a cake.

Eight

❖

PORTIA STOPPED DEAD with the urge to bake a cake.

The need hit her hard and strong, surprising her. She hadn't woken to, or felt a single stab of knowing since she'd made the meal that first day in the apartment. But the image of that same chocolate cake she had woken to that day circled through her, making it difficult to breathe.

"Control, Portia," she whispered. "You're in control of your life now. Not Robert. And certainly not the knowing."

Despite the hamburger debacle, not to mention her dwindling bank account, she felt freer than she had in years. For the first time ever, she was living her own life. For the first time, she wasn't at the mercy of things she couldn't control. The money situation had to be solved, sure, but that didn't negate the fact that she felt alive.

Her walks through the streets of New York amazed her that she lived here. She didn't care that she made solemn-faced neighbors scurry away from her wide Texas smiles. "*I am here!*" she wanted to shout. She was making a new and fabulous life! Or would! Hope made her buoyant.

She had managed to avoid Gabriel for another two days, but obviously it wasn't going to last. Based on his repeated comments about the conversation they needed to have, she figured the man's lawyer hadn't given a good enough explanation as to why she had backed out of the sale.

But she should have known that no explanation left on an answering machine would be good enough. Gabriel Kane wasn't the sort of man who ever gave up. If he wanted something, he would take it. She had figured that out the day she saw him from the front steps.

Just as with the other aspects of her life, she had to take control of this, too, and make it clear why she couldn't sell. So when the dinner invitation slid under her door, she decided it was time to address the situation head-on.

She reread the invitation, then felt a surge of surprised worry when she noticed the mention of cake. But she pushed that aside, too.

Instead, she focused on what she had been meaning to do since she had slipped through the front door. Clean.

Before fleeing to New York, she hadn't seen the apartment in years. During the first month she had been in Manhattan, she had stayed with Cordelia in her fancy Central Park West duplex apartment and had been too consumed with loss to give any thought to what she would do next or where she would live long-term. But after that month of staying with her sister, she had been hit with the certainty that she couldn't stay with Cordelia and her husband any longer. With that thought she knew exactly where she would go. Great-aunt Evie's garden apartment.

Standing in the apartment now, Portia took in the dark draperies and grime. The apartment flowed back to French doors that opened onto the garden, which sat a few steps up in the rear. The kitchen was rustic, with a cast-iron stove, a sink, an ancient refrigerator, and an old stone fireplace that Portia couldn't imagine had been used in years, if not decades. The slate floor in the entry and the hardwood throughout the rest of the apartment were murky and scuffed, uneven in places. The bathroom was dingy, but had a beautiful antique ball-and-claw tub. Portia felt sure there was potential.

She unearthed cleaning supplies from the kitchen cabinet and got to work. She pulled every stick of furniture out into the back garden. She rolled up all the rugs and dragged them out, too. Once the apartment was empty, she tied a scarf over her nose and took down the dusty curtains she planned to wash. She swept down the exposed-brick walls and hardwood floors, and even found a hand broom to tackle the fireplace.

When she finished and looked around, sweat rolling down her back and streaking her face, nothing looked any cleaner than when she had started.

So she started over, this time with hot water, Clorox, rags, and a mop. She scrubbed everything in sight until her hands were raw and red. By the end of the day, she was covered in grime and soot, her hair a tangle. But when she drifted off to sleep, the apartment was clean, and she had a deep sense that for whatever reason, she had come home.

The next morning, she woke with a groan. Every bone in her body ached. But when she glanced around and saw what she had accomplished, excitement drummed through her. She also thought of the dinner invitation. Though she shouldn't have been, she was excited about that, too.

She gave a thought to giving in and making the cake herself, then pushed it away. She hurried out to purchase the least-expensive dessert she could find. Once she had that taken care of, she resorted to her great-aunt's closet again. She found a fabulous pair of long, flowing, gray flannel, pinstriped pants with wide cuffs by Yves Saint Laurent, and a simple cotton blouse made in Paris as well. Then at five minutes before seven that evening, Portia headed upstairs with the cake.

Inside the vestibule, next to the front door, a series of work permits had been posted. Portia hadn't been in New York City long, but it didn't take a genius to figure out that her neighbor was in the process of renovating the rest of the town house.

Out of habit, she knocked. In all the years she and her sisters had spent summers with Aunt Evie, the doorbell had never worked. When no one answered, she knocked again, this time more loudly. Eventually

Ariel peeked out the curtain over the side window. "What are you doing just standing there?" Ariel asked, pulling open the door.

"I knocked."

"Haven't you heard of a doorbell?"

The girl looked at Portia like she was crazy, popping out and pressing the button like a game show hostess demonstrating how to spin the wheel. Bells sounded, a sign that the new owner wasn't content with broken stuff.

Portia felt an odd feeling of displacement at the thought, as if the work permits and new doorbell meant her old life was really gone. Which was ridiculous. Her husband divorcing her had put that particular pony to bed, not a stranger remodeling her great-aunt's former home.

"My great-aunt used to live here," Portia said, distracted. "Back then, the doorbell was broken."

"Seriously? Someone you know used to live here?"

"Yes, my great-aunt," Portia repeated, walking farther into the town house.

The structure was the same, but nothing else. The entire inside had been gutted and refurbished. The old Victorian wallpaper was gone, stripped, the walls redone with a bright white textured plaster. Portia shouldn't have missed the water stains shaped like butterflies and dragons, but she did.

The carpet had been pulled up, the wood underneath refinished and covered with Oriental rugs. Expensive art hung above expensive furniture. Everything was perfectly done, and in the back of Portia's head she knew it was beautiful. But that was *way* back in her head, pushed aside by the fact that the work she had done in her own apartment suddenly felt inadequate compared to this. Glumly, she noted that one of the man's rugs could no doubt have paid for an entire year's worth of property taxes that Portia now had to figure out how to pay.

"Where's your aunt now?" Ariel asked.

"She died. A few years back." The words came out more abruptly than Portia intended. She thought for a second that Ariel flinched, but then the girl rolled her eyes.

"Was she old?"

"Yes, but very lively and dear. She left the building to my sisters and me. My sisters sold the upper floors to your dad."

"So that's why you're in the basement. I take it she didn't like you as much as the others."

Portia laughed. "She left me the garden apartment, not a basement. She knew I love gardens."

"My mom's dead," Ariel said. "Like your aunt. But my mom wasn't old." She turned away as if she hadn't said anything all that important.

It took Portia a second to absorb the words. Was that why she felt a connection to Ariel when she barely knew her? Did girls who had lost mothers have a hidden bond?

"That looks like a store-bought cake," Ariel said, shifting gears before Portia could respond.

"It is."

"You were supposed to bring one of those amazing cakes you make yourself."

Ariel gaped. "You did both the other night."

"Sorry. That was then. This is now."

Ariel's shoulders slumped. But then she drew an exaggerated breath. She shrugged. "I can only do so much."

Portia followed the girl toward the back of the house. Unless there had been major structural changes, Portia knew they were coming to the sunroom, her favorite part of the house.

But it wasn't the room that she saw. It was Gabriel.

"Damn it, Dan, that isn't acceptable," he said into a cell phone. "I've told you, I'm not going to relent. Make them pay."

He stood with his back to them, looking out the tall windows, phone pressed to his ear. Everything about him felt barely controlled, hardly contained. Without warning, he turned and saw her.

The dark of his eyes grew intense as his gaze met hers before it slowly drifted over her.

"You remember our neighbor, Daddy," Ariel said, sweet as pie, emphasis on the word *Daddy.*

Portia hadn't seen him since the burger incident three days ago, and he seemed to take her in, assessing to determine if she was fine.

She scowled at the memory of the incident, which made him raise a brow, his lips quirking.

A voice squawked anxiously from the phone he was holding. "I'm here," he said smoothly, seeming reluctant to turn away. But eventually he did, concentrating on the call.

Ariel leaned close. "I use the whole Daddy thing to soften him up. For some reason, he likes it. Go figure." She cocked her head. "Come on. Let's put that *store-bought* cake in the kitchen."

Portia followed Ariel through a swinging door and into the kitchen. The heat of the oven hit her along with the bright yellow and white walls, white trim and crown molding. The kitchen had been redone as well, but instead of making it into something different, it had become a newer version of its old self. She had to concede she loved it.

An older woman stood at the wide granite counter, making a salad. She didn't say hello or glance up.

"Come on," Ariel said, taking the cake and setting it on the counter, then herding Portia through another swinging door into the dining room. "That's Gerta, and she hates being interrupted. Dad hasn't had very good luck finding housekeepers. We should wait in here."

But before Portia could do anything like question, sit, or bolt for the front door, Gabriel walked into the room. Heat filled her like milk and honey coming to a slow boil. Truth to tell, she felt nervous, what with her promising herself to deal head-on with this man regarding the apartment, and nervous was bad.

He leaned his shoulder against the doorjamb, arms crossed on his chest. "So," he said.

"So?" she countered.

"What's with the outfit?"

She looked him up and down. "People don't really call clothes *outfits* anymore, at least not guys." She considered him for a moment. "Take that, combined with the whole obsession-with-talking thing, and I have to ask: Is your favorite color pink? Have you ever worn tight jeans and cuffed them at the hem with loafers and no socks? No, wait; have you ever worn man clogs?"

His lips twitched. "Hardly. Never. And no. But you, on the other hand, look like you just stepped out of *Saturday Night Fever*."

"I was going more for *Annie Hall*. Same year. Smarter movie."

Ariel looked traumatized, as if she couldn't imagine how or where this type of conversation was coming from. Portia shook the sarcasm free. She drummed up a good, if strained, Texas smile. And Ariel grew visibly relieved. Gabriel just looked like he was trying not to laugh.

"What's going on?" An older, more put-together version of Ariel walked in. She had to be the older daughter Ariel had mentioned.

Unlike her younger sister, this one's light brown hair was long and straight, and she had grown into her eyes and mouth. She wore a lime green T-shirt tucked into a short, fitted denim skirt that flared around her thighs, and multicolored tennis shoes with a wedged heel. "Nana's here," she said. She looked Portia up and down. "Who are you?"

"She's our new neighbor," Ariel supplied dejectedly.

Miranda gave her a once-over, then shrugged. "Cool clothes."

Portia shot Gabriel a triumphant smile.

Footsteps resounded from behind Miranda's shoulder. "Where is everyone?"

A woman of about sixty-five walked into the kitchen. Beautiful and elegantly put together, she seemed like a woman who was used to commanding attention. "There you are. Miranda, I saw you walk by without opening the door, which was astonishingly rude. I had to use my key. Gabriel, if I've told you once, I've told you a thousand times, don't let these girls run roughshod over you."

"As if that were possible," Miranda muttered.

The woman shot a pointed look at Gabriel, but a clatter of pots and pans in the kitchen interrupted.

The woman started to say something, but then she saw Portia. "Oh, I didn't realize we had company." As if she weren't a guest. "I'm Helen Kane. Gabriel's mother."

"Hi, I'm Portia Cuthcart. I live downstairs."

"Downstairs?" Yet another person who gave Portia a once-over. "I thought the apartment was empty," Helen continued. "Have you lived there long?"

"No, not long. My great-aunt used to own the building and left it to me and my sisters." Portia knew she was babbling, but she couldn't seem to stop.

Helen turned to her son. "I thought you were buying it for Anthony."

"Mother, I'm handing this."

"Gabriel, don't tell me you didn't go through with the deal. I know you don't want Anthony here, but I won't forgive you if you decided against buying the garden level just to keep him away."

"Mother, enough."

The woman composed herself with effort, turning back to Portia, who felt more uncomfortable than ever.

"Do you have people here, dear?" the woman finally asked. "Friends. Family. I'm sure there are plenty of places you'd rather live than downstairs in the godforsaken apartment."

Portia didn't know what to think or do. Clearly it wasn't going to be as easy to explain not selling as she had hoped. "My sisters are here."

"How lovely. Family really is the most important thing." Helen said the words with more emphasis than necessary, turning back to Gabriel. "Where is your brother?"

If possible, Gabriel's expression grew even more guarded. "I told you, Mother, he isn't coming. We both know that Anthony only shows up when he needs money. Another reason why he doesn't need me to buy him an apartment that he won't spend time in."

"That's not true. He's coming." Her voice rose. "He promised."

Miranda's head shot up, fingers stilling on her iPhone, eyes brightening with excitement. "Uncle Anthony is coming?"

Gabriel opened his mouth, but his mother cut him off. "Yes, he is. He's coming to town and he promised he'd arrive by dinner." The grandmother shot Gabriel a glare. "When he arrives, he'll be staying with me, for obvious reasons."

"Dinner," the cook announced.

"We need to wait," Helen Kane said, rummaging around in her Chanel bag until she found a cell phone.

"Mother, how many times has Anthony said he's coming to town, then failed to show up?" Gabriel refocused on Portia. "Thank you for stopping by," he said. "Ariel, show Ms. Cuthcart to the door?"

Portia blinked.

"Dad," Ariel interjected, "I told you, we invited her to dinner."

Gabriel stared at his younger daughter, irritation riding across his face. "No, you didn't tell me."

"I didn't? Oops, bad me."

"Ariel, doesn't your father know that you invited me to dinner?"

Ariel wrinkled her nose. "Not exactly."

Just great. "I'll go."

"You can't! You brought a cake. Dad, you can't kick her out after she brought us a cake."

"Way to be polite, Dad," Miranda said.

Was that a hint of desperation in his eyes?

Gabriel ran his hand through his hair. "Sorry for the confusion. Please. Join us."

"Really, I—"

Ariel grabbed Portia's arm and pulled her toward a chair. Without jerking away, there wasn't much she could do.

The dining room had been transformed into a breezy space. Billowing lightweight curtains framed French doors leading to a Juliet balcony. It was beautiful, in a picture-perfect magazine sort of way. But there was nothing personal about it.

"Nice, huh?" Ariel said.

"Absolutely lovely!" She might have added too much enthusiasm in an attempt to cover up a real lack of it.

Gabriel raised a brow, but didn't comment.

Helen Kane managed to delay the meal for another ten minutes waiting for her other son, but finally gave in when Gabriel pointed out that Anthony was already forty-five minutes late. The family sat in silence as they were served a meal of tough beef tenderloin, overdone asparagus, underdone potatoes, wilted salad, and slices of plain white bread.

Portia thought of her own grandmother, of the cookbooks, of the knowledge that charred beef would fill a person with heated anger. The last thing this family needed was more anger.

Miranda's phone rang, and she started to answer.

"What did I tell you about phone calls at dinner?"

"But, Dad!"

"No buts."

Miranda glared.

Gabriel pretended not to notice. Ariel sighed. The grandmother kept looking toward the door.

This family was unhappy. This family needed food—light, nutritious meals. Happy food. Menus rushed unbidden through Portia's head. A fluffy quiche. Arugula salad with a light balsamic dressing.

The thought surprised Portia, and she pushed this one away, too.

Miranda glared. "You're a terrible dad, you know? Nobody I know has to put up with this stupid stuff at home."

Portia opened her mouth, and closed it again. Gabriel's face closed, his eyes expressionless. Helen raised a brow much like her son did so often.

"Hey, Dad?" Ariel said, breaking the silence. "I think you're doing a great job."

Apparently the task of peacemaking had fallen to Ariel.

The tense silence was interrupted when the doorbell rang.

"That's him!" Helen lit up like a Christmas tree.

Miranda bolted from the table and dashed to the door.

"Uncle Anthony!" rang through the town house.

Portia heard a deep voice laugh and footsteps headed their way. Helen stood. For his part, Gabriel remained seated at the head of the table, his jaw visibly tight. But as his brother entered the room, he rose to greet him as if ingrained manners took over.

The man who entered couldn't have been more different from his brother. It wasn't that they didn't look alike; they did. They had the same dark hair and dark eyes, the same set to their jaw. But something about the way Anthony Kane's features came together made him seem like light to Gabriel's dark—Beauty to the Beast.

Gabriel extended his hand. Anthony smiled and pulled his brother in for a bear hug.

When they stepped apart, Portia saw that Gabriel's face hadn't eased.

Anthony just laughed, and turned to his mother. Helen Kane looked as if she was on the verge of tears.

"It's about time you noticed your mother," she said, opening her arms.

Portia watched as Anthony pulled his mother into another fierce hug, then set her at arm's length. "God, you are the best-looking woman I've seen in a long time." He actually twirled her around, like two dancers on a stage.

Then, suddenly, the force of Anthony's attention turned to her.

"Hello there, beautiful. Who are you?"

Portia felt Ariel's surprised glance, Helen's narrowed-eye glare, even something decidedly tense coming from Gabriel. But no one introduced her.

"I'm Portia Cuthcart," she offered. "I live downstairs."

Anthony took Portia's hand and lifted it dramatically in the air. "Oh, to have a neighbor like you," he said, his eyes laughing. He leaned down to kiss the backs of her fingers.

"Good Lord, Anthony," Helen said. "I can see you haven't lost any charm while you were away." She sounded both jealous and proud.

"I wouldn't call it charm."

Gabriel hadn't moved, but Portia felt his tension settle into something deeper, more nuanced as he said the words.

Anthony dropped into a chair next to his mother. He snatched up the woman's hand and peppered kisses up to her wrist, making her scoff and bat him about the head.

What would it be like, Portia wondered, to be the less-favored child? She felt an instant desire to defend Gabriel. Then she shook the thought away. If anyone in this room needed protecting, it definitely wasn't Gabriel Kane.

"You can't believe how good it is to be back in the States, sitting at a real table, eating civilized food," Anthony said, his lightning-quick attention span shifting to the serving dishes in front of him. After a closer look, he made a face. "Two out of three isn't bad."

"Where've you been, Uncle Anthony?" Miranda asked.

"Here and there," he said, serving himself a plate. "Mostly there."

Miranda giggled, though Ariel's face stayed as expressionless as her father's.

Anthony glanced at his brother. "You'd hate the places I've been. We never know when we're going to get shot at. No showers for days. We spend weeks hiking to where we need to be. No cushy Easy Street for us."

If Portia hadn't met either man and she'd had to guess which one lived a less civilized life, it would have been Gabriel.

"What do you do?" Portia asked.

Gabriel glanced at his brother. "Yes, Anthony, what do you do?"

Anthony ignored his brother. "I'm a writer. I've done a bunch of work for newspapers."

"Yes, like *The Alliance Sun* and *The Waco Citizen*," Gabriel interjected.

Anthony glared, but then shrugged. "Right now I'm working on a book proposal."

Gabriel began sawing at the leathery meat on his plate. "Translation: He's out of a job."

Anthony's jaw set.

Ariel jumped in. "Speaking of jobs, Dad! Did you know that Portia is a cook?"

Anthony stabbed one of the rock-hard potatoes and waved it in the air. "Maybe you should hire her to cook for you, given the bang-up job you're doing as 'Mr. Mom.'"

Gabriel looked him in the eye. "Maybe you should worry about finding your own job."

"Me? I'll get a job. But, frankly, I'm in no hurry."

"Interesting. I assumed the only reason you showed up this time was because you were broke."

Anthony glared right back at his brother. "Turns out, I'm about to come into some money," he said coolly.

"Really?" Gabriel asked. "Then you signed the documents?"

"What documents?" Helen demanded.

Anthony's easy smile returned. "I haven't signed a thing yet, big brother. I've got to make sure I'm getting the best deal."

The tension that had wound around Gabriel like a rope pulled tight.

Anthony turned to his mother. "But let me tell you, I've lucked into the most amazing opportunity. It's a deal that helps the environment *and* promises to pay back investors tenfold. All I need is five grand."

The light in Helen's eyes visibly dimmed, and Portia knew with a sinking sense of certainty that Anthony had sprung many "deals" on his mother before.

Gabriel opened his mouth, but luckily his cell phone rang. He glanced at the screen. "If you'll excuse me. I have to take this." He directed a humorless smile at his brother. "It's about a real job." Then he stood up and left the room, saying, "Dan, is the Global deal done?"

Portia wanted nothing more than to hightail it out of Dodge. Apparently the rules regarding no cell phones at the dinner table applied only to adolescents. Which gave her the perfect way out.

"Oh dear, I forgot all about a call I have to take, too." She hopped to her feet. "This really was lovely, but I have to go. If you'll excuse me . . ."

Helen gave her a measured smile, and Anthony a lavish one. Miranda barely looked up from her own cell phone, which she had grabbed the minute Gabriel left the room.

Ariel looked miserable. "Sorry."

"There's nothing to apologize for," she said, keeping her tone bright. "You were sweet to invite me. Bye!"

Nine

⋅⋅⋅⟐⋅⋅⋅

THE NEXT MORNING, Ariel stared at her open journal, her neat block writing, the consistent Bic pen–blue ink. She always used her blue pen for the journal. All those lines of static blue ink should have made her feel better, but didn't.

Her family was a mess. But unlike perfect block letters or math problems, there didn't seem to be any orderly solutions in sight.

She missed her mom in a way that was so big that it constantly wanted to burst out of her. Mom had been so smart, but in a different sort of way. Not math smart, like her, or even money smart, like her dad, but something way more useful really. She knew how to deal with problems. She wouldn't have come up with some lame plan of getting another woman to distract anyone.

Tears burned in the back of her throat. Not that crying would do any good. During the last year since Mom had died, Ariel had learned that over and over again.

She considered giving up on playing matchmaker between her dad and Portia. No question it was a ridiculous idea, and felt traitorous to her mom. Plus, Portia was weird. The only thing was that there was the whole *Portia had made her dad laugh* thing when she'd had on that burger suit. Which led Ariel right back to the fact that she didn't have a better plan.

A few minutes later, Ariel found her dad in the kitchen dressed for work, peering into one of the big pots Gerta normally used to make her awful soup. Bread was toasting in the toaster oven.

"Hey," Ariel said, coming up beside him. "You're cooking?" She looked over at the toaster oven, then into the pot, and wrinkled her nose. "What is it?"

"Oatmeal." He stirred it a few more times, like that would make it edible.

"Where's Gerta?"

"She quit."

"Quit?" She stepped back. "Ugh. Dad. That's totally burned. Can't you smell it?"

He jerked the pan off the stove, dumped it in the sink, and turned on the water. A sizzle and fog rose when the water hit the pan. Then he yanked the burned bread out of the toaster. By then, Ariel would have bet the whole house smelled liked a campfire cookout gone awry.

Grumbling, her dad opened the refrigerator and pulled out some milk. Then he stuck it on the table with three bowls and a box of cereal.

"Oh, joy, Wheaties."

Her father scowled at her.

"Miranda!" he bellowed in the general direction of the doorway.

Ariel sat down at the table. "You know, I was serious the other day," she said, deciding that if there was no other option than the Portia Plan, then there was no time like the present for a Portia Pitch, "about Portia cooking for us. But if you don't want to hire her outright, have you ever thought of, I don't know"—she made a show of considering—"dating her?"

He sliced her a look that she could only classify as irritated. "I'm not interested in dating Portia," he said, pouring milk on her cereal. "As for hiring her, didn't she say something about *not* cooking?"

Ariel tried to look serious and pensive. "I happen to know differently. But that's neither here nor there."

"Neither here nor there?"

"Dad, seriously? You sound like Miranda. Whatever, we're talking about Portia. It's probably good you don't want to date her." She nodded, just like the Shrink did whenever she bothered to say something, as if that would encourage her to start yakking away. "Now that she's had a chance to get to know you, she'd never go out with you, anyway." Didn't every man like a challenge?

Unfortunately, other than snort, her dad didn't take the bait. "I am not dating the woman downstairs."

"She's not just any woman. She's Portia, who can cook regardless of what she says." She shot him a broad, encouraging smile. "Portia, who could provide your growing daughters with much-needed food, even if she just bought it and brought it home to us." She dragged the last word out just a hair. "I mean, really, she *is* looking for a job."

"Are you suggesting I date a woman for convenience?"

"I've heard of worse reasons to ask someone out. In fact, I was watching *Jersey Shore*—"

"What were you doing watching *Jersey Shore?*"

"Stay with me, Dad; that isn't the point."

"The point is that you shouldn't be watching cr—" He cut himself off. "Trash. You shouldn't be watching trash."

"Does this fall into the category of kid blocks on computers and 'No, Ariel, you're too young for a cell phone'? Because, seriously, just think what would happen if I got lost and I didn't have a cell phone? If I had a cell phone, all I'd have to do is call you and say, 'Hey, Dad, guess where I am?'" She wrinkled her nose. "Hmm, I guess that wouldn't work since, given the whole lost thing, I wouldn't know where I was. Whatever—"

"Not 'whatever.'" Her dad glared even more. "No twelve-year-old needs a cell phone."

"You've forgotten that I'm almost thirteen, but I won't mention that since you're probably sensitive about forgetting things. And, really, Dad, you could do a lot worse than Portia. Her hair is great, for one thing."

Her dad just shook his head, though Ariel wasn't sure why. Maybe it was about the way Portia looked. Truthfully, who could blame him? He had seen Portia in all her flowered-Keds-and–strange-clothes glory. Maybe if Ariel figured out how to fix Portia up some, he'd take the bait. Hair, clothes, attitude. But how to make over an adult?

Great. Something else she had to figure out.

She picked up her bowl, set it in the sink, and headed for Trident Prep. But if managing the illogical workings of the standard American family was tricky, three and a half hours later she decided the whole middle-school hierarchy thing was preposterous when she sat at a back lunch table in the school cafeteria and her tiny world erupted in a battlefield of peer pressure and social awkwardness.

It wasn't like she had been popular in New Jersey or anything, but Ariel was her sister's sister and she had lived there forever, so people left her alone. But now she was the new girl, and no one had even heard of her sister—who went to a different school anyway. Ariel was on her own. Plus, Mindi Hansen thought she was the head of the world and— no surprise—she couldn't stand Ariel.

Ariel was sitting by herself doing homework when Mindi came over. "So, uh, Ariel, right?"

"Last I heard."

Mindi obviously couldn't take a joke. "What are you?" she demanded, tone biting. "A geek, a nerd, a moron?"

Mindi's friends all laughed as they walked away.

"Actually," Ariel muttered to the girls' backs, "I'm someone who doesn't need other people's approval to understand my self-worth."

Quite frankly, she blamed her dad for what happened next. If he hadn't made her go to the Shrink, she never would have known anything about self-worth and outside approval.

Mindi froze in her Tory Burch ballet flats. "What did you say?"

"Nothing." Her heart pounded like a fist on a drum. But because she just never learned, she opened her mouth and added, "There's no point in repeating it because you'd never understand."

It was that or give in to the knot of total sad-anger raging inside her—which she had no intention of doing. What would come out? Crying? Disappearing right then and there instead of the slow melting away it felt like she was doing every day?

Mindi leaned closer. "So, Ariel"—saying her name as three long, drawn-out syllables—"where's your *mom*?"

The question caught her by surprise.

Mindi tapped a pink nail on her cheek. "Let me see. Is your mom, like, dead?"

Ariel just stared at her.

"And not dead of, like, cancer or something. She wrecked her car driving like a maniac in New Jersey, right?"

Ariel's mother *had* died in a car accident, slowly disappearing as she bled out before the ambulance could get there. Ariel knew, because she had been in the car.

"That's not cool," one of Mindi's friends said, grabbing her by the arm. "You're putting the B in Bitch, girl. Let it go."

Mindi tossed her hair, smiled, and walked away.

Ten

❖

PORTIA GASPED AWAKE with the taste of apples in her mouth—crisp green apples smothered in brown sugar and spice. She needed to bake.

Lying tangled in the sheets, she tried to calm her racing heart. She tried to write off this urge, too. It was nothing more than a knee-jerk reaction to moving to the Big Apple. But no matter how forcefully she told herself she had stuffed the knowing back down, she realized that she hadn't. Not really. When she should have smelled bleach and sundried cotton, it was the scent of apples and buttery caramel that swirled in her mind.

The urges to bake and cook were getting stronger, the knowing coming back to life like simple syrup spun into cotton candy.

For those first couple of weeks she had managed to feel alive and carefree. But with every day that passed with her unable to find a real job, the images of food growing more persistent, panic started to grow. The only thing that kept her from a full-blown panic attack was the promise of Robert's settlement.

Groggy and disoriented, Portia made it out of the bedroom just when

Cordelia arrived. Maybe her sister knocked, maybe not, but whatever the case, Cordelia walked right in using her own key, holding her cell phone to her ear with her other hand.

"I'm here. I've got to go," Cordelia said, looking at Portia. "I promise," she added quickly. "I'll call as soon as I know anything." She dropped her phone into her handbag.

Cordelia wore a cream blouse with a camel cashmere sweater tied around her shoulders, camel pants, and brown suede Chanel ballet flats. Her hair was pulled back in a demure twist at the nape of her neck, pearls at her ears. She looked just like a politician's wife. No politician's wife would be caught dead in Aunt Evie's old dress, which Portia was now wearing regularly.

"Who was that?" she asked, trying to pull herself together. She had no interest in letting Cordelia know she was out of sorts.

"Oh, just Olivia."

"*Just* Olivia?" Portia sliced her a look. "What do you need to let her know?"

Cordelia waved the words away. "Nothing." Then she looked around. "My God, you must have worked around the clock." She brushed past Portia, walking into the kitchen. "The place is still hideous, but at least now it's clean."

Cordelia sat down at the table and pulled out a stack of books and two magazines from her shoulder bag. Portia sat down opposite her. Her oldest sister was infamous for the self-help articles and books she distributed like a librarian encouraging a reluctant reader.

"I thought you might like some company," Cordelia said, setting the assorted reading on the table.

"Did you think I'd be driving myself crazy by now?"

"Something like that." Cordelia didn't smile, didn't laugh. Instead, she pushed the stack across the table.

Portia's eyebrow flew up. "*Bon Appétit*? *Fine Cooking* magazine? *Restaurant Management for Dummies*?"

With a shrug that didn't match the determination in her eyes, Cordelia pulled a plastic shopping bag from the tote. "I stopped at the market."

"How sweet," Portia said, trying to sound sincere. "But I have more than enough groceries."

"What do you mean?" Cordelia scoffed. "I bet you hardly have anything in this place. Plus, I brought you a surprise. A present."

Portia stared as Cordelia began pulling items out of the bags with the efficiency of a nurse preparing an operating room for surgery.

"Remember that fresh apple cake you used to make?"

Portia's heart practically stilled in her chest.

Cordelia continued, laying out ingredients on the counter. She looked through the window, momentarily distracted. "It made me think about how much I miss The Glass Kitchen. For days now I've done nothing but think about that place."

Portia's heart surged into her throat. "You hated everything about The Glass Kitchen."

"I did not. I might have been too young to appreciate it, but I didn't hate it. But that's beside the point. I would be over the moon if you'd make me one of your famous apple cakes."

Portia stared at the ingredients her sister had lined up with perfect precision on the scratched countertop. Apples. Butter. Brown sugar.

Cordelia cocked her head. "What is it?"

"Nothing," Portia said, her voice weak. "It's just that I'm not in the mood to bake, is all."

That was a lie. Her fingers itched to dive in, peel, and core, sift the flour, fold in the softened butter and brown sugar. Again and again since moving into the apartment she'd had to ignore her tingling fingertips and the smells of chocolate and vanilla that didn't really exist. She had thrown every bit of food in the apartment away, and it still hadn't helped.

"I don't believe you," Cordelia said. "You want to bake like nobody's business. I can see it in your eyes."

"No."

It was panic that glittered in her eyes. It was her fingers that wanted to betray her.

But her brain knew the real cost of baking. She didn't want to be someone who knew things. She didn't want to sense that something was going to happen and have no idea what that was until it was too late.

The *knowing* spelled worry and stress and desperately trying to save people. Under no circumstances did she want the stress and uncertainty of the knowing back in her life. "No," she repeated, determined.

Cordelia sat there, quiet and watchful. After a second, she said, "Just hear me out."

"Cordelia—"

Cordelia raised her hand, stopping her. "Olivia and I were talking. We want to open a restaurant."

Portia felt the blood drain from her face.

Cordelia didn't let up. "A café, really. Something small. A quaint version of, well, The Glass Kitchen. We thought, maybe, you had brought Gram's cookbooks with you."

While Portia didn't want any part of the knowing, she *definitely* wanted nothing to do with another Glass Kitchen.

"It makes all the sense in the world," Cordelia continued, with more of that calm efficiency. "And, of course, you'll do it with us. Olivia and I agree."

"You and Olivia?" As if that decided everything. Apparently, nothing had changed after the loss of her grandmother, her home, her husband. She was still the little sister to be bossed around.

"Yes, and it will be fabulous—"

"No."

"Portia, it could be like old times."

"What has that got to do with old times? You and Olivia weren't there. You had nothing to do with The Glass Kitchen. You were *here*, in New York. You—" Portia cut herself off, forcing herself to be calm.

"No," she reiterated, and to make sure her point was understood, she walked to the front door and opened it. "I have a million things to do."

Like throw herself back in bed and never get up.

"Just listen." Cordelia stopped herself and drew a deep breath. After a second, she continued. "If you must know, I haven't been completely . . . forthcoming." She pursed her lips, lines showing age in a way Portia hadn't noticed before. "The truth is, Olivia and I need a Glass Kitchen."

Portia studied her. "What do you mean?"

"I need something." Cordelia said, looking away. "I'd be great running a restaurant with my sisters. I see it so clearly. I see you and me and Olivia creating the sort of place you can't find in New York. Magical food in a magical space. Gourmand Texas style. How can it not be a huge success?"

"Cordelia, opening a restaurant is a hugely iffy proposition under the best of circumstances, and it's not like any of us are in a strong position right now."

Cordelia blushed, surprising Portia even more. Cordelia had always been so sure of herself. But then she pulled her shoulders back and looked Portia in the eye.

"I want to open a Glass Kitchen because it's my legacy as much as yours. But more than that, James was wrong. Everything isn't going to be all right. It's one thing to lose our savings. But James took out a substantial loan against his next bonus—that would be the bonus he won't receive. Portia, I have to find a way to make money, make a living for my family. And Olivia is no better off than I am, teaching yoga, arranging flowers, or whatever it is she does between boyfriends. She's spent every dime she made when she sold her part of this place. We need this."

Portia felt light-headed with worry. Then anger. How many times had she saved her older sisters when they were growing up?

Portia closed her eyes, recalling the time Olivia took a job as a caterer with a mom-and-pop shop that was The Glass Kitchen's only real competition. As the middle sister, Olivia had been determined to be independent, to prove that she wasn't reliant upon Gram or Cordelia or even Portia. Portia had been planning the night's menu when she knew she had to make bouillabaisse—but not for dinner. The next afternoon, when the bouillabaisse was perfect, with loaves of French bread just done, Olivia flew in through the back door of the Kitchen.

"I promised the mayor's wife I could cater a French meal for her party tonight. I promised it would be great! But everything I've made is a disaster."

Portia stood silently as Olivia glanced over at the old cast-iron stove and took a deep breath. "I have to have it, Portia," she said. She didn't need to be told the answer to her dilemma was in the pot.

Now Portia stood in the small apartment in New York City, Cordelia in front of her again, tension thick in the room.

"Yes, but remember the strawberry preserves?" Cordelia said quietly, as if she were reading Portia's mind.

Of course she remembered. She couldn't forget any of it. The bad. The good. She remembered the strawberries, could smell them as if they were sitting in front of her on the counter. It had been a day when she and her sisters had argued. Afterward, all Portia could think about was making strawberry preserves. She had ended up making a huge vat of the preserves only to realize she didn't have anything to can them in. Cordelia and Olivia had shown up with boxes of Ball jars they'd gotten at a yard sale for a penny apiece. They had ladled in tense silence, filling jars, setting them aside to cool, much as their tempers cooled.

Once they were done, without a word of apology, Olivia had smiled with that impudent glint of hers, and pulled Portia and Cordelia into a dance. Then they took the preserves to an outdoor flea market and made enough money to pay for the dress Cordelia needed for her wedding to James.

The knowing had provided the bridge back to each other, a way for Olivia to keep her job, a way for Cordelia to pay for a dress she couldn't afford. Some of the few times the knowing worked for good, when it made Portia's world better, rather than signaling a loss to come.

"I love James," Cordelia said now. "I'll do whatever it takes to help him. But I need help. Olivia needs help. And, sweetie, so do you."

That had always been the way with the Cuthcart sisters. Fighting, furious, but unable to live without one another.

Portia hesitated. "Tell me this, Cord. Do you really want to open a café, or is it that you don't know what else to do?"

Cordelia answered. "Both. Did it ever occur to you that maybe, just maybe, you might not have been betrayed by your husband if you hadn't been suppressing who you really are? Did it ever occur to you that turning your back on the . . . that trait Gram swore by made you blind to what was really going on with Robert and Sissy?"

The words hurt more than they should have. It wasn't as if Portia hadn't wondered exactly that. But it didn't change anything.

"Just think about it," Cordelia said, then gathered her things and left.

Portia paced from room to room in her small apartment. Small, at least, compared to the Texas house she and Robert had lived in. Size was relative in New York City. A closet in Texas was a million-dollar bargain in the city.

An hour later, the chirp of her cell phone caught her off guard. She grabbed her phone only to be brought up short by the display.

Robert Baleau.

She grabbed the counter, ducking as if her ex-husband could see her.

"No, no, no," she whispered, letting the call go to voice mail.

As soon as the line was free, she dialed Cordelia.

"I'm at Saks; I can't talk."

Portia blinked. "You were just here. How can you be at Saks now, especially if your husband is out of work?"

"I'm just browsing. It's like . . . therapy."

"Tell me you didn't just say that."

"What do you want, Portia?" Cordelia shot back.

"Robert just called."

"Oh, my Lord! What did he say?"

"I don't know. I didn't answer." Her phone beeped. "He left a message."

"Listen to it and call me back."

Not a minute after she was done listening, her phone rang again and she answered to Cordelia, saying, "I've patched in Olivia."

"What did that rat say?" Olivia demanded.

Portia's hand shook as she held her phone. "He said he wants to talk to me. He wants to know where I am."

"He doesn't know?" Cordelia was surprised.

"No. And I don't want him to know. If he calls either of you, you know nothing."

"What about his lawyer?"

"Everything is going through *my* lawyer."

"Have you gotten your settlement yet?" Olivia asked.

"No. Not yet."

"Yep, typical male crap," Olivia added. "I swear, you should have told the world about how he treated you. Why you haven't told anyone who would listen what an ass he is makes zero sense."

"I've told you. I have no interest in being in the news, and me telling the world that the good Christian politician Robert Baleau divorced me so he could marry my ex–best friend puts me smack dab in the middle of the news as yet another pathetic wronged-politician's wife. I've already told you, no thanks."

Olivia scoffed. "Portia—"

"No. I am not going there. Listen, I've got to run."

She couldn't breathe. She had to get out.

She pressed end, then threw on one of Evie's old sweaters, grabbed her purse, and bolted. She didn't slow down until she came to Columbus Avenue and the same bakery where she'd bought the cake for the Kanes: Cutie's.

Before she thought it through, she was inside buying a baker's box full of every variety of cupcake they sold. She couldn't have explained the impulse if she had tried. She barely managed to cover the cost from the money she had in her wallet. Then she carried them home, nearly running all the way back, before slamming into her apartment. The minute she launched herself into the kitchen, she tore into the cupcakes like an alcoholic plunging into a binge.

Maybe thirty minutes later, maybe an hour, the door opened and Ariel walked in, finding Portia at the kitchen counter, half-eaten cupcakes spilling across the scarred linoleum.

"What are you doing?" Ariel said, gaping.

"These are terrible!"

"What do you mean, terrible?"

"Awful, hideous, dry. I tried one and couldn't believe it. So then I started testing more of them, and so far they've all failed!"

"You're testing cupcakes? Are they supposed to answer directly, or are you giving them a multiple-choice exam?"

"Ha-ha," Portia said, taking a bite of a bright pink cupcake. She swallowed with a gulp of water. "Gah, these are awful."

"They can't be awful." Ariel picked up the box. "Cutie's Bakery. These are, like, the most famous cupcakes around."

"So I've heard. Have one."

"No thanks. I had a bite of that cake you brought from them. It wasn't even close to as good as the one you made that first night. Hint hint."

The words hit Portia in the gut, swirling around like plump, juicy blueberries folded into the kind of thick, sweetened batter perfect for licking off a spoon. Abruptly she stood, her mind whirling, when a huge *bang* sounded outside.

She and Ariel ran up the stairs and out the open door.

Gabriel was already there, two steps down. He wore faded Levi's and a navy blue T-shirt that stretched across his chest. The sun hit his hair, the brown so dark it was nearly black. He looked great, Portia thought. Really great. No surprise there. What *was* a surprise was that he was howling with laughter, talking to a guy who was obviously a contractor.

His eyes crinkled at the sides when he grinned like that, making him look downright approachable. Who would have guessed the beast had it in him?

Portia forced herself to focus, noticing for the first time that the outer front door had been ripped out. She gasped. "You can't do that!"

Gabriel turned. "What's all over your forehead?"

Portia swiped her skin, coming away with frosting. "Don't think you can distract me with your, your . . . scowl."

"My scowl?" He looked amused.

"You cannot rip out my aunt's front door. I'm going to call someone, the historic society or something. I'm sure it's listed. You can't just rip out doors!"

"This is none of your business," Gabriel said, the laughter disappearing.

"This is my home—of course it's my business!"

He raised a brow.

"Okay, so it's both of our homes. You on the top, me on the bottom."

That got a different kind of raised brow.

"Errr!" Portia grumbled. "That door belongs to both of us!"

Gabriel's jaw set.

"Well?" she demanded. "I bet we're something like one of those insane apartment building co-ops they have in Manhattan, you know, giving everyone who lives there equal rights. I have rights to that front door, just as much as you do."

"The door was rotting. And if you don't like what I'm doing, you can always leave."

"Funny. But I can't. I have nowhere else to go." Belatedly, she realized that after all her ranting, he just might ask her for half the price of the rotting door.

It flashed through her mind that maybe she should just sell him the apartment and be done with it. She had been scouring *the New York Times* real estate section, and she knew she could make a small fortune by selling.

Gabriel clearly saw her moment of vulnerability because he suddenly looked like a shark circling a floundering cruise ship tourist. He sensed blood. "Ariel," he said, "can you give me a second to talk to Ms. Cuthcart?"

Ariel glanced between the two of them, shrugged, and trotted back inside.

Gabriel took two steps up. There was an intent look to his face that . . . well, Portia had the distinct idea that he was going to reach out and kiss her, never mind the work crew milling down below on the sidewalk.

But at the last second Gabriel's eyes cleared and he said, "Why are you here?"

Portia blinked—then blinked again, hating the implication that she didn't belong.

That was the thing. She *did* belong. Ever since that first morning she woke up in the garden apartment, she had felt as if her whole life had been bringing her to this place. Texas wasn't home anymore. New York City was.

"I belong here," she said. Then found herself blurting out, "You don't like me, do you?"

That threw him. He gave her a look as if to say, *"You are such a girl."* And who could blame him?

Aloud, he said, "I don't even know you."

Unbidden, the image of the way he had looked at her after peeling her out of the burger suit came to mind. He had wanted to know her that day, at least on some level.

"This is not about liking or not liking you," he stated firmly.

"Dad!" Miranda marched out the front door. "There isn't a thing to eat in the whole house! Are you trying to starve us? Huh? Is that what you really want?"

Gabriel took a deep breath. "Give me a second, Miranda. I'll fix it."

"Yeah, right. Sure, you will."

She wheeled back inside.

"Listen," Gabriel said, dragging his hands through his hair. "You need a job, right? Given the demise of the burger suit, I mean."

"And?" Portia said carefully.

"The girls need someone to make meals for them. Breakfast and dinner, on school days."

Portia felt her blood begin to boil. "Are you offering me a job as your cook?"

He eyed her. "I guess I am."

"Either you are or you aren't."

"Fine, yes. I am offering you a job." He told her an amount he would pay, and her stomach actually rumbled at the thought of all the boxes of cereal, not to mention fabulous food, she could buy with the amount. But then she remembered.

"What is the matter with everyone? How many times do I have to say that I don't cook? Not anymore!"

Though she wanted to. God help her, she did.

Portia reminded herself of things that were normal. White picket fences. Food that didn't come in visions. She took a deep, steadying breath.

"Ariel says you do. And you couldn't be worse than me. Just give it some thought. In the meantime, I suggest you get out of the way before the workmen run you over."

He left her standing on the steps. When Portia gathered herself and glanced around, she noticed the old man next door. Despite the closed window, the man raised a challenging eyebrow, as if he'd heard every word.

Her great-aunt Evie had followed her dream and moved to New York when it became clear that her future didn't lie in Willow Creek, Texas.

"The measure of a person isn't the bumps you hit in the road," Gram had always said. *"It's how you pick yourself up and move forward."*

She could almost hear Gram asking a question: *"Who are you, Portia?"*

Every direction she turned, she was hit with images and urges, thoughts and knowing. Then something else hit her, harder than it had before.

If she had been true to who she really was, would Robert have been able to deceive her, as Cordelia had said?

And suddenly she lost the fight. Before she could think better of it, she dialed Cordelia, who answered on the first ring.

"Get me the names of some investment bankers."

A beat passed before her sister spoke. "What for?"

"We're going to open The Glass Kitchen in New York."

Third Course

❖

Salad

Grapefruit and Avocado Salad
with Poppy Seed Dressing

Eleven

❖

PORTIA GROANED over what she had done.

But there was no turning back, and as night fell later that day she managed to nurture a flicker of hope. She was giving in to cooking. She would bake. She would open a Glass Kitchen with her sisters. But she would do both like a normal person.

That was the key. It would be three normal sisters opening a normal restaurant in New York, serving the kind of normal food that was the opposite of the tiny portions so often served in Manhattan. None of that fancy food that was better to look at than to eat.

But Portia knew there was something else she had to do.

Stepping out into the dark garden, she noted the metal fire escape that zigzagged up the back of the town house.

The maze of metal ladders and landings used to be a dangerous wreck, but she'd bet anything that Gabriel would have had it fixed. She had no doubt he was a man who took care of his own. He was a man her grandmother would have respected.

The thought surprised her, left her off-balance.

She glanced up to the higher floors of the town house and found that the third-floor light was on. Back in the day, the room had been her great-aunt's library. Gabriel Kane must have left it as a library, because through the sheer curtains she could just make out his large shape as he stood in front of the tall windows.

Without thinking, she started climbing the fire escape, just as she'd done as a girl. She didn't want to go to the front door and ring the newly working bell. She didn't want to call—not that she had his number. She didn't want to wait until morning. If she waited a second longer, she would change her mind.

Her handholds were firm as she climbed, the years slipping away until she was just a girl with her sisters in New York for the summer. She had loved climbing the fire escape. Cordelia had not.

"Portia! Get down here," Cordelia had always demanded, her voice bouncing against the tall buildings surrounding them.

Olivia had always laughed, egging Portia on. "Keep going, Portia!"

But even Olivia had never followed Portia up the narrow ladders and landings. Portia was the only one who scaled the metal stairs like a cat, slipping into one of their bedrooms or Evie's library. Cordelia and Olivia would fly into the house, then dash upstairs to find Portia already curled up in Evie's favorite chair with one of their aunt's magazines.

All these years later, with each handhold and step up the stairs, she came to the third floor once again, but this time Gabriel Kane stood inside.

Gossamer-thin draperies covered the library windows. Portia knocked and nearly fell backward when Gabriel whipped aside the curtains, something dangerous in his face.

"Oh," she squeaked.

Before she could fall, flee, or figure out how to get back down without killing herself, Gabriel's face shifted from dangerous to fierce. She felt like kindling in front of a flame. It wasn't nearly as comforting as a welcome mat, but Portia would take what she could get, given a plunge to the earth made his harsh expression seem appealing.

At least that's what she thought until he wrenched open the window, grabbed her arms, and pulled her inside.

She wasn't a big woman, but still. Gabriel lifted her with the ease of a bodybuilder lifting a can of peas. "What the hell are you doing out there?"

He was angry, she realized. Really angry.

"You could have killed yourself on that thing."

She remembered him giving her that glass of water and making her drink. Now this. The man seemed oddly protective for a guy who clearly wanted nothing to do with her.

The fire in his eyes made Portia feel alive and reckless. "But I didn't!" She gave him a sunny Texas smile. "More than that, I thought about your offer. Of a job."

She watched as he visibly reined in his anger. "That was fast."

She cocked her head. "That's me. Fast, decisive." In her dreams, sure, but he didn't have to know that. "Are you impressed?"

"I'm impressed you didn't fall and break your neck."

She scoffed. "I've been climbing that fire escape since I was in grade school."

"You're certainly acting like you're in grade school."

"Sheesh, Portia," she said out loud. "You handed him that one."

He looked at her as if he hadn't a clue what to make of her. "Who are you?"

She laughed, delighted. "Have you noticed that every time you see me, you wonder who I am?"

Gabriel ground his teeth.

"But that isn't what you meant."

His narrowed eyes showed he still wasn't amused.

"All right. If you want the truth of it, then I've come to tell you that I officially accept the position as the Kane Family Cook."

It all made sense. It would give her an income while she and her sisters got the business going. The job wasn't full-time, and there wasn't much in the way of commuting, so she'd have plenty of time to work on The Glass Kitchen.

Gabriel stared at her long and hard, not uttering a word.

Portia glanced around the room and noticed that everything about her aunt's library was gone. The books, the bookshelves, the paintings. "You've ruined this room, too!"

"I didn't ruin it."

Her head shot around. "You did too—"

He didn't let her finish. "You make me forget I'm a man who doesn't do things without knowing every possible consequence," he said, then pulled her to him, his mouth coming down on hers.

Of all the responses Portia had expected, kissing wasn't one of them. She tensed, her hands coming up to his chest to push him away, though she didn't do it. Instead, her body melted and she opened her mouth to him.

"God, you drive me insane," he said raggedly.

"Same page," she answered, her arms circling his neck as she leaned into him. His muffled groan sent heat through her. She wanted him, even though nothing good could come from getting involved with a neighbor—a neighbor who had offered her a job. Would he take back his offer?

Right then, she didn't care.

Gabriel's hands ran down either side of her spine. Her breath caught when he cupped her hips, pressing her to him. The kiss wasn't soft. It was demanding, his tongue tangling with hers, and she gave up all hope of breaking away.

He backed her against the wall, his hands flattened on either side of her head. In the past, with Robert, she had always wanted more, wanted some deeper connection, but she had contented herself with a white-picket-fence sense of normalcy. Nothing about the way Gabriel Kane made her feel had anything to do with white-picket fences.

"You have driven me mad since the day I walked up to the steps and found you sitting there," Gabriel said, his lips trailing down her neck.

"You with the compliments."

"It wasn't meant to be."

Her head fell back, her eyes closed. "Of course not," she breathed.

Portia felt the strength of his muscles beneath his button-down shirt. At his waist, she hardly believed it when she tugged up the material. She wanted to feel skin, feel heat. When his shirttail came free, she slipped her hands underneath to his abdomen, her palms sliding up over warm, taut skin, the single line of hair from his navel to his chest.

She felt his breath shudder before he reclaimed control of her body, and she did nothing to stop him. Portia wanted more, moaning as he gave it to her, his hand slipping beneath her shirt, his thumb dipping into her navel. Their kiss grew wilder, a kind of craving that she'd never experienced, and certainly never succumbed to. But right then, she would have given him anything.

The tips of his fingers brushed against her hip, then slid back, cupping her hips and pulling her to him.

"God, you taste good," he murmured against her lips. "Like honey."

He tasted like nothing so tame as honey. He was a decadent, caramelized brandy that made her press against him like a madwoman. Those clever fingers found her lacy boy-short panties, sliding his palm under the elastic, his foot nudging her legs wider.

She trembled, her breath catching in her throat. He deepened their kiss, turning it fierce, just as he brought his hand around and his fingers slid low.

"Dad?"

A paralyzed moment passed before Portia realized Ariel was headed their way.

"Fuck!" Gabriel ground out.

Right this second, she wished.

Instead, she sagged against the wall, trying to steady herself.

"Dad? Where are you?"

Portia could hear footsteps coming down the hall now, and she pushed him away so she could straighten her clothes. Gabriel shoved in his shirttail, turning to the closed door, ready to face his daughter. Portia, on the other hand, chose the coward's way out and slipped back out onto the fire escape.

He pivoted back to her. "Don't leave," he commanded, his voice low and fierce.

"I'll start work in the morning," she said, throwing herself down the stairs, her heart pounding.

Back in her own kitchen, she looked around, as if the room would have changed. But everything looked the same, despite the fact that her world had just been rocked.

Twelve

❖

ARIEL WAS ALMOST CERTAIN that her dad had been messing around on the fire escape.

That, of course, was totally impossible, since he had forbidden her and Miranda from going anywhere near the escape, even after he'd had workmen practically rebuild the thing.

Ariel had no problem obeying. While she wasn't about to admit it, even the thought of having to go up or down the narrow metal stairs and landings terrified her. But Dad's laying down the law had sent Miranda into one of her fits.

"*So, what are we supposed to do if there's, like, a fire?*" Miranda had snapped in the tone of voice that never failed to get a rise out of their dad.

Tit for tat, Ariel thought.

Whatever. There was no reason why her dad would have been doing anything anywhere near the fire escape.

"What are you doing?" she asked, coming over to look past him. The garden below was dark. "Is Portia down there?"

She glanced sideways at him, thinking he would scoff at her, but there was a strange look on his face. Almost a guilty look. "You've been peeking!" She went right up to the glass and peered out. "You know, Dad, that's, like, a crime or something."

"I was not peeking out the window."

It wasn't hard to imagine Portia out in that garden dancing or something.

"I read *Harriet the Spy*," she said, craning her neck. "I know what people get up to in New York. Next thing I know, you'll get yourself a pair of binoculars. I'd better warn Portia."

"*Ariel.*" Even she knew better than to keep going when he had that tone. It meant business.

"Good night!" she said cheerily, running back out of the room before he could launch into some sort of lecture.

But the next morning, if the possibility of her dad doing something on the fire escape was a surprise, breakfast was a real Lollapalooza of surprises.

"Good morning!"

Ariel blinked at the sight of Portia standing in their kitchen, wearing another pair of her whackjob high-waisted, wide-bottomed pants, a white T-shirt, and an old-fashioned apron tied around her waist.

"What are you doing here?" Ariel asked, still frozen in the doorway.

"Believe me," Portia said, "I'm as surprised as you by this turn of events."

"What do you mean?"

"I'm your new head cook and chief bottle washer."

"Seriously? Dad hired you?"

"He did." Portia got a weird look on her face, then shook it away.

Ariel came over and peered inside the pot on the stove. "Sheez, what are you making?"

"Doughnuts."

"Dad actually took my advice, amazing. And does anyone other than Dunkin' make doughnuts?"

"Your advice? Then thank you. I guess. And funny."

"I thought you didn't cook anymore."

"I wasn't." Portia gave the big spoon a swirl around the pot of boiling oil. "But sometimes we have to be brave in order to dig deep and find answers. Even if we're not sure we're going to like the answers."

"I don't want to be mean, but you sound like a really bad infomercial."

Portia laughed, and started extracting golden-brown fried balls. After placing them on a paper towel–covered plate, she tossed them into a brown paper bag and started shaking.

Ariel's mouth started watering. "Powdered-sugar doughnuts!"

Footsteps stopped in the doorway. "My favorite."

Ariel and Portia turned; Ariel blinked. "Uncle Anthony."

"None other." He sauntered into the kitchen. "And look who else is here," he added, winking at Ariel, then smiling big and wide at Portia.

Ariel liked her uncle well enough, though she probably would have liked him better if Miranda didn't act like an airheaded nitwit whenever he showed up. It was the same with their grandmother. Nana was totally mean to Ariel's dad, but she gushed like a demented schoolgirl when her younger son came to town. Ariel figured Nana was in hog's heaven now that Uncle Anthony was staying with her.

Thankfully, Dad wasn't like Nana. Ariel was pretty sure he loved both her and Miranda the same. And if she was ever a mom—not that she was going to be, because it was a seriously awful job, as far as she could tell—she'd love all her kids the same. Even if one of them was as mean as Miranda.

Uncle Anthony walked over the stove, never taking his eyes off their neighbor. "Portia, right?" he asked.

"Yes, Portia Cuthcart."

"From downstairs," he added.

"Right again."

Just in case Portia and her dad were getting something going, the last thing Ariel needed was her uncle getting in the way. You only had to be around Anthony for five minutes to realize that grown ladies turned into mush the minute they saw him. Which made no sense since he was like a math equation with only one answer: He never committed. So how come she, twelve-nearly-thirteen-year-old Ariel Kane, had figured this out when full-grown women hadn't?

Anthony picked up a doughnut and popped it into his mouth. "Amazing," he said, licking his fingers. He actually sounded surprised. "So amazing that I'd like to take you out to dinner to show my appreciation."

Portia laughed, swatting his fingers away. "No thanks. Hands off my doughnuts."

He stole another, anyway.

"You're like a ten-year-old who's used to getting his way."

"You've pegged my little brother so quickly."

Dad to the rescue! Ariel gave him a big grin.

"Gabriel," Anthony said, minus the big grin. He looked at Portia. "Even as a kid, he was a wet blanket."

"Not everyone can make it through life on the largess of others."

If Ariel wasn't mistaken, something weird was happening with Uncle Anthony's jaw, sort of like a spasm. A definite sign that he was mad. But then her uncle just laughed, making her think she'd imagined it.

"Ms. Cuthcart," her dad said in clipped tones.

The two of them exchanged a massively weird glance, and for half a second Ariel thought her dad was going to fire Portia on the spot. That, or Portia was going to up and quit.

Instead, Dad glanced at the doughnuts on the counter. "This is what you've chosen to feed my children for breakfast?"

"No." Portia opened the oven door and pulled out a platter. "For the girls, eggs, turkey bacon, whole wheat toast." From another pot on the stove, she whipped off the lid. "Oatmeal." Then, like some crazed hostess on a game show, she walked over to the refrigerator, from which she produced a bowl of cut-up fruit and some orange juice.

"Covering all bases, I see," Dad said.

"Yep, that's me." She threw him a look, kind of sideways under her lashes. "Though now that I think about it, not so unlike you last night covering a few of your own."

Dad's jaw dropped, then snapped closed. There was that weird look in his eyes again, though.

Portia turned away, like she had surprised herself.

"Isn't this interesting," Uncle Anthony said in a kind of sour voice. Which was even weirder.

Miranda walked in just then. She scowled at their dad, for whatever reason, this time. Then she saw Uncle Anthony. "Hi!" she said with a big smile.

"Hi, yourself," Anthony said, grinning back.

Her dad got that frustrated look about him, but instead of saying something mean, he just asked, "Anthony, what are you doing here?"

Ariel could feel tension in the room like she felt heat coming from the oven. It made her stomach clench and worry come up in her throat, a worry that was always there these days.

She didn't dare tell the Shrink about the worry, because he would tell her dad, and then there would be hell to pay. Dad would watch her like a hawk, just like he watched Miranda. As it stood now, Ariel knew her dad felt pretty certain she was under control with the whole journal and Shrink thing. She wanted to keep it that way.

Miranda glanced at Portia, seemed surprised, though not in a good away, then sat down.

Ariel focused on serving a plate. She really hated all this weird family mess that, even as smart as she was, she hardly understood.

It took a second before something occurred to her. "How did you know what our favorite stuff was?"

Portia bit her lip. "Really? I mean, I figured I'd just make a little bit of everything."

"I have to get to work," Dad said.

"But you haven't eaten!" Portia blurted.

Dad gave her a look, grabbed a piece of toast, and then he was gone.

"Are you staying for breakfast?" Miranda asked Anthony.

Anthony was frowning after Dad, but he looked back and his smile returned. "I wouldn't miss it."

They all sat around the kitchen table. Portia was still cooking and didn't sit down, but Uncle Anthony yakked at her the whole time anyway. "So, are you going to go out with me?" he asked again.

She just laughed and said, "No."

"We got an assignment at school," Ariel said, breaking in. "We have to write about our family tree. Uncle Anthony, can you tell me something about Mom that you think I don't already know. Like, when was the first time you met her? Did Dad do the *bring his date home to meet the family* sort of thing and there she was?"

Uncle Anthony looked totally weird. "Your mom?" But then he got a faraway look in his eyes and a kind of dreamy smile. "The first time I met your mom I thought she was the prettiest girl I'd ever seen." He focused on Miranda. "You're the spitting image of Victoria."

"Really?"

Ariel scowled. She wished she looked like their mom. But no, she looked like some mongrel dog.

"So when did you meet her?" Ariel asked.

Anthony sat back. "Actually, I met your mom before your dad did."

"No way!" Miranda breathed.

Great, more unstable ground. Sheesh.

Miranda came over and sat next to Uncle Anthony. "What was she like when you met her?"

"Well, like I said, she was beautiful. She walked into this place I used to go with a bunch of friends. Downtown. You know, music, dancing. We were young. Or younger," he added with a twist of his mouth. "Vic walked in like she owned the place. She gave off so much wattage that you saw nothing but her." Uncle Anthony gave sort of a half laugh. "Victoria

Polanski. God, was she a handful." He cleared his throat. "Like I said, she was just as gorgeous as Miranda here."

Ariel ignored that and persisted. "Where was she from? New Jersey? Long Island? Did she grow up by Nana on the Upper East Side?"

Anthony blinked, coming back to himself, then leaned over and chucked Ariel on the chin. "Ask your dad that, A. I'm sure he'd love to talk about the old days."

Yeah, right. She'd jump all over that. Not.

Her uncle glanced at the clock. "Gotta go." He stood and walked over to the stove, where Portia was taking another batch of doughnuts out of the pot.

"You're sure you can't spare a few hours to keep a guy company?"

"I'm sure."

"I guess I'll have to settle for another of your doughnuts." He grabbed one up. Just before he popped it in his mouth, he added, "At least for now."

Thirteen

❖

PORTIA FIRED UP THE LAPTOP she had borrowed from Cordelia and spent the next hour figuring out what a business plan looked like. She knew all about the practical elements of running a café, having learned the ropes at her grandmother's side, so it wasn't too hard. Plus, Cordelia and Olivia were coming over later to help.

Quite frankly, her intent was as much about work as it was about filling her head with something besides the memory of that kiss. She hardly knew how to square it away in her brain other than to chalk it up to the greatest kiss known to man. Which was melodramatic and completely absurd, especially given the fact that she hadn't much to compare it to. She snorted. She didn't need anything to compare it to. The man could kiss.

By the middle of the afternoon, her head was ready to explode with numbers and business details. She told herself that what really mattered was her ability to create food that wowed people. Which made her think of those Cutie's cupcakes. And she knew with certainty that she could fix them.

The doorbell buzzed just as she was starting to put everything together, and Ariel walked in. "Are you baking?"

"Yes."

"Something good."

"One can only hope."

"Interesting. You don't strike me as the sarcastic type."

Portia rolled her eyes, which she noticed Ariel ignored as she started rooting around in her backpack. The girl pulled out notebooks and magazines and set them on the table. Portia went back to her I Can Do Better Than Cutie's cupcake. She had all the bowls and utensils out by the time Ariel was ready, her own project set up. Poster boards, magazines marked with Post-its, and some sort of list.

"What's that?" Portia asked.

"Think of me as your fairy godmother."

"You're on the young side. Shouldn't I be the fairy godmother?"

"My clothes are fine. Yours? Not so much. I'm going to fix you up. You can thank me with one of those cupcakes."

"Fix me up?"

"So you can catch a, well, guy."

Portia's mouth fell open.

"I know you're divorced and all. Still, you're not so old that you can give up dating for the rest of your life. Right?"

"Are you sure you're a child?" Portia asked faintly.

"I prefer preadult female. Now, stop talking and listen."

Two minutes into Ariel's "presentation," Portia decided to ignore her and focus on the hideous Cutie's cupcakes. If she wanted a makeover, she could ask one of her sisters. Well, not Cordelia.

Of course, Ariel just kept talking. She had ripped out a load of "perfect outfits" from *Teen Vogue.* But if Portia ever had money again, she wouldn't be buying short, pleated skirts and platform tennis shoes.

The Cutie's cupcakes were missing something. The more Ariel talked, the more Portia craved the cupcake fix. She mixed the dry ingredients in a bowl, stirring slowly, feeling a sense of peace come over her. Ariel battled on, talking about how tights could be coordinated with a short skirt.

Portia finished her first "fix" on the cupcakes, writing down what she had done, just as her grandmother had taught her.

Ariel peered at her. "Are you sure you're listening to me?"

Portia put the batch in the preheated oven. "You bet," she answered.

"I don't believe you."

"Don't you have homework to do?"

"I spent a lot of time on this. The least you could do is listen."

"I am! Think of me as a multitasker. I can bake and listen. Tell me more about stockings."

"Not stockings," Ariel said with disgust. "Tights! There's a big difference, you know."

"Sorry. Of course."

Ariel's eagle eye stayed on her as Portia went back to the mixing bowl and started on a second batch. An hour or so passed with Ariel talking and Portia baking.

Oddly, it felt good to have Ariel's high voice providing a counterpoint to the sounds of baking. But by the time cupcakes covered every inch of counter space, Ariel was running out of steam. "Looks" from *Teen Vogue* and *Tiger Beat* battled with the cupcakes for space on the counter and kitchen island.

"I just can't believe that *Tiger Beat* is still in business," Portia said. "And you know I'll never wear pants like that, don't you? I'm not seventeen."

"These are totally swaggy pants," Ariel said indignantly. "Justin Bieber—not that I'm a Belieber or anything, but still—he wore them on his last tour. In leather."

"Do I really look like a woman who would wear *swaggy* leather pants?"

"Well, the other things, then. I got these magazines out of Miranda's room. She totally knows how to dress and she marked the pages, so everything I told you about is like picked by an expert."

"Picked by a teenager," Portia said, pushing the cupcakes on the table closer together so she could put out another tray. "*For* a teenager."

"My dad says she dresses like she's sixteen going on twenty-six. You can't be much older than twenty-six. Right?"

"I'm twenty-nine, and fashion isn't a priority for me right now."

"Like I didn't already know that."

Portia just laughed and kept working.

"You know, you're not really like other adults. Just saying."

"Why not?"

"You don't get worked up like the teachers at school. They always look mortally wounded or bear-woken-in-winter mad whenever I start talking without thinking my words through, which is pretty much all the time."

Portia just laughed again, concentrating on the elaborate designs she was swirling into the cupcake frosting.

Everything was nearly done when the doorbell rang.

"I'll get it," Ariel said, as though she lived there.

Miranda followed Ariel back into the kitchen, which was unexpected.

"Hi, Miranda," Portia said.

The girl stood there scowling, not looking even a bit happy to be there. "Yeah, hi—" The words froze in the air, and she stared at the table. "Oh, my gosh! How did you know?"

Portia took a deep breath. "Know what?"

"The cupcakes! How did you know I needed cupcakes? We're having a sophomore class bake sale and everyone has to bring something."

Portia couldn't speak. She hated this feeling, hated that she couldn't just bake like a normal person. In the morning she'd had the Kanes' favorite breakfast without knowing a single thing about what they liked to eat. Now this.

"Awesome!" Miranda exclaimed.

Gabriel chose that moment to walk into the apartment. "I rang the bell, but no one heard," he said.

When he saw Miranda laughing, the hard planes of his face eased, if only slightly. "I got your text that you needed cupcakes," he said to Miranda. "There's that cupcake place on Columbus." His eyes shifted to the kitchen counters. "What's this?"

"Cupcakes," Ariel said.

Portia tried to ignore the way Ariel eyed her.

"Can you believe it! Portia already made them," Miranda crowed. But then she seemed to realize what she was doing and stopped, the glower firmly back in place.

"How did you know?" he asked Portia.

"I didn't. I was experimenting." She refused to give in to the queasy emotions she felt. Maybe she just made the cupcakes because of Cutie's. And maybe she was going stark raving mad. She turned to the girls. "Can you find some boxes to put them in? How many do you need, Miranda?"

"A lot. Like six dozen," Miranda said.

Portia didn't need to count. She knew on a sigh that if she did, there would be exactly six dozen sitting on the counter.

The girls went out to find boxes, which left Portia and Gabriel standing alone.

"You have batter on your face. Again."

"Last time it was frosting."

She would have sworn he swallowed back a smile.

She wiped her cheek and found a swipe of strawberry shortcake cupcake mix.

"How did you know about the cupcakes? Really."

"I didn't. I was trying to come up with a way to make Cutie's cupcakes better. And I did." She took a mock little bow. "The German chocolate cake was easy. So was the vanilla buttercream. But the strawberry shortcake gave me fits. Turns out, the final fix came when I baked a fresh strawberry in the middle of a vanilla sour-cream batter instead of strawberry batter with chunks of strawberries. Here, try one."

"No, thanks."

"What, you're watching your boyish figure?"

Gabriel gave a surprised bark of laughter, snagged the cupcake, and took a bite. The amazement on his face made her smile. He stared at her concoction almost suspiciously before looking at her.

"And?" Portia prompted.

"And what?"

"What do you think?"

"I think you can bake."

"I'll take that as your way of saying you think it's good. Thank you." She shot him a saucy look, to which he raised a brow, his eyes intent on her.

The memory of him dragging her through the window and pulling her close made her light-headed, and she wondered if he was thinking about the same thing.

After a second he focused and saw the books. He picked up one with his free hand. "*'Hospitality and Restaurant Practices'*?" He cocked his head. "What's this for?"

"My sisters and I are going to open a restaurant."

Saying it out loud thrilled her and terrified her in turn.

For a second she thought he was going to laugh. She just held his gaze.

"You're serious."

"As serious as an accountant at an IRS audit."

His face closed off, reminding her of the ruthlessness she had first noticed about him on the front steps. "You have no business opening a restaurant."

"Says who?"

"Says the guy who watched you try to extricate yourself from a burger suit with a knife."

Her mouth fell open. "Burger suits and restaurants are two different kettles of fish."

"Kettles of fish? Now there's great business terminology."

"Yep, Texas style."

"You're in New York, sweetheart."

"I am not your sweetheart, thank my lucky stars."

"Another of your quaint Texas sayings? What was the last one I heard you use? 'Bless your heart'?"

She sliced him a tooth-grinding smile. "While you might not like them, you can bet your backside that a café that serves the kind of fare we create in Texas would have people lined up around the corner. Or, as we say in Texas, till the cows come home."

He raised a brow as he eyed her. "Did you know that sixty percent of all restaurants fail?"

"Really, I thought the number would be higher."

"Eighty percent in New York City."

She refused to gulp. "Wow, I thought the number was more like ninety-five percent."

"Some statistics put the number that high."

Double non-gulp.

"Is it possible that something has left Portia Cuthcart speechless?"

She glared at him. "Okay, funny guy."

His head cocked, but she kept going.

"I stand by my belief that a Glass Kitchen in New York will work."

"Then tell me, if you're such a prodigious businesswoman, what's your cost-to-baked-goods ratio?"

"What?"

"Don't know? How about margins? What kind of margins do you expect to achieve?"

She stammered.

The way he looked at her liquefied her insides, and she felt sorry for anyone who went up against him.

"Nope?" he said. "Then how much does a bushel of flour cost? Or how about the cost of small-business insurance?"

Her eyes narrowed.

"There's more to running a café," he finished, holding up her cupcake for demonstration, "than being good in the kitchen."

Finally she broke free of her shocked stupor and walked over to him. "One, bakers don't buy bushels of flour. We buy it by the pound, and last I checked—namely, this morning—a five-pound bag was going for $4.95; ten pounds, $8.95; twenty-five, $20.50. As to *two* on your rapid-fire list of insulting questions, small-business insurance varies, depending on the size of the small business, how many employees, what the business is, not to mention the city and state in which said small business is run. Having been a *prodigious* part of my grandmother's restaurant, The Glass Kitchen, back in Texas, I'm well aware that there's more to running a café than being a good cook."

She stopped directly in front of him. "My sister Cordelia has plenty of access to investors, all of whom will be interested to hear how I took a famous but hideous tasting Cutie's cupcake and turned it into the mouthwatering delight you now hold in your hand." She snatched the partially eaten cake away from him. "Or should I say, held in your hand."

She expected him to be embarrassed or, short of that, at least contrite. But no, not Gabriel Kane. He just looked at her, assessing, and she had to remind herself she wasn't intimidated by him.

"Good-bye," she said pointedly.

Gabriel raised a brow, then surprised her when he licked the frosting from his fingers. "Insulting. Rapid-fire. You're cute when you get feisty."

"Ack!" It was all she could do not to launch the cupcake at his head.

"Before you get carried away," he went on, smooth as butter, "I have something for you."

She eyed him. He pulled a key from his pocket and handed it over. "For my place. This way you can come and go when you need to, from the job that actually pays you money."

She reconsidered launching the cupcake.

"I'll leave money on the kitchen table to buy food. Later, I'll show you how I order online, if you want to do that instead."

Then he reached out, surprising her yet again, and wiped a smudge of frosting from the corner of her mouth. His gaze locked with hers as he sucked the sugar from his finger. "How is it that again and again, you make me forget the type of man I am?"

Portia felt heat rising in her cheeks. This was ridiculous. She didn't like aggravating men. In all the years she had known Robert, he had never once aggravated her, at least not before he divorced her. And then he had devastated her, which wasn't the same.

Truth to tell, for the first time since Robert had come home with his big announcement, Portia felt that maybe he had done her a favor.

When she dragged her gaze from Gabriel's lips, their eyes met. For a second she thought he would kiss her again. But then his mouth went hard, his eyes shuttering, and she was certain irritation ran along his body like an electric current.

"There will be no more of that," his expression told her.

Relief mixed with disappointment.

"I couldn't agree more," she shot back wordlessly.

He nodded and disappeared through the doorway.

Fourteen

⋅⋅⋅⋅

T HREE DAYS LATER, Portia forgot to set her alarm and ended up
dashing up the stairs at ten minutes after seven, having barely thrown
on cargo pants and a white cotton tee, and hastily brushed her teeth.

Gabriel leaned against the kitchen counter, reading the newspaper, a
cup of coffee in his hand. His hair was still wet from the shower, a little
long and raked back. He looked better than her cupcakes. Damn, damn,
damn.

She had hoped to get breakfast done early; she had a lunch meeting a
block away on Columbus Avenue with a potential investor. Cordelia had
made the arrangements, and her sisters were supposed to meet her there.
But Olivia had already e-mailed that she couldn't make it; she had been
asked to sub for an advanced yoga class.

"*Since Olivia's bailing, you have to be there, Cordelia,*" Portia wrote back.
"*When you made it a lunch meeting, you promised to pay.*"

"*Stop worrying, P! It's lunch; it won't cost much. And I'll be there.*"

"Late?" Gabriel asked, breaking into her thoughts. "Only three
days in?"

"It's seven o'clock," Portia stated. "Okay, seven-ish."

"I didn't realize that in a professional workplace seven sharp was more of a loose term."

"God, you're funny."

He gave her a strange look.

"What? No one's called you funny before?"

"No," Gabriel said, the word quiet.

She looked at him, but before she could probe, he folded the newspaper and tossed it on the counter. "The girls should be down any minute. I have a meeting at eight. Though maybe the Civic Board really meant eight-ish. And at two I'm meeting the contractor here. Or maybe it's two-ish."

She shot him a look. "That probably *is* what they meant."

His shout of laughter surprised them both.

She smiled at him then. "I won't be late tomorrow, promise."

A remnant of his smile seemed to fight with his standard glower. "Good girl."

The words caught her off guard. *Good girl.* She had always been just that. Fun, maybe, but not much more than that. Always good.

She realized she was tired of being the good girl. What would happen if she wasn't, if she gave in and lost herself in Gabriel Kane?

The girls entered, though it was a second before she realized Gabriel had already left. So much for losing herself in him.

"Good morning!" Portia said.

"What are you? A cheerleader?" Miranda grumbled.

"Hey, I made you cupcakes. Seems like you'd be in a better mood."

"Yeah, okay, thanks."

"Now, now, Little Miss Sunshine," Portia teased, setting her own concerns aside.

Ariel grimaced. "You're kidding, right?"

Miranda went over to a cabinet and pulled out a box of sugar cereal. "Maybe she thinks she'll get paid more if we give her a good report."

"Aren't you the cynic?" Portia said, swiping the box away.

"Hey! That's my breakfast."

"Not as long as I'm in charge of feeding you." Portia rummaged in the refrigerator. "Who's up for eggs, bacon, and toast?"

Miranda and Ariel exchanged a glance. "Ah, no one."

Portia made them eggs, bacon, and toast anyway, which Ariel ate and Miranda picked at, but picked at enough that Portia gave her a thumbs-up.

"Surely she'll take it down a notch after she's been here a while," Miranda said to Ariel as the girls headed out the door.

"I heard that," Portia called after them.

"You were supposed to."

⁖

Once Portia finished up in the kitchen, she returned downstairs to get ready for the lunch meeting. After a quick bath, she dressed with care. Ariel wasn't wrong about Portia needing a different look. Vintage clothes weren't going to win her any prizes for business professionalism. So she did what she could with the clothes she had. Texas politician's— wife clothes. Navy blue St. John Knits. Not a staple on the Upper West Side of Manhattan, but sure to instill more confidence than Annie Hall one-offs.

Ready to go, Portia fired up her computer to check her e-mail. The headline of Google News caught her attention.

Gabriel Kane Brings Global Inc. Down

Gabriel Kane? Her Gabriel Kane? Or, rather, her neighbor Gabriel Kane? Portia quickly amended.

The article was definitely about her neighbor, who, it turned out, wasn't your Average Joe. His primary concern wasn't going into one of those dime-a-dozen glass-and-steel office towers by day and bossing around a stream of people redoing his apartment by . . . well, the rest of the time. If the article was to be believed, his raison d'être appeared to be very publicly destroying some company named Global Inc. The reporter further went on to say that once Gabriel's investment in the company went sour, he vindictively went after Global Inc., driving their stock price into the ground.

Portia headed out, her mind spinning. Yikes. While Gabriel looked ruthless, she couldn't help but remember the way he had made her drink water after spilling out of the hamburger suit, or how he had seemed fierce about the danger on the fire escape. Not to mention the way he was trying to do right by his girls. She had to believe he was fair. That he wasn't a man to bring people down ruthlessly. The article had to be an exaggeration. But on top of that, she realized that her neighbor was an investor.

With the thought tumbling around, she walked into La Maison five minutes early and was seated outside. Five minutes passed and Cordelia still hadn't shown up. Portia checked her phone; nothing. After ten minutes, Portia dialed her older sister, but the call went straight to voice mail.

"You better be just about here, Cordelia," she muttered into the phone.

Russell Bertram showed up by himself after a few minutes. "Portia?" he said, coming up to her and extending his hand.

According to Cordelia, he was the most promising of the investors on their list. He was handsome, with fair skin and coppery brown hair longer than a Texas banker would have allowed. He wore a brown sports jacket with blue pinstripes over a white button-down shirt and jeans. He didn't seem anything like an investment guy. He definitely seemed too young to have enough money to invest in a café. But before more than a few words had left his mouth, Portia realized he was utterly charming.

"Sorry I'm late. I volunteer at my old school. They have a young-entrepreneur's group." He gave her a lopsided grin. "Once a month I spill out words of wisdom. If only they knew what a lousy student I was back then."

Portia laughed. "Maybe you should tell them. It would be inspirational."

"So tell me, how's Cordelia? And James? I don't know either of them well, but James helped me a lot when I put together my own fund."

"They're both doing great. James has a lot of amazing stuff going on." She prayed it was true.

"That's good. I was worried when I heard he got caught in the Atlantica General blowup. But if anyone could land on his feet, it's James."

Portia liked Russell more with each minute that passed. He ordered a surprisingly big meal, and when he suggested wine, she thought about how tired she was of being a good girl. She laughed and agreed.

They talked about the best restaurants in the city—ones he had been to, ones she had only read about, given her whole no-money problem. They even delved into Manhattan real estate, if only because no meal in New York was complete without mention of a street address or a co-op. There wasn't a single mention of why they were actually there.

When Russell ordered a second glass of wine for each of them, Portia didn't refuse. He leaned forward and looked her in the eye. "So, tell me, I hear you work with Gabriel Kane."

The wine must have muddled her brain. "Pardon?"

"Don't go coy on me." He grinned, his blue eyes shining with schoolboy charm. "When I asked Cordelia about your experience, she said you work with Gabriel Kane."

Portia's head jerked back. Why would Cordelia say anything about her cooking for Gabriel?

But a second later, it hit her. Cordelia had known Gabriel was an investment guy all along. She had used his name as bait to get the meeting. No wonder her sister hadn't shown up.

She ground her teeth. "You know him?" She tried to smile, trying to figure out how to salvage the lunch. She wouldn't out and out lie, but she saw no reason to tell this guy that she not only didn't work for Gabriel in any investment capacity, but that Gabriel had made it clear what he thought of her opening a Glass Kitchen.

Russell gave a modest shrug. "I know *of* him. Who doesn't? But I've never met him." He leaned forward, his elbows on the table, his forearms encircling his wine. "I have the greatest investment opportunity, one I know will blow Kane away. I've tried to get in to see him, but no luck. When you invited me to lunch, I figured you must have heard about it. I take it you do legwork for Kane."

Portia blinked. "Legwork?"

"You know, get the lay of the land. See if something is worthwhile to show Kane?"

"You're here because you have an investment opportunity you want to present to Gabriel?"

He smiled, excited. "Yes! This is awesome."

Suddenly he seemed exactly as young as he looked. This was a man who thought he was getting the chance of a lifetime. He had no money to invest. He needed investors.

Disappointment seeped through her, every ounce of wine making itself known.

"Not so awesome," she replied wearily.

Russell's blue eyes stopped sparkling. "What do you mean?"

"I'm not here about your project."

"Kane didn't send you?"

"No."

Freckles she hadn't noticed before popped out on his pale skin as he hunched forward.

For a half a second he just sat there. Then he glanced at her expensive St. John suit and managed a guileless smile. "So," he said, "even if you're not scouting for Kane, are you looking for your own investment opportunities?"

He looked so dejected and sweet with those freckles and tousled red-brown hair, not to mention so fruitlessly hopeful, that she felt a nearly maternal need to comfort him, despite her own stinging disappointment. She reached across the table and squeezed his hand. "I wish I was."

"Then why did you want to meet . . ." His voice trailed off as he looked at her hand on his. "I'm being stupid, aren't I? Now I'm embarrassed. Your sister told me you were divorced and had just moved to New York."

A heartbeat passed as she tried to make sense of what he was saying. Then it hit her, blood searing through her cheeks, and she jerked her hand way. To her horror, Russell blushed, too.

"Look," he said awkwardly, "lunch was nice and all. I mean, I enjoyed meeting you. But, well, I'm not—I have a girlfriend."

Her mouth opened, then closed, then opened again.

But before she could think of what to say, he jumped to his feet.

"Listen, I've got to go. But I'm glad you invited me to lunch." His blush deepened. "I mean, you're great. And if I was the kind of guy to have a fling, I would love having a fling with you." If possible, he blushed even more. "Sorry, that came out wrong. Okay, anyway, gotta go. Thanks for lunch!"

Then he was gone.

She was mortified, aghast. But seconds later, she was frantic. Forget that he thought she was trying to have a fling with him. He'd left her with the check.

She scrambled into her purse, praying she'd find more than she knew was actually there. Sure, she expected that she, or rather Cordelia, would pay for lunch when it was meant to be their pitch to him, sans wine and steak. But steak! For lunch! The minute he'd ordered wine, Portia had assumed he would pay.

And it was all Cordelia's fault. What had her sister been thinking, giving him the impression that she could help him gain access to Gabriel Kane?

Portia really was going to kill her sister.

Her hands trembled, a trickle of sweat forming beneath her fancy suit as she pulled out her credit card and handed it over. Not more than a few minutes later, the waitress returned. "Ma'am, I'm afraid your card was rejected."

She cringed. "You're sure?"

"Sometimes the machine just doesn't like the card. Do you have another?"

"Well, no." Part of Portia's alimony deal with Robert was that he would pay her expenses for six months while she got settled—but she had only the one credit card, which he obviously wasn't paying. Why was she surprised?

"Then it'll have to be cash."

Portia rummaged through her wallet again, but no wad of bills miraculously appeared. She started counting out what she had, but didn't come close to the $150 bill.

All she could do was call Cordelia. But Cordelia still didn't answer. Neither did Olivia. Not that Olivia had more money than she did.

Portia counted her money again.

In the end, she left her driver's license with the manager and ran across the street to the ATM.

As soon as she paid, she went straight home. With every step she took, her anger grew. *I can't believe Cordelia did this to me*, she raged as she took the steps to the town house. *I am absolutely, positively going to kill Cordelia*, she promised herself as she slammed into her apartment.

She came to a dead stop when she heard the noise, and a smell biting at her nose.

"Portia, is that you?"

"Cordelia?"

Portia marched into the kitchen to find Cordelia there, an apron tied over her perfect clothes. The counters and stove were covered with pots and pans. Fingerprints and swipes marked the thin coating of flour that covered the surfaces like a child's watercolor painting project.

"What in the world are you doing?" she gasped.

Cordelia laughed, delighted, though there was something off about the look in her eyes. "What does it look like I'm doing?"

"Making a mess! And where were you at lunch?"

Cordelia paused mid-stir. "Oh my Lord! Lunch! Sorry. But just look at this. I'm cooking and baking! I woke up this morning," she rushed on, "thinking of food. Just like how it happens to you. I have the *knowing*!"

"What?" Portia tried to make sense of the scene. After a second, she noticed that Cordelia's clothes weren't so perfect, after all. In fact, for the first time she could remember, her sister wore wrinkled pants, the blouse not coordinating with the rest of the outfit. And her hair. Cordelia usually spent a great deal of time at the salon having her tresses professionally done. Portia speculated that Cordelia hadn't been to the hairdresser in a while.

"Cord, are you okay?"

Cordelia whipped around, spoon in hand, some sort of liquid flying across the room. "I'm fine! Don't I look fine? Of course I look fine. You're just saying that because I forgot about lunch. I am sorry, Portia."

"Okay, sweetie," Portia said carefully, coming closer. "Not to worry about the lunch."

Behind her, she heard the front door open and close.

"Hey!" Olivia called out, then stopped in the kitchen doorway. Her long, curly blond hair was pulled up in a messy twist, her full lips shiny with a nude gloss, her standard yoga attire fitting like a second skin. "What happened in here?"

Portia and Olivia exchanged a glance. Portia shrugged carefully. "I came home to this."

"Why isn't she cooking at her own place?"

"I wondered the same thing."

"She looks off."

"Don't mention it to her. She's sensitive."

"I'm standing right here, and I am not one bit sensitive. I'm cooking! It's perfect. And it's a sign that opening a Glass Kitchen in New York is going to be even more perfect! I'll be able to cook, too!"

Portia and Olivia exchanged another glance. "Everything is burned," Olivia mouthed.

"I know," Portia mouthed in return, picking up a bowl filled with wilted lettuce swimming in dressing. She sniffed and tasted. Butter lettuce with, perhaps, a raspberry vinaigrette.

Olivia walked up to Cordelia, as if approaching a wild animal. "Sweetie, give me the spoon. I'll keep stirring, then you can tell us all about waking up with the knowing."

It looked like Cordelia would protest, but then her fake cheer and shoulders sank, like a rock in water. She relinquished the spoon, then walked over to one of the stools and sat.

Olivia set the utensil aside, then sat next to her.

Cordelia looked around, seeming to notice the mess for the first time. "I don't have the knowing, do I?"

Olivia took her hands and squeezed. "Probably not." She leaned forward and pressed her forehead to Cordelia's. "Which you didn't want anyway, remember?"

Portia turned away from them, wishing not for the first time that she had the same confidence with people that seemed to come to Olivia as easily as breathing. Portia focused on the pot on the stove and tasted whatever it was in the pot. She grimaced. "It's not the worst stew I've ever tasted."

"It's supposed to be cream sauce. I was going to make creamed beef on toast."

Portia turned off the heat, set the spoon aside, and walked over to sit next to her sisters. "Creamed beef?"

"Daddy's favorite," Cordelia said, the words quiet.

"Oh my God!" Olivia laughed. "That awful stuff?"

"You didn't love it?" Cordelia asked.

"Seriously? Toasted bread slathered in creamed beef? No one loved that meal. Not even Daddy."

Portia joined in, smiling as she remembered. "No, Daddy didn't love anything about creamed beef on toast. But he loved Mama, and I swear she never knew that he barely choked every bite down." She looked at the scratched linoleum. "What I'd give to have even half the love that Daddy felt for Mama."

The sisters were quiet then. Portia knew they were lost in their own thoughts, their own memories of their parents. Then all of a sudden, Olivia leaped up.

"No dancing!" Portia said automatically. "And no singing!"

"Ha! Do I look that predictable? No. Let's play Spit!"

Another of Daddy's favorites.

Olivia raced into living room, and Portia heard her rummaging around in one of Aunt Evie's cabinets.

"I am not playing Spit," Cordelia stated.

Portia felt a trickle of relief. Cordelia was sounding more like her normal self again.

"Don't be a stick in the mud," Olivia teased with a wry twist of lips when she returned with a deck of ancient playing cards.

When they were growing up, their father had loved teaching his girls the rough-and-oh-so-impolite game called Spit, a game completely at odds with their mother's book on manners. How many times had Daddy teased Mama about turning his girls into sissies, making Mama laugh until they ended up in the back of the trailer, the laughter shifting into something that pushed the girls out the door into the hardscrabble yard?

"You only want to play because you always won," Portia said, smiling, grabbing up cards the minute Olivia handed her a pack.

Olivia and Portia played a quick hand, Cordelia looking on with a jaundiced eye.

"I win! And I'm starving!" Olivia said, as she started separating the cards.

Portia whipped up a quick meal for her sisters to eat from the few things left in the refrigerator. Sandwiches and a grapefruit and avocado salad topped with poppy seed dressing. The two sisters played and ate, while Cordelia only ate.

"You might win," Cordelia said, finally picking up her deck of cards "but only because you always cheat." With a put-upon sigh, she set up to play without having to be reminded how.

"I did not cheat," Olivia said, then cried out, "Spit!" to start the game just before Cordelia was ready.

"See! Cheating," Cordelia yelped, her fingers stumbling as Portia and Olivia started working their cards.

Portia lost herself in the game, worry fading away, laughing, as she slid a 2 onto a 3 just before Olivia got her own card there.

"Rats!" Olivia cried, slapping down a King, Queen, Jack, and a 10 with rapid-fire quickness, then threw up her hands. "I win!"

Portia was just a few cards behind. But Olivia leaped up and cheered. "I won! I won! You guys are turtles!"

Cordelia took a deep breath, then set her cards down. "Sorry about the mess, Portia. And sorry about lunch. But I better get home." She ate her last bite of poppy seed–covered avocado, took off the apron, and smoothed back her hair before gathering her handbag. She walked to the kitchen doorway, then abruptly turned back. "Oh, and I probably should mention, it looks like James is going to be indicted."

Fifteen

⁂

THE NEXT DAY, Ariel walked into the town house after school. She loved asking questions, though she wasn't big on answering them, as the Shrink had learned. But what was weird was that the Shrink didn't even seem to know what the right questions were, much less know to ask them. Her mom died over a year ago now, but he kept asking her to tell him what she felt. Hello, lousy.

She wanted him to tell her something massively smart that would make her feel better, like: *"Given the trajectory of matter over time, the miasma of your mind will not stay stagnant, therefore your sorrow will morph and change, making you feel more hopeful soon."* Or: *"Given how incredibly smart you are, Ariel—a genius, really—your astounding brain is sifting through the data and soon it will make sense out of the senseless occasion of your mother's death, and then you'll start feeling better."* Even a lame: *"Everything is going to be okay"* would do in a pinch. But nope, he never spoke a word that made her feel anything other than that he really was a quack.

Whatever. Plus, what did it matter? Her mom was dead. Dead. She wasn't coming back. How did that ever get better?

It didn't.

But right then, Ariel had other problems. The report on her dysfunctional family, or what was left of it.

Yesterday she had roughed out a few pages, mainly in her journal. But that just made her realize she didn't know anything about her family. It was like some sort of twisted nursery rhyme. Her mom was dead. Her dad made money. Her uncle was sort of sleazy. And her grandmother . . . Ariel hardly knew what to say about her. Nana was bizarre. The woman didn't seem anything like a grandmother, or even a mother.

And then there was Miranda, who could be summed up as completely nuts. Or, maybe, nympho.

Just that morning she was muttering in her cell phone the way she always did, but Ariel managed to overhear her anyway. She was talking about a dare. With a boy.

Which meant it was time to raid the journal again, because someone had to look out for the family, now that Mom was gone. And poor Dad was just too clueless when it came to Miranda.

Ariel dropped her bag in the foyer, checked around the house, then snuck into Miranda's room and found her journal.

A big, boldly written **DARE** blazed on top of a new page.

"Bingo," Ariel whispered.

Tuesday, October 1

I don't totally hate school anymore. I met some girls who are pretty nice. Not as nice as my old friends back in Jersey, but they'll have to do. One way or another, I am going to get back to NJ. God, I miss our old house and Kasey just down the block. My new friend Becky lives on the Upper East Side, and her mom is a total stay-at-home type who is always there, or at least someone is always there. I'm the only girl I've met so far who doesn't go home to someone. Actually, though, I'm lucky because I can do stuff and they can't. Becky dared me to

ask Dustin Bradford over after school. DARE. No question Dad
would go Dark Side if he found out.

The sound of the front door opening took a second to register. Ariel
slapped the journal shut and shoved it under the mattress. She was just
shutting the door when Miranda rounded the bend in the staircase.

Her sister stopped short. "Were you in my room?"

Ariel scoffed. "No."

"Then why are you standing in front of my door?"

"I heard you coming up the stairs."

Miranda's eyes narrowed; then she waved Ariel away like she wasn't
important enough to spend another second dealing with. "You are *never*
allowed in my room."

"Like there is anything in there that I'd want." *Nympho*, she added
silently.

She ran down the stairs and surprised Portia in the kitchen, unpack-
ing groceries. "Hey, Ariel."

"Hey? Is that a Texas thing, too?"

Portia laughed. "I take it you don't say *hey*."

"Nah. I pretty much stick to *hi* or the occasional *how do you do*—you
know, when I want to throw off an adult."

"Throw off an adult, huh?" Portia pulled a chicken from the bag. Next
came onions and celery, carrots and brown rice.

"Most adults are clueless."

"I'm an adult."

"The jury's still out on you."

Portia laughed. "Tell me something I don't already know."

The woman definitely wasn't easy to peg.

Ariel stood there a bit longer until Portia glanced over at her. "What?"

"I've been at school. All day. I'm a kid."

"And?"

"Aren't you going to ask me whether I have homework to do? Or whether I was bullied in gym? Or whether I threw up?"

"You don't really look like the throw-up type."

She had her there.

Miranda practically danced into the kitchen.

Portia glanced over her shoulder. "Hey, you."

Miranda didn't say a word. She walked over to the refrigerator and pulled out a bottle of VitaminWater, then circled back to lean against the stainless-steel door and sighed, a weird smile on her face.

"What's wrong with you?" Ariel asked.

"Nothing's wrong. Everything's great."

Portia turned back to the sink. "She's in love."

Miranda's eyes went wide. Then she did an even bigger sigh, tons of dreamy slathered on. It made Ariel want to gag.

"Maybe a little." She giggled.

Portia kept working on dinner, washing the chicken, putting it in a pot.

"So who is it?" Ariel asked.

"Like you'd know him," Miranda scoffed.

Portia still didn't say a word, but then Miranda went off like a race-horse.

"His name is Dustin. He's the cutest boy in school. Becky says so."

Uh-oh. Dustin was coming to fruition.

"He's in my algebra class." Miranda said. "I hate algebra. Sooooo, I asked him to come over and help me! Not that he's any better at it than I am, but he's going to come over." She glared at Ariel just as Portia walked into the pantry. "No telling Dad," she hissed. "I told an adult I have someone coming over. I told *her*." She nodded toward the pantry.

Who would have guessed Miranda was smart enough to come up with a way to win a dare without breaking the letter of the law? Dad's law, that is.

"Me? Do I look like a snitch?"

Of course Ariel had already thought of several ways she could use this information to her advantage. But she really didn't tattle.

Portia returned to the sink, and Miranda walked over to stand next to her.

"What are you making?"

What? The girl who hardly ever came out of her room except to barely eat and fight with Dad was making conversation?

"A cross between chicken and rice and chicken soup," Portia said.

"Cool."

Cool? Who was this girl? First, a non-adult adult, now a non-glowering teenager?

"My mom never cooked," Miranda said. "But she loved my dad. And he loved her. A lot." Miranda's smiled shifted and changed. "In fact, just because you cook for us doesn't mean you can take her place."

"Miranda!" Ariel gasped.

Portia turned her head, didn't look one bit ruffled. More like she looked determined, like she had been reminded of something totally true.

"Not to worry, Miranda," she said. "I'm not trying to take her place. I'm just working for your dad. Your mom is your mom, and always will be."

Hello, *our* mom.

But Ariel didn't say that, either. She didn't care to go into Miranda's story about how their mom and dad brought home the wrong baby when they picked up Ariel, but then the hospital wouldn't take her back. Sure, Ariel was smart enough to know that this was in no way possible. But Miranda said it with such authority that Ariel was half convinced there was some truth to the story. Maybe just that her parents hadn't believed someone who looked like Ariel could be their child. Thank God Ariel had their mom's weird green eyes, so no one could pretend she wasn't their kid.

Miranda took a carrot and chomped down on it, turning away from Portia so she could glower at Ariel. "She might not have cooked, but she was fun."

"Mom? Fun?"

The words were out of Ariel's mouth before she could swallow them back.

Miranda glanced at her. "Of course." Like Ariel was a moron. "You heard what Uncle Anthony said. She was the life of the party. And she was totally fun when . . ."

The words trailed off.

Portia glanced over at Miranda, but still didn't say a word.

"Mom wasn't fun," Ariel said, "she was, like, beautiful. Always the perfect clothes and hair, always had her nails done. Totally beautiful."

Miranda eyed Ariel, seemed on the verge of rolling her eyes, but relented. "She was all that. But she was fun, too. At least she was totally fun before you landed on our doorstep looking like a troll."

Ariel felt the blood rise in her face. As always in circumstances like this, words eluded her. Her quick brain slowed; her heart hurt.

"Miranda." This from Portia.

"What?" Miranda snapped back.

"You know what."

Now Portia was being an adult. She had that steady gaze thing down pat. And Miranda backed down.

"Whatever. Mom was fun even after you arr—"

Another look.

"Fine. After you came home and weren't a total troll." She drew a breath. "She really was fun. When you were a baby, she could make you laugh and laugh."

Ariel's throat went tight, the same way it did whenever the Shrink asked her to talk about their mom. Then a memory hit her. "I remember a time, once, when Mom dragged me into the backyard to plant violets and watermelon. She laughed and said it would be fun." The kitchen grew comfortably quiet. Finally, like giving in or something, Portia asked, "Do you have a photo of your mom?"

Miranda shrugged, then pushed up. "I do." She went upstairs, then returned in a flash. "This is her. It's the only one I have since Dad packed all the others away. But it's a great one."

The photo made Ariel's throat tighten even more. It showed Miranda, Mom, Dad, and Ariel, all laughing, Mom leaning up against Dad.

But the photo had been taken when Ariel was little. Other than in this picture, she had never seen her mother laugh or lean against Dad.

"You should put it out," Portia said.

Miranda gave her a look. "Yeah, so Dad can bite my head off? No thanks."

Ariel explained. "He doesn't like being reminded of Mom. Which makes it really hard to do the report I'm working on."

"What report?"

"The one on our family. We have to write a paper on our family tree, without it just being a family tree. I ask, what does that even mean?"

"I had to do one of those when I was in middle school," Miranda said. "I just asked Mom a bunch of questions. She told me stories about herself as a kid."

"Really? What did she say?" Ariel asked, the words kind of breathy.

"Not much. I just wrote about her wanting to be a princess when she was young, and how it was special to me since I wanted the same thing when I was her age. I got an A." Miranda looked at Ariel wryly. "You could hand in the same report, but I don't think anyone would believe that you ever wanted to be a princess."

Ariel's heart twisted even more. Her mom had wanted to be a princess?

Miranda's cell rang. One glance at the screen and she dashed from the kitchen, then out the front door.

Ariel and Portia watched her go. After a second, Portia poured a glass of coconut water with ice and handed it to Ariel. "I bet you have your own stories to tell about your mom, stories that are completely yours."

"How do you know?"

"I'm a sister, just like you. And I'm a younger sister, just like you. All you have to do is dig around, find the memories. They'll be there."

"Dig around?"

"You know, ask questions, search out answers?"

"Like a detective?"

Portia laughed. "Exactly. Ariel, the Twelve-Year-Old Detective."

"I'm nearly thirteen!"

"All the better."

Portia turned back to the pile of food on the counter. Ariel took the glass and then headed out of the room to her dad's office.

She felt a little better. She could look for some memories, like Portia said. She could get her own A, and not with some idiotic story about a princess, either. She would do an Internet search.

In the office, she fired up her dad's computer, the one that didn't have any kid blocks. She opened her backpack and rummaged around, looking for a pen and some paper. She really needed to clean out her backpack now. Before she knew it, she'd be thirteen. And, seriously, what self-respecting teenager carried around a calculator covered in stickers; a painted inhaler; or crazy socks with individual toes, like gloves for feet. She had outgrown them all.

But then there was the whole thing she couldn't get out of her head. Her mom had given her the stickers. Her mom had whipped out the nail polish and painted Einstein on the inhaler after Ariel had refused to carry it around because it was stupid.

And the socks? She'd found those after her mom died, like some sort of weird relic from the past. Her mom had been super fancy. How many times had Ariel wondered how a girl who owned those socks could grow up to be a woman who always wore boring clothes and tons of pearls?

As usual, there were more questions than answers.

Ariel went to Google and typed in her mom's name. Photos popped up. Ariel had seen them before. After all, she'd Googled her mom a zillion other times. No new photos. No new news, either. Just the same articles, the ones about all the good works Mom did, and all the variations on "Social Scion Dies in Crash."

Pressure built up behind Ariel's eyes.

Quickly, she moved on. This time, she typed in the name her uncle had used, Victoria Polanski. The computer spun for a second, and up popped a whole new batch of images. Mom way younger than Ariel had ever seen her. Mom with a group of girls glammed up like that old group the Spice Girls, arms linked, drinks in hand. The caption read: *Beauty Times Four.*

The article went on about Mom and a whole bunch of other people attending a big bash at a bar opening in Union Square.

Ariel couldn't have been more shocked if she'd read that her mother was a vampire. This image, and the one that was lodged in her head, didn't match. At all.

She kept scrolling down until she came to a photo of her dad. Actually it was of her dad and uncle, standing on either side of her mom. This time, the caption read: *Two Beauties and a Beast.* It said that her mom was a beauty, sure, but it was mainly about how her uncle was the beauty to his older brother's beast. The thought made her hurt a little bit more.

Quickly, she clicked on another link, anything to distract herself. But what popped up made her flinch. An obituary. She hated obituaries. Avoided them like the plague.

On second glance, she breathed a little easier when she realized it wasn't for her mother. Instead, it was for a man named Bohater Polanski. *Bohater Polanski?*

Ariel scanned the notice. The man was born in Poland; immigrated to the United States when he was a teenager; married, then lost his young wife; was a longtime maintenance engineer at the Amsterdam Houses, the same complex where he raised his only daughter, Wisia "Victoria" Polanski.

Her pulse slowed.

The photo included with the notice showed an old man with no smile but clearly proud of the teenage girl standing next to him, as if it were the only photo of the man to be found. Even Ariel couldn't deny that the girl was her mother.

With her heart in her throat, she Googled "Amsterdam Houses."

Ariel stared at the screen. Her la-di-da mother, who refused to socialize with anyone who wasn't from the "right" family, was raised by a man she had never bothered to mention, in a housing project in an iffy section of the Upper West Side.

That was the woman who could paint Einstein in lime green nail polish and who owned crazy gloves made for feet.

Sixteen

⬩⬩⬩

A CRASH STARTLED PORTIA and she dashed out of the Kanes' kitchen.

"Ariel?"

"Everything's fine! No need—"

Portia came to a stop in the doorway to what looked like Gabriel's office. The room had heavier furniture than the study one floor up. Ariel stood at a mahogany desk with a drinking glass at her feet, a spray of coconut water and ice cubes splashed across the floor.

"Ah, clumsy me." Ariel closed the computer window, then turned off the machine. "I guess I made a mess."

Portia eyed the computer. "What are you doing?"

"Homework."

"That didn't look like homework."

"Portia, seriously, you're showing your age. This is how we do homework now. On computers. We do research on the Internet, then write intelligent reports suffused with impressive detail." Ariel stepped high over the water and drinking glass. "I'll get some towels." She walked across the hall and retrieved two hand towels from the half bath. "But don't worry, I don't think less of you for not knowing that." Her smile widened, and she dropped down and mopped up the mess. Portia dropped down next to her, and they had it all cleaned up in seconds.

"Ariel, seriously," Portia said in a perfect version of a teenage accent, if she said so herself. "Do I look like I just fell off the turnip truck?"

Ariel eyed her. "You probably don't want me to answer that."

Then she surprised Portia when she leaped up, tossed the towels back in the bath, and grabbed her hand. "I'm starved."

Portia was still worried about Cordelia. After her announcement about the possible indictment, she had later explained that the authorities had started probing not just the bank, but James as well. James had not left the apartment in days.

Portia's unease grew when she and Ariel returned to the Kanes' kitchen and found that Miranda was back, this time with a boy.

Ariel stopped so fast that Portia bumped into her.

"Ariel," Miranda snapped. "Shouldn't you be upstairs or something, doing homework?" She eyed Portia. "And aren't you, like, finished playing maid for the day?"

The boy actually laughed, though he also gave Portia a once-over like a bad imitation of a lech in a seedy bar. He looked older than Miranda, though he wore the same school uniform. His blond hair was shaggy, but somehow seemed professionally cut that way, as if he—or his mom—had paid two hundred dollars for the trim.

"This is your maid?" he asked. "My mom needs to fire whoever finds our housekeepers. Ours are always old and major ugly."

Portia wrinkled her nose. "Do kids in New York really talk like that?"

"Huh?" the boy said.

"Ignore her," Miranda said. "Come on, Dustin, let's go upstairs to my room."

Ariel's eyes went wide. "You can't take a boy to your bedroom! Dad will kill you!"

"Well, he won't be home for hours, so he won't ever know. Right?"

"I guess," Ariel muttered.

"Right, Portia?"

"Don't get me involved in this. I'm just the *maid*, remember?"

"Whatever. Come on, Dustin."

Portia cursed under her breath. "Miranda, I don't think it's such a good idea to go upstairs. Stay down here, in the garden room."

Miranda jerked around and gave her a look. "Dad hired you as a cook, I get it. But guess what? That doesn't make you my babysitter!"

The boy laughed. "Dude," he said with a nod.

"Your dad won't be happy if he finds out you took a guy to your room. He might well decide that you *need* a babysitter."

Portia didn't register the sound of the front door opening until Miranda's eyes went wide.

"What's up?" Dustin asked.

"It's Dad," Ariel said. "He's going to kill you. *Dude*."

"You have to go," Miranda added. "Shit, how do we get you out of here? What is Dad doing home so early?"

Before Portia could intervene, Miranda pushed the boy out the window and shooed him down the fire escape.

"Portia's door is always open. I'll take him out through there once Dad's inside," Ariel said as if Portia weren't standing there.

Miranda nodded. "Great."

"Hello, Dad!" Ariel sang frantically, blowing by him as he walked into the kitchen. "Back in a flash."

Gabriel stood, taking in the retreating form of Ariel, and then turned to take in Miranda and Portia. "Did I miss something?"

"No," Miranda blurted. "Not a thing. Right, Portia?"

Gabriel glanced between Miranda and her. What would she do if he asked her what was going on?

Just a few minutes later, Ariel burst back in.

Finally, he asked, "What's for dinner?"

"It's only five o'clock," Portia said.

"I thought I'd come home early. See how my girls were doing."

"Ah, yeah. Great," Miranda stated. She tucked her hair behind her ear and strode past him.

"*I'm* glad you're home, Dad," Ariel said, as if trying to reassure him that he was loved.

Gabriel smiled. "Thanks, sweetheart."

Then his cell phone rang, and he disappeared into his study. Portia was left alone again to finish dinner and was on the verge of leaving when Gabriel, Miranda, and Ariel reappeared.

"Dinner's ready," Portia said.

"Why don't you stay?" Gabriel said.

Portia glanced around to see whom he was talking to. "Me?"

"Yes, you."

"Thanks, but I can't."

"Come on," Ariel chimed in. "Stay."

Miranda glared.

Portia shook her head. "Nope. But thanks." No way was she getting roped into another dinner with this crew, despite the fact that she was starving.

At six, she found a can of tuna in her cabinet downstairs. At seven, she had eaten and cleaned, then started to pace. At eight, she called Olivia to get away from her thoughts. At nine, she called to check in on Cordelia, though her call went to voice mail. At ten, she went out, hoping to stop her circling thoughts. She was worried and irritable over one unavoidable fact. She was running out of money.

She walked for nearly an hour, but didn't feel one bit better. When she returned to the apartment, Gabriel was sitting on the front steps, his forearms on his knees.

He didn't say a word as she approached.

He always took her breath away, the mix of power and brutality, stirred together with an ache that was only visible if you looked closely.

She didn't need to be with any man right then; she had enough complications as it was. Not to mention the fact that this man had his own set of problems, the biggest of which being that he had lost his wife—the mother of his daughters—the one who didn't cook but was fun, at least according to Miranda. More than that—if she needed more than that—was the fact that she worked for him. To top things off, if . . . no, *when* things fell apart, they would be stuck in the same building, coming and going through the same cramped vestibule.

She hated that he made her want to forget everything and dive into him.

"I want a raise."

He cocked a brow, leaning back, planting his elbows on the step behind him, a grin sliding across his face. "Last I heard, *Hello* was the accepted form of greeting in the U.S."

She slapped her thigh. "God, you with the jokes. But I'm serious. And as you just pointed out, this is the U.S. Haven't you heard of redistribution of wealth? You appear to have lots. I need some. Hence the raise."

His grin hitched into a smile. "You've barely made half a dozen meals."

"A half dozen of the best meals you've had in a long time."

"It's pretty hard to get breakfast wrong."

"You'd think. But I have a nose, Mr. Kane, and the smell of burned oatmeal wafted from your kitchen the other morning."

"Wafted?"

"Don't change the subject."

His dark hair looked black as night in the sun, the waves reflecting the light, his matching eyes so dark that she couldn't tell where the pupils ended and the irises began.

"You're a good cook. I'll give you that."

"And then there were the cupcakes."

"True."

"Then you'll give me the raise?"

"No."

She heaved a melodramatic sigh, somehow feeling better already. "This really isn't funny," she said.

"Actually, it sort of is. You look like you're sucking on a lemon."

She shook her head with a jerk. "Untrue!"

"Nope, true."

"Do men your age say words like 'nope'?"

"This from the woman who just used the word 'wafting.'"

For a second, she thought he was going to laugh outright. Again. This man who people said was ruthless. But then the lightness dissolved, his face shifting back into hard, unyielding edges, and he stood. "Haven't you heard how intimidating I am?"

She rolled her eyes. "Who could have missed Big Bad You on the front of *The New York Times*?" She patted his shirt. "Go scare those poor guys at Global Guppy, or whatever company you're trouncing. I'm not afraid of you."

He actually looked a little insulted.

"One article does not a ruthless magnate make, Gabriel. What're you doing? Warming up to doing a Donald Trump 'You're Fired'?"

"Me channeling Donald Trump is about as likely as me giving you a raise."

"Well, you do have better hair."

His head fell back, and he looked up to the sky. "Three females in one suddenly small town house, not a one of them who listens to a word I say."

"Ariel listens."

He glanced back at her. "When she wants to."

They walked up the stairs and into the vestibule, but when she reached the entry to her apartment, she turned back. He was watching her, hands jammed into his pockets.

"For the record, I don't believe a word of that article," she told him.

He studied her. "You should. Every word of it's true. I get what I want, Portia. And I crush anyone who gets in my way."

She blinked, then broke into laughter. "If you're not careful, someone's going to ask you to star in your own reality-TV show."

His eyes narrowed in a way that gave her a flutter of alarm.

"Were you sitting out there for a reason?" she hurried on.

He appeared to debate letting her change the subject. "I rang your bell and you weren't home."

"I was out."

"What, no business plans to refine?"

"Ha-ha. You with the joking."

He stood there for a second. "I'm guessing Miranda had a boy here this afternoon."

Portia stiffened.

"I'm not an idiot, Portia. I assume he went out the kitchen window after I came in the door."

She debated. "Yeah, he did."

They stood in silence for a moment or two longer.

"I didn't know much about the girls before my wife died," he said, surprising her. "Now it's just me taking care of them. And I know what those boys are thinking. That's one thing I know about, being a kid lusting after a girl. You don't think about the fact that one day you'll probably have your own daughter."

"You know what they say about karma," she said delicately.

"I say it's a pain in the ass," Gabriel muttered.

Portia smiled at him. "There's more to raising girls than protecting them. You need to figure out how to have fun with them. Let them see that you *can* have fun. Make them feel at ease so they'll open up to you."

Gabriel's jaw set. "I know how to have fun."

"Really?" she challenged.

"Really."

"Prove it."

He glanced at her. "I don't have to prove anything."

"Maybe that's true in business. But with your daughters? Do you really believe you don't have to prove anything, especially when you admit that you weren't a big part of their life before their mother passed away?"

"What am I supposed to do?"

The noise of New York felt distant, as if just the two of them existed in this city of millions.

"Make something up," she suggested.

"What?" The word came out as a snap.

"I don't mean lie. I'm talking about simple kid things. Like looking up in the sky and finding shapes in clouds."

"I am not a child."

"No, you're a dad who's trying to connect with two daughters. You need to remember what it's like to be young, Gabriel."

He grumbled something, and then said, "There are no clouds."

"You can't see them because of the streetlight. But I bet if we go up on the roof," she said, her tone teasing and singsong, "we could see some."

"It's night."

"There's a full moon."

"We are not going up to the roof."

She ignored his glower, then headed for the front door. "Come on. It'll be fun."

"Ms. Cuthcart—"

"Don't go all 'Ms. Cuthcart' on me. I've wanted to see the roof again ever since I got here."

She stood in the vestibule, waiting expectantly at his front door, his hard gaze locking with hers. She caught her lower lip in her teeth, trying to look sweet and innocent.

"That would work better if I didn't know you're only sweet around me when it suits you."

She gave a surprised burst of laughter. "Touché."

After a second, he relented and put his key in the lock. Before he could change his mind, she slipped inside and started tiptoeing up the stairs.

Amazingly, Gabriel followed, floor after floor, quiet so the girls wouldn't hear them. When they came to the doorway that led to the roof, Gabriel reached out and opened it for her.

The minute she stepped outside, Portia smelled the cool evening air. She felt like the clock had been turned back, Gram still alive, Great-aunt Evie still here, the summers filled with promise of a very different kind of adventure. Portia had loved New York when she was younger, but in a way that was so different from what she felt for Texas, with its giant blue sky and easygoing charm, like sweet tea over ice on a hot day. In New York, nothing was easy; everything was dense, nothing fluffy about it, like bagels slathered with thick cream cheese.

Of course, Gabriel had renovated the space. Latticework provided privacy from the town house next door, a cabana-like structure creating a private space. The long swathes of roofing had been covered with a wooden deck. A table perfect for rooftop picnics stood to one side, with two chaise lounges perched at the far end.

The sky was a dark blue, almost black, the buildings like silhouettes. Only a hint of clouds could be seen.

"It's too dark," Gabriel stated, then turned back as if either this space, or the night sky, or maybe Portia, made him feel too much.

"Not so fast." Without thinking, she grabbed his hand.

He glanced down, and Portia felt the shock of his skin on hers. He didn't tug away when he dragged his gaze back to hers, but the expression on his face was unfathomable. "Are you intimidated by anything?" he asked softly.

Portia let go and walked away from him, with the same overwhelming awareness that he made her feel sliding through her like a warm sip of brandy. "Of course I am," she called back.

"Like what?

The future. A life derailed. Twice. Not understanding what I did wrong, or what I could have done different to make things turn out right.

But she didn't say any of that.

"Hmmm, like what?" She studied the wide black sky. "Like sports metaphors, navigating the Thirty-fourth Street subway station—I mean, seriously, how many subway lines do they have down there?—and SquareBob SpongePants. Or is it SpongeBob SquarePants? Whatever, I don't get him or his underwater bikini world."

She heard what sounded like a reluctant snort of laughter as she went over to one of the chaise lounges that sat side by side at the edge of the roof. After a second, she said, "Up here I feel completely alone, despite all the windows, the lights burning. Or maybe it's because I know that even if someone does see me, here, in New York, no one cares. It's freeing." She lay down and looked up at the sky. Finally she looked over at him.

"Come on, Gabriel. The girls are asleep. They'll never know you were up here instead down in front of your computer, slogging away like a efficient hamster on a wheel."

She was almost certain he muttered a few curse words and that he would storm back downstairs. Instead, he stood there for a second before he strode across the roof, those broad hands of his shoved in his pants pockets. After a moment more, he lay down on the chaise next to hers, so close that they nearly touched.

"What do you see?" she asked finally.

When he didn't answer, she rolled her head to glance over at him. He was looking at her, and this time his eyes held unmistakable heat.

The night air drifted between them, something charged. She told herself that she hadn't had sex in well over a year and that of course a guy like Gabriel with all his barely contained control would make her think of just that. Sex. It made sense that he intrigued her despite the fact that she knew nothing good could come out of getting involved with her neighbor. Besides, he had kissed her. Sue her, she wanted another taste. Which, despite all her bravado about him not intimidating her, was about as sane as thinking it was safe to pet a cuddly-looking grizzly bear.

"The clouds. What do you see?" she asked.

He stared at her. "I see a woman who is tilting at windmills."

Her eyes narrowed, thoughts of kissing and sex gone. "What does that mean?"

"Not a fan of Don Quixote?"

"Stop showing off and explain."

His shout of laughter seemed to surprise him. "'Showing off.' You are priceless."

She scowled.

"Fine, Don Quixote went around—"

"With Sancho Panza, trying to rekindle chivalry. Got that, but really don't know how it applies to me."

"So you know more than you're letting on."

"And you don't do the same thing?"

She made out his smile in the dark.

"Don Quixote kept fighting battles that he couldn't win."

She sucked in her breath.

"As when he tried to battle windmills that he thought were giants that could be beaten."

"I take it in your oh-so-*not* subtle way you're telling me I'm fighting a losing battle," she said.

"You sound like Ariel."

"You should sound more like Ariel."

He shook his head, but he still smiled.

"Just so we're clear, which battle am I losing?" she asked.

"The Glass Kitchen."

Portia bristled. "The Glass Kitchen is not a losing battle." It couldn't be.

"The way you're going about it certainly is."

"What does that mean?"

"You're not asking enough questions."

"I ask plenty of questions."

She forced herself not to cringe at the memory of her disastrous investor lunch.

"What questions should I be asking?" she asked, her tone completely even.

"According to Henry Ravel, you didn't ask him anything other than where did he prefer to meet. Midtown or Upper West Side."

"Ack! How do you know about Henry Ravel?"

Henry Ravel had been at her second ill-fated investor meeting. The second meeting that had ended abruptly when he learned she wasn't associated with Gabriel Kane, at least in terms of investing.

"He called me."

"About what?" Though she was afraid she knew.

"Somehow he got the impression that you're working with me."

Portia groaned. "Sorry about that. He's the second person my sister has done that to. But Cordelia's out of sorts, and I haven't found a good time to scream at her."

"I'm not worried about the calls," he said. "But here's the thing: Even if I thought you should open a Glass Kitchen—which I don't—you're going about it all wrong. As I said, you're not asking enough questions."

Portia looked up at the sky. The clouds were riding high and fast, like horsemen chasing across the sky. As much as she knew she should jump all over his advice, she just didn't want it. "Okay, you want questions, how about this: If you can't see or hear a tree fall in the forest, has it really fallen?"

"You're impossible," he muttered, and before she knew what was happening, he reached over and dragged her into his arms, her legs sliding between his as they lay together on his chaise.

"Oh," Portia whispered, their mouths only inches apart.

"Yes, oh," he whispered.

Her heart beat hard. She wanted to feel his lips on hers again. She wanted him to wrap her in his arms and make her feel all the things that she hadn't felt in years, if ever.

But just when he ran his hands up into her hair, she couldn't help herself. "I do have one important question. Why have you erased all traces of the girls' mother . . . your wife?"

They were so close that she could just make out the way his pupils contracted, the only sign of anger.

He didn't respond. He just looked at her. After a long second, he put her aside as if she didn't weigh anything at all and got up. He didn't help her to her feet. He didn't wait for her as he headed for the door.

"See," she called after him. "No one likes the important questions. Not even you."

He didn't respond, and the door shut closed firmly behind him.

Seventeen

❖

WHAT'S WRONG?"

Portia found Ariel at the table, head on forearms, a loaf of bread and a jar of peanut butter by her side, a knife sticking out of the peanut butter like a metal pole planted in a pot. "Ariel?"

The girl stirred and groaned. "What's going on?"

"You tell me," Portia said, pulling out a chair next to Ariel and sitting down.

It was four in the afternoon. She planned to make breaded veal cutlets, mashed potatoes, and green beans, then leave it for the Kanes to eat. Between the cupcakes and the cooking, not to mention the trip up to the roof with Gabriel, Portia felt she was getting pulled into this family despite her best efforts to resist them.

With a silent sigh, she pressed the back of her hand to Ariel's forehead to see if she had a fever.

"What's going on?" Ariel repeated groggily, then winced at the sight of the peanut butter. "Oh, yeah. I was hungry. But I never got around to making the sandwich."

"Didn't you eat lunch at school?"

"Not really."

"Why not?"

"The lunch room is not the best environment for eating."

"What is that supposed to mean?"

Ariel rolled her head and looked at her. "It means that it's not a five-star restaurant, okay?"

Portia studied her for a second. "Not feeling well?"

But Ariel wasn't hot. She didn't sound sick either. She sounded more dismayed than ill.

Stop getting involved with this family, Portia warned herself. *Remain detached. You are the cook. The* maid, *as Miranda said.*

"So, do you want to talk about whatever's bothering you?" she asked instead, cursing herself even as the words came out of her mouth.

Ariel eyed her for a second and then shook her head. "Nothing to talk about."

Portia debated, then shrugged. "Okay, then I'll get started on dinner."

She could feel Ariel's eyes on her back.

"Portia?" she said after a few minutes.

"Yes?"

"Did you mean it when you said that if you want answers, you need to dig, even if it makes you uncomfortable?"

Had she said that?

"You totally said that," Ariel said, yet again reading her mind.

"We were talking about your report."

"That's what I'm doing. Trying to write a good report."

Portia stopped working for a second and thought about it. "Yeah, I guess I meant it. We all have to dig sometimes. We all have to ask questions. Even if we don't really want to hear the answers."

Ariel grabbed the peanut butter, pushed up, and headed for the door. "Thanks."

Portia eyed her. "Are you sure you're okay?"

"I'm fine," Ariel answered. "Really."

An hour later, dinner prepared, Portia thought she heard the outer front door open and close. But she didn't hear the bell ring.

A few minutes after that, she heard a door again. This time, the bell rang.

Curious, she made her way to the foyer and opened the front door. In the vestibule she found Anthony Kane and her sister.

"Olivia?"

"There you are." Her sister smiled that particular brand of smile she had, like a single-malt scotch mixed with honey, both sophisticated and sultry sweet. Her long curly hair was loose, her long-sleeved white T-shirt tucked into jeans, a gossamer scarf twisted artfully around her neck. Of all the sisters, Olivia was the most comfortable in her own skin, throwing clothes together with an easy flair that made other women try to emulate her. On Olivia, the clothes made her look like a muse in an artist's painting. And no doubt Olivia had served as an artist's muse. Clothed, unclothed. Olivia had never been shy.

"I went downstairs, but no one was home," Olivia said. "Lucky me, when I was leaving," she added, her Texas accent stronger than usual, "I ran into this gorgeous man."

Portia rolled her eyes. Anthony laughed appreciatively.

"Nothing better than a female who speaks her mind," he said to Olivia.

The outer door opened and Gabriel walked in. He stopped at the sight of Anthony.

The four of them stood in the entry foyer of the Kanes' house as Gabriel curtly acknowledged Olivia, glanced at Portia, and then gave his brother a particularly forbidding smile. "You're here," he said.

His younger brother put out his hands, palms held up. "In the flesh," he said, his smile wide and charming. "You said you'd have a check for me. Of course I'd be here."

Gabriel's jaw ticked. More than ever, he looked the part of the beast. "My study. Now. We'll discuss."

"Discuss? I know what that means." He took Olivia's arm instead of following. "Maybe you should take a second to think about just what there is to discuss, Gabriel. In the meantime, I think this is as good a time as any to get to know Portia's beautiful sister."

"Anthony," Gabriel stated.

"Just give me a few minutes, big brother. I have no plans for the rest of the night." He looked at Olivia. "At least not yet."

Olivia laughed and let him guide her out the door.

Portia glanced at Gabriel. He gave her a hard look.

"Hey, he's your brother," she said.

"And she's your sister." He turned on his heel and headed for his study.

A few minutes later, Portia found Anthony and Olivia sitting at her kitchen table downstairs, each of them with a glass of fresh-squeezed lemonade.

"I came by to make sure we are still on for tonight," Olivia said. "The Bandana Ball, remember?"

Portia grimaced.

"Portia." Olivia eyed her. "Tell me you didn't forget."

"What's a 'bandana ball'?" Anthony asked.

"It's the best party in all of Manhattan," Olivia said. "Every year Texans in New York put on a huge gala event to raise money for Texas charities. This year is a push for Texas literacy. And every year Portia and her—" She cursed. "Well, Portia came to town to join us. This year she's already here." She sliced Portia a look. "Here and going."

"Do you dress up in ballgowns made of bandanas?" Anthony asked with a laugh.

"Actually, no. You dress up in Western wear. Boots, hats, jewels. We bought four tickets, but Cordelia is . . . well, a bit out of sorts these days, which means we have two extra." Olivia turned to Portia. "You can't back out on me, too."

"I'm sure you have plenty of friends to take."

"No way. You're going with me if I have to dress you myself and drag you to the Mandarin Oriental Hotel."

"I'll go." Anthony said.

Olivia gave him the once-over. "Perfect." She paused. "In fact, I have an idea. I think we need to get your brother to come as well. How can Portia say no if her *boss* is going?"

"He's not my boss."

Olivia gave her a look. "Do you work for him?"

"Sort of."

"How do you *sort of* work for someone?"

The *boss* chose that moment to walk in, without so much as a knock.

"If there is anyone who can *sort of* work for someone, Olivia, it's your sister."

Olivia laughed appreciatively. Portia scowled. But it was Anthony whose expression shifted the most when Gabriel turned to him.

"I'm running out of patience, Anthony. I have the papers ready upstairs," Gabriel said.

Olivia interrupted without an apparent thought for the tension that crackled through the room. "Come to the Bandana Ball with us, Gabriel Kane." She turned to Anthony. "Convince him to join us. Two Kane guys, two Cuthcart girls."

"Olivia," Portia snapped. "Stop."

"I think it's a great idea," Anthony said. "We'll go together. Dance up a storm." He glanced at the clock. "Gotta go if I'm going to have time to pretty up! I'll sign tomorrow, Gabriel."

Olivia grabbed Portia's hands and leaned close. "And don't you dare wear something boring."

⸙

"I can't believe I got talked into this," Gabriel stated.

Portia sat at a table underneath the vaulted ceiling of the Mandarin's ballroom on Columbus Circle, looking out over Central Park, hardly believing she was there either. But Olivia had pointed out that by not going, she was letting her ex-husband take away something else from her that she loved.

Country-western music filled the hall, the strings and crooning at odds with the elegance of the modern hotel. Bales of hay and old-fashioned wagon wheels decorated a room full of men dressed in tux jackets, bow ties, jeans, and cowboy boots. The women wore diamonds the size of Texas, denim skirts of varying lengths, and stiletto heels straight off the runways of Paris.

Texas women might like their hair styled and their diamonds big, but you wouldn't find a single self-respecting Texas female in a pair of cowboy boots.

Gabriel looked as if someone had picked him up and landed him on the moon.

"Having a touch of culture shock?" she asked.

He gave her a wry look.

He wore a black suit and a silver-gray tie. Hot, yes. Texas Bandana Ball? No.

She glanced out at the dance floor. Anthony and Olivia were already there, laughing, having fun. Gabriel hadn't moved since they had arrived.

"Hey, I know," she said, her tone needling, "why don't we do something no one would expect us to do and, say, dance."

"I don't dance."

"That's how the whole *unexpected* thing works—doing something you wouldn't normally do."

"I've already exceeded my quota of the unexpected for the night."

"How's that?"

"I'm here."

She laughed at that. "Fine, don't dance. But could you go sit someplace else then?"

"What?"

"Someone else might ask me to dance," she explained, "but not if you're sitting here with me. And as long as I'm here, I plan to dance."

"I'm not leaving you at this table alone."

She wrinkled her nose. "It's hardly a dangerous street corner in the Bronx. And I'm hardly alone. We're surrounded with hundreds of people. Oh! There's a guy I know. I bet he'll dance with me."

She jumped up, but she hadn't gotten a step away when a woman came toward the man and led him onto the dance floor. When she glanced back, Gabriel looked exasperated but amused, too.

"If you'd worn running shoes, you could have gotten there faster."

She shot him a sharp look.

The music coming from the speakers stopped, and a band appeared onstage. At the sight of the country-western band Asleep at the Wheel, the crowd erupted in wild applause; minutes later, the dance floor filled to overflowing.

"What are they doing?" Gabriel asked, his face a mask of disbelief.

Portia laughed. "It's the Cotton-Eyed Joe."

Lines of dancers formed spokes, looking like a wheel turning as they danced side by side, shouting out the words. Namely, "Bullshit!"

No surprise, Anthony was at the center, Olivia next to him, her head tossed back in the sort of abandon that drew men in.

Portia watched, wishing she were out there, wishing she possessed her sister's ease, if not her abandoned behavior. Portia had been in Manhattan for only a few months, but already Texas felt distant. The women with their diamonds flashing in the glittering lights, heels high, fabulous attire, be it short skirts or long. The men with their wide, friendly smiles. But as much as she missed the only place she had ever called home, more and more she was finding that she felt as though she belonged here in New York. She wasn't even exactly sure why.

She was startled out of her thoughts when two women stopped abruptly on the opposite side of her table.

"Portia? Is that you?"

Portia blinked, then felt her heart squeeze to a halt in her chest. "Hi, Meryl. Hi, Betsy."

The two women gasped and hurried around to her. "Oh, my Lord! I never in a million years thought I'd see you again, much less here! How are you, honey?"

"Yes, how are you?" Betsy added with her own gasp.

Meryl Swindon and Betsy Baker had been a part of Portia's world since elementary school. And, like Portia, they had married into the better part of Willow Creek. But unlike Portia, they had moved easily in the new world of heirloom pearls and Francis 1st silver. The only event Portia had truly loved was once a year when she and her husband had traveled to New York to attend the Bandana Ball. Here, in New York, these proper Texans let down their hair. They were more at ease, feeling a camaraderie in a foreign place that they didn't share at similar events in their hometown.

"I'm doing great!" she replied with that thick cheerfulness she had nearly forgotten about in the few months she had been in Manhattan. "You both look fabulous!"

She felt more than saw Gabriel's raised brow at her exaggerated cheer.

"You do, too!" Meryl and Betsy said.

"You look, . . . different," Meryl added.

"Truly fabulous," Betsy said. "I swear, after Robert divorced you, I thought the next time I saw you, you'd be a wreck. I mean, who wouldn't be after Robert made it so public that you weren't the woman for him."

By then, Gabriel had stood, every inch the gentleman. Portia felt a sizzle of tension coming from him, filling her with a disconcerting rush of embarrassment. Meryl and Betsy looked at Gabriel, and seemed to assess him with a Texas woman's eye.

"You're obviously doing better than we possibly could have imagined," Betsy continued on, then introduced herself.

The women wouldn't ever have known that he wasn't perfectly happy to make small talk with them. But Portia could feel tension run through him, a tension she didn't understand as he turned to look at her, studying her while Meryl and Betsy went on about something else.

Finally, they walked away and Portia looked up at Gabriel. "Come on," she all but begged, not wanting him to ask a single question. "This is a party. Dance with me!"

The song ended, the next starting up, and Anthony returned to the table. "I can't believe you two are just sitting here."

Olivia came up beside him. "Once upon a time, Portia used to be a great dancer. That is, until she married that ass—"

"Olivia!"

"Don't you give me that look, Portia," Olivia said, undaunted. Instead, she came over to Portia, sitting down next to her and forcing her to turn, her always languid eyes fierce. She took Portia's hands and gave her a little shake. "I saw Meryl and Betsy come over to you. I know how they are, no doubt going on about Robert. But let me tell you, you are better than all the Meryls and Betsys put together. And you certainly deserved better than that philandering prick. If I could, I'd castrate him myself."

Portia felt the sting of embarrassment at Olivia's words, the brutal honesty that she was never uncomfortable with. But mostly she was embarrassed that Gabriel heard the truth about her marriage.

A man Olivia had promised a dance to came up. Olivia didn't look at him. "Are you okay?" she asked Portia.

"I'm fine. Really. Go dance."

Olivia appeared conflicted.

Portia would have stood, wanting to get away from Gabriel's questioning gaze, but Anthony caught her arm while she was still sitting down. "Come dance with me."

He ran his hand down to her fingers, trying to pull her away from the table. She sensed more than felt the tension that flared through Gabriel. She saw the two men look at each other, Gabriel like a dangerous jaguar, Anthony like a spoiled Abyssinian cat.

"Thank you, Anthony, but I can't dance with you," she said.

She wanted to dance, but not with Gabriel's brother.

Just then another man walked up to them.

"Gabriel. Anthony," the newcomer said by way of hello.

He was tall and good looking, with blond hair and blue eyes. The quintessential all-American boy.

"William," the brothers said in unison. The man extended his hand to Portia. "William Langford," he said.

"Hello, I'm Portia Cuthcart."

"Portia. A fan of Shakespeare?"

"That would have been my mother. First Cordelia, then Olivia, and finally me, Portia."

William laughed easily. He had charm, but not the bad-boy variety. His was more the elegant man about town. "Would you like to dance?" he asked.

"Forget it, Langford," Anthony said with a proprietary smile. "She's dancing with me."

"Actually, she's dancing with me."

Gabriel stepped closer.

Anthony cocked his head, eyes narrowed. Portia could only look at Gabriel, take in the harsh angles of his face.

But as he took Portia's elbow, to help her from her seat, she jerked to a stop.

Anthony laughed. "Second thoughts about dancing with my big brother?"

Portia gave Anthony a look, one learned at the knee of her grandmother, a woman who didn't put up with anything.

"Hard to go anywhere when I'm pinned down." She nodded toward Anthony's foot. "You're standing on my shawl."

The group looked down to see Anthony's fancy boot on the tail end of Portia's gossamer-thin, golden scarf, which had partially unwound and drifted to the floor. Tiny translucent sequins glittered in the ballroom lights.

"Though I guess I don't need it," she added.

She stood, letting the wisp of fabric unwind completely, slipping from her shoulders, leaving them bare.

Every ounce of darkness in Gabriel shifted to heat.

When the scarf had been draped elegantly, no one had noticed that Portia wore a strapless gold brocade bustier she'd found in her aunt's trunks. Instead of the traditional blue denim skirt, she wore a gold denim she suspected Evie had worn to some Texan event of her own, back in the day.

Olivia's eyes sparkled with a sister's pride.

Portia focused on Gabriel, who stood next to her, his expression indecipherable.

"Our dance, Mr. Kane," she said, taking his hand and allowing him to guide her onto the floor. But once there, he held her stiffly as they stepped into a country waltz.

He was a good head taller than her, despite her heels. Portia felt tiny, delicate—and definitely undesirable, despite the flash of heat she had seen in his eyes seconds before.

"You're maddening, you know. One minute you step forward like some warrior staking your claim for the dance. The next you're holding me like I haven't had a bath in a week. You could at least try to pretend you're enjoying this dance."

"I'm not."

"Then you shouldn't have asked!"

"I didn't. You asked. More like you begged. Twice. It was pathetic." He smiled at her then, his body easing. "I felt obligated. I don't usually do pity, but there you have it."

"I bet you make girls swoon regularly with speeches like that."

"You got what you wanted, didn't you?"

The country waltz was beautiful, reminiscent of an earlier life spent in Texas, her parents dancing under the stars outside the trailer, and Gabriel's steps settled. They made their way around the floor, each turn easier as they learned each other's rhythm.

"True, I did."

Portia felt her tension ease and they circled the floor in earnest, his hand at her waist, her palm resting on the hard muscles of his shoulder. After a few minutes, she said, "Admit it. You're enjoying yourself."

"Not true." But she caught a glimpse of his smile.

The music shifted, changing without stopping, to a soulful country three-step, still basically a waltz. Gabriel didn't miss a beat. He shifted his step with the song, pulling her even closer. He smelled like Texas on a summer morning, the heat simmering, but the harshness lost in the overnight cool. Portia thought of long grasses and wild plains. She itched to press even closer.

"I can see how happy you are," he said, his voice lower. "Your eyes shine when you're happy, Portia. Did anyone ever tell you that?"

She tripped, but he caught her easily.

They made another circle of the floor.

"I miss this," she said finally.

"Dancing?"

"Yes. Dancing, and country music."

"What else?" he prompted softly.

"Kissing," she said.

She felt the sudden surge of tension in his shoulder.

"I miss being carefree, driving along two-lane country roads, stopping at Willow Creek Lake, walking along the sandy edge in bare feet."

"Kissing and . . . ?"

"Just kissing. Sweet, innocent kisses from teenage boys with more hormones than they knew what to do with."

"Was one of them your husband?" he asked.

"No. No sweet kisses from my husband. Or ex-husband."

The music came to an end, and Gabriel cupped her chin and tilted her face until she met his gaze. "Your husband's an ass," he said. The intensity of his expression melted her heart, melted her dark thoughts.

"Ex-husband," she repeated.

"Come on," he said, taking her hand. "I saw some games."

"The carnival booths!"

Portia had never been good with beanbags or horseshoes. But when they came to a baseball booth, she stopped.

Gabriel eyed her. "A woman who wants to throw?"

"You'd rather I just bat my eyelashes and drink sweet tea?"

"Do you even know how to bat your eyelashes?"

She tucked her chin and gazed up at him, her eyes sultry, then did just that.

He laughed out loud.

"I used to watch Olivia practice in the mirror when we were growing up."

He shook his head, his smile easing the harshness of his features. "All right." He handed over a set of tickets.

"You go first," Portia offered. "I want to watch, see how it's done."

"Fine."

Gabriel took up one of the six baseballs set in front of him, aimed, threw, and sent the ball through the small round opening with ease.

"Not bad," she conceded.

Standing tall, his expression intent, Gabriel sent three more through the opening in quick succession with the ease of a major-league baseball player. A small crowd formed around him. By the time he had made five of the six, the crowd was bigger and more raucous.

"Do you think I can make the last one?" he asked her, his smile challenging her.

"You've made five of six easily. I'm guessing you'll make the last."

He turned back with a grin on his face. Taking aim, he pulled his arm back, then threw, but not before the group of men whooped—then groaned—when he jerked slightly and missed.

"Oops," Portia said, walking forward with a deliberate sway to her hips, her gown glittering in the lights as she held out a hand. "My turn."

Gabriel handed over the three necessary tickets. He smiled at her, playful, wicked.

She felt a shiver of joy at the sight of this man. "Thank you," she told him as the vendor set out six baseballs, the crowd quieting.

"Ready?" the vendor asked.

Portia nodded, focusing. She threw once, twice, not stopping as the crowd started to go wild. *Thwack, thwack, thwack,* until she'd made five of the six throws. Tossing the sixth ball in her hand, one corner of her mouth turned up, she said, "Not bad for a girl, huh?"

Gabriel laughed out loud. "I take it you've played baseball."

"My daddy made a diamond in a field not far from our trailer."

She noticed the way Gabriel's brow twitched at the mention of their trailer. But by then, the crowd of men cheered and stomped in their tux jackets, bow ties, and jeans. Gabriel looked at her with an amused smile, and for half a second, she would have sworn he was proud.

Turning back, her heart slammed against her ribs. She had indeed thrown a baseball since she was big enough to hold a ball, then played this exact game at carnivals since she was six. She could throw in her sleep. But with Gabriel looking on, not taunting her as she had expected, yet somehow looking at her in a whole new way, her nerves flared. But then she forced herself to stop thinking, aimed, threw, and sent the ball dead center through the opening.

The crowd erupted, and Gabriel tipped his head back and laughed again. He took her elbow.

"Hey, mister. Don't you want the stuffed animal?"

"No, thanks."

Portia tugged away and dashed back. "Of course we want it!" She grabbed all two feet of the plush giraffe and hugged it close.

Gabriel laughed and guided her through the crowd, back toward their table, but the last thing she wanted was to spend another second inside.

"I've had the perfect night. But now it's time for me to turn into a pumpkin."

"I'll take you home," he said.

"You don't have to. Stay. Enjoy yourself."

He gave her a look. "You can't be serious."

Which made her laugh. "Good point."

Gabriel guided her out into the night, barely stopping at their table to gather her shawl. It was late, but Portia started to walk.

"We're not walking home dressed like this. Not to mention the hour."

"You're forgetting how safe New York is now."

"I'm not forgetting. It could be three in the afternoon and I still wouldn't let you walk in that dress."

Normally she would have bristled at his tone, but she refused to let him ruin her perfect night.

"All right. How about a bus?" She hurried across Broadway, then Central Park West, to the opposite side of Columbus Circle.

"No way am I taking a bus," Gabriel said, still beside her.

"Then you'd better find yourself a cab!"

She came to the M10 bus stop on the north side of the circle just as a lumbering bus pulled to a stop. She dashed inside. Gabriel stood at the bottom of the steps for half a second before muttering a curse and leaping up beside her just as the doors closed.

"Does everything have to be your way, Portia?"

"You're just used to everything being *your* way. I know how to compromise."

Given the hour, the bus was empty expect for the driver and a man clearly getting off from the night shift, half asleep at the back. Portia slid onto a hard-plastic two-seater. Gabriel hung his head and sat down beside her.

They headed north on Central Park West, her knee brushing against his as the bus swayed like a boat on a gentle sea. The sky was dark but crystal clear; the sidewalks were crowded even at midnight. To the right beyond the sidewalk, the old stone wall of Central Park surrounded the giant rectangle of trees, lakes, and winding paths. To the left, mostly prewar apartment buildings lined the way like a wall of ancient stone and brick. This new world was nothing like Portia's old one back in Texas, but the longer she was in Manhattan, the more she fell in love.

"Thank you for coming with me tonight."

He was silent for a moment. "You're welcome."

When they reached the Seventy-second Street stop, Gabriel took her hand and pulled her off of the bus.

"Let's take a carriage through the park," Portia said.

"It's late."

"You go on." She started to walk toward the carriages lined up at the entrance to the park, but he caught her around the waist.

They looked at each other before he glanced at her mouth. "I thought you were open to compromise," he said.

"Ha!"

He didn't say anything else. When he grabbed her hand and started walking up Central Park West, she followed. And when they came to the town house, a thrill ran down her spine when he guided her down the steps to her apartment.

Eighteen

⬩⬩⬩

Portia felt nervous. "Well, thanks again for going with me."

Gabriel had leaned back against the wall.

"You have an amazing throwing arm," she offered, her voice clattering. "Almost as good as mine."

He just studied her.

She kept chattering. "It was fun. Lots of fun."

His lips quirked up as she rambled. And really, she did have pride.

"So then, good night." She raised her chin and squatted as gracefully as she could to retrieve the key she kept under the mat.

That wiped the quirk off his mouth. "I told you not to keep a key there."

"You tell me a lot of things."

He pushed away from the wall, dragging his hands through his hair. She saw the flash of frustration she made him feel on a fairly regular basis. And right alongside all that pride she'd just had was a wide swath of sympathy, for him. She cocked her head and gave him a sympathetic smile.

"Don't you dare look at me like that," he bit out.

"Like what?"

"Like I'm some sort of lost . . . puppy."

"You? Hardly. More like a wounded beast."

That surprised him. And she certainly hadn't intended to say any such thing. The words had just slipped out.

His frustration turned to something darker.

"I'm sorry," she said. "Really."

The frustration shifted again and he drew a deep breath. He nodded, and she realized that he was going to leave. Without thinking yet again, she caught his hand.

He stilled, and looked at their fingers, his expression wary. Then slowly he looked up at her. He was fighting, she could see it, and he had no intention of giving in to her.

"Good night," he said, pulling away.

She should have been embarrassed. Instead, she reached up on tiptoes, slipping her hands on either side of his head, and pulled him down to her. She had dreamed of his kiss since the night he had dragged her through the window. After an evening of carefree baseball throwing and dancing, she felt lovely and alive. Careless. She didn't want it to end.

They were close, she looking into his eyes. Then she pressed her lips to his. Soft. Barely a kiss. And he groaned into her mouth.

She could feel the way he dragged in a breath, the way he worked to marshal control. Then he gave in with a groan, or maybe a curse, and he crushed her body to his.

Portia closed her eyes and inhaled the scent of him. There was nothing sweet or chaste about their kiss now. It was hot and consuming. She tasted the smoky sweetness of bourbon on his tongue. She melted into him when he ran his hand down her spine, pressing her even closer.

"Give me that damned key."

He unlocked the door and they crashed into her apartment, hands tugging at clothes, searching out skin. The kiss turned desperate. He tangled his tongue with hers, gentleness gone. He cupped the side of her face, tilting her head back, forcing her to look at him. Her breath shuddered as he ran his thumb across her lips. "I want you," he said.

More proof that Gabriel wasn't a man who asked. He demanded. And this demanding man wanted her. The feeling was heady and emotional.

He swept her up into his arms and headed unerringly for her bedroom. It was the only room she'd had time to paint. Small even by New York standards, it was painted a pearly blue that reminded her of a Texas sky—not on a hot day, but a cool one by Southern standards.

She saw the room through his eyes. Upstairs, everything was decorated with exquisite, refined taste that was paid for. She'd lived that life, albeit with Texas rather than New York style. This room was all *hers*. She'd stenciled the moldings with cream fleur-de-lis and hung luscious silk drapes in her tall windows. No need for anyone to know that the silk had once been a ball gown of her aunt's. In the dim light it gave the room an unmistakable luster, a touch of what she believed Paris would be like on a moonlit night.

He set her down, letting go of her legs but holding her close, bringing her body into line with his. He dipped his head, kissing the bare skin of her shoulder. "What's this?" he asked.

It took a second before she realized what he was talking about. "A scar," she said, her stomach twisting at the memory of running into that sudden storm, crying, as she fought to reach her grandmother—and then the lightning throwing her to the ground in a tangle beside Gram, both of them like rag dolls in the dirt.

She began to push away.

"Stop," he said, kissing the scar in a way that made her shiver with something more than desire.

She forgot about scars, her grandmother, the past.

The kiss in his library had been amazing, but this was different. He backed her up until her thighs hit the side of the mattress, his hands cupping her face.

"I've been trying to get you out of my head, but you keep creeping back in. You distract me, make me lose focus." His hands drifted lower, his thumbs brushing her lips, then even lower until they brushed against her collarbone. "But I can't stay away."

She closed her eyes as he swept her up and put her on the bed.

He came over her. The scent of him filled her, like spice and wild grasses. He slid his knee between her legs, nudging one to the side before he sank down into her, and she could feel every inch of his erection through her skirt. With his arms on either side of her head, he kissed her, coaxing her mouth open, his tongue slipping inside.

Portia ran her hands up his arms, her fingers touching his face. Reality unraveled around them like thread from a spool. Nothing in the world existed but the two of them, touching, kissing, his body pressing into hers. Just when it seemed he couldn't get enough, he broke the kiss and pulled back to look at her. She could see restraint trying to seep back to the surface. But then it was gone.

With one twist, he had the ties on her bustier falling to the sides. She gasped as cool air hit her skin. His palm came to her breast, pushing it high, his thumb brushing against her skin, an inarticulate sound breaking from her throat.

She arched to him, felt his hand skimming up her leg, gathering the hem of the skirt. Then with a quick jerk, he dragged the skirt off her body and tossed it on the floor.

He slid his hand down her stomach, slipping beneath the thin silk of her panties. The more he took, the more he seemed to need as he reclaimed her mouth.

She moaned, couldn't help it when she thrust against his hand.

"Yes," he murmured.

He was slow and sensual, caressing her, kissing her until she couldn't take it anymore. She bit his lip, groaning against him. But just when he tangled his hand in her hair and entered her, hard, her senses suddenly jangled. She jolted as the images of fried chicken, sweet jalapeño

mustard, mashed potatoes, cole slaw, buttermilk biscuits, and strawberry pie flashed through her mind. It was the meal that had first come
to her when she was sitting on the front steps and Gabriel had appeared
like a promise.

But a promise of what?

Nineteen

∴

Ariel still didn't know much of anything about her mom's family, other than that they had lived in a housing project only blocks from her dad's town house, and her granddad was named Bohater. Bohater? Seriously?

Not that she knew much more about her dad's family that wasn't the standard brown-haired, brown-eyed sort of stuff. Not the ingredients of an A-plus social studies report.

Determined to find something that fell between boring and the whole "My really fancy, rich mom used to be a wild partier and never bothered to tell anyone that she grew up in a really bad part of town" that would get her killed by her dad, she went back to the Internet. Googling her parents still didn't bring up anything she hadn't already learned.

Then it occurred to her: She had never heard a peep about her mom and dad getting married. Didn't that stuff show up someplace? And if her parents had been in the news for parties they attended, didn't it make sense they'd be in the news when they got married? Didn't weddings make for great stories? A wedding report had to get her something decent, right?

She Googled that, too, but found nothing. If only she knew the date they got married. Didn't there have to be some kind of record?

After more searching, all she came up with to find records was the City Clerk's Web site. She'd have to go downtown, which was practically like going to New Jersey. No way.

The house was super quiet; Ariel was home only because her school was off a half day for teacher training. She hadn't bothered to tell her dad, since she had a key to the house and could take care of herself. Besides, she had wanted time alone at home. All the better to exercise her detective skills.

Well, no time like the present. Her dad was at work; Miranda's school didn't have a half day; Portia was probably down in the basement cooking her brains out, or whatever she did in her spare time. Even if Ariel couldn't make it to the City Clerk's, she had time for a house search.

She bolted up the steps to the top floor that her dad used more for storage than for anything else. There were cedar closets and cabinets filled with drawers that lined the walls. There was a TV and a sound system in there, not set up, sort of like extra. And her old bike was there, too.

She ignored the stairs that continued on to the roof and started going through every nook and cranny. Surely there had to be more stuff about her family. A wedding date. Birthdays.

Looking in drawer after drawer at all the stuff the movers had unpacked and put away, Ariel found nothing. She grew more frantic with each cabinet she finished.

She had nearly given up when she found a box marked MIRANDA in the back of a closet. Not exactly what she was looking for, but she'd take what she could get.

Inside was a baby book. Date of birth. Footprints. A hospital bracelet. A photo. Miranda's first curl. First tooth. But then the book went blank.

It was as if their mom had gotten tired of documenting her first child's existence.

No matter how much she dug, Ariel couldn't find a corresponding book for herself.

"Figures," she muttered to the empty room. Maybe she'd always been a little bit invisible.

When she'd searched every corner, Ariel stopped and looked around the room, mystified. She knew that the only stuff her dad had brought with them from the old house was important stuff like papers and files. But even with that, it was like her mom had disappeared, too. Her mom, her parents' marriage. Her stomach churned.

Returning to the kitchen, she realized what she had to do. It was already after one, but if she took a cab, she could be down at the records office, get her parents' wedding record, and hightail it home before her dad even thought about leaving his office.

Yanking on a light jacket, counting out a wad of ones and fives, and even a ten-dollar bill, Ariel flew out the front door. A cab was driving by, and she waved her arm.

When she barreled inside, the cabbie barely glanced at her.

"The City Clerk's office," she said in a tone of voice that meant business.

He craned his neck. "Where?" His accent was thick, and he looked like he ate little girls for breakfast.

"One forty-one Worth Street. It's downtown."

"I know where Worth Street is."

"Okay then, good."

He snorted, turned, and threw the car into gear. They were off.

Panic set in as soon as they turned left onto Columbus Avenue. "Be brave, be brave, be brave," Ariel whispered to herself.

She hadn't given much thought to the fact that she was going to be in a car. The kind of car that wrecked. Just like when she was with her mom. She had barely been in a car since.

Ariel reached up, wrapped herself securely in the seat belt, and prayed.

The cabbie careened through traffic, clutching the steering wheel with both hands and talking the whole time into his cell phone headset. She couldn't understand a word. There was a ton of traffic, but that didn't faze him.

Ariel closed her eyes, concentrating. "If you take one yellow cab," she whispered to herself, "moving at one hundred miles per hour for five-second intervals, how long will it take the cab to go three miles?"

But word problems didn't calm her.

"You say something?" the cabbie called back to her, their eyes meeting in the rearview mirror.

"No. Not a word. No reason to look back here. Best to look up ahead." *Where the traffic and cars are,* Ariel added to herself.

They took rights, then lefts, and swooped under a bridge. By the time they arrived in front of a building made of huge rectangular bricks, Ariel's legs were rubbery. On the backside of a heinous cab ride, she wasn't sure she was up to the task of sleuthing out any information.

But which was worse? Stay in the cab and ask to be taken home, or get her sea legs back and continue her mission? The decision was made for her when the driver barked out the fare.

"Eighteen?" Ariel squeaked. "You mean eighteen dollars?"

He jerked around, eyes murderous. "Eighteen! If you don't have money, you should no get in my cab!"

"Oh, no, it's fine. I have the money."

Keeping her hands from shaking by sheer force of will, Ariel counted out eighteen dollars. She knew she was supposed to tip, so she added some more. The cabbie grabbed it, waved her out of his car, and raced off, leaving her standing on the curb with only three dollars.

As much as she couldn't imagine getting back in a cab, the thought of taking the subway home paralyzed her. She didn't have a clue how to take the train home from downtown.

She started to panic.

"Buck up, Ariel," she chided herself. "It's a subway. You take it on the Upper West Side all the time."

She turned to face the imposing heights of the City Clerk's office. "You are fine," she whispered to herself.

Inside she was confronted by intense security. She made it through, though not without a few raised eyebrows, and stopped at the information desk. "I'm here for the records department."

A gruff woman with steel-gray hair looked down at her. "What kind of records?"

"Marriage."

"You seem kinda young to be getting married."

A man behind the desk glanced up from whatever he was doing and chuckled. "A mite young, indeed."

Great. A couple of jokesters. "I'm doing a report for school." Ariel tried to look young and smart and like she had a really good reason for them to let her in. "We have to document a city record's search. I'm going to write about my experience working with New York City and the kind of treatment one gets while pursuing their rights within the law."

"Whoo-whee," the man said with a chuckle.

The woman got serious. "Are you some kid reporter?"

"Well no. Just doing a report for Miss Thompson's social studies."

The woman glanced at her watch for the first time, probably noting that as it was early afternoon, Ariel should have been in school.

"It's a teachers' training day. I'm using the time to finalize the details of my research."

God, she was good.

"Whoo-whee," the man said again. "A smart one."

The woman debated, and then nodded toward a hallway. "Third door on your left."

"Thank you," Ariel said. "I appreciate how helpful you've been."

Maybe that was a little much, she conceded. But she was glad she had thought of the whole research angle. She was even gladder after waiting in line for nearly an hour only to learn that she had to be one of the spouses to get the record.

"But, ma'am, I'm just doing a report. I don't want the actual record. I'm just reporting on how it's done." Ariel trotted out the whole social studies angle, eyes wide and earnest. "So if I could just look up a record and explain how the process is handled, you know, how easy it really is for New Yorkers to get the things they need from the government, I would appreciate it."

This woman gave her a strange look, half disbelief, half worry. No one wanted to be shown up by some kid publishing a tell-all blog.

And her dad said the Internet was a bad thing.

"Fine," the woman said. "Go to that door over there and tell Ida I said to help you."

Thankfully, Ida couldn't have cared less who Ariel was, why she was there, or what she wanted. Ariel blurted out her mother's maiden name and father's name, and with a few keystrokes, Ida came back with a date. "June 27, 1998."

Ariel wrote it down so she wouldn't forget it. Something seemed wrong, but she couldn't place what. She gave her parents' names again. "That's definitely the date for them, right?"

"Yes."

Ida clearly wasn't one to waste words. "Is that all you want?" she said. "It's 3:15. We close at 3:45."

"Really?" That seemed really early to close an office. But then Ariel realized she had to get home before anyone found out she was gone. And she still had to figure out the subway route. She slapped her notebook shut. "I mean, no problem."

But outside, her heart raced. Spotting a policeman, she raced over to him. "Where is the subway? Ah, sir."

The guy gave her a crooked smile and pointed. "At that brown building, take a right. The subway is a few blocks up on Canal Street."

She followed his directions. Sure enough, when she came to Canal

Street she saw the station. But it was for the N and R trains. She had never even heard of the N or R train.

Fear started to creep up, the kind of fear Ariel rarely allowed herself to feel. "You are not a panicker, Ariel," she muttered.

Shaking herself, she found one of the posted subway maps. The spider's web of multicolored lines wasn't for the faint of heart, but Ariel wasn't faint of heart, she reminded herself.

With her remaining three dollars, she purchased a single-ride Metro-Card and made it to the uptown platform just as a train arrived. She hopped on. The bell rang, the doors slid shut, and Ariel offered up another prayer that this train would get her somewhere close to the Upper West Side.

"Excuse me," she said to a lady standing next to her.

The woman narrowed her eyes at her.

"Does this go to Seventy-second Street on the Upper West Side?"

The woman hesitated, and in the silence, another woman answered. "No, sweetie, it doesn't. You'll need to get off at Thirty-fourth and change to a B. Or, if you need a 1, 2, or 3, you'll have to go to Forty-Second and change there."

Ariel's head spun with a plethora of numbers and an alphabet soup of letters. She concentrated with every ounce of her ability as they came into each station. Prince. Eighth Street. Fourteenth Street. Stop after stop, the train getting more and more crowded, making it harder and harder to see station signs. Finally Ariel caught a glimpse of a sign when they pulled into the Thirty-fourth Street station. She squirmed out, relieved, only to find that she didn't have a clue what to do next.

"Excuse me, I'm looking for the B train."

She made it to a B just as it arrived in the station. On board, her heart pounded at stop after stop until she recognized Seventy-second Street.

When she came up onto street level across from Central Park, she was only a block from home. Ariel had never been so glad to see the horse-drawn carriages and masses of people taking photos of the building where some singer named John Lennon had been shot. And when she blew into her house, falling back against the closed door with a gasp, she nearly broke down in tears.

"What's wrong with you?"

Her head jerked up. Miranda stood at the top of the stairs, scowling.

Ariel blinked furiously. She had no idea what to say. She had been fixated on the maze of subway tunnels and platforms, and hadn't yet thought about the information she had found: Their mom and dad's wedding was on June 27, 1998.

Miranda was born on November 19, 1998. Five months after their parents were married.

Twenty

❖

A T FIVE, Portia bolted upstairs to make dinner. From the sunroom, she was surprised when she heard Gabriel's and Anthony's heated voices. She hadn't seen or talked to Gabriel since he'd slipped out of her bedroom that morning. She felt her body in a way that she hadn't in years, if ever. He had allowed her no modesty. He had taken what he wanted. But, if she was completely fair, he had given as well. Her body shuddered and sighed at the thought. "Bad, bad, bad," she muttered to herself.

There was no denying that the whole fried chicken–meal thing had thrown her.

The other issue that threw her was that Robert had called three times during the day, but without leaving much by way of messages. Then her lawyer had called, saying that her ex was contesting the small amount he was supposed to pay her.

Her stomach twisted at the thought. She had to breathe through her nose to try to stay calm, releasing her breath slowly into the quiet kitchen. She didn't have the money to fight him. Very soon, even with the money she was making from working for Gabriel, she wasn't going to be able to survive in New York.

For the first time she was having to admit to herself that she might have to sell the garden apartment. No question the clock was ticking on her dream of building a new life in the city.

She left lasagna and garlic bread warming in the oven and a salad in the refrigerator and tiptoed out of the house. Once she was outside, the beads of panic didn't lessen. Nothing was going as planned in New York. She felt as if she was trying to start over, transform her life, remake herself in quicksand. The harder she tried to get free, the deeper she sank. Trying to cook without embracing the knowing wasn't working; it popped up constantly without warning. Trying not to fall for Gabriel? Also not working. Creating a viable way to support herself and help her sisters? Going the way of women wearing hats.

With no answer in sight, she began to walk. Traffic was heavy on Central Park West before she crossed into the park, veering onto the bridle path. Trees overarched like a canopy of green, runners passing her, generally in pairs, followed by two mounted policemen on giant horses. Portia walked fast, trying to outpace her thoughts. But even when she came to the Reservoir, she couldn't slow her brain.

She headed out of the park, then turned south. She walked forever, hooking over to Broadway and the crush of tiny shops.

It was right outside of the Sabon bath shop that it hit her, the scent of luscious soaps drifting out into the street. Inside, the space was filled with soap and lotions, bath washes and candles. Her senses were filled, surrounded. Teased.

In an instant, after hours of walking and trying to stay out of her brain, a glimmer of an answer came to her like disparate ingredients coming together to make an unexpectedly perfect whole.

She couldn't get home fast enough. Banging into the apartment, Portia went straight to the cabinet where she had stored the Glass Kitchen cookbooks. She pulled out volumes one and two, skimming through the first. Then she took up the second book, leaving the third volume where it was stored. Holding the second in her arms, close to her chest, she drew a deep breath.

The answer was here, she realized, in this cookbook. She just had to find it.

She cracked open the old spine and started flipping through the pages, taking notes. Once she had five pages of hurried scribbles, she condensed things down into one single shopping list. Then she began to turn the vision into reality, and a week later, a week of barely managing to avoid Gabriel with an odd assortment of excuses and meal preparation at even odder times, Portia was ready. She had finally put into place exactly what she needed to prove that a Glass Kitchen would work in New York City.

Fourth Course

❖

Palate Cleanser

Blood Orange Ice

Twenty-one

⟡

W HAT IS GOING ON here?"

Gabriel stood in the doorway of her apartment, dark tension carved into his features, and for a heartbeat Portia forgot all about what she was doing. She just stared at the man.

He wore a simple black T-shirt that showed off his chest and arms, his dark hair raked back. He looked rugged and sexy, and memories of his hands and mouth on her body made every inch of her thrum to life.

Bad, bad, bad, she reminded herself.

His dark gaze narrowed.

"We've created a version of The Glass Kitchen," she hurriedly explained, giving him a sunny smile.

Olivia and Cordelia came out of the kitchen to stand behind her. Cordelia glanced from Portia to Gabriel, then back. "Portia, didn't you clear this with him?"

Cordelia still wasn't herself, her husband's problem growing deeper. Portia and Olivia did everything they could to keep her mind occupied, and Portia still hadn't had the heart to question Cordelia about implying to people that somehow Gabriel was involved with The Glass Kitchen.

"Actually, it's more a venture where I'm cooking the food of The Glass Kitchen, and people can come to try it."

After reading the second Glass Kitchen cookbook, she had taken its advice to heart. Losing herself in the words, she had put them into action.

For a meal to work truly, it must be an experience. From the moment a guest arrives in The Glass Kitchen to the moment they set their napkin down, they must be enchanted. More importantly, the giver of food must believe that they have the power to enchant. No person, whether she is a scientist or a cook, can find success if she doesn't first believe that she holds power in her hands—not to use over people, but to use for the good of another. Food, especially, is about giving. A cook must find a way to make the recipient a believer, for what is a person who sits down to a beautiful meal but someone who wants to believe?

As she read the words, Portia had finally set aside her own misgivings and opened herself up to what might come. It had been then that solutions appeared. Her sisters had shown up without her having to ask, the three of them working day after day in a way that gave each hope that a Glass Kitchen really could happen. For a week they had pulled down Aunt Evie's dark draperies, replacing them with a cheerful gingham Cordelia found in the huge sale bins in the Garment District. Olivia filled the space with flowers. The sisters had bought white paper bags and pink baker boxes, then sat around the kitchen island drinking wine, laughing, and hand-decorating them.

Once the apartment was ready, Portia had begun to plan out what foods they would showcase in this little glimpse into a Glass Kitchen world. Her sisters couldn't help her with this part. Portia had let go, and dishes had come to her, all of which she wrote down and prepared to make. Then, at eight that morning, she got to work. Olivia and Cordelia served as *sous*-chefs; they started by making a decadent beef bourguignon. Olivia and Cordelia washed and chopped as Portia browned layer after layer of beef, bacon, carrots, and onion, folding in the beef stock and wine, then putting it in to slow bake as they dove into the remaining dishes. They opened all the windows and ran four swiveling fans Portia had bought and found that pushed the scent of the baking and cooking out onto the sidewalk. Then they had put up a fairly discreet sign in the window, hand-painted by Olivia: THE GLASS KITCHEN.

Portia had gotten the idea while walking down Broadway and passing the French soap store. Scents had spilled into the street from the shop— lavender and primrose, musk and sandalwood—luring passersby inside. Portia had realized that the best way to get investors interested was to show them a version of The Glass Kitchen. The food. The aromas. She had realized, standing there on Broadway, that she needed to create a mini version of her grandmother's restaurant to lure people in. This way, they'd have no monthly rent as they would if they tried to lease out space somewhere else. No extra utility bills. It was perfect. Standing there now with her sisters flanking her, she explained as much to Gabriel. "Ta-da!" she finished. "What do you think?"

Gabriel's jaw hung slack for a second before he snapped it shut. "You can't open a restaurant here."

"But that's the thing! It's not a restaurant."

"Definitely not a restaurant," Olivia confirmed, then raised a brow at Gabriel's pointed glower.

"It's just an example of a restaurant," Portia hurried on. "At best, it's more like counter service to go!"

He narrowed his eyes.

She gulped and persevered. "We're showcasing the fabulous food we'll be making at the *real* Glass Kitchen when we open it somewhere else.

This way, people can get a taste, get the feel of what our café will be like, get excited."

She spread her arms wide to encompass the old pine table they had painted robin's egg blue, lightly sanding it in places so the white primer showed through. She had pulled out Aunt Evie's moss green platters and bowls, filling enough of them with everything from cheesy quiches to creamy chocolate pies, butterscotch cupcakes to the beef bourguignon to cover every inch of counter space. The place smelled heavenly.

"Admit it, you're drooling."

"You can't open anything here. Not a restaurant. Not even an example of a restaurant." Each word enunciated.

"Says who?"

"Says the zoning laws," he bit out.

Portia felt his exacting gaze all the way down to her bones, and not in a good way. She ignored it. All they were doing was giving people a taste of her food. Granted, they would be charging for those tastes. But they weren't doing anything close to opening a real retail establishment.

"Olivia and I will let you two talk," Cordelia said, gathering her bag.

"Seriously?" Oliva protested. "This is just getting interesting."

Gabriel turned to Olivia with an expression that made her shrug; then she strolled out the front door after Cordelia.

Portia swallowed as Gabriel stepped closer. Then she squared her shoulders. "Has anyone pointed out how moody you are? One minute you're all—" She searched for the right word.

"*I'm all* what?" The words were deep, sensual, but still exacting.

"One minute you're, well, nice. Then the next you go all Sybil on me and out comes the big bad beast."

The words flew out, yet again, before she thought them through, and emotion shot through Gabriel's eyes. But a second later that implacable façade was back in place.

"This is just an experiment, Gabriel," she hurried on. "We're going to show investors how much people love my grandmother's food. That's it."

Portia felt a flash of panic. She had spent the rest of her meager savings pulling it together. "This is just temporary, and only a way to show investors how great our food is," she pointed out.

"You can't run a restaurant out of my home!"

"My home. And it's not a restaurant!"

His gaze slammed into hers, then took a deep breath, dragging his hands through his hair.

The doorbell rang.

"Now what?" he snapped.

Footsteps clattered down the steps before Cordelia and Olivia dragged a woman inside.

"Our first customer!"

"Seriously?" Portia squeaked. "I mean, yay!"

"Ah, well," the woman looked a little frightened by the sisters' enthusiastic welcome. "I was just walking by, smelled the heavenly aroma, and noticed your sign tucked in the window. I thought . . . well, I thought this was a restaurant, not a home."

"Actually, it's just three sisters cooking!" Portia emphasized for Gabriel. "Cooking and baking very real food! Think of it as a kid's lemonade stand. Come in!"

"I don't know."

"Don't worry, we're from Texas, which might mean crazy, but definitely not dangerous. Just look at all the wonderful things we have."

Hesitantly, the woman came farther inside—though one glare from Gabriel made her stop dead in her tracks.

"Don't mind him," Portia said. "He's not as ornery as he looks."

The woman saw the fragrant dishes on the counter, and every bit of hesitation evaporated. "This is wonderful!" she said, walking straight past Gabriel. "Quiche? And pie? Is this a tart?"

Portia explained the dishes while Cordelia offered samples. By the time the woman headed out, she was loaded with food Olivia had wrapped up. At the door, the woman stopped and shook her head. "I just have to tell you, you saved me."

"What do you mean?" Portia asked cautiously.

"I'm having a book party for a friend tonight, and the caterer canceled. Last minute, said she had an emergency and no backup plan. I had no idea what I was going to do. I turned down Seventy-third by accident." She beamed at all three of them. "At least I thought it was an accident."

The woman left in a rustle of white bags and pink boxes. Cordelia and Olivia started talking. When Portia turned, Gabriel was still there. Their eyes met and held. Despite herself, a slow pulse of heat went through her body. He was like the darkest, richest hot chocolate she could have imagined. She remembered the way he had stared at her, hard, his jaw ticking, then the ruthless control that seemed to shatter when she had reached up on tiptoes and kissed him. Barely a kiss, tentative, before he crushed her to him with a groan.

A breath sighed out of her at the memory, and his gaze drifted to her mouth. But then the buzzer rang again, making her blink, and he seemed to remember that they weren't alone.

"This isn't over," he said, his voice curt.

He left before she could respond. She drew a breath, pushed worry from her mind, before all three sisters squealed in delight and danced it out in the seconds before their next customer arrived.

⋯⋰⋯

For the next two days, Portia cooked and baked like a dervish while Cordelia sold The Glass Kitchen's fare to a growing line of people who had heard about their amazing food. She still cooked breakfast and supper upstairs as well, though there were no more cheeky conversations in the kitchen with her employer. Actually, she didn't see Gabriel at all, as if he stayed away intentionally.

But after the third day of sales, with every minute of her last three days filled to overflowing, she was lying in her bed, still damp from a shower, completely exhausted, when there was a knock on the garden door. She opened it to find Gabriel. Surprised, she glanced from him to the fire escape.

He stood there and looked at her, just looked, his jaw working, his eyes narrowed in frustration. "Even with strangers traipsing in and out, I can't stay away from you."

His voice was hungry, and he reached for her even as the words left his mouth.

They fell back into her apartment, he kicking the door closed. He made love to her with an intensity that made her arch and cry out, his hands and mouth possessively taking her body. There was a near desperation in the way they came together, both of them knowing it was a bad idea, but neither able to fight it. He lost himself in her body until early dawn, when he rolled over, kissed her shoulder, and said, "I have to get back upstairs before the girls wake up."

Portia felt drugged, her limbs deliciously weak, her body sore and aching in a wonderfully used way. "Be up soon," she murmured, burrowing into the sheets and covers. "Making huevos rancheros for you guys this morning."

⁘

A few days later, she finished another breakfast upstairs—after Gabriel had pulled her behind a door, slammed her against the wall, and kissed her until her head spun—then she came down to her apartment to start cooking for The Glass Kitchen. She decided to make salmon baked in a touch of olive oil, topped with pine nuts, and served over spinach flash-fried in the salmon-and-olive-oil drippings. She added brown rice that she had slow-boiled with the herb hawthorn. Just as she finished, Cordelia arrived with a woman she had found standing on the sidewalk out front.

"My husband has high blood pressure," she explained, negotiating the stairs down into Portia's apartment with care. "He's never happy with anything I make for supper, so I should tell you that you probably don't have anything that will work for me."

Cordelia took a look at the meal, raised an eyebrow at Portia, and then turned to the woman. "This is the perfect meal for your husband's high blood pressure. Fish oil, nuts, hawthorn, whole grains."

Next, a pumpkin pie went to a woman who couldn't sleep.

"Pie?" she asked in a doubtful tone.

"Pumpkin," Portia clarified, "is good for insomnia."

An apricot crumble spiced with cloves and topped with oats and brown sugar went to a woman drawn with stress. Then a man walked through the door, shoulders slumped. Cordelia and Olivia eyed him for a second.

"I know the feeling," Olivia said, and fetched him a half gallon of the celery and cabbage soup Portia had found herself preparing earlier.

The man peered into the container, grew a tad queasier, and said, "No thanks."

"Do you or don't you have a hangover?" Olivia demanded, then drew a breath. "Really," she added more kindly. "Eat this and you'll feel better."

He came back the next day for more.

"Cabbage is no cure for drinking too much," Cordelia told him.

He just shrugged and slapped down his money for two quarts of soup instead of one.

The knowing was steering Portia with a force and intensity that she had never experienced before. She tried to be happy about it, but it was hard not to worry. Yes, the knowing had brought good into her life, but the good was far outweighed by the bad. So she worked all day, and then when Gabriel came down the fire escape to her, they made love half the night. She didn't tell her sisters. He was her secret. They behaved with circumspection when they met in the kitchen (most of the time); they never went on dates; they never talked about anything serious. When it came to The Glass Kitchen, they existed in a sort of wary standoff, too busy losing themselves in each other to talk about it.

Ariel started wandering into The Glass Kitchen after school and doing her homework at a space she had carved out for herself in a corner. It was easy to forget she was there. One afternoon about two weeks into their new endeavor, Olivia jumped when Ariel spoke.

"Sweetie, you scared me." Olivia laughed. "When you scrunch up like that, doing homework like a mad little scientist, it's like you're practically invisible."

After that, Ariel planted herself at the end of the kitchen counter, where no one could help but see her.

A few days later Portia was upstairs completing the Kanes' meal of grilled lamb chops, sliced potatoes roasted in olive oil, and sautéed broccoli rabe. After having found a stack of blood oranges at a street cart on Columbus, she planned to surprise her charges with a blood orange ice she had thrown together, minus the orange liqueur Gram had always included.

Miranda walked into the kitchen, ignoring Portia and Ariel. She pulled out some green tea in a tiny bag, threw it in a cup of water, then slammed it into the microwave.

Miranda's phone beeped with a text. Her fingers flew over the keyboard as she responded, forgetting as the tea circled. Portia wasn't paying close attention when Miranda pulled the cup out and immediately took a drink.

"Ahg!" the girl cried, dropping the cup to the counter with a splash.

Portia had just finished chopping the flavored ice. She instantly put a scoopful into a glass. "Put this in your mouth!"

The girl gasped and gagged, closing her eyes, and she sucked on the shards of ice. After long seconds, she sagged back against the counter and swallowed, then just stared at Portia.

"It's weird, you know," Ariel said, looking at them.

"What's weird?"

They turned and saw Gabriel walking into the kitchen, going through the mail.

"Hey," Portia said softly.

He shot her a look under those thick lashes of his that made her remember the way he had shuddered the night before when she had kissed a path down his abdomen.

After a second, he shifted his gaze to his daughters.

"What's weird, A?"

The girl shrugged. "Portia makes stuff downstairs, and then random people show up who need whatever she makes. Or even here. She made some strange ice just before Miranda burned the cra—I mean, crud—out of her mouth. It's, well, weird. Like magic."

"Ariel," Gabriel stated, his voice crisp. "There's no such thing as magic. It's a fact of life that people see what they want to see. They adjust their expectations to what they see in front of them." He turned to Miranda. "Are you okay?"

"I'm fine," she snapped.

"See, you're fine now, after the ice," Ariel persisted. "I've seen it happen, lots of times."

Portia felt a shiver of unease. "I wish I had a magic wand," she said with a laugh she didn't feel. "But the truth is that I make whatever I feel like, and hungry people want it. End of story." She displayed their dinner. "Just like you all want to eat tonight."

Ariel rolled her eyes. "There's that you all thing again."

"Yep, you all better eat before it gets cold." Portia walked over to the door as casually as she could.

"See ya!"

She waved, bolting when Gabriel gave her a curious look and started to say something.

Twenty-two

⬥⬥⬥

ARIEL HAD BEEN SITTING at her spot in Portia's kitchen for days, brewing over how she could get more info on her mom and dad, while the sisters cooked. She did her best to keep the whole invisible thing to herself. If she hadn't already been going to the Shrink, mentioning the invisible thing would definitely have gotten her carted off to one.

Somewhere between a batch of cheese tarts and custard-filled cream puffs, Ariel realized that with some careful questioning, surely her grandmother would spill some info on Mom and Dad that would help with the report. Which left Ariel figuring out a way to get to Nana's house that didn't involve a taxi. Subways, Ariel had learned, didn't go across town north of Fifty-ninth Street.

It was a few days later when she finally managed to sneak her old bike out of the town house. Of the few things from the old house they had brought with them, she wasn't sure how a bicycle had made the cut. But, yay, it had.

She hopped on the bike without bothering to change out of her school uniform. She had a good three hours, maybe four, before her dad came home—plenty of time to get to her grandmother's, then back.

She went straight into Central Park at Seventy-second Street because obviously that was way safer than riding around with all the taxis at her back. She hadn't ridden the bike in years. But now that she was wheeling down the curving road into the park, streamers on the handlebars fluttering in the wind, remembering just how much she used to love riding Ethel.

She named her bike that because of watching reruns of *I Love Lucy* with her mom. As much as Ariel would have liked to be Lucy, she knew she was more the sidekick. She was Ethel. Mom never agreed with her, but Ariel went ahead and named her bike that, to mark the truth of it. Moms always think their kids are lead actors, even when it's obvious to the whole world that they aren't.

All she had to do was cross at the Seventy-second Street transverse, then take the walking path to the pedestrian exit at Seventy-seventh Street on the east side. Bikes weren't allowed on the walking path, but still she decided it was better to risk getting chased down by a park ranger than to ride on the park road because of all the cabs.

It didn't take Ariel more than fifteen minutes to make it from her house to her grandmother's. After chaining the bike to a pole on the sidewalk, she rang the bell on the towering stone town house. Ariel's town house was nice and all, redbrick with a fancy green tin mansard roof, but her grandmother's was like a mansion. Big blocks of stone, curlicues carved everywhere, and a massively imposing door. Even after her dad managed to buy the basement of their town house from Portia, it would never be this fancy.

Ariel buzzed a second time before the intercom crackled and the housekeeper's voice floated out.

"Hi, Carmen. It's Ariel. I came to see my grandmother."

"Oh, *chica*. Does your *abuela* know you are coming?"

"No. But I wanted to surprise her."

True. She didn't want her grandmother to put her off.

"So sweet. Such a good *nieta*." The door lock buzzed. Ariel grabbed the handle and pushed inside. Her grandmother was coming downstairs with a confused look on her face when Ariel walked into the living room.

"Ariel?"

Helen Kane didn't look happy. Not that it was a surprise. She wasn't exactly the milk-and-cookies type of grandmother.

"Hi, Grandma!"

Helen shuddered.

"Oh, sorry," Ariel said, adding, "Nana."

Helen drew a deep breath, as if Ariel tried every last ounce of her patience. Ariel had always assumed that it was her mom who made Helen crazy. But Mom was dead, and her grandmother hadn't changed.

"Why are you here, dear?"

At least she got a *dear* out of the deal.

"I thought I'd stop by and say hello." Hopefully put some of her weird worries to rest. "Now that we live so close, it seems like a shame not to see you more!"

She could tell from Helen's hard gaze that she wasn't buying that fib.

"Is Uncle Anthony here?"

Helen hesitated. "No, he's out."

"Oh, darn." Not.

"You're here to see your uncle?"

"I'm mainly here to see you. But I was just thinking about all the amazing things he's done in his life."

Her grandmother's hard gaze softened. "Yes, he has done a lot."

Forget the fact that the man didn't work—or so her dad said—but whatever. Ariel knew that complimenting the golden boy would soften Helen Kane right up.

"Yeah, I was thinking about Uncle Anthony's trip to Africa. It sounded really awesome."

Her grandmother raised an eyebrow. "Anthony told you about his trip?"

Actually, no. Ages ago, Ariel had heard about the Africa trip when her mom and dad were fighting. Dad had used Africa as an example of her uncle's irresponsibility. Mom said it showed he was adventurous. But Nana didn't need to know that.

"Actually, my dad talked about it."

"Well, I suppose it was a long time ago."

"Totally. But I don't remember when exactly he went. Ages and ages ago, right?"

"It was nineteen ninety-eight."

Helen walked through the living room and went into the kitchen. Despite the lack of invitation, Ariel followed.

"Carmen, I'd like my tea now," Helen said.

"*Si, señora.*" The housekeeper gave her employer a meaningful look and nodded toward Ariel.

Helen sighed. "Ariel, would you like some tea?"

"Sure. Tea would be great."

She followed her grandmother into a back sitting room that overlooked the gardens one level below. The gardens at Ariel's house were a mess, though she had seen Portia out there a time or two digging around.

"Oh, yeah, I remember now. Uncle Anthony went in nineteen ninety-eight. I wasn't even born then."

Carmen brought a tray filled with fancy china stuff and made a big to-do about serving, like Nana was a queen or something.

"So, you were telling me about Uncle Anthony going to Africa," Ariel prompted, taking a sip, trying her best not to spill anything.

"Was I?"

"Yes, you said he went in nineteen ninety-eight? Did he go in the spring or summer?"

"Why do you want to know?"

Ariel wasn't about to answer that question, at least not truthfully. "I just can't quite get it in my head. You see, I'm writing a social studies report." That was true. "About our family." Also true. "About cool things our family does." Sort of true. "And Uncle Anthony is the King of Cool Stuff."

Nana smiled, but it was a sad smile. "Yes, he is. Always has been." She sat back and looked out into the garden. "You should have seen him as a little boy. The most beautiful child anyone had ever seen. Everyone said so. I couldn't go anywhere without people stopping me—on the street, mind you—and commenting on what a beautiful child he was."

Ariel refrained from asking where Dad had been in all this walking-the-beautiful-baby-around business. She wanted answers and while she didn't completely have her head wrapped around the thoughts bubbling to the surface, she figured it was better to avoid bringing her dad into it.

"When he was young," Helen continued, "Anthony went on any adventure his father and I allowed. When he was six, he asked to go to sleepaway camp in Vermont. Sleepaway camp at six!" Helen chuckled. "At ten, it was camp in Colorado. Then Montana. I couldn't believe it. At seventeen, he wanted to travel to Costa Rica on summer break to build houses for the less fortunate."

In some recess of her mind, Ariel remembered another conversation she'd overheard. Her dad and uncle going at it, yet again.

You had to go everywhere I did, her dad had shouted.

I looked up to my older brother. What of it?

You didn't go because you admired me. You went to show that everyone, everywhere, loved you better.

Ariel had expected her uncle to deny it.

And they did, didn't they?

Silence, followed by her dad's cold voice.

Yes. They always loved you more.

Ariel hadn't understood at the time, and she hadn't thought of it again until now. Sitting with her grandmother, a sick feeling started to build in her stomach.

"Yeah," she said with a laugh she didn't feel. "Uncle Anthony is amazing. Costa Rica at seventeen. And you said he went to Africa in nineteen ninety-eight?"

"Yes. May nineteen ninety-eight. He hasn't lived in New York full-time since."

Ariel's heart pounded so hard that she bumped the teacup, the china clattering. Helen jerked her gaze away from the window, her normal smooth beauty pinched as she took in Ariel. "It's your father's fault that he left, you know," Helen said, as if trying to gain supporters to her cause.

"What do you mean?"

"It's a very sad thing when one brother is jealous of another," Nana said, her mouth sort of pinching together. "I'll tell you for your own good, since you have a sibling as well. And so you can understand that your father is just plain being unfair to your uncle. Your father has always hated the attention Anthony received. So when Anthony wanted to go to camp, Gabriel made us send him, too. Vermont. Colorado. Costa Rica."

Ariel wasn't quite sure how to respond to this. *I believe it was the other way around* didn't seem to be what Helen had in mind.

"And then Anthony met Victoria." The pinched look turned bitter. "Even more than your father, Victoria was responsible for everything falling apart. As much as I'm not one to speak ill of the dead, the first time I met her, she looked like—" She cut herself off and focused on Ariel, her lips pursed hard. "Like a girl raised in a housing project. But your mother was smart. The next time I saw her, she was wearing a sweater set and pearls. She played Gabriel against my Anthony. In the end, she ran Anthony off to Africa, heartbroken, when she chose Gabriel over him. I've always wondered what Gabriel did to win her. He'd never won against Anthony. Ever."

By then, her grandmother was leaning forward, intent, lost to her own words. Then she sat back abruptly and eyed Ariel warily.

Ariel sat, stunned. She couldn't believe what her grandmother was saying. Uncle Anthony had said he met her mom first—but he'd dated her? More than that, how could Nana say this stuff about her dad?

She sat up straight. "A mom shouldn't love one kid more than the other."

Helen glanced out the window. "Mother or not, there are some people who simply pull everyone to them. Anthony is like that." She looked back, directly at Ariel. "Your father always made it hard to love him."

Ariel's chest was burning so much that she couldn't even think of what to say. So she jerked up from her seat and dashed to the front door, slamming out into the street. As soon as she managed to free her bike she pedaled as fast as she could back across the park to the Upper West Side, tears flying in the wind along with the streamers.

Twenty-three

❖

PORTIA LOVED THE SMELLS of cooking and baking. It turned a house into a home.

It was October, barely two weeks after she and her sisters had opened up the test version of The Glass Kitchen. Standing at the sink, she washed her hands, getting ready to start cooking for the day. Ariel had been quiet lately, sitting at the end of the counter, busy doing homework and writing in her journal. But sometimes she just sat there, lost in thought, her brow creased. Portia had asked if anything was wrong. Ariel had blinked, then scoffed, diving back into homework.

And then last night Portia had dreamed of apples again. When her mind swirled with images of her grandmother's moist apple cake, she had gasped awake, her heart pounding. Between Ariel, Gabriel, and her rapidly dwindling money, Portia felt as if a noose were gradually slipping tighter around her neck. And with every day that had passed, the knowing grew a little bit more. Part of her reveled in it. But the other part still held out against it, worried about what it meant to give in to the knowing completely.

Given the dream, she shouldn't have been surprised a few hours later, as she stood at the counter making a fresh batch of sweet tea, when Cordelia arrived.

She looked tired and disheveled, distracted as she walked in carrying a bag of groceries. "I thought we could give that cake a second try."

"What cake?" Portia asked carefully.

"The apple cake."

The only thing that surprised Portia was the pure, unadulterated spark of excitement that flared inside her, as if finally she could let go of any remnants of worry.

Cordelia looked at her, though her eyes were dull. "I knew it. I knew that today was apple cake day. Just like I know that my life is over."

Portia stiffened. "What?"

Olivia walked in next. "What do you mean your life is over? What's wrong now?"

Cordelia looked her sisters in the eye, seeming to come to a decision. "You mean what's wrong besides lying to people and telling them that Portia works with Gabriel Kane in order to get meetings?"

Portia's head snapped back. "You really did it?" She had hoped there would be some explanation, some misunderstanding.

Cordelia pressed her eyes closed, then sighed. "Yes, I did it. I started out doing it the right way when I first tried to get appointments with investors. But I never got past the receptionists. Then I sort of casually mentioned that you knew Gabriel Kane, which morphed into you worked for Gabriel Kane, which morphed even more into you worked *with* Gabriel Kane." She cringed. "That had people lining up to take a meeting with you." Her face was red with strained emotion. "I shouldn't have done it, I know. But with all this mess with James, I felt desperate. It was like getting the appointments was proof that I could make something happen in my life."

Portia came over and took the bag away, setting it down. Olivia joined them.

"Hey, sweetie," Olivia said, wrapping her arms around Cordelia. "It's okay. It will all work out. Things always do. Just like it will all work out with James."

"But it won't. It turns out there's an e-mail trail a mile long."

Olivia couldn't seem to help herself when she snorted. "Who, in this day and age, leaves an e-mail trail?"

"Obviously my husband." Cordelia drew a shaky breath, and when she spoke, her voice cracked. "Me. Dirt poor. Again."

Portia took her sister by the shoulders. "Not a single one of us wants to go back to our trailer-park roots. But whatever happens, I know you'll get through this. Daddy taught us to be fighters. And I just realized that not one of us has been fighting for ourselves. Not really. Not well enough. We've been hanging in the wind, at the mercy of what comes our way. Daddy would hate that."

She saw the shift in Cordelia's eyes; she even saw it come into Olivia's eyes, as if the mention of their father brought his strength into the room.

"You've been dealt a bad hand, Cord," Portia continued. "But it's time you started taking control in the right way. You've got to pull your head out of the sand, start fixing your life."

Cordelia pressed her eyes closed. "But how?"

"I don't know," Portia said honestly. "But we'll figure something out, just like we figured out how to open a version of The Glass Kitchen without money, and it's working."

She prayed she wasn't lying.

"Now," she said, stepping away with a decisive nod, "we are going to drink to that." She retrieved three glasses and poured lemonade into each.

Portia and her sisters raised their glasses. "To Earl Cuthcart," she said.

"May his daughters do him proud," Olivia continued.

Cordelia drew a deep breath. "To taking charge . . . and responsibility."

The three of them clinked, then drank, and more of what Portia thought of as her father's strength swirled through the room like a warm Texas breeze.

Just then, someone knocked. A second later, Gabriel walked in.

As always, everything about him spoke of a man who took his power for granted. Portia watched as he surveyed the scene.

Cordelia didn't bother with so much as a hello. Her chin rose, the glass still in her hand. "I've been using your name to get appointments for us with investors. I'm sorry. I knew it was wrong, but I did it anyway."

Olivia gave a snort of surprised laughter. "Way to jump into it, Cord."

Gabriel's expression grew scary. Portia held her breath. But at the same time, she couldn't have been prouder of Cordelia.

"Gabriel," Portia started to say as he strode over to them with a slow, predatory gait. This was a man who crushed people, happily, for less than using his name without his consent.

Portia's heart all but stopped when he halted in front of Cordelia. Portia scuttled closer to her sister protectively as Gabriel looked at Cordelia hard.

"I appreciate your honesty," he said finally, surprising Portia. "I appreciate you telling me face-to-face. There are more than a few men who don't have it in them to do the same."

Cordelia's squared shoulders started to round, relief putting out the fire.

"Hey," Gabriel said, this time softly. "Things have a way of working out like they should." Surprisingly, a smile eased his face.

The smile he gave her sister made Portia's knees weak with gratitude. And when he turned to look at her, she nearly threw her arms around his shoulders. As if he understood, one side of his mouth crooked up in a smile as he took her glass, drinking a long, slow pull.

Somehow the gesture felt intimate, as if they had kissed rather than shared a glass, and Portia blushed.

Thankfully, Cordelia was too caught up in being let off the hook to notice.

Flustered, Portia swiped the glass back. "Would you like me to get you some lemonade?"

"No need." He took hers again, turning back to Cordelia as he leaned against the counter. "If there's anything I can do to help, I will."

If Cordelia had been anyone else, and Gabriel a less formidable man, Portia was sure her sister would have flung her arms around him. Instead, Cordelia steadied her trembling lip and said, "Thank you. I appreciate it."

Gabriel nodded, took one last pull on Portia's lemonade, then handed it back. "I have a meeting and won't be here for dinner. It'll just be the girls." He focused on her. "I won't be home until late."

Up went Olivia's radar and eyebrow, and Portia felt another blush coming on. But still, Cordelia was too caught up in anything but her own misery as Gabriel said his good-byes and was out the door.

Portia was doing a little shaking of her own as she began cooking. Olivia started to say something, but Portia jerked her head in Cordelia's direction. Olivia relented and got on the computer. Cordelia managed to find a smile and chat up the customers who trickled steadily through the door.

But just as Portia finished the regular items on their menu and was about to start on the apple cake, she froze, having to brace her hands on the counter.

"Portia? What's wrong?"

She couldn't answer. Her head spun; her heart pounded. The knowing was getting stronger. It had never felt like this before. It had never *demanded.* "I need figs," she said, her eyes closed, the words labored. "And chocolate. And chili."

"What?"

When Portia opened her eyes, she saw that Cordelia's face radiated concern.

"I need it. Now."

They left the place a mess, and she and Cordelia dashed to the store, leaving Olivia to man the counter.

"I spoke too soon about the knowing. I hate this part of it," Cordelia muttered as they flew through the small Pioneer market just a block from the town house. "The sudden bursts? The way everything used to come to a standstill, our lives, everything on hold while Gram went off on a cooking tangent? That was when we were little. Later, she'd have you doing the cooking." Cordelia grabbed a packet of chili powder and tossed it into their basket with more force than necessary.

"You're the one who pushed me to get back into this. Do you think I like being at the mercy of a bunch of figs, for pity's sake?"

Cordelia gave a shout of wry laughter.

They made it through the market in record time, returning to the apartment just as the timer went off for a small potato casserole. Cordelia's phone buzzed with a call from James, so she had to go. Olivia took off for the yoga class she was now teaching regularly, and Portia dove back into the kitchen as if the very thing she had been running from for the last three years could save her.

After twenty minutes, her nerves started to calm. Not a single customer found their way to the front door to disrupt her. After forty minutes, her breathing had slowed. And after another hour, she was lost in the rhythm, following the knowing as if it were steps to a dance she'd learned as a child.

She brought port wine, sugar, and chili powder to a boil and let the mix simmer until she had a fragrant syrup. At the last minute, she added cinnamon. Setting it aside, she melted bittersweet chocolate, stirring until the mixture was smooth.

With every stir of the wooden spoon, images danced in Portia's head. Of happiness, of love, of forbidden fruit that promised sex. She thought of Gabriel's chest as he reared over her at night, his gaze locked with hers, and felt a shiver that went down her fingers and made the spoon shake.

For some reason, she didn't dip the figs whole, but decided to chop them into bite-sized morsels, then dipped the pieces in the chocolate and set them on a waxed paper–covered baking sheet to cool.

When that was done, she realized she had plenty of the chocolate-chili-cinnamon concoction left over—along with a bag of unsalted peanuts. Refusing to question it, she dipped the peanuts and set those out, too.

That afternoon, after the candies were cooled and wrapped in cellophane bags, she escaped the apartment and perched on the front steps outside. The day had gotten surprisingly cold.

The old man next door, whom Portia had only seen sitting in the window, emerged from a cab. He looked dapper in an ancient but immaculately kept sports jacket with equally ancient pants, perfectly polished cordovan loafers, and steel-wool gray hair.

"Hello," Portia called out.

The man nodded, walked toward the curb in front of his town house, his posture severely stooped. When he got to the curb he took a step toward it, but his cane stuck on a crack in the sidewalk.

Portia dashed over and offered a hand.

The man gave Portia a wry little smile and took her hand. Together they managed the steps one at a time. Halfway up, the man had to stop to catch his breath. "It's awful getting old," he told Portia. "Just in case you're wondering."

"It's not for sissies," Portia answered. "That's what my grandmother always said."

The old man snorted. "Not for sissies, indeed. It's this blasted chest cold I can't get rid of that makes me so weak. Congestion, I suppose."

"Really? You have congestion?"

He peered at her. "You don't have to look pleased about it."

"No, no! Not pleased that you're congested. It's just that this morning I made chocolate-and-cinnamon-chili-coated peanuts. The cinnamon and chili are perfect for cold congestion, the peanuts provide protein for strength, and the chocolate, well, chocolate gets your endorphins going so you'll feel better." She laughed, delighted and relieved. The demanding sense of needing to make the candies hadn't meant anything bad was going to happen. "Can I give you some for your cold?"

"That's the most absurd thing I've ever heard. Chocolate peanuts for colds."

"Chocolate *cinnamon-chili* peanuts! Just try some. They certainly aren't going to make you feel worse."

Before she could say anything else, another man came down the stairs to meet them. He was equally old, dressed equally well, but was more mobile. Where the man on Portia's arm had wiry gray hair, this man had dyed his red. His skin was smoother, his carriage erect.

"Well, look what we have here—the woman from next door." He stopped in front of her, beaming. "Even prettier up close."

Portia smiled back, charmed.

"I'm Marcus, my dear. And while this old grump bucket probably hasn't mentioned a word about it, he's Stanley."

"Hi, Marcus. I'm—"

"Portia, from next door. We know. Stanley has been giving me regular reports on his sightings."

Of course she'd seen him at the window, but . . . "You've been watching me?"

"*I* haven't," Marcus said. "But Stanley here has done little else." He smiled wickedly and leaned forward. "Very *Rear Window*, don't you think? And, rest assured, you've provided more entertainment than we've had around this place in ages."

The whole thing was a little weird, but Stanley's complete lack of guilt and Marcus's smiling charm made it difficult to do anything but laugh a little herself. "But how do you know my name?"

Marcus hooked his arm through Portia's free elbow. "Didn't you know that the postman knows everything? And he's about the only company we get these days."

Stanley coughed.

"The peanuts!" Portia said. "I have to get them."

"I'm not eating anything you make. How do I know they aren't poisoned?"

"Ha! Do you think I'd get you all this way into your apartment only to poison you?"

"Portia, love, go get whatever it is you're talking about," Marcus said. "We could use some new nuts around here."

Portia laughed, dashed out of the men's apartment and into hers. Grabbing two bags of peanuts, she wheeled back next door, flipping the OPEN sign to CLOSED. When she returned, Marcus was helping Stanley back into his favorite spot by the window with a caring devotion.

Embarrassed to be walking in on such a sweet scene, Portia set the bags down quietly and started to leave.

"We knew your great-aunt," Stanley said, his eyes still closed, his head back.

"You knew Evie?"

"She bought her town house around the same time Marcus and I bought ours. And let me tell you, this wasn't considered a good neighborhood back then. We didn't spend time together, really. She was an actress," he said, tone at once disdainful and amused. "I was a Broadway producer, and Marcus here was an agent. Actresses always tried to befriend us, and we learned to keep our distance."

He sat up a bit straighter and opened his eyes. "Evie was different. She didn't want any favors from anyone. Swore she would make it on her own, and she did. Even after she found success, we didn't socialize, but we watched out for each other. How could we not, all of us living in these giant town houses? Just me and Marcus, and Evie by herself. Plus, there was the Texas thing. I was born in Texas to a Southern mother who loved to cook. Evie's sister loved to cook—well, you must know that if you're her niece." Stanley gave Portia that wry little smile of his. "I remember you, too," he continued, "along with the rest of Evie's wild Texas nieces. Running up and down the fire escape at all hours. I was sure one of you was going to fall to your death."

Portia smiled back. "It was just me on the fire escape. And I survived."

"Yes, you did. And now that man and his daughters have moved in. Are you living with him?"

"No!"

Stanley snorted.

Marcus wiggled his eyebrows at her. "I still haven't managed to catch a glimpse of him. Though Stanley says he's something to be seen. All rugged and manly."

"Good God, man, you can't let the neighbors know that I'm ogling them!" Stanley said.

Marcus laughed, and Stanley began slowly eating his nuts. A few minutes later, Portia found herself in their kitchen, making a cup of hot chamomile tea. She brought it back out to Stanley, who sipped it, and soon his breathing grew easier. A tension in Marcus's face, which she hadn't realized was there until it was gone, also eased.

"I'd better go." Portia wrote down her cell number. "If you need anything, I'm right next door."

"Evie always said you were like her own children. She loved it when you came to visit."

"We loved visiting." Portia squeezed Stanley's hand, hugged Marcus, and headed home. That was one of the things she had made herself forget when she pushed the knowing away: It always brought about unexpected interactions with strangers. Food had a way of bringing people together.

But every peaceful thought evaporated when she walked into her kitchen and found that someone had taken all the candied figs and nuts. The question circled in her head. Why? And, more important, who?

Twenty-four

✦

ARIEL USED HER KEY to get in the town house. The muted sound of rock music drifted down to her through the walls. She dropped her backpack in the foyer, tilting her chin up to look at the ceiling, trying to understand where the noise was coming from. "Dad?"

But Dad wouldn't be home. It was barely three. And he sure as heck wouldn't be listening to any sort of music that thumped and buzzed.

"Miranda?" No answer.

"Portia?" No way Portia would be playing loud music in their house.

She headed up the stairs to the second floor, then on to the third, the music getting louder the higher she went. The whole thing made Ariel feel nervous. But she was pretty sure Miranda was up in the attic doing who knew what.

When she got all the way up, the door was closed, but the music was impossibly loud now, thumping through the wood door. Ariel hesitated, her hand on the knob, then opened the door.

If she thought the music couldn't get louder, she was wrong. The beat pounded through the room, making her body buzz and her eardrums hurt. No one noticed her, not any of the three guys who lounged around the floor, or the two girls, plus Miranda, who sat Indian style next to them. Ariel only recognized the creep Dustin.

All of them were laughing hysterically. Not that Ariel could hear the sound of their laughter over the music, but she could see how their faces contorted and moved, like watching a silent movie where everyone on-screen was laughing.

It took another second before the smell hit her. A weird sweet smoke smell. And wine. Like her mother used to drink in their house in New Jersey with its big formal living room and dining room, the giant kitchen and den. Ariel still held out hope that her dad would see the light and take them back to Montclair. Weird stuff like Miranda smoking pot and drinking alcohol didn't happen back in New Jersey.

Ariel stood there frozen, smoke wrapping around her stinging her nose and eyes, as she wondered what to do.

The teenagers still didn't know she was there. They kept laughing and throwing little chocolate-covered balls, trying to get them into each other's mouths. As if this were really funny.

The creep noticed her first. He reached over and turned down the sound system. "Hey." Dustin laughed. "Dude."

Seriously?

"What's up?" he added.

Miranda jerked around, her hair flying around her shoulders. When she saw Ariel, her eyes narrowed to mean, thin slits. "Are you spying again?"

"I am not spying!"

"I am not spying!" Miranda mimicked cruelly, making the other kids laugh.

Ariel felt a burn, thinking it was embarrassment, but even that didn't deter her. "You're smoking pot. And drinking. Dad could come home any minute."

"Yep," one of the girls said, still laughing. "She's spying. Little sisters are a pain in the ass."

Miranda glared. "Dad isn't home. And he's not coming home anytime soon. So just go and mind your own business, freak."

The name hurt worse than it should have. Ariel knew people thought she was a freak. Even she had put the description in the title of her journal. But Miranda had never called her that. Since their mom died, Miranda hadn't been that nice to her, but she hadn't been outright cruel like she was being now.

Ariel pushed back the tears in her throat, dashing at her eyes that burned and teared, and not for the first time she wished she were a tougher sort of sister, one who would put shaving cream in her sister's bed, or pour ice-cold water on her feet when she was sleeping. "You're going to get in trouble, Miranda," was all she managed, the words sticking in her throat. "Big trouble. You're smoking *pot*."

All of a sudden, the creep leaped at her. Ariel felt her eyes pop open like some sort of cartoon character and she started to back up.

He grabbed her around the shoulders and spun her around. "She isn't a spy! She's cool! Right, dude?"

Everything around her rushed by. It was beyond insanity, she knew, but she felt something. Noticed. Which was ridiculous. Appalled at herself, she pushed at his arm. "Put me down, you Neanderthal!"

He did, then offered her a chocolate ball. "For the lady," he said, sweeping a bow. "In fact, you can have all of mine." He pushed a little bag filled with chocolate at her.

Ariel scowled at him. But his smile, his bow, his offer of perfect chocolate candy drew her in and she took the bag.

"You have the coolest hair," the other girl said, as if she were her greatest friend, then turned a pointed look at the girl who had called her a spy.

"Oh, yeah, majorly cool," that girl added.

They all started talking to her then, each of them offering her chocolate. Miranda rolled her eyes.

Ariel didn't need Miranda to tell her that the kids didn't really think anything about her was cool; they just wanted to make sure she didn't tell on them. But the whole not being invisible thing seduced her even if it wasn't real.

"Don't you dare tell Dad," Miranda said, dragging a deep pull of the joint into her lungs before blowing it out in a rush.

Ariel just stood there, holding tight to the bag of chocolate, smoke wrapping around her as she tried to figure out what she should do. She had just decided that it was her dad's problem, not hers, when she realized that the burning in her throat and lungs had gotten worse. It happened fast then. Her throat started to close off in a way it hadn't in years, teasing her into believing that she had outgrown stupid reactions to weird things in the air.

In a flash, she could hardly breathe.

Miranda and the other kids had fired up the sound system again, and the walls throbbed and swelled. Trying her hardest not to panic, Ariel dropped the chocolate and pivoted toward the door. She half ran, half tripped down the stairs to her room, frantically digging around in her backpack as she tried to suck in gasps of breath. Calculator. Antibacterial gel. Socks. Pen after pen. Her head started to throb and swell like the walls upstairs, the music growing fainter even as some part of her realized the music was really getting louder. But just as a massively tired feeling swelled through her body, her fingers clamped around the inhaler, and she jerked it out. The nail-polish picture her mother had painted on it fluttered in front of her eyes. Without thinking, she jammed Einstein into her mouth, squeezing as hard as she could, praying he was smart enough to save her.

Twenty-five

Portia walked into the Kanes' house at five that evening. As she was walking in, a small crew of what she knew were Miranda's friends came out. The boy Dustin wagged an eyebrow at her. She glowered back in what she hoped was a stern schoolteacher sort of way. The boy only laughed.

Portia had been spending her days doing exactly three things: cooking, baking, and telling herself to stop thinking about Gabriel Kane. Actually, that made it four things, the fourth being the time she spent thinking about Gabriel. Which was a lot.

Then there had been the nights. But she really tried not to think too much about those. She still found it hard to believe that she was having utterly passionate, completely uncommitted sex with her upstairs neighbor. Her, Portia Cuthcart. Always safe. Always careful. Always proper. She still hadn't even been out on a date with him. The Bandana Ball didn't count. Olivia had all but forced him to go.

Sure, something in her old Texas soul whispered unhelpful things about cows and milk for free. But everything in this newer New York soul had her reveling in being someone so unlike the woman she had become in Texas—soft, a ghost of her former self.

Her thoughts were interrupted just as she was finishing up dinner for the Kanes when Ariel walked into the kitchen looking a bit gray. She sat down without saying more than a listless hi.

Miranda followed a few second later. "What is Ariel telling you?" she demanded, more belligerent than usual.

Portia considered. "What's going on with you two now?"

"Nothing," they said in tandem.

Miranda shot her sister a sharp scowl, then wheeled around and left. A moment later Ariel got up and walked out, too. Portia heard first one bedroom door slam, then another.

Don't get involved, she told herself. *A smart woman doesn't get involved with her secret lover's children.*

Which just got her mind circling back to the same thing she wasn't supposed to be thinking about. Gabriel.

Last night he had come down the fire escape in that way he did. When she had opened the door, she found him standing there, his hair still damp from a shower, raked back with his hands. He wore a T-shirt instead of a button-down, old jeans that hung low on his hips, and a pair of Converse with no socks. He stepped inside without asking, as if he couldn't do anything else, a strong man giving in to her in a way that made her feel heady with a foreign sort of power. This strong man wanted her. This powerful man couldn't stay away from her. A thrill ran through her at the thought.

Standing at the door, he showed no trace of the civilized businessman who stepped out of his town car every evening. He walked into the room as if he owned it and pulled his T-shirt over his head, throwing it to the side.

The twist in Portia's stomach at the sight of him was so raw and primal that she couldn't shape words.

"Portia," he said finally, the word dragged out on a breath, then just stood there.

"Gabriel, are you okay?"

He pressed his eyes closed, blowing a hard breath out his nose. "No."

Then he dragged her into his arms and took her over to the old wrought-iron bed. They made love with a kind of ferocity that made the bed slam against the wall. But even that wasn't enough, and five minutes after, they started over, sweaty bodies turning over each other, the only sounds ragged gasps and moans. At some point, he flipped her on her back and pinned her down, his face wild as they gave in to sensation without words, he never taking his eyes off her.

Finally, later, when they were lying next to each other, gasping, it was Gabriel who broke the silence, the edge in him eased, if only slightly. Lying in the semidarkness, he came up on one elbow, demanding to know everything about her, pinning her down when she was elusive.

So she told him about her parents, her grandmother, the stories all whitewashed and pretty. Evie and the town house, the way it had looked in its prime, the way she had loved it. The way she and her sisters used to play dress-up with their aunts' old costumes.

He listened intently, his fingers running along her arm and shoulders, circling slowly across her collarbone, as if drawing her words along her skin.

But at some point he captured her hands with his and rolled over on top of her, breaking off her sentence. "Portia," he groaned against her mouth, his free hand sliding down her body, no longer lazy, rather intent.

She lost herself to his touch. But at the back of her mind she worried. What they shared was sweaty and complicated. Despite all her talk of uncommitted sex, he refused to let her keep her boundaries. With the exception of that one earlier kiss, he maintained control of her, her body, of his. But she also knew that he let down his guard with her. Gabriel was a man who was used to control. What would he do if he lost what he no doubt felt defined him?

The bang of the kitchen cabinet yanked her out of her thoughts.

"Dinner still isn't ready?" Miranda demanded. "Hello, I'm starving."

Portia blushed as if the teenager could possibly know what she had been thinking. Miranda made a strangled scoffing sound. "Dinner. In this century."

By the time Ariel and Miranda were seated at the table and Portia was neatening up from preparing the meal of juicy pork chops, green beans with almonds, and creamy cheese-filled grits before she left, she heard the front door open, and her knees went weak.

She glanced up and saw Gabriel coming down the hallway. He stopped in the doorway and just looked at her.

"Jeez, what's up with you, Dad?" Miranda sneered.

Portia jerked her head down and focused on the stove. Instead of snapping at his daughter's tone, Gabriel walked over and kissed the top of Miranda's head. "Sorry, honey. It's been a good day."

For a second, Portia was certain Miranda was about to cry. But then she jerked up from her chair.

"A good day?" she bit out. "Have you looked outside? It's, like, totally cloudy."

She slammed her chair back and stomped off, leaving her nearly full dinner plate behind.

"Miranda!" Gabriel snapped, all that ease disappearing from his eyes as he started after her.

Ariel dropped her head and concentrated on the food Portia had set in front of her.

Later, after the girls had gone to bed and Portia was sound asleep, he came down the fire escape.

"This is New York," Gabriel said, his tone sharp, waking her. "You need to keep your windows locked."

"I do," Portia murmured. "You came in through the glass door. Using a key you shouldn't have. There has to be a law against that."

She was dimly aware that he carried the cardboard sign she had posted earlier. "I take it that among your plethora of skills, reading isn't one of them?"

"I read." He tossed the sign aside, then slid between the sheets, pulling her close.

She rolled over onto her stomach, burrowing deeper into the sheets and blankets, hugging the pillow. Gabriel lifted up her hair and ran his lips along the nape of her neck. Then other kisses, his hands leaving her hair. "You think I'm sexy," he said.

She groaned. "Of course that's what you took away from the sign."

"'All Sexy Cat Burglars Keep Out.'"

"I should have just written 'Keep Out.' Simple. To the point." It had just seemed too mean. But she wanted him to stay away. The more he came down the fire escape, the harder it was to remain in the frame of mind of being okay with an arrangement where they were nothing more than two single adults having casual sex. She was turning into a pathetic, old-fashioned cliché. The more she had sex with him, the less casual it felt. Given the man she realized he was, there was no way this could end well. She had come to understand that he wanted something from her that he hated needing. Hated that he gave in to repeatedly.

"That isn't fair," she gasped when he pulled the sheet low.

"What isn't fair?" he asked, running his tongue along the shell of her ear.

"I'm exhausted. I've been cooking all day."

"I'm the one who's exhausted," he countered, sitting up briefly to rip off his shirt and kick his shorts away. Falling back to her, he rolled her over, her arms above her head, loosely pinning her wrists with one of his large hands. His eyes flared as he took her in, her breasts high through the old T-shirt she wore. "I haven't slept since I met you."

"At all? Not one second of sleep."

He grinned down at her. "Barely." His free hand slipped beneath the soft cotton of her tee, his thigh sliding over her hips. Portia moaned into his mouth, tasting him.

"You're like a demented cat burglar," she murmured, gasping as his thumb brushed the peak of her breast.

"A *sexy* cat burglar," he reminded her, running his tongue along the same path his thumb had just grazed.

"You're also my boss," she managed. "My upstairs neighbor. A man, need I remind you, who is trying to kick me out of my apartment."

He had the good grace to tense at that.

"Basically," she continued, trying her hardest to stay focused as he resumed his attention to her body, "this all adds up to a really bad idea. Beyond that—if you need a *beyond that*—one of these days someone is going to figure out what is going on here. My money is on Ariel. And as much as she likes me, I'm not sure she's going to like *you* and me. I know Miranda won't."

"Let me worry about my daughters. Besides, at one point, Ariel was trying to get me to ask you out."

"Really?"

"Really. She thought it a small price to pay for a decent meal."

Portia snorted.

He tugged her shirt over her head and left it tangled around her wrists, his hand holding her wrists secure. There it was again. Gabriel maintaining control. "You're beautiful, you know."

This time, she scoffed. "I'm cute, at best."

He met Portia's eyes with an intensity that made her breath catch. "You are beautiful," he said in a way that dared her to contradict him.

She loved the sound of the words, the fact that she could tell he believed it. He dipped his head, making love to her with his mouth, going slowly, never rushing. She felt the electric pull between her legs.

"Oh, to hell with the sign," she whispered, and stopped thinking altogether.

He still held her captive, but she turned as best she could to press up against him. He laughed when she cursed at him, his palm sliding over her stomach, then lower to her hip. Portia felt as if she had stopped breathing when he brought one of her knees up, nudging her legs apart, the palm of his hand skimming down the inside of her thigh. But he avoided her center.

"Gabriel, please," she pleaded, twisting again to free her hands, but he held her secure. She wanted more.

"I know," he murmured against her skin. "But not yet."

He dipped his head back to her. Her breath came in pants as he refused to allow her to move.

He stroked and kissed, then surprised her when he dropped his hand from her wrists and slipped down her body, pressing her knees farther apart.

Reality flashed into her head like lights flipped on with a switch. She had never done anything like this. She sat up and tried to pull free. "Gabriel!" she said, pushing at him.

But he was far too strong for her. "Shhh," he said, nipping the skin of her inner thigh.

"I just don't do that," Portia said, even as her body shook. "I'm not comfortable with that. It's private."

"Not private," he stated against her skin. "Mine," he said so softly that she felt certain he was saying it to himself rather than to her.

She fell back at the first touch of his tongue to her core, and when he pressed her legs even farther apart, she allowed that, too. Sensation rode through her, the kind that lust lends to a girl who isn't used to being wild. She let go, she opened to him, and when she gave in so freely, she felt a shift in him.

With a groan he reared over her like he could do nothing else, entering her hard, his careful control lost. He didn't say anything else, just moved, fast and sure, needing something, reaching, bringing her to another orgasm. Only when she cried out did he let go completely, his body tensing and shuddering.

He collapsed on top of her and they lay that way for minutes, or maybe longer, connected, her eyes closed. She could feel his warm breath on her neck, his breathing ragged. When she opened her eyes, he pushed up on his elbows and stared at her. "What are you doing to me?" he whispered.

"Gabriel—"

He pressed his forehead to hers, then rolled away. She expected him to keep going and get off the bed. Instead, he dragged her to him, wrapping her in his arms.

"Go to sleep, Portia."

"But—"

"Portia, sleep."

She debated. But then he tucked her close, his chest to her back, the tension finally easing out of him completely, and she drifted off to sleep.

Twenty-six

⬩⬩⬩

"D AD, REALLY, I don't need to go to the Shrink anymore. I'm fine. You're fine. Miranda's fine." Ariel plastered a big fat smile on her face. "We're all fine, remember?"

Which was far from true, but Ariel was tired of figuring out ways to avoid talking to the Shrink. It was exhausting to come up with new and increasingly inventive ways not to talk about anything that mattered.

Her dad sat at the desk in his study, looking out the window instead of at all sorts of business stuff spread out in front of him. Just sitting. Just looking. So not like her dad.

She felt a flicker of worry. No way her dad could die on her, too, surely.

He turned back and studied her. She studied him right back. Something was definitely different about him, though thankfully as best she could tell, he looked perfectly healthy.

An image of her mom popped into her head, dancing around her dad, laughing. *"What can I do to wipe that scowl away?"*

Her dad would look back at her mom in that way of his, massively intense.

Her dad was scary, but he was really great, too. Like, she remembered that when he got home late from his office, he would come sit on the edge of her mattress even though she pretended to be asleep. He wouldn't say anything; he'd just have a look and then lean down and kiss her forehead. She knew he did the same thing to Miranda. Miranda had told her once. Of course he hadn't sat on the edge of either of their mattresses since their mom had died. As far as she knew, anyway.

"First off, Ariel," he said, "I don't appreciate you calling Dr. Parson the Shrink."

Ariel swallowed back the retort that no amount of lipstick on a pig was going to make that pig anything but. Calling the Shrink Dr. Parson wasn't going to make him less of a quack.

"Second, Dr. Parson said that when you're in his office, you refuse to speak to him."

"I talk."

"About the weather. Or you grill him on his credentials."

"I ask: Does a man who lives and works in the twenty-first century seriously wear a goatee and round tortoise-shell glasses? I have two words for you: Fake Freud."

"Ariel."

"Okay, so maybe I shouldn't judge him based on his Freud facial hair, but come on, he has a black leather sofa. Seriously, Dad, I know everyone says you're a genius, but maybe money smarts don't translate into regular street smarts. I tell you, the guy isn't for real."

Her dad looked amused for a nanosecond before he wiped the humor from his face as fast as good old Wink swiped his big block letters from the dry board at school.

"As much as I appreciate your assessment of my intellect, I assure you that Dr. Parson is for real. And *for real* you have to go tomorrow."

Sure enough, at 3:30 the next afternoon, Ariel found herself on that black sofa.

"Have you ever considered getting one of those Victorian-type couches, or whatever they're called? Chesterfields. I Googled that for you. I think Freud must have had a Chesterfield in his office." Ariel made a production of considering the idea. "Tell me, Dr. Parson, do you think Freud would have had a leather sofa in his office if they'd been available back then? Because, really, I don't think yours is working."

Ariel could have sworn that the guy actually blushed—at least as much as a guy with a beard could blush. No matter how hard she tried, she never managed to flummox her dad. She had to give him that.

"Ariel," Dr. Parson finally stated, "we are here to discuss the unfortunate things that have happened to you, not my furniture choices—"

"Maybe you *should* talk to someone about your unfortunate furn—"

"Ariel." He barked her name before pulling himself together. Ariel's personal diagnosis? The guy was losing it.

He leaned forward. "We've been talking for three months. I've been patient. I've let you discuss whatever you want. I've asked you to write your feelings down in a journal. And I've done this in the hopes that you'd learn to trust me."

She barely held back a snort.

Dr. Parson narrowed his eyes. "Ariel," he said. "There's one question I haven't asked you directly, the one question that matters, the one question that I shouldn't have to ask because you should want to talk to me about it on your own. Since that hasn't happened, tell me: What happened in the car?"

Her heart came to a full-blown stop.

Ariel had to force herself to breathe, air in, air out. She felt the sweat on the palms of her hands. It took a second to drum up a smile.

"I don't know what you're talking about."

"I think you do."

Life had been so simple before. One dad, one mom, one sister—all of them living in a house in Montclair, New Jersey.

"You're only hurting yourself by bottling it up."

He leaned even closer, his elbows on his knees, his tablet and pen set aside.

"Why won't you talk about it, Ariel? Are you protecting someone?"

The words were like a kick to the stomach. She searched for something to say, something sarcastic, something to distract him. But she couldn't find anything. The facts were just facts. Life could change in an instant.

She turned her head and focused on all those degrees framed and lined up on the plain white walls. One frame was slightly off. She had told him several times. Once he had stood up all of a sudden and strode over, straightened it, and then turned back. *"There,"* he had stated.

Ariel had seen that he regretted his show of temper. It was the only time she had liked him. It was the only time she had thought about showing him what was inside her. But then he had come back to his chair, drawn a deep breath, and settled back into his Fake Freud persona.

Now the frame was crooked again.

"I'm not keeping a secret," she said finally. "There's no one to protect."

"Tell me about the accident, Ariel." He hesitated. "Please."

A sigh escaped her lips. "Fine. My mom was driving me to a Mathlete competition in Paramus. I was in the backseat; she was in the front." Her leg betrayed her, swinging too fast and hitting the coffee table. She made it stop. "She was driving really fast on the Garden State Parkway. We were late. We swerved. We wrecked. The car flew over the rail. Mom died. I didn't."

The guy sat there for something like a full minute. Ariel knew, because she was counting, not to see how long it would take before he talked again, but to keep her mind focused on something besides the accident.

Finally he found words again. "How did that make you feel?"

How did it make her feel? How did he think it made her feel?

She glanced at the clock and stood. "Oops, look at that. Time's up."

Startled, the Shrink glanced over at the clock and blinked. "Ariel," he said.

But she was already banging out the door.

Twenty-seven

⬩⬥⬩

FOR THE LAST THREE WEEKS Portia had done little more than cook for The Glass Kitchen. Now she stood in the middle of her apartment, the day's assortment of menu items already sold and out the door, and her head swam with images of cake. But not just any cake: a festive concoction loaded with candles. She closed her eyes and knew she needed to plan a birthday party.

But for whom?

She'd have to make the cake later because she needed to get upstairs to make dinner for the Kanes. When she walked into their kitchen, Miranda and Ariel were sitting at the table. Ariel was pretending to do homework; Miranda was staring at her silent cell phone.

"Hey," Portia said.

"Hey," Ariel replied with little enthusiasm. Miranda just rolled her eyes.

"What's up?"

"Nothing," Miranda snapped.

"She's waiting for the creep . . . I mean, Dustin . . . to call," Ariel explained hastily.

Miranda shot her little sister a glare. "You didn't think he was a creep the other day when you—"

She stopped abruptly, glancing at Portia. Both girls jerked back to what they had been doing.

Miranda looked back down at her cell phone, her jaw set, but a moment later her lips started to tremble. "He's not going to call. He broke up with me. He says I'm not mature enough for him."

Portia sighed. "Boys can be real jerks," she said, leaning her hip against the kitchen counter. "Let me guess: You wouldn't . . . sleep with him, right?"

Ariel gasped.

Miranda scowled. "It wasn't like that."

Portia just waited.

"Okay, maybe it was like that. Don't you dare tell Dad!" She dropped her head to her arms. "I hate New York! I miss New Jersey!"

With a mental sigh, Portia walked over to Miranda and, after only a brief hesitation, stroked her hair. "Oh, sweetie."

Miranda drew a shaky breath. "My mom used to call me that." She started to cry. "It's her birthday today. Or it would have been."

A shiver ran down Portia's spine. The birthday cake. Not for some unknown someone who would show up at the apartment.

Once again, her first instinct was to run, but she sat down and hugged Miranda instead. Ariel looked on with that same expression she'd had when Portia and her sisters were dancing it out. Portia extended her other arm, and Ariel tucked under it like a baby bird. With another sigh, Portia realized she was getting pulled in closer and closer to this family.

"I miss her," Miranda choked out, sobs racking her body.

Ariel didn't say anything. She just squeezed in closer.

"When my sisters and I were your ages," Portia finally said, "our parents died. So I know how awful it is."

"B-b-both of them?" Miranda asked.

"Yep. We went to live with our grandmother." Portia hesitated one last second, then plunged ahead. "And every year on our mom's birthday, we celebrated with a party. What do you say we make a cake and have a birthday party for your mom?"

Miranda sniffled and straightened up. "I guess so."

Ariel peered across from under Portia's arm at her sister. "But what if it makes Dad too sad?"

Miranda's features hardened. "Erasing her is the wrong way to miss her."

That's all it took. Instead of making dinner, Portia showed the girls how to make a birthday cake. And then she let them do it by themselves, trusting that the act of making something for their mother would be healing.

Portia started on party sandwiches, little small square bites of cucumber and cream cheese, smoked turkey with gouda, ham and cheddar nestled inside bread with the crusts cut off while the girls worked together as a pair. When Ariel saw what she was doing, she laughed, the clear, bright laughter of a child rather than the mini adult she so often sounded like. "It's going to be a real party!" Ariel cheered.

The three worked together in a surprising harmony, and soon the cake was done. When Portia finished making the sandwiches and putting them in the refrigerator, she went downstairs and found streamers and an old HAPPY BIRTHDAY sign in Aunt Evie's boxes.

By the time they heard the front door open and close, they had the dining room set with birthday paraphernalia, party sandwiches covering the table, and a cake at the center of it all.

"I smell something good," Gabriel called out when he came in the front door.

Portia held her breath. She had simply followed the knowing without a thought for the consequences.

"What's this?" Gabriel asked as he came around the corner. He took in the balloons and the banner. "Whose birthday is it?"

No one spoke. Portia watched as understanding dawned, and she went cold. The hard planes of Gabriel's face crumpled, sharp edges going weak.

He didn't look like he was on the verge of crying. It was more that some aching part of his soul had escaped the carefully controlled façade.

Miranda must have been watching his face, too, because when she spoke her voice was harsh. "It's a birthday party. For Mom."

Gabriel couldn't seem to find words, but he looked every inch a wounded beast.

"All you want to do is forget her!" Miranda accused him when he didn't say anything. "You want us to forget her! You made us come to this awful place and be with these awful people who break up with us and don't like us and tell us we don't fit in—all because you don't want to think about Mom. Well, guess what, *we* loved her! We miss her!"

"Miranda, that's enough," Gabriel said, the words catching in his throat.

"No, it's not! I hate you! I hate you for moving us here!" She bolted from the room, her steps rapping a staccato beat up the stairs.

Ariel's small face looked so thin and fragile that Portia was shocked. The girl was obviously taking in everyone's pain, with no idea what to do about it.

"I'm sorry if we hurt you with the party," Ariel choked out, and ran from the room before Gabriel could speak.

He looked at Portia. The hard planes were back in place. "What in the hell is going on?"

Portia took a deep breath. "The girls were upset when I got here. Miranda's boyfriend broke up with her."

He narrowed his eyes at the boyfriend mention.

"But the real problem, Gabriel, is that they feel they can't talk about their mother."

"I'm paying a fortune to a shrink so they have someone to talk to!"

"They need to talk to you."

He plowed his hands through his hair. "So you got it in your head to throw a party for a dead woman."

"Exactly," Portia shot back. "My grandmother did the same thing for me and my sisters after our mother died. It made us feel as if she was still with us, somehow."

He strode to the table and stared at the cake.

"Of course you miss her, Gabriel, but your daughters are still here. They need to celebrate their mother. If they're at all like me, they're terrified that they'll forget her, that at some point a whole day will pass and they won't even remember it was her birthday." Idiotically, tears pricked Portia's eyes.

Gabriel turned to leave, but stopped at the door, his back to her. "Things are fine, Portia. Just leave it alone."

Her mouth dropped open when he left. "Things aren't fine," she called after him. "You're smart enough to know that."

He disappeared up the stairs without replying. Stunned, Portia stared after him. Was he going to leave it at that?

She had promised herself that she wouldn't get involved, wouldn't open herself up to this family. While she had opened herself to the knowing, she had promised herself that she wouldn't use the knowing with Gabriel and the girls. Look what had happened when she had. She'd made a cake for the man's dead wife, wrecking all three of them.

Go back downstairs, she told herself.

Instead, she followed Gabriel, taking the stairs two at a time up to the office level. He wasn't there, so she kept going, hearing noise from the floor above. She tiptoed up the last flight and stopped in the doorway of a room that she had barely noticed the night they had gone to the roof. She saw now that it was being used for storage. There was an old bike and boxes, though there was also a sound system and television, even though there were no sofas or chairs.

Gabriel stood inside a closet, pulling a box that seemed to have been hidden in the very back on a high shelf. He strode over and set it down with a thump, wrenched off the top, and pulled out several framed photographs.

Something aching and painful twisted inside her: jealousy. Every time

Gabriel came into her arms, she conveniently forgot about his wife. But watching Gabriel stare at the photos of the woman, she had a blinding reminder of why she had told herself to stay away from this man. She started to turn away.

"I'm selfish."

His voice stopped her.

"You asked weeks ago why I didn't have photos out, why I wasn't keeping the memory of my wife alive for the girls. Miranda's right. I didn't want to remember."

Portia's heart twisted a little more. "You loved her, and now she's gone," she said, her voice coming out a near whisper. "It's okay to want to avoid the pain."

He hesitated. "It's not that." He ran his hands over his face. "How am I supposed to know what's right or wrong? For the girls? They don't come with an instruction manual."

Portia gave him a faint smile. "You just have to keep trying. That's all they want."

He swallowed, nodded at her. "Get the girls, will you? I have an idea."

Portia found Miranda lying on her bed, curled on her side, eyes squeezed shut, earbuds in her ears. Portia knocked, then knocked more loudly, but there was no answer. With no help for it, Portia walked through the open door and sat on the bed. In for a penny, in for a pound. "Hey, kiddo."

Miranda rolled her eyes. "Who calls people 'kiddo'?" Her voice rasped a little from all the tears.

Portia knew Miranda was lashing out because she was hurting. "Your dad wants you and Ariel to go upstairs."

"What's he going to do, lock us in the attic?"

"Oh, honey, he's figuring things out as he goes. He's bound to make some mistakes along the way."

The girl snorted. "You think?"

"He's trying right now. Give him a chance."

"What? You're telling me that he's planning to sing Happy Birthday? Dive into the cake?" But Miranda sat up and scooted off the bed.

Portia didn't have the faintest idea what Gabriel had in mind, so she just said, "Let's get Ariel."

They walked down the hall. Ariel's bedroom was empty.

"Where is she?" Portia asked, frowning.

Miranda gave her a funny look, walked into the room, and knocked on the closet. "Hey, A, you in there?"

"No," came the muffled reply.

Miranda pulled open the door. Portia could just make out Ariel sitting cross-legged in the corner, writing in a journal.

"What part of *no* didn't you understand?" she snapped.

"The part where Dad doesn't take *no* for an answer when he wants us upstairs."

Ariel scowled.

"Supposedly, he sent Portia down for us," Miranda added.

Ariel glanced between Miranda and Portia, then closed the journal and started to put it away, only to stop. "Turn around," she instructed them.

Once the book was hidden, Portia, Miranda, and Ariel headed up the stairs to the top floor and found Gabriel standing in front of a television set.

Miranda glared at him, not making it easy.

"I thought we could watch some DVDs."

"You made us come up here to watch TV?" Miranda demanded.

Gabriel didn't let the sarcasm deter him. "Not TV. Home movies. Ones of you girls and . . . Mom."

Ariel flew forward. Miranda just stayed by Portia in the doorway, visibly tense.

Gabriel looked at her. "There's that great one of you and Mom dressed in matching clothes for Easter."

Miranda bit her lip, and then came forward reluctantly. As she got close, Gabriel pulled her into a hug and then pulled Ariel in with them. "I'm sorry," he said.

Portia felt tears backing up in her throat. She began to turn away.

"Where're you going?" Gabriel blurted.

"It's time for me to get home," Portia said, summoning a smile.

"No!" Gabriel and Ariel said. Even Miranda gave Portia a half smile. Ariel raced over and pulled her into the room.

In addition to the DVDs, Gabriel had gotten four slices of cake and a tray full of the party sandwiches. The four of them sank down onto the floor to eat and watch.

Victoria Kane had been a beauty. Dark hair, deep blue eyes, and the sort of rosebud mouth that made men go wild. She seemed about twenty-five in the first DVD. She danced for the camera and winked before pulling Gabriel close and kissing him. The kiss was deeply intimate, like a movie kiss between two characters in love. Portia had to swallow hard.

But both girls were smiling. "Mom was beautiful," Miranda breathed.

Gabriel took a deep breath as he stared at the screen.

They watched Miranda's third birthday, an elegant Christmas party, and Ariel's sixth birthday before they were finally done. At the end, Ariel threw her arms around her dad's neck, and he hugged her fiercely. Miranda conceded a nod, and he nodded back, though Portia could see that he wanted more.

The girls trooped downstairs to go to bed. Gabriel sat quietly, staring without seeing. Portia went over and slipped down next to him on the floor, their backs against the wall.

"That was a lovely thing to do for the girls. But obviously painful for you."

"Painful?"

"It's not just the girls who are grieving," Portia said, stumbling over what to say. "You have to remember that you're in pain, too. I could see how much you loved her."

Gabriel reached over and took Portia's hand, running his thumb over her knuckles. Then he said, in an absolutely even tone, "I never loved her at all."

She barely understood the words. "What?"

He heaved a sigh, dropping his head back against the wall. "We never should have married. She loved partying, just like Anthony. We wouldn't have gotten married, but she got pregnant."

Portia was stunned. Gabriel didn't seem like the kind of man who got anyone pregnant by accident. "So you married her?"

"I figured I wouldn't be the greatest father, but I couldn't allow a child of mine to be raised by a woman who liked partying as much as Victoria did. The only way I could make sure that my child was taken care of was if I married the mother." He sat quietly for a moment, then added, "Victoria wasn't very maternal, but she did her best. And she loved the girls. You can see that."

Portia leaned her head on his shoulder. Gabriel had intrigued her, maddened her, filled her with desire. But now all that swirled together into something stronger. She thought of how he had handled Cordelia's confession. How he struggled to be a good father. "You're a good man, Gabriel Kane."

There was a long pause. "Tell that to Miranda."

"She'll come around."

He sighed, then stood, taking her hand and drawing her to her feet. "Will she?"

He looked exhausted and ravaged, as if his young daughters could bring him down in a way that multinational conglomerates couldn't. He might have been ruthless when it came to business, but this man was anything but when it came to Miranda and Ariel. This man loved his girls, but he didn't know the first thing about how to manage his way through their lives.

Portia reached up and wrapped her arms around him. He leaned over, pulling her into him, burying his face in the crook of her neck. Seconds ticked by before she felt his body ease.

"Thank you," he whispered into her hair. "Thank you for tonight."

Finally, he let her go, and together they cleaned up the mess. Downstairs in his kitchen, they worked like two cogs in a wheel. When they finished up in there, she realized that finger sandwiches and cake couldn't possibly be enough for him to eat.

"Sit," she told him softly, gently pulling him over to the table. When he tried to pull her to him, take control, she spun away.

He watched her with greedy eyes, greedy for her, greedy for the food, as she made an omelet gooey with melted cheese, bacon on the side, along with thick slices of homemade bread slathered in butter and jam. It was the kind of meal her mother used to make for Daddy when he came home late and exhausted from one of the manual jobs he had managed to drum up. Food that comforted as much as it sustained.

Portia set the plate in front of Gabriel. He looked from the food to her, something deep and nearly overwhelming in his eyes.

"Thank you," he whispered to her again.

When he picked up the fork and took a bite, she knew that the emotion in his face was about a great deal more than how delicious it tasted. And she realized then that with his mother, his brother, and even his wife, this was a man who had always taken care of everyone else. No one had ever taken care of him.

She remembered the way he had taken her the night before, holding her down, kissing her so intimately. She had expected to feel awkward afterward. Instead, she felt only a flare of slow carnal desire at the memory. And rightness.

She realized something that had been there for a while, but she had been reluctant to admit it, even to herself. She wanted more from him than a secret love affair.

At the thought, she sucked in her breath when images of food hit her. The fried chicken, the sweet jalapeño mustard—the same images that had hit her the first time when he walked toward her on the sidewalk, then again after the first time they made love. Gabriel's Meal.

Every day it had shimmered just beyond her thoughts, like a heavy pan of sauce simmering on a back burner. The more they made love, she realized, the stronger the image of the meal became. That was what she had been trying so hard not to think about.

Was it a gift? Or a warning? Good news or bad?

She didn't know.

But if she wanted more from him, more for them, then she would have to find out. She would have to make Gabriel's Meal.

Twenty-eight

❖

L IFE, ARIEL KNEW, often made no sense, a fact that could make even
a smart girl want to trade in her brain for an obsession with acne
cures and makeup tips. Almost.

Life didn't hand out easy equations with perfect answers. Instead, there
were things like one minute your mom was there, and the next she was
gone. One minute your sister was awful, and the next she was nice. But
how long before Miranda turned mean again?

The second Ariel figured her dad was asleep, she snuck back upstairs
and retrieved the DVDs. Back inside her room, she curled up in her closet
and popped one of the discs into her laptop, fast-forwarding to all the
scenes with her mom.

There were days when she could hardly remember what her mom looked
like—at least, how Mom looked before the accident. What she mostly
remembered was the way Mom looked in the car.

Ariel's stomach hurt at the memory, which never did anyone any
good. What's more, a real shrink should have gotten that. Shouldn't he

know that talking about the accident was massively screwed up and to-tally a waste of time?

Of course, in all her trying to convince her dad that the guy was a quack, she couldn't talk about the accident because she had zero interest in letting him or anyone else know that she had to watch her mom die in the car. If Dad knew she had been conscious while it happened, he'd have her locked up for good, figuring she was about to go all *Girl, Inter-rupted* or something. So she kept quiet. Besides, it would just make him feel worse. That was something she'd figured out since the accident: Why say the stuff that hurt other people? No point.

Sitting in the closet, Ariel started to fall asleep to footage of her own birthday party the year before. But she jolted fully awake when she heard a crash in the entry hall. Sharp voices sounded, com-ing all the way up the stairs and into her closet. Miranda and her dad.

Ariel focused on the computer screen. "Everything is fine," she whis-pered, tracing the lines of her mother's image as she brought a store-bought cake from the kitchen, birthday candles flickering.

But her father's voice boomed, making it hard to stay focused on the screen. "Where the hell do you think you're going, young lady?"

"Out, Dad. I'm going out!"

"Like hell you are!"

Miranda sounded as angry as their father, the truce from earlier swept away like store-bought or even homemade cake scraped from a plate into the trash.

Ariel started to hum. She found another DVD, one they hadn't watched, and popped it in the computer. She could ignore the fight if she tried hard enough. She would pretend that everything was fine.

She clicked on play and Mom and Miranda flared to life, laughing as they chased each other around the den. Mom was dressed up in a tight red dress that stopped just above her knees, her hair teased and puffy, and her lips painted a darker shade of red. Ariel's own voice from behind the camera asked where she was going.

Her mom laughed. *"Where am I going?"* She made a big production of considering the question. *"A book party, darling. Yes, one of those book groups where people talk about characters who are happy and lead exciting lives."*

"Is Dad going, too?" Ariel heard herself ask.

For a second, her mom's smile tightened. *"Dad is busy."*

Mom had put makeup on Miranda, who was in seventh grade back then, and her sister strutted into the frame, primping for the camera. *"I'm fabulous,"* she cooed into the lens. *"Simply fabulous."*

Ariel heard herself snort in the background.

Miranda stuck out her tongue and twirled away.

Pulling the computer closer, Ariel focused on the screen, remembering the details of their old house. The dark hardwood floors, the huge rugs, the fancy furniture. Her mother had liked fancy. Her dad never had.

"All you have to do is pay for it, Gabriel. It's not like you live in it all that much."

The memory leaped out from somewhere, jarring Ariel back into watching the DVD. Their old doorbell rang and Ariel watched her mother's expression change, her laughter gone as she smoothed her dress.

"How do I look, sweetie?"

"Perfect," Ariel heard herself say.

In the background of the spinning footage, Miranda raced to the door while her mother stood, waiting.

"Turn that thing off, A."

But she hadn't, and Mom had forgotten she was there. Miranda ran back into the room, excited, and suddenly Ariel remembered what had happened next.

Her heart started to pound as Uncle Anthony walked onto the screen, dressed in a sports jacket, blue shirt, and jeans. He stopped when he saw her mom, smiling at her.

"Anthony!" her mother cried.

Then the footage snapped off. She could remember hitting the power button and going over to say hi.

Uncle Anthony had come in and out of their lives for as long as she could remember. And for as long as she could remember, he made her mom smile and made her dad really mad.

The difficult thing about life was that once you learned things, you couldn't unlearn them. Like remembering her uncle walking into their house in Montclair. Her uncle loving her mom first, before her dad came along. The date of her parents' marriage and Miranda's birthday. It was like her parents had done everything they could to hide the date they got married. Ugh. Her heart thumped in a way that made the back of her eyes hurt and her throat swell.

Suddenly, she heard Miranda flying up the stairs.

"Your acting out stops now, do you hear me?" Dad roared, his voice thrumming through the walls as he followed after her.

"Up yours!" Miranda shrieked back.

"You do not sneak out of this house," he ground out.

Ariel shut the laptop and pressed her hands to her ears.

"No, no, no," she whispered. Whispering *no* never did any good, but she did it anyway. Same as she had in the car, lying there with her mom.

The memory made her get to her feet, unsteady at first, before she threw open the door. This time she wasn't locked down by a seat belt and crumpled metal. This time she could do something. Help, maybe.

She opened the door to her bedroom just in time to see Dad walk by, gripping Miranda by the arm, propelling her toward her bedroom. For a second, she barely recognized her sister. Miranda wore a tight dress that she definitely didn't buy with Dad in tow, and she held a pair of those super-high heels. The five-inch ones that Miranda would never have been able to walk in. Not that she was going to get a chance to try since Ariel was pretty sure their dad would kill her first. Or lock her away until she was twenty-one.

"You can't do this! My friends are waiting for me! It's hard enough to make friends around here without you making it impossible!" Miranda screamed.

Not that Dad listened. He forced Miranda to her room. "What kind of friends are you meeting?" he demanded. "Dressed like that?"

Ariel backed up and closed her door, then ran over to her window that led out to the fire escape. When she pulled it open, cool air struck her face, bringing the sound of the city with it. Ariel clenched her teeth as she stepped out onto the thin metal landing. She hated heights, hated the fire escape, had loved it when her dad had forbidden both her and Miranda from going anywhere near the fire escape. In her nearly thirteen years, Ariel had never completely defied her father. She had left that to Miranda. But the only way she knew how to help was to distract her dad from how mad he was at Miranda. She would make him mad at her.

Clasping her fingers tightly around the railing, ignoring the fear that the metal would disintegrate under her feet, letting her crash into the garden below, making her disappear, Ariel crawled over to her sister's window. By then, her dad stood inside Miranda's room lecturing, Miranda screaming back.

Just then the wind gusted and the fire escape swayed, the metal groaning in protest. Ariel's stomach heaved, and she realized she was acting like an idiot. She leaped up, but her sneaker caught in the metal grating and she fell against her sister's window.

Faster than she would have thought possible, her dad was across the room. He had never been pretty, not like Uncle Anthony. But now the look on his face was terrifying. For one thing, he didn't recognize her at first. The minute he did, he wrenched open the window and hauled her inside.

"Oops," she managed, a smile faltering on her lips. "I guess I'm in trouble now."

Ariel watched the gears in his head churn, emotion flashing across his face. Miranda was staring at her like she was crazy. Which she probably was.

"Go to your room, Ariel," her father said. The words seemed to stick in his throat.

"You know how you always think I should talk?" she said instead. "Well, guess what, I'm ready."

"Go to your room!" he shouted.

He didn't wait for her to leave. He turned around and went down the stairs without another word.

Ariel stood frozen, hoping he wouldn't leave the house, leave them. Instead, he slammed the door of his study.

"Are you crazy?" Miranda hissed.

Ariel forced a smile she didn't feel. "Me? Nah?"

"You did that on purpose."

"Get caught on the fire escape on purpose? Now *you're* crazy."

Miranda looked at her, and suddenly Ariel couldn't stop herself. "Mir?"

"What?"

"Couldn't you be a little bit nicer to Dad?"

Miranda's lips pursed. "Why would I do that? Dad's an ass."

"So—so he doesn't get, like, so mad that he leaves us," Ariel whispered. "He could just hire someone to deal with us, you know, and go back to work all the time."

For a second, Miranda looked shocked. Then the hardness returned. "No. I cannot be one bit nicer to Dad, and frankly, if he hired someone to be here with us, all the better. My friends talk all the time how they just have to pay their nannies or help or whoever twenty bucks every time they want to sneak out." She flopped on her bed, grabbed a pillow, and hugged it tight. "I'm going to pray he hires someone. Anyone's better than him."

Ariel bolted out of the room before Miranda could say another hateful word. She didn't know how to explain that while Miranda might not be a perfect sister, and their family was massively broken, they were all she had left. It was like a punch in the gut to think that Miranda didn't care one bit what happened to what was left of their sorry family.

❖

Ariel waited an hour past the Vesuvius blowup before she tiptoed downstairs. She was starving. Drama did that. If this family stuff didn't get
fixed soon she'd probably get as fat as a beach ball. Whatever, she told
herself. Again.

She had pretty much repeated that word over and over in the last
hour. Wasn't there some sort of three-strikes rule? Crawling out onto the
fire escape was her first offense. Two more to go before her dad did something like send her off to boarding school.

After eating a sandwich, she saw a dim light coming from her dad's
study, so she peeked inside. At first she didn't understand what he was
doing. He was sort of lying in his big leather chair, the one with oversized
padded arms. Sound asleep. She couldn't remember a time when she'd
seen her dad sleeping. Lying there, he looked almost peaceful.

It was a strange thought, and Ariel felt stupid tears well up. She, the
non-crier.

Just like with the fire escape, before she could think better of it, she
slid carefully down into the big chair right next to him. They used to sit
that way sometimes, back when he would read aloud to her. She was still
skinny, so she fit next to him, like a cork in a bottle. He didn't wake up.

"Sorry I climbed the fire escape," she whispered.

He didn't move.

He had one of those clocks that actually ticked, and Ariel's eyelids
started to get heavy. She wondered if the Shrink had told her dad about
their last session. If he had, her dad hadn't mentioned it.

Just as her eyelids were fluttering closed, she whispered, "What would
you do if I told you why I was really in the car with Mom? Why we were
going so fast?"

He didn't answer, his breathing still deep.

Ariel didn't remember drifting off, but when she woke the next morning she was tucked into her bed.

Twenty-nine

⬥

NOT EVEN A MONTH after Portia and her sisters opened the doors, so to speak, word of mouth about The Glass Kitchen rippled through New York City like a YouTube video going viral. Sure, the food was great, but it didn't hurt that Portia was able to provide everyone who came to her door with just what they needed, and Cordelia made sure they knew it. It also didn't hurt that Olivia was a natural with social media on the Internet. The Cuthcart sisters had become a perfect team.

But what Portia was really thinking about was that it had been two days since she had made Gabriel the plate of eggs and realized she wanted more from him. But as it happened, since that realization he hadn't come down the fire escape once. He hadn't so much as stopped by. It was odd, not to mention disconcerting, since she'd been trying to drum up the nerve to make the Gabriel Meal.

She was on the verge of finding some schoolgirl way to run into him when he walked through her front door.

Her heart squeezed with a mix of disappointment and relief when he didn't rush toward her with a kiss. Not that he was the rush-toward-her sort. But still.

Instead, he had that dangerous look of his, and his greeting consisted of precisely seven words. "You are not meeting with Richard Zaslow."

Portia stiffened. "How do you know I'm meeting with Richard Zaslow?"

"Did you really think I wouldn't hear about it?"

Portia's eyes narrowed.

"Don't get that look," he said, his expression guarded. "He's not for you."

"Not for me? He has billions of dollars, is famous for turning food businesses into huge successes, and he called us. How's that not for me?"

"Let me guess. He called you after he saw the photo in *The New York Observer*."

"So?"

"The three of you looked great, kind of like Charlie's Angels in aprons. Richard likes women. And he's especially good at making things happen for business owners he sleeps with."

Portia gasped. "I don't believe for a second he was sleeping with Bartalow Bing when he turned him into the Fat Chef."

"Bing was an exception."

"I think his ex-wife is the exception." Everybody knew the story of how struggling cookie baker Rachel Turnbell met Richard Zaslow. Pretty soon they were rumored to be sleeping together, then they married, and all the while he poured millions into making her business a success. Not long after she was dubbed the Cookie Queen, Rachel had filed for divorce, but not before her business had started selling about 35 percent of all cookies sold nationwide. "My guess is he learned his lesson about mixing business with pleasure."

She finished setting out the day's fare with a little more energy than was needed. *Bang!* went the brussels sprouts and pancetta. *Slap!* went the flour tortillas next to the fajita meat.

He came up next to her and turned her back to him, his hands surprisingly gentle. "Look at me, Portia."

Reluctantly, she did.

"He's not for you."

"Really?" Portia sliced him a wry expression, stepping away. "Do you have someone better in mind? Are *you* offering up the money?"

She had tossed out the words without thinking, but he looked at her long and hard.

She held up her hand. "Don't bother answering with that 'Restaurants in New York City have an eighty percent failure rate.'"

He still stared at her.

The doorbell buzzed. Gabriel went to the door before Portia could. "Dick," he stated, pulling open the door.

Richard Zaslow looked surprised. "Gabriel, what are you doing here?"

"Actually, I'm here trying to convince Portia that you're not a great investor match for her."

"Gabriel!"

Both men looked at her, and then Gabriel swung back to Richard. Richard gave Gabriel an appraising grin that Portia didn't like one bit. She realized belatedly that these two men were friends.

"She has you by the short hairs, doesn't she?" Richard said.

Gabriel grunted, not so much a threat as a primal acknowledgment between two men who were man enough to admit how things really were.

Richard slapped Gabriel on the back. "Good luck with that," he said, then turned to Portia. "Take him for everything he's worth," he teased, then left.

Portia's mouth fell open. "What was that all about?"

Gabriel looked dangerously pleased, a full-watt smile that made Portia want to laugh despite the fact that she was furious.

"I guess he wasn't all that interested," Gabriel said with an innocent shrug.

Portia's answer involved the kind of profanity that would have made her ex-husband faint. But not Gabriel. He grinned at her, and then hooked his arm around her waist and pulled her to him, kissing her in that way that made her knees weak.

⁎

That night he came to her with no words, just strode up behind her as she sat brushing her hair at her great-aunt's vanity. He took the brush and began slowly pulling the bristles through her thick hair. It had grown out and bore no resemblance to a blown-out pageboy perfectly contained by a velvet headband.

Their eyes held in the mirror.

"I'm giving you the money," he said softly.

She blinked, then stared back at him.

"I'll take care of you. You don't need to worry about money anymore."

Portia jerked around to face him. "What are you talking about?"

"You want to open a Glass Kitchen. I'll provide the money." To prove his point, he pulled a check from his pocket.

She gasped at the amount, followed by a slow burn starting under her breastbone.

"You can stop wearing your aunt's castoffs—"

She cut him off. "Are you giving me this money because you believe in The Glass Kitchen?"

He stared at her. "Does it matter why I'm giving it to you?"

"Of course it does! I don't want you giving me money just because you're sleeping with me!"

Gabriel's expression darkened. "This has nothing to do with us sleeping together. You need money. I have money. And before you rip up that check, if I were you, I'd ask your sisters what they think of the offer. I'm not so sure they'd be as quick to turn my money away."

She ground her teeth. She knew he was right, but still. He believed she would fail. Could she take money from a man who didn't believe in her? Part of her cheered with a resounding *yes*. But another part of her, this newer part that was trying hard to prove she could make it on her own merit, cringed.

Finding an investor who genuinely believed in The Glass Kitchen held more meaning to her than simply being provided with the money. It was symbolic. Gaining an impartial investor would prove that someone truly believed in what she was doing. Finding an impartial investor struck her as a powerful step toward proving that she wasn't dependent on a man in her life. Her husband had supported her, given her a home, provided her with a life. But the minute he got tired of her and wanted to move on, all of that had been swept from underneath her like feet giving way under a wave.

She felt her chin set.

His eyes narrowed, but there was a glint of laughter in them, too. "Stubborn females will be the death of me."

❖

During the next week, despite Gabriel's frustration at her refusal to deposit his check, Portia cooked and baked for potential investors. Every night when she was alone, she pulled the check out of The Glass Kitchen cookbook, where she had hidden it. With each day that passed, her bank balance ticked lower, and she knew she couldn't afford not to take his money. But every night she ended up tucking the check back into the book.

Cordelia set the table again and again with the pitted silverware and stoneware dishes. Olivia arranged everything until the setting was a worthy tableaux for an elegant country-style magazine. Portia fed them food that made them melt, made them happy. And then it began to happen. The food began to work. By the end of the week they had offers from four different investor groups, as if the food combined with Gabriel's check in the cookbook had worked like a magician conjuring up a rabbit in a hat.

Cordelia, Olivia, and Portia sat around the table on Friday evening going over each offer, as stunned as they were thrilled.

"Can you believe it?" Olivia laughed.

"I'm amazed," Portia said.

"I am not," Cordelia said, shaking her head. "I've said it all along. In this age of cooking madness, who wouldn't want to invest in three sisters from Texas cooking food to die for?"

Portia's mind froze, memories of her grandmother springing to her mind. The storm. The meal of pulled pork and the lightning.

Cordelia reached across the table. "Sorry, sweetie. I wasn't thinking."

Olivia jumped up from her seat. "Let's celebrate!"

After no more than one circle around the living room to Toby Keith, Ariel must have heard and poked her head in the door, dancing her way inside without waiting for an invitation.

Two songs in, Olivia headed back to the kitchen. "This calls for margaritas!" She glanced at Ariel. "And a virgin margarita for the kid."

Cordelia went in search of chips. Portia made a batch of fresh guacamole. Ariel threw herself onto a stool, grinning madly.

"You guys are the weirdest adults ever. You know that, right?" She took a sip of the sweet drink. "So what are you celebrating?"

"Great investor meetings, and"—Olivia dragged out the word—"a newspaper interview with *The New York Post* coming up!"

"That's good, huh?"

"It's fabulous," Cordelia confirmed.

"Dad'll be happy, too."

"No need to tell your dad," Portia said instantly.

"But he'll want to know!"

"Of course, he will. But could I surprise him?" Portia wanted to tell him herself. Return his check. She felt certain that he would grumble at her, but that deep down he would be proud of her.

She also hoped that it would be the beginning of a shift between them. If she felt she was making her life work, she could breathe again, she could believe things were supposed to work out. She could make Gabriel's Meal without fear.

Ariel blinked, but then she nodded. "Okay, you tell him." She glanced at the clock. "I've got to go."

Portia, Cordelia, and Olivia lifted their glasses as she left. "To The Glass Kitchen!"

"To three sexy sisters in New York City!" Olivia cheered.

Cordelia made a face. "You'll have to carry that flag by yourself. I'm too old, and Portia hasn't had sex in months."

Portia choked on her margarita.

Cordelia and Olivia stopped and studied her. "Portia?" they said in unison.

"What?" She tried to look nonchalant. Innocent.

"Hell," Olivia snapped. "Who are you sleeping with?"

"No one!"

"Liar! You're blushing!"

"Stop!"

"We are not stopping," Cordelia persisted. "Who in the world are you having sex with?" She blinked in confusion. "One of the investors?"

"Of course not!" Portia exclaimed.

Olivia laughed as she sat back. "Then who?"

"That's private."

Olivia raised a brow, glanced at Cordelia, then back. "How very un-Portia like. Our little sister has a secret lover."

But when Portia looked closer, she was sure Olivia knew just who that secret lover really was.

Fifth Course

✥

The Entrée

Fried Chicken with
Sweet Jalapeño Mustard

Thirty

⬧⬧⬧

PORTIA'S LIFE WAS falling into place. The money was coming in for The Glass Kitchen. The sisters were working together in a way that gave her hope that it was a good idea. And she wanted to believe there could be more between her and Gabriel Kane.

Which meant she couldn't put off making Gabriel's Meal any longer.

She remembered her grandmother's meal. She remembered what turned out to be Cordelia's meal, which she'd had to make when she woke up with the knowing after moving to Manhattan. Both had foretold bad news.

But there had been good meals, too, she reminded herself. Meals that had saved her sisters. Meals that had helped people since she had been cooking these last several weeks. Though, really, each of those instances had been the result of single items. A pie. A pot of French stew. A soup. A bag of spicy chocolates.

A tremor of nerves raced along her skin. Entire meals coming to mind had been few and far between.

She wrote out the menu she had seen in her head. Fried chicken,

sweet jalapeño mustard, mashed potatoes, slaw, biscuits, and pie—
strawberry pie with fresh whipped cream piled high. Her hands shook
as she started to prepare. Once she opened the floodgates to the meal, a
relentless, nearly strangling need filled her.

What scared her most was the pie. It was her grandmother's decadent
concoction—a definite sign. But, again, of what?

Next, Portia started a list—not of ingredients, but of people whom
she felt certain she needed to invite. Powering up her computer, she composed a short e-mail.

> Dear Friends and Family,
>   I'm preparing a meal tonight at 7:30. No need to bring
> anything. I hope you all can join me. Love, Portia

Just that.

She sent the e-mail to Cordelia, Olivia, Gabriel, Miranda, and Ariel.
However reluctant she was, she also knew she had to send it to Gabriel's
mother and brother.

The last two guests made her the most nervous. Why would she need
to invite them? Was this meal a way to start building a connection between Gabriel's family and hers? Or proof that there was too much distance between their two worlds to cross?

As she always did, Portia went to Fairway to pick up the ingredients
she didn't have. The chicken, the cabbage, the potatoes. Milk and butter.

The strawberry pie again gave her pause; strawberries weren't in season. Was she setting out to fail before she ever got started? But then she
remembered she was in New York City, a place where anything could be
found at any time. Strawberries were in season somewhere, and they made
their way without fail to the city that had everything.

As soon as Portia returned home, she got to work. She didn't check
the answering machine. She didn't check e-mail for responses. If she had
learned anything about the knowing, it was that whatever was to come

was beyond her control. Guests would come or not. Once the invitation was issued, nothing she could say would make a difference.

Before she started cooking, she raced out and got flowers, though her instinct to buy freesia, delphinium, and hydrangea didn't offer any insight to what was coming.

She took great care in setting the table, pulling two smaller tables together in the living room. She added an antique linen tablecloth that had belonged to her aunt, candles, and the flowers in the center. By the time she had shopped and done the prep work, she had only three hours before the guests were due to arrive. The apartment was ready.

Now for the food.

The sense of peace came first. A smile broke out on her face, and she even laughed. She felt better and better by the minute.

First, the chicken, filling a brown paper bag with flour and seasoning. Then the potatoes, peeling and cutting, putting them on to boil. The apartment grew hot, and she wiped her hands on her apron, then raced into the living room to open the back French doors.

She mixed up the biscuit dough and set it aside in one of Evie's old mixing bowls. The pie came next. She cut up brilliant red strawberries and sugared them, a feather-light crust, whipped the cream, and put it in the refrigerator. She would have to fry the chicken after she bathed, but that couldn't be helped if she wanted the crispy outside to be perfect.

Then she took a bath, soaking in lavender, and dressed with care. A crisp white cotton blouse and floral skirt, with low heels. At the last minute, she found a pair of old pearls that had been Evie's. "This is the right thing to do," she told her reflection.

By the time she returned to the kitchen, she had only thirty minutes left. She mashed the potatoes, mixing in more butter than was good for a person.

Her front door opened, startling her. How had the time gone so fast?

"What's going on?" Olivia called out.

Her sister wore workout clothes, hair pulled back in a messy ponytail.

She took one look at Portia and stopped in her tracks. "Really, what's going on? Nice clothes. Your hair. And you're wearing makeup." She narrowed her eyes. "Your e-mail only said dinner. Who all is coming?"

The bell rang, and Cordelia walked in, dressed in a casual way that wasn't Cordelia at all.

"Why didn't you answer my e-mail?" Cordelia said. Then, like Olivia, she took in Portia's attire. "What's going on?"

Cordelia glanced back into the living room and saw the table settings. The two older sisters exchanged a wary glance.

"You had to make a meal," Olivia said, her voice hard.

"I hate this!" Cordelia said.

Olivia scoffed. "How is it possible that you, who pushed Portia back into the knowing, are acting like this is a surprise? You know the weird meals you get with the knowing. It's not her fault."

"Look at me!" Cordelia exclaimed, gesturing to her clothes. "Based on that table, this is a dinner for more than just the three of us. I look like a bag lady." She glared at Portia. "Why didn't you warn me?"

"You should have known," Olivia said. "The e-mail said 'Dear Friends and Family.' When was the last time Portia had us over for dinner with that kind of an invitation? I should have known."

Portia's smile flatlined, her heart leaping into her throat.

The bell rang again and Ariel burst in. "Miranda can't come. She got Dad to let her stay with a friend."

More bad news. Miranda was supposed to be there.

Ariel didn't look any happier than Portia felt. But before Portia could ask about Miranda, the smell of burning potatoes hit her.

"Oh, no!"

She was barely aware that Helen Kane and Anthony were at the door before she dashed into the kitchen. She couldn't think of anything right then, other than saving the meal.

Thirty-one

❖

ARIEL SLIPPED OUT of Portia's living room, escaping the suddenly crowded apartment, the smell of weird, burned potatoes stinging her nose. She snuck out the back door, then up three brick steps leading to the town house's garden. She curled up in an oversized sweater she'd found up on the storage floor, one that must have been her dad's. She tucked herself out of sight, huddling against the growing cold, her thick wool, multicolored socks with toes shoved into a wild pair of boots that she had been certain Portia would love. Except Portia had been too worried about her cooking to notice.

She tucked her chin against her knees. She was starting to feel as if she was really losing it. Sure, she had beaten back the Shrink's questions and not spilled her guts. But it didn't mean she'd stopped *thinking*. In fact, she couldn't stop thinking, and all her thoughts were weird. Like why was her sister being so awful.

"Miranda," she said to the empty garden, "why can't you just give Dad a break?"

Like that would work. Miranda would just slam the bedroom door in her face.

Plus, she didn't even feel like talking to Miranda, because she felt a little guilty about reading her journal. Which she was now mostly doing to learn anything she could about her family. The problem with that was that every time she dug Miranda's diary out from underneath the mattress, she found out that her sister was getting deeper and deeper into trouble. Miranda was determined to be friends with the popular kids, and that meant doing whatever the creep Dustin wanted her to do. But it wasn't as if Ariel could *do* anything with that information. She wasn't a snitch. She wasn't a spy.

But, seriously, how was it possible Miranda could be so stupid?

Voices coming from inside Portia's apartment caught her attention.

"Mother, just tell Gabriel to give me the money!"

"What, so you can leave?"

Ariel peeked back in through the door and saw her uncle and grandmother standing not two feet inside the living room. No one else was in sight. The sisters had have been in the kitchen. Ugh. The last person Ariel wanted to talk to was her uncle, but still, her grandmother's question made her curious. Uncle Anthony wanted to leave? Already?

"You've been gone for over a year, Anthony. Why can't you stay and get a job here in the city?"

"I don't need my mother or brother to take care of me, or make decisions for me. I'm a grown man!"

"Then act like one!"

Ariel couldn't see Uncle Anthony's face because his back was to her, but he must have been really mad, because suddenly Nana was hanging on his arm in a massively pathetic way.

"I'm sorry, Anthony. I didn't mean it. I just wish you wouldn't stay away so long."

Nana made a sad weepy sound that almost—almost—made Ariel feel sorry for her, except the woman was so completely awful to Dad and not to Anthony. It wasn't fair.

"I feel that the only reason you come back is to get money from Gabriel."

"He owes me!"

Nana sighed. "Fine. Then sign his papers and he'll pay you."

"A pittance. No thanks. I'm not leaving until he pays up, big-time. And not until he hands this apartment over to me. That was the deal. The money and the apartment. It was supposed to be mine! I saw the papers, for God's sake. He's already bought the damned place. All he has to do is sign it over to me!"

"Keep your voice down! You promised to stay quiet until he got it worked out with Portia."

Ariel frowned. The apartment was supposed to be Anthony's?

"What are you talking about?"

But it wasn't Nana or Uncle Anthony who spoke this time. Ariel practically fell into the apartment as she swung her head toward the kitchen. Portia stood there, frozen, holding a smoking pan of burned chicken with two oven mitts, her brow furrowed as she looked back and forth between Nana and Anthony.

"What are you talking about?" Portia repeated. "The apartment is mine, not Gabriel's, and certainly not yours, Anthony."

Only then did Ariel notice that Portia wasn't the only person who had shown up unexpectedly in the living room. Her dad stood just inside the front door, looking totally like he was going to kill someone.

Thirty-two

❖

T HE MEAL was ruined.

The chicken had burned; the mashed potatoes were a sea of soupy lumps; the biscuits were charred rocks of hardened dough.

Portia held the pan of burned chicken and tried to understand what Anthony was saying. She took in the fury on Gabriel's face and the guilty delight on his brother's as they both looked at her.

"That's right, Portia," Anthony said, swiveling his head to smile at his older brother. "When Gabriel bought the apartment, he promised it to me."

"Damn it, Anthony," Gabriel bit out.

Portia blinked as she tried to make sense of it. She looked at Gabriel. "But the apartment isn't yours. I didn't go through with the sale."

Gabriel dragged a hand through his hair, and suddenly the pieces came together like a Rubik's Cube settling into place.

Her mouth fell open. "That's impossible! I never signed the documents."

He stared at her, and she could see the way he willed things to be different. "The papers were signed, Portia. And notarized."

Her knees went weak, recognizing the truth. Suddenly, a lot of things made sense. Gabriel demanding to know what she was doing in the apartment. All the times he had started to say something, only to cut himself off.

Robert must have gone through with the sale by forging her signature.

Portia felt sick, angry, and betrayed. What's more, with each piece of the puzzle that fell into place, this meal made more and more sense.

Burned chicken for betrayal by Robert, who had not only sold the only thing she owned, but had also kept the money.

Soupy potatoes for a relationship with Gabriel that had no true bond.

Coleslaw she had mixed with dressing that went bad for a Glass Kitchen in New York, a sour idea from the start.

Rock-hard rolls for a stubborn woman who had repeatedly refused to make a meal that would have led her much earlier to a greater truth— the reality that when she had seen Gabriel, and the shimmering images of fried chicken and sweet jalapeño mustard had come to her, it had foretold disaster between her and Gabriel Kane.

"Welcome to my world, babe," Anthony said with a laugh. "My brother does what he wants, when he wants, regardless of how many people he hurts in the process."

"Fuck," Gabriel ground out.

"Is that why you let her stay here, big brother? So you could fuck her?"

Portia's head jerked up just in time to see Gabriel fly across the room. Anthony's eyes went wide.

"Gabriel, no!" their mother shouted.

Gabriel ignored her, jerking Anthony up and throwing him against the wall. "Damn you!" he roared.

Anthony lunged back at Gabriel, screaming. But he was no match for the bigger man. Gabriel had him pinned to the wall in a moment. "You leave Portia out of this."

"What in the world is going on here?"

Portia jerked around. A man she had never seen before stood at the open front door.

The newcomer's face was wrinkled with distaste. "I'm a New York City inspector conducting an unannounced property visit. Our office was notified that someone is illegally running a retail establishment out of a ground-floor residential building." He glanced around. "Based on the sign in the window and the posted hours, I'd say the report is correct." His mouth twisted. "A restaurant and, what, a fight club?"

The inspector walked straight in and began snapping photos—of The Glass Kitchen sign, the daily menu. He also snapped the shocked faces and Anthony's bloody nose. He had an unobstructed view straight into the kitchen, the pots and pans lined up on the counter like ship-wrecks on a worn linoleum sea.

"I can explain," Portia said hurriedly, stumbling over to the table and dropping the pan of chicken down.

"Don't bother. Save your explanations for zoning court."

Thirty-three

✦

ARIEL SAT ON the edge of her bed, shoes hooked over the side bed-rail, her feet jiggling as she tried her hardest to calm down. After the disaster downstairs, she had flown to her room to get away. She hadn't left since.

Things were getting worse. Anthony and Dad fighting. Some inspector guy showing up. Portia getting in trouble.

But the worst was seeing the look on Portia's face when she learned that she didn't own her apartment. Talk about surprise. Ariel had been as surprised as Portia. How come none of them had known? And why hadn't her dad said something sooner?

Just then there was a strange noise outside her bedroom door. Miranda giggled, tiptoeing down the hallway toward her own bedroom, even though she was supposed to be spending the night with a friend. Ariel started to confront her, but then she heard someone else laugh, the sound deeper, and she knew it was a boy.

"Shhh!" Miranda whispered, with another giggle.

"I'm being quiet. You're the one making all the noise."

Dustin. Ariel realized that Miranda was giving in to the guy. She was going to have sex, right there in their house, their dad somewhere downstairs, probably in his study.

Her legs started jiggling again as she heard Miranda's door click shut, then louder, muffled giggling. She fell back on the mattress and planted the pillow over her head.

Minutes ticked by. A muffled quiet. Slowly, Ariel started to breathe again and she pulled the pillow away. She hated to think what the silence meant.

But then something worse happened.

"Miranda?"

Ariel gasped, and leaped off the bed and raced to her door, flinging it open. But it was too late.

Her dad stood in front of her sister's closed door. "Miranda, open this door right now."

"Go away!"

Dad grabbed the door handle, but it was locked. He pounded on the hard wood. "Open this door," he demanded, banging on the door.

"No! I hate you! You ruin everything!"

Dad didn't wait another second. He was a big guy, strong. So it shouldn't have been a surprise when he rammed his shoulder into the door and it crashed open.

It looked like the movies, the sound awful, like a huge, splintering crack that went straight to Ariel's gut. She could hardly believe what she was watching. What had happened to her normal family?

"What in the hell is going on here?"

"Whoa, dude!"

"Don't you *fucking 'dude'* me, you degenerate. Get the hell away from my daughter."

"Dad! This is my room! You can't just barge in here!"

"I am your father. You will do what I say!"

Ariel figured her dad must be looking way scary, because the next thing she knew, Dustin was dashing down the hall, pulling on his shirt, his belt unbuckled. She felt even sicker now.

"I hate you!" Miranda shouted the words so loud that Ariel could practically hear her spit.

"So you said!" Dad bellowed back.

Then he pulled a deep breath. "Damn it, Miranda. What do you think you're doing? You're barely sixteen years old."

"Dustin loves me! And I love him!"

"*Dustin* is a hormonal asshole who just wants to get laid!"

Ariel squeezed her eyes shut. Who was the man shouting like that? How could that guy be her dad?

"Oh, really?" Miranda spat. "You know that from experience?"

"I am trying," their father stated, his voice cold and angry. "I have put up with your antics. I have put up with your sarcasm. I have put up with you talking back. But I've had it."

"Have you?" Miranda sneered. "Well, guess what? I've had it, too! If Mom were here, she'd want me to have a boyfriend."

"Your mother isn't here! And you sneaking a boy into this house to . . . to . . . do—"

"Do what, Dad?" Miranda scoffed. "Fuck? Like you and Portia?"

Silence. A great big painful silence.

Dad and Portia? Ariel felt light-headed. She remembered what Uncle Anthony had said. She didn't know why, but she thought she was going to throw up.

"Like I didn't know," Miranda spat.

It seemed like forever before her dad said, "You are grounded."

"Great, there's an original response, *Dad*. But I'd think you'd have a bigger bag of tricks than that. You think grounding me will keep me away from Dustin? I love him! You wouldn't understand love. I know more than you think about you and love!"

Ariel jumped back as their dad slammed out of the room, then hammered his way downstairs.

The only thing left in the hall was part of the door panel and the shiny brass doorknob that had rolled out of Miranda's room like Humpty Dumpty after the fall.

Thirty-four

PORTIA WAS VAGUELY AWARE that morning had finally come. She had spent the whole night cleaning up the disarray of pots and pans. The city inspector was long gone. But he'd left her with a general citation. Plus, he reeled off the list of things he could and would cite her for if she didn't cease and desist immediately—everything from improper sanitation to a ten-thousand-dollar fine for illegal posting of a sign. After her head stopped reeling, with tears streaming down her face, she had ripped The Glass Kitchen sign out of the window.

No matter how she looked at it, the testing version of The Glass Kitchen was over.

Portia dropped into one of the ancient living room chairs and thought of the last meal she had made for her grandmother, a meal for just one person. When Gram had seen it, she'd been shocked. But after long minutes she had pulled a deep breath.

"It's your time now, Portia," *Gram had said.* "It's your legacy."

"Gram, I just cook! You're the one people come to see. You give them advice. You tell them the kinds of food that will restore them. You are *The Glass Kitchen*."

Gram had looked at her for an eternity, seeming to consider. Then finally: "My sweet Portia. I lost the knowing years ago. I woke up one morning and it was gone. I didn't want to believe it, and I kept cooking, trying to pretend it wasn't true. But the Kitchen began to fail. Nothing I cooked was right. When I still had the knowing, no one gave a thought as to why they were drawn here, because they always left sated, with answers, with calm.

"Even after the food started to fail, they continued to come since by then I was famous. But once they started leaving unsatisfied, they had to find a way to explain why they were drawn to me, to my food, in the first place. Suddenly answers mattered. As people do, they found excuses. That's when people started calling me crazy.

"Ever since the day your knowing found Olivia, the day your mother brought you to me, I told myself I needed to teach you the ways. But," she hesitated, "I couldn't do it. I told myself that it was because I wanted you to have a normal life. Truth to tell, I didn't want to share the spotlight. That's why I didn't help you develop the knowing. Only when I realized that I had lost mine did I accept that I needed you to save The Glass Kitchen. To save me. If you knew what to cook and bake, I'd know what the people needed to be told to find their calm. So I brought you into the kitchen in earnest then, but to cook, only to cook. Still not teaching you. But you developed the knowing anyway, more powerfully even than me.

"But none of that matters now. It's your time to do it all, Portia. I know you're tired of not being set free to explore. And you've shown me by making this meal. Making it for one."

"Gram, I don't want to do this without you! That's not why I made the meal for one."

Then why had she made the meal for one? Why had she known what to prepare, how to set the table? Deep down, she had wanted to fly.

"*Hush, child,*" Gram had said.

Then she had walked out into that Texas storm, shocking Portia.

She had married Robert and suppressed the knowing, as if that could keep her guilt at bay.

But marriage to Robert had failed. If she was truthful, deep down she had wanted more. She had wanted a Glass Kitchen. She had wanted passion. She had wanted to fly, just as Gram had said.

Portia's head fell back, and a word escaped her mouth that was, frankly, blasphemous. After her failed marriage, she had thought she had found passion and a Glass Kitchen in New York. But that had all been a lie as well.

She went to the closet and pulled out the two suitcases she had put away, throwing the few things she had brought with her from Texas back inside. This wasn't her home. She should have understood that the moment Gabriel Kane had first seen her in the apartment and demanded to know why she was there.

But the most humiliating thing of all? He must not have told her because he had wanted her. She had seen the way he looked at her from the very first time. The heat. The desire. And he was nothing if not a man who got what he wanted.

She had slept her way into free rent.

She bit her lip savagely for a moment before she had the tears under control. She refused, absolutely refused, to cry. If she started, she might never stop—not with the gut-wrenching pain of Robert's betrayal mixed together with that of Gabriel, whom she had thought was different.

Her cell phone rang, and Cordelia's number popped up. Portia had to figure out what to do next, but she couldn't do that at either sister's apartment.

Thoughts of chocolate drifted through her head. She tasted it, smelled it. She pressed ignore on the phone as it occurred to her where she might go.

-:::-

Twenty-four hours later, her cell phone was still ringing every time she turned around. Cordelia, Olivia. Gabriel. Everyone wanted to know where she had gone.

This time, it was Cordelia, her fifth call in an hour. Portia turned back to the TV.

"How can you watch that garbage?"

She ignored the question, though she shot her hosts a half smile. "You know," she said, "Texas hair gets a bad rap for being big. But it has nothing on New Jersey hair." Portia took a particularly unladylike bite of a Little Debbie cake, her words muffled by the premade pastry. "Not a thing."

"I guess they didn't teach you manners in Texas when they were teaching you how to do hair?"

Portia swallowed and glanced over. "Seriously, Stan, have you tasted these things? They're amazing."

Stanley rolled his eyes, shuffled over, and sat in the chair next to her. "How long do you plan on staying here?"

"You said I could stay as long as I liked."

"No, Marcus said you could stay as long as you like. The only reason I didn't slam the door in your face when you showed up like a half-drowned cat in a storm was because I felt indebted after those chocolate nuts you gave me." He sniffed. "Lucky for you, you showed up when I was experiencing a moment of weakness."

Portia shot him a dark grin. "You better work on your gruff thing. A person only has to know you for more than a minute to realize you're a softie."

Marcus strode into the room. "He's a mean old man, don't let him fool you." But he leaned down and kissed Stanley on the top of his head.

A twist of yearning hit Portia's gut at the sight of two people committed to each other for so many years. That was what she had wanted out of life: a partner who knew all her traits, good and bad, and loved her anyway.

She unwrapped another cake in a crackle of clear plastic, then took a giant bite.

Stanley scoffed. "Where's the woman who made all those chocolate nuts and figs? The one who cooked and baked, the one who went on and on with all her talk about the joy to be found in food."

Portia raised the half-eaten prefabricated cake in the air. "Don't know her, never met her. But if I did, I'd tell her to stuff a Little Debbie cake in her obnoxiously cheerful face. And, really, you can't be tired of me yet."

"I'm hiding the Hostess Sno Balls," Stanley grumbled.

Marcus laughed.

After Stanley and Marcus went back to the kitchen, Portia slouched lower in her seat. Stanley was right. She had hardly moved from her spot in front of the television. For all her pull-herself-up-by-the-bootstraps pep talk about fixing her life, she didn't have the first clue how to do it. So she hadn't. For the first time ever, Portia was just sitting around and feeling sorry for herself.

Even in Texas, when everything had gone to hell in a handbasket, she had been proactive. Sure, she had fled. But she had actively fled.

Right now, all she wanted to do was flip through cable stations until she found yet another show filled with people who probably couldn't spell *kitchen* much less know what to do in one.

And she refused to feel one bit guilty about it.

Thirty-five

✦

P ORTIA WAS GONE. Vanished.

For three whole days, Ariel listened and watched as her dad tramped up and down the stairs to Portia's apartment. Every time he returned back upstairs he still didn't have any idea where she was. For all three of those days, Ariel tucked in her shirt, folded her ankle socks neatly around her ankles, brushed her hair, and even wore a headband she thought her dad would like. Like that would help.

He only looked at her oddly, and didn't say a word. He also didn't say a word about their missing neighbor.

She even tried to get him to talk about it, doing her best Shrink Speak, but finally he snapped, "That's enough, Ariel. She's gone."

Anyone who didn't know him would have sworn he couldn't have cared less. But Ariel knew better. She knew he was hurting. Her dad dealt with stuff just like she did, swallowing it back, not letting on. It was one of the ways that she and her dad were exactly alike.

Plus, every night he went down the fire escape like a lovesick burglar.

Of course he didn't stay down there long, because really, what was there to find?

The problem was that unless her dad went out and found her, Portia wasn't coming back. And there was no sign that he was planning to do that.

It was getting her worried. What if he didn't get the Portia Problem fixed? She'd have to do it for him.

But she had promised to be a good daughter and let him fix things. So she continued to tuck in her shirt and worked hard to smile and be polite. Being a perfect daughter was proving even more difficult than her genealogy report.

But on the fourth day, she'd had it. She woke up knowing that her dad wasn't going to get the job done. Here she was being, like, so perfect, and what good was that doing?

She started thinking, taking notes in her journal, figured things out. With a start she realized that she was doing perfect wrong! She needed to do the kind of perfect Mother Teresa did, and based on every photo she had seen, Mother Teresa didn't worry about tucking in her blouse. She was out there doing, helping, mucking around doing the dirty work. If it had been up to Mother Teresa, she would be out helping Dad right along with the lepers! She wouldn't sit on the sidelines!

As quietly she could, Ariel sneaked downstairs to Portia's apartment, using the key Portia kept hidden under the mat, regardless of the fact that Dad always did the whole growling thing whenever something came up about it. Once inside, she walked from room to room, looking for a clue.

"Where are you, Portia?" she said aloud, feeling like an idiot, especially since the walls didn't talk back. "Where did you go?"

Finally she ended up in the kitchen. She was about to leave when she saw a slip of paper on the floor. She read it a couple of times before dashing upstairs, bursting into her dad's study, and handing over the sheet of paper.

He gave it a quick look, then eyed her. "What's this?"

"A recipe!"

"I know that, Ariel. But why are you showing me?"

"Dad," she said as nicely as she could, since she was still sort of trying to be the perfect daughter, even if it was the Mother Teresa version, "it's a *recipe*. For chocolate-covered peanuts and figs."

Her dad sat back in the leather chair and stared at the piece of paper. Ariel saw the resistance on his face. But she wasn't completely sure what he was resisting.

"Dad," Ariel repeated. "Like Portia always said, some things are true whether we believe them or not."

She watched as he looked back at her, his eyes narrowing.

"She left us, Ariel. Even if I were inclined to look for her, I don't know where to find her, and a fig recipe isn't going to tell me."

Ariel's mouth gaped. Finally, she gave in and rolled her eyes. "Seriously? You can't figure it out based on the chocolate chili recipe? The one Portia made. The one she told you about because all the extra bags disappeared."

The chocolates that had drawn her in like a pathetic puppy to her sister's soiree. Not that her dad knew that part of it.

"You can't figure it out based on that?" She enunciated each syllable, unable to hold back the sarcasm any longer.

Her dad's eyes narrowed even more, but then he drew a breath and his face kind of softened. "I'm glad to see my old Ariel is back."

She peered at him across the massive desk. "What do you mean, the 'old Ariel'?"

"The one who doesn't measure her words." Then he stood. "What you're telling me is that Portia's been right next door all this time."

"There's hope for you yet," she cheered, racing around the desk and throwing her arms around him.

Thirty-six

❖

PORTIA JERKED IN SURPRISE when she heard Stanley and Marcus's buzzer.

"Well, well, well," Stanley said, glimpsing out the window. "Look who's here?"

"Who?"

"Our neighbor."

"Ariel? Miranda?"

"Nope. Their father."

"I'm not here!"

Marcus tsked. "You're here. You're sitting right there."

"No way! He lied to me! He . . . he . . ." She cut herself off. There was nothing to explain. "I am not here."

Finally, Marcus conceded, and told Gabriel she wasn't available.

"That's not the same as I'm not here!"

"True, but it also isn't a lie."

He had her there.

Portia stayed in front of the TV. In fact, she sat there for the whole next day, too. A *Top Model* marathon kept her glued to the screen. Stanley threw up his hands and grumbled. Marcus *tsked*, but was utterly kind. Finally, after a total of five days, Marcus said, "Portia, sweetie, don't you want to go outside? Get some fresh air?"

Portia sat in front of the television, wearing a pair of old Adidas sweat pants Marcus had donated to the cause, and a misshapen *Chorus Line* T-shirt he had given her outright when she had run through the few clothes she had of her own. But she couldn't leave. She couldn't talk to Gabriel. What would she say? *How could you not have told me that you owned the apartment? How did you make love to me over and over again, all the while you knew that you owned the only thing I thought I could call my own?* How could she ever trust him?

Or even, to herself: *What in the world am I going to do with my life?*

"How about we take a walk in the park?" Marcus suggested. "Or, say, you change up your clothes?"

"I changed. I wore a *Cats* T-shirt yesterday. And before that, I wore the one I found in the bag headed for the thrift store: *Ain't Misbehavin'*."

"Of course. How could I forget the black Magic Marker you used to cross out *Ain't*?"

She glanced over, eyeballing him to see if sweet Marcus was being sarcastic. "You're sounding an awful lot like Ariel."

As soon as the words were out of her mouth, Portia felt even worse. She missed Gabriel more than she knew how to say. But she also missed Ariel. Even Miranda, a bit. Still, she couldn't bear thinking about Gabriel making love to her while knowing he owned her apartment and not telling her.

She groaned, then slid down even farther front of the TV. Obviously, she should feel guilty about camping out on Marcus and Stanley's overstuffed chair, not facing her problems head-on—especially after that whole *don't be a chicken* speech she had given Cordelia. She was starting to feel guilty. But just a little.

"I'm fine," she said.

She heard Stanley shuffle in; the two men whispered for several moments. Portia heard phrases like: *Not natural for a woman to let herself go, Too much TV isn't good for her psyche,* and, Ain't Misbehavin, *really was one of the most overrated musicals of the 70s.*

"I can hear you two."

"We just think you're a bit, well, discombobulated." This from Marcus.

"Pshaw. She's a wreck. And she looks like one, too." Stanley.

Portia jerked up. "Fine. I'll go take a bath, wash my hair."

"Sweetie," Marcus said, his grimace apologetic. "We weren't talking about your hair, which, by the bye, is hideous. But we aren't ones to judge."

Portia scowled.

"We're referring to your mental state. *You* are a wreck. We discussed it after breakfast and decided we had no choice but to take matters into our own hands."

Portia narrowed her eyes. "What did you do?"

The door buzzer sounded.

"Seriously, what have you done?"

"It's for your own good," Marcus said.

Stanley scoffed as he shuffled to the door. Next thing she knew, they had guests.

Portia jumped to her feet. "Traitor!" Portia glared at Marcus and Stanley. "You know I'm not in the mood for family!"

Marcus grimaced. Stanley shuffled back to his seat by the window, not one bit apologetic.

"You are the traitor!" Cordelia shouted. "Not taking our calls. Going MIA without a single word to let us know you were okay and not dead in a ditch."

"I don't do worry!" Olivia stated.

"Good God, look at you," Cordelia went on. "You *do* look like you've been in a ditch."

Stanley snorted in agreement.

"You need to stop with this nonsense." Cordelia walked over to Portia, took her hand, and pulled her toward the staircase. "It's time you rejoin the living." She glanced over at Marcus. "I take it there's a bathroom upstairs with a sink, running water?"

"Up the stairs, second door on the right," Marcus supplied. "Her meager stash of belongings is in the bedroom one door beyond that."

Portia didn't know if she wanted to scream or cry as Cordelia and Olivia herded her up the stairs.

"I don't need the two of you marching in here thinking you can boss me around!"

"We aren't bossing you around," Olivia said. "We're taking charge while you're mentally incapacitated."

"I'm tired of this!" Portia snapped. "I'm tired of both of you always in my business. I'm tired of trying to live the kind of life I want, only to get upended every time I turn around!" Lord, it felt good to let it out. "And I'm tried of always having to save—"

She cut herself off. It only felt good for so long. She was angry at her sisters. But, really, she knew she was angry at the world. She had never been one to intentionally hurt anyone.

"Tired of having to save us," Cordelia supplied for her.

"Of course that's what she thinks," Olivia said to Cordelia. "Poor little Portia is sure she wouldn't be in this mess if the two of us hadn't browbeaten her into this whole Glass Kitchen fiasco. And if she hadn't been busy trying to get the café started, then she would've been able to find a real job and not have to take one cooking for Gabriel, which is the only reason she got involved with him and HAD SEX!"

"Olivia!" Portia snapped.

"Of course she knew," Cordelia said. "She's Olivia. And of course she told me."

"It sucks being you," Olivia added with more than a little sarcasm.

Portia ground her teeth as her sisters pushed and prodded her down the hallway of Stanley and Marcus's old town house. "You don't know the first thing about what it's like to be me."

Olivia held up her hand, seesawing her thumb and forefinger, much as she used to do when they were children. "The world's smallest violin is playing for you, baby sister."

Cordelia rolled her eyes. "The fact is, Portia Desdemona, you have a gift or talent or maybe even a curse, which is really nothing more than a wildly in-tune intuition that freaks you out. For that matter, it freaks me out. But so what?"

Olivia nodded like a member of the choir. "So what!" she echoed.

Portia's frustration bubbled up. "You don't understand!"

"Stop feeling sorry for yourself!" Cordelia barked. "Did it ever occur to you that I would love to have a gift? Any gift? That I'd give my eyeteeth to feel special, to feel like I'm someone other than a woman who just tries to get by in a regular life in a regular world that falls apart for no good reason?"

Olivia and Portia stopped and gaped at Cordelia.

"Who knew?" Olivia said. "At least about feeling regular. How come you forgot to act regular, if you're feeling that way?"

Tears suddenly welled up in Cordelia's eyes.

"Olivia!" Portia snapped, and turned to her older sister. "Cordelia, honey, your world isn't falling apart. James is going to be fine. You all are going to be fine."

Yet again, it was always this way with them. Sniping, fighting, arguing, taking sides as alliances ebbed and flowed through each encounter. Now the sisters stopped and stared at one another, then did what they always did best: They sighed—half a laugh, half resignation—then hugged.

"We don't care what you do, Portia," Cordelia said, choked up. "Just do something. Stop hiding. You can't keep living a half life, not embracing the knowing, but not embracing anything else, either. You've got to find a way to live your life, sweetie. Not Gram's, not Robert's, not ours. Yours. And that takes being strong enough to stand up to whoever is trying to sway you. Even if it's us." Cordelia gave Portia a little shake. "Now, clean up. Olivia and I are here to help. But you have to let us know what you want help with."

The sisters left Portia standing in the bathroom. She looked in the mirror, giving herself a hard glare. "You are not this person," she said to her reflection.

Thirty minutes later, Portia was bathed, dressed, and sitting cross-legged on the floor in her borrowed bedroom. Cordelia and Olivia had left, but not before she promised to call them tomorrow with a plan.

Portia took a deep breath, unzipped her suitcase. She sat there for long minutes more, then nodded her head and pulled out all three Glass Kitchen cookbooks. Whether she liked it or not, the knowing was her legacy. It had led her in so many ways, giving her answers, even if she didn't like the answers it had given. But she couldn't deny that the answers were true.

She didn't bother with the first two books. She went straight to the third volume. The one Gram had always said wasn't for novices. The one she hadn't read until now.

She cracked the old spine and found spidery handwriting on the first page.

Every kitchen should be filled with glass—to drink from, to see through, to reflect the light of a wonderful meal prepared with love. To ensure that the light is not lost, I have filled these pages with everything that has been passed down to me from earlier generations of Cuthcart women. I hope each generation to come will do the same.

Imogen Cuthcart
The Republic of Texas, 1839

Portia started to read the fragile pages, first tentatively, then greedily. Images swirled as she read. Stews and roasts, herbs and spices, broth and gravy, cookies and pies. Sweet and sour. Joy and laughter, pain and sorrow. No life could be without these.

The language was stilted, the meals old-fashioned, but the advice was progressive, considering how old the book must have been. Each time Portia came to a notation, she recognized the ones that her grandmother had made, modern takes on antiquated forms of cooking, be it the update of a gas oven from coal-stoked, or a mixer to replace beating a cake by hand.

There were as many recipes for folk medicine as for meals. Obviously food had been the main source of healing for her forebearers. Gram had traded in her own version of food as a great healer, both physically and mentally. What surprised Portia was how each of these older, more complicated entries made so much sense to her, as if she already knew the wisdom she found copied down so carefully over the years, as if she had been born with a knowing that was far deeper than her ancestors', truly deeper than her grandmother's, as Gram had said.

Portia turned the last page and the breath rushed out of her. Gram had written this page herself, years after the book was originally compiled.

I dreamed a meal. A big meal. A final meal. I keep telling myself that it's impossible to know for sure. My knowing is coming in fits and starts these days. But the images of food in this meal are strong, and I've been at this long enough to know, to feel certain, that when I see this meal, it will be time for me to stop. What I don't know is what I will do when my turn is over, when it is time for me to pass the baton. How will I be able to bear it when my whole life has been the knowing?

Though that shouldn't be my worry. I should worry that I haven't taught Portia what she needs to know. Why is it so hard for me to let go? Why is it so hard for me to teach her? Why won't I let her read any of these books, and most especially this one?

Because I'm jealous that she has always had more power than me, and if she reads it, she'll realize that she doesn't need me at all.

The Meal

*Chile cheese and bacon-
stuffed cherry tomatoes
Pulled pork
Endive slaw
Potato pancakes
Homemade catsup*

Portia stared at the entry. Her chest constricted.

It wasn't *her* selfishness coming to fruition through the food and the single place setting that had pushed Gram into the lightning. It had been Gram's meal, Gram's knowing, that had been realized in Portia's cooking.

She felt weak with relief, freed—a feeling followed quickly by a burst of frustrated anger.

"It didn't have to be that way, Gram," she whispered to the empty room.

If Portia had known her grandmother had lost the knowing, she would have worked with her to find a way forward for both of them. If she had known, she wouldn't have fallen into the trap of living a half life with Robert. Trapped in a half life of guilt thinking she had made a meal that had killed her grandmother.

But it also meant that now she finally knew how to move forward.

Thirty-seven

⊰⊹⊱

ARIEL CRAWLED OUT her window to the fire escape. She still hated the fire escape, but crawling out onto the thin metal stairs moved all her worry away from her disintegrating family and onto the fact that at any second, she could plunge to her death. Okay, so maybe that was an exaggeration, but try telling that to her brain. Three stories above ground seemed really high when she was standing on two-foot-wide thin slates of metal.

But tonight even the precariousness of her perch on the fire escape wasn't helping. It had been a week since Portia had left them, and she needed someone to talk to. Not the Shrink. Not her dad. And definitely not Miranda, since Miranda was the person she needed to talk about. Which left Portia, and Portia was gone.

Not that her dad was doing anything about it. Hello! He should have been dragging Portia back where she belonged—downstairs in the garden apartment that should have been hers.

The thought of that made her smile, since Ariel had spent the whole first few weeks Portia had lived there calling it a basement. But just like Portia, Ariel had fallen in love with the old place.

With her legs dangling off the sides, she rested her forearms and chin on the metal side slat and looked out at the big buildings all around her. It was so different here in New York from their house in New Jersey. There, the house nestled into the cliff, gardens built up the back side, with stone steps taking you higher and higher. Her mom had loved those gardens. It felt weird to think that if Portia ever saw them, she'd love them, too.

Would Portia ever see their house? Maybe they would move back now that things were getting so awful with Miranda.

The sound of the door opening to the garden broke the quiet.

"Yep, I could easily live here."

Ariel scooted back against the wall. Peering through the floor slats, she watched as her uncle walked out into the garden. She couldn't in a million years imagine her dad buying the place for Anthony to live in. The two guys practically hated each other. So it didn't make sense.

"Anthony, you don't want to live here any more than Gabriel wants you here."

Her grandmother.

Anthony laughed, a sound that didn't seem very happy. "No, he doesn't, does he? I can't think of a better reason to move in. That should up the ante for what he's willing to pay me. Or if he gives it to me, like he promised, I'll sell the damn thing, take the money and run."

Her grandmother made a disgruntled noise, then walked back inside.

This whole thing was about money. Ariel took a deep breath. If she could figure out a way to convince her dad to give his brother what he wanted, then Anthony would be gone. It made so much sense. It was perfect. It would make everyone happy. Well, not Miranda, but she couldn't solve everything. But wasn't she good at talking to her dad, getting him to see her point of view?

Leaping up, she staggered, then grabbed the railing as she hurried as fast as she could down the zigzag of fire escape steps.

Her uncle looked up. "Ariel, what the f—"

She made it to the ground, safe, almost breathless, and gasped, "I'll get you the money, Uncle Anthony!"

"What?"

"I can tell you don't really want to live here! And Dad would hate it."

At the mention of his brother, Anthony's face creased hard.

"Don't you see, it's the perfect solution? I can make Dad see it. How much money do you want?"

As the words hurtled out of her mouth, she felt all the pieces of her world finally coming together.

"Why?" he said carefully. "Why would you do that?"

"Because!" she blurted out, "I know you're Miranda's dad!"

The words tumbled out before she could think them through, as if they had been dammed up and finally broken free. "I know you're her real dad. And I think she knows it, too, which is why she's acting worse and worse and getting in more and more trouble. It's because you're here and not being her dad, don't you see? But you don't want to be her dad, and if you stay, you make my dad mad. If you do stay, eventually something is going to explode and everything will come out, then everyone will know your secret, including my dad. Then what're you going to do?"

"Miranda's dad?" Uncle Anthony said. "What are you talking about? Jesus, I'm not Miranda's dad. Have you lost your mind?"

Ariel didn't believe him for a second. "Just tell me, Uncle Anthony. Tell me how much it will take to make you go away?"

His expression hardened, anger filling his eyes.

She drew a sharp breath. "Sorry! That came out wrong, I swear. It's just that we both know you'd be way happier not hanging out in New York. You love all that great mountain-climbing stuff, and wrestling with lions, or whatever it is you do."

"I do not wrestle lions."

He spaced the words in a really furious way. In fact, she'd never seen him so angry. "Sorry!" she repeated, thinking fast. "I swear, cross my heart, I won't tell a soul about you being Miranda's dad."

"I am *not* Miranda's father."

"Okay, seriously. You're forgetting who you're talking to. Me. The smart one. Of course you are. I saw when my mom and dad got married. I know Miranda's birthday. And your mom said you and my mom were in love before you left for Africa." She was on a roll, every last bit of what she'd learned spilling out. "Don't you see? If you stay, all you'll do is make things worse. For yourself!" she added quickly. "I swear, I can find a way to convince him to give you more money."

"Ariel—"

She had no idea she was crying until she felt the tears streaming down her face. "You have to *go*, Uncle Anthony. You can't let anyone know you're Miranda's dad!"

"Damn it, Ariel. I am not Miranda's dad! I'm yours!"

Thirty-eight

⋄⋄⋄

A SOUND LIKE OCEAN waves rushed in Ariel's ears and the world jerked.

"What? No," she breathed. "No, no, no."

Her head spun, images of her mother dancing through her mind, like the home movies running in slow motion. Mom laughing. Mom dancing. Mom and Anthony. Always Anthony coming back into their lives.

Her mom had loved Anthony Kane, not his brother, Gabriel.

And, worst of all, awful Uncle Anthony was . . . was *her* father.

Ariel dashed back up the fire escape, Anthony muttering and cursing just behind her. But she didn't stop, didn't look back. She bolted up to Miranda's window instead of hers before Anthony could get her, and banged.

"What are you doing?" her sister demanded when she opened her window, Anthony flattened back into the shadows.

Coward.

The word rippled through her. The man who said he was her father was a coward. The one who was strong and great wasn't her real dad. How could that be true?

Ariel threw herself inside Miranda's room. She wanted her to do something, make the awful words go away. She wanted her sister to look at her like she loved her, like she cared. She wanted someone in this wacky world to see her, not let her disappear any more.

"Seriously, Ariel, what is your problem? You're not allowed out there."

"Uncle Anthony says he's my dad," she whispered, realizing that her hands shook. "You don't think it's true, do you?"

For half a second, Miranda's eyes widened. Then her cell phone rang. "Look, if it's true, it totally sucks. But I don't believe it. As much as I like him, we both know he'd do just about anything to get up in Dad's face." Her phone rang again. "Seriously, forget him." She flipped open her phone. "Hey, Dustin."

Her tone changed completely, her whole body going soft as she listened to whatever the Creep was saying.

"I'm totally ready," she said. "I'll meet you at Port Authority. The De-Camp bus to New Jersey."

Ariel gaped. "You're going to New Jersey?"

"Shit, I've gotta go. I'll meet you there." She glared at Ariel. "Don't you dare say a word. I'm already totally late. I'm going to the old house."

"What? Why?" Ariel gasped.

"We're going to . . . hang out."

"You're going out there to have sex with him!"

"What if I am? Are you going to be a total baby and tell Dad?"

At the mention of their dad, Ariel felt her lip tremble.

Miranda sighed, impatient. "Listen. We'll deal with the whole dad thing tomorrow. I mean seriously, what are the chances that it's true? Uncle Anthony can be so lame, and everyone knows he hates Dad. He probably said it just to be mean."

Ariel felt a sickening mix of gratitude that her sister said something nice and a sizzling worry about what Miranda was getting ready to do.

"Why do you have to go all the way out there to . . . do it?"

"Dustin thinks it will be fun. I shouldn't even tell you this, but the first time is supposed to be special. He has a surprise for me."

"But he broke up with you! Now he's saying you've got to go out to New Jersey to have special sex with him? That just seems weird."

"It is not weird! Kids go out to New Jersey all the time."

"Really?"

"Yes, really. We're taking the bus. Totally easy."

"But what will Dad say when he finds out?"

"He won't find out. He thinks I'm spending the night with Becky."

"This is a really bad idea, Mir."

"Tell Dad, and you're not my sister anymore." Miranda said it flat and mean; then she grabbed her bag and slammed the door on the way out.

⁘

Ariel paced her bedroom. She felt sick and weird and terrified at the possibility that her dad wasn't her dad. Panic stuck in her throat, making it hard to breathe.

A lump swelled in her throat. What would she do if was true? What if Anthony took her away? What would she do if she had to go live with him? She couldn't imagine her dad not being her dad. She couldn't imagine him not coming in and checking on her in the middle of the night. After a whole life of him being Mr. Busy Working Guy, it seemed unfair that he'd get taken away now, when he was staying at home so much of the time.

Her uncle had to be lying. Just like Miranda had said.

The thoughts went round and round in her head until she felt as if she was going to throw up. But there was something else. Miranda had gone to New Jersey. To their old house.

Ariel buckled over, clutching her stomach, other memories pressing in on her. The fact was, their old house held something she hadn't wanted to face.

"Do you remember my memory chest, Ariel?"

The words hit Ariel hard, words she had refused to think about. They were her mother's words as she lay trapped in the car, blood streaking down her face.

"Mom," Ariel had cried. She hadn't cared about any chest. *"You have to be okay!"*

Ariel had watched, terrified, as a tear rolled down her mom's temple, into her hair. *"You're a big girl now, A."*

"I'm only eleven!"

"Nearly twelve," her mother breathed.

Ariel still hadn't understood how she could be unhurt while her mom was such a broken mess. Plus, it was Ariel who had made her mom so angry that she had driven fast, too fast.

"Ariel, pay attention." Her mother had struggled to speak. Ariel had experienced the awful feeling that she was watching her mother disappear.

"Listen to me, Ariel. I was an idiot. I didn't think. But now you've got to find the box. It's in my study. Upstairs. In a little cabinet behind my memory chest. You have to get the box." She had tried to move and moaned. *"Find it. Make sure you give it to Gabriel."*

Ariel was crying by then, hard and loud. *"What do you mean?"*

But her mom hadn't answered, her eyes fluttering closed, and Ariel watched her mother disappear.

"Mom! Mommy!"

Police and firefighters had arrived on the scene, pulling Ariel out of the car. But they hadn't been able to free her mom.

Over a year had passed since then, and Ariel hadn't done what her mom had asked. She hadn't wanted anything to do with the chest, or the box her mother must have hidden behind the chest. She had tried to pretend that her mother hadn't even said the words. She had resented the Shrink for wanting her to remember. But Portia had said that sometimes you had to dig deep to find answers. Ariel had hated when Portia said that. But now she knew she had to do it.

She flew to her stash of money, hoping she could catch up to Miranda. She'd have to sneak out of the house. So she wouldn't run into her dad. Or non-dad.

She swallowed back tears, shoved the money into her backpack, and made it out the front door without being caught.

⋯⋯

It wasn't nearly as hard to get out of Manhattan as Ariel had thought it would be. She'd been saving money since the whole city clerk-cab fiasco. Every chance she got she asked her dad for money for this and that. Her dad never asked to see the birthday presents she supposedly bought for her nonexistent friends. She wasn't ever going to get caught in some random place again without enough money to get home.

Who knew that the next "home" she would need to get back to would be her old one in New Jersey? That was weird.

Of course she had always known that she'd have to go back someday.

She took a taxi to the Port Authority Bus Terminal and made it on to a DeCamp bus without anyone questioning her. By then, she'd missed Miranda, probably by a couple of buses, but she managed it herself. Pretty soon she was looking out the window of the bus as it hurtled through the Lincoln Tunnel, focusing on the way her ears popped as they drove deeper under the Hudson River. Better than focusing on what she'd find when she got to Montclair.

What would she do if she walked in on Miranda in bed with Dustin?

A few tears escaped, but she used her sleeve to swipe them away and kept staring out the window so no one could see.

When they came out of the tunnel, she saw the giant buildings of Manhattan standing like a wall of cement and glass just across the Hudson River. Twenty minutes later, the bus pulled into the parking lot by the Upper Montclair train stop. Everything looked the same as when they'd lived there before the accident. But of course it wasn't. It felt like some weird awful song.

She hitched the backpack over her shoulders and got off the bus. She went to the line of cabs, then asked the front driver to take her to the house.

He looked at her in the rearview mirror, then shrugged. "Sure."

They turned right out of the parking lot, drove over the railroad tracks, followed by another right, a left, then one more right on to a road tucked into a hill, exactly as she and her mom had done a hundred times, even down to Ariel sitting in the backseat.

The house stood on the left, giant with the long green lawn—all lit up like a Christmas tree, teenage kids going in and out of the front door.

Ariel pressed back against the seat.

Miranda wasn't out here having sex.

She was having a massive party.

Thirty-nine

✦

PORTIA SAT DOWN in Stanley and Marcus's living room, ready to get on with her life. Finally. She hadn't so much as turned on the TV since her sisters left. She had made a list. A bunch of lists, actually.

She had cleaned up, put away the last of the prepackaged food, cooked Stanley and Marcus a big, early dinner before her hosts took off for Lincoln Center and the opera, leaving her alone. But the moment she turned to the first of her lists, the doorbell rang, surprising her.

Portia peeked out the window. Gabriel stood on the steps, looking out at the street rather than at the door. He looked typically Gabriel—tall, fit, ruggedly beautiful in his own beastly way. The very sight of him sent a stab of ridiculous lust through her, followed by a wave of panic.

Like a criminal, she dropped to the floor, not wanting him to see her. He had proven to be an addiction, and there was no better way to cure the need than going cold turkey.

Not that he was making it easy. He called her cell phone practically every hour. The messages had started simple. *"Portia, we need to talk."* Gruff, impersonal, so very like Gabriel. From there, they had escalated.

"*Portia, call me. We need to talk about the apartment.*" Before he moved on to a tightly controlled anger. "*Damn it, Portia. Let's deal with this like adults.*" Then a sigh, as if giving in. "*Please.*"

Which only pissed her off more.

After a few minutes, she heard Gabriel going back down the front steps. She rolled to the side, sitting up on the floor with her back against the wall. And thought about violets. Watermelon.

The images surged in her head. She could taste the sweet juicy meat of watermelon crunching in her teeth. She smelled the gentle scent of violets. And something else, sharp and pungent. Burning. Like fire.

She leaped up and yanked open the front door. "Where's Ariel?"

It came out in a bark.

Gabriel stopped halfway up his steps next door. The fierceness of his face softened, barely, but enough that she noticed.

"Portia." Nothing else. Just a note of relief.

She looked at him, just looked, frozen for a tiny second as if she could do nothing more than memorize all that beautiful harshness of him, the strong jaw, the dark eyes, the dark hair winging back, the obstinacy, imprinting him on her mind.

But then the relief was gone, and the man in control returned. "We need to talk."

"Gabriel, where is Ariel?" She ran down the stairs, then up his.

He scowled at her. "In her room."

"Are you sure?"

"Of course I am."

"Have you seen her?"

"What? Why should I? She's been in her room for hours doing homework."

"You know that for a fact? You haven't left?"

He frowned at her again. "I went downstairs once, to talk to Anthony."

"Anthony was here?"

"Now that it's vacant, he wants your apartment." He said it flatly, unforgiving, as if it were *her* fault that the apartment was free.

Her jaw went tight. "You might as well give it to him. It obviously isn't mine."

He hesitated, his tension palpable. "I should have told you about owning the apartment." As if this was all he had to say.

"Yes, you should have," she snapped. "Though obviously I've been an idiot about everything regarding the apartment." She laughed bitterly. "I should make a list of how rock-bottom stupid I've been. Let's see: I married the kind of man who would forge my signature to betray me. I moved into the place and set up shop, all the while not realizing I didn't own it. You did! But, hey, it gets better! The whole time I was staying there, I didn't realize that the guy I was stupidly falling in love with was giving me free rent to pay for all the free sex he was getting!"

"Fuck," he breathed.

"Yep, fuck," she snapped. "Convenient, huh? You didn't even have to pay cab fare to get me home. God, could I be any more stupid!" she practically shouted into the air. "I fell for the same kind of guy! Twice! For once, why can't I meet a man who'll be honest with me?"

She marched past him to the front door, hating him, hating that she still wanted him, hating that he wasn't the man she had believed him to be. And the minute she made sure everything was all right with Ariel, she would move farther away and cut Gabriel utterly and completely out of her life. She would not be stupid any longer. "We're going to check on your daughter."

The outer door was locked and she didn't have a key anymore. She had set it on the counter when she left. She turned back. Gabriel just stood there, staring at her. As always, she had no idea what he was thinking, but his jaw was rigid.

"I know you don't believe me," she stated, "but humor me. Open the door, Gabriel."

He pulled out his key, came up next to her, and turned the lock. But his arm blocked her way when she tried to enter.

"Now what?"

He touched her cheek barely, softly. She tried to jerk away, but she was trapped by his other arm. Gabriel stared at her forever, not allowing her to look away. She could see the emotion in his eyes. "We are going to talk about this, Portia. As I said, I should have told you. At some point you have to forgive me."

Her jaw dropped as she stared at him.

"Say something," he stated, his voice strangely rough.

Just forgive him? Like all he had to do was command her and she'd do his bidding?

"I think," she said deliberately, "that there is absolutely nothing to be gained from us talking. Now *move aside*."

His mouth went tight, but he moved.

Portia raced up the stairs, fighting back the burn in her eyes.

"Ariel?" she called, knocking on her bedroom door, Gabriel coming up behind her.

He knocked, louder than she had. "Ariel?" He turned the knob and pushed in. "Ariel!"

The room was empty, books lying out on the desk, the window to the fire escape open. A piece of paper was lying on Ariel's desk.

Portia says that sometimes you have to be brave and dig deep for answers.

Gabriel's jaw leaped, fury in his eyes. "What the hell is she talking about?"

Portia's head spun with images of food and flowers. "Violets," she whispered. She shut her eyes and concentrated. "And watermelons. Lots of watermelons."

"What are you talking about?"

"At your old house. In New Jersey. Ariel told me she and her mother planted violets. Then watermelons, and the watermelons went wild and took over the entire patch."

Gabriel's eyes narrowed, as if he were trying to remember. Something snagged. "What does that have to do with Ariel and this note?"

"She's gone home."

"Home is here."

"She thinks New Jersey is home, and she's gone there."

His face was a mask of disbelief mixed with denial, like grapefruit mixed with cayenne pepper. "You're telling me that my twelve-year-old daughter fled to New Jersey to return to our old house?"

"She's nearly thirteen," Portia said. She almost laughed but it turned to a strangled cry. "I think so."

"You *think?*"

"Yes. She's been searching for answers for a while."

"Answers to what?"

"I don't know. But whenever Anthony was around, she was asking questions."

His jaw worked. "About what?"

"Her mother."

"Why the hell didn't you tell me?" He leaned close, his expression harsh, his voice clipped. "Why the hell did you encourage her to ask questions?"

She refused to let his anger scare her. "A better question might be, is there something for her to find?"

He rocked back. "Damn it!"

She saw anguish in his eyes and she almost reached out—but managed to snatch back her hand. "I'll take that as a yes. You need to find Ariel. And I would start at your old house."

"Just like that. Because you thought of watermelons."

"And violets," Portia added.

"That's crazy," he snapped. "Hell, *you* are crazy. Ridiculous."

Crazy. Like her grandmother.

In yet another way, this man was no different from Robert. He wanted her to be normal. Not that any of it mattered anymore.

He pulled out his phone.

"Who are you calling?"

"Miranda. She's at a friend's house." He pressed a number, put the phone to his ear, then waited. He cursed. "Voice mail."

He strode out of the room and downstairs. He found a phone number scribbled on a piece of paper, then dialed.

"This is Gabriel Kane, Miranda's father. May I speak to my daughter?"

Portia watched as tension rose through his body.

"She's not there? She told me that she was spending the night."

More listening, fury building.

"Please ask your daughter if she knows where Miranda is."

The words were polite, but the tone was not. She could imagine that whoever was on the other end scrambled to do his bidding.

"What the—" He cut himself off. "Thank you."

He disconnected and looked at her. "Miranda and her friend aren't there. According to a brother, the girls are in New Jersey. Throwing a party."

"Ariel must have followed her." She met his hard gaze. "Some things are true, whether you believe them or not. Now, go. Find Ariel and Miranda."

He muttered a curse, then took her arm.

"What are you doing?"

"Like you said, I'm going to New Jersey. And you're going with me."

Forty

⟡

ARIEL WALKED UP the front path, the gentle curve of flagstone winding through the lawn, blue-black against the deep green grass. The weather was almost cold, much cooler than it had been just thirty minutes away in the city. She shivered and pulled her backpack tighter to her body.

The oversized front door was still painted red with giant black hinges, the mullioned glass inset like a portal to the way life used to be—as if her mom would be waiting on the other side. But if her mom was home, there wouldn't be teenagers drinking beer on the lawn.

Her entire body deflated, those stupid tears burning again. She made herself stop thinking about her mom. Miranda was in so much trouble if anyone found out about this party. With the drinking and everything, she'd probably be grounded for life.

As soon as Ariel walked through the front door, music hit her along with the smell of alcohol and smoke. No one gave her so much as a second glance. She walked through the entry and then three steps up into the main foyer. To the left, kids sprawled on sofas and chairs in the giant living room, white dust covers ripped off and tossed aside, lying around on the floor like melting ghosts. Two guys laughed as they tried to build a fire in the fireplace. Bags of marshmallows, a box of graham crackers, and a stack of Hershey's chocolate bars sat on the hearth.

They were going to make s'mores? In the fireplace? Did they think they were at summer camp or something? Idiots.

Ariel jerked away and crossed into the dining room. Two teens sat at the long dining table, beers in front of them. Ariel ignored them and walked on into the kitchen. But Miranda wasn't there either, or in the den just beyond that.

Retracing her path to the foyer, she weaved through a knot of teenagers as she started up the stairs. Halfway up was a small landing with a window seat. From the large, multipaned window Ariel could see the lights of Manhattan in the distance. For a second she just stood there, looking.

Growing up in New Jersey, she hadn't given any thought to the city. She knew her mother thought it was the greatest thing ever to have the view. Looking at it now, it made Ariel feel all the lonelier. A year or so ago, she would never have believed that she wouldn't still be living in this house. That her mom would be gone. That she would have moved to the city that had always seemed like a whole other planet, regardless of the fact that she could see it out the window.

A year ago, she never would have believed that her uncle would claim he was her father. Maybe she could ignore it? Would her uncle regret having said the words, maybe pretend he hadn't said them at all?

But Ariel wasn't going to take any chance that things could go haywire, catching her unaware. If the truth was here in this house, she was going to find it.

"I am not a baby," she told herself, climbing the rest of the stairs to the second floor, music thrumming up the walls, smoke following her. "I am not afraid of what I'm going to find."

Though the truth was, she was scared out of her wits. She could hardly believe she'd gotten herself down to the Port Authority, on a bus, then a taxi, and was now getting ready to dig around in her mom's study. Dad was going to kill her.

Which brought her back to the fact that Dad wasn't her dad. Or so Uncle Anthony said.

She felt another one of those disconcerting surges, like she disappeared just a little bit more. Shaking it off, she slipped into the study, closing the door behind her with a *click.* The music faded away as she walked to the big wooden chest that sat low on the floor, the hinged top covered by a thick cushion that matched the curtains.

Carefully, Ariel pried open the top, images flashing through her memory of the last time she had snuck into the room. She had been home sick from school, just a month before her mom died, and had woken from one of those feverish naps. The house felt so different in the middle of the day, during the week, the neighborhood weirdly quiet. She had woken up and went to find her mother, discovering her kneeling in front of the chest.

"*Mom?*"

Her mother had jerked up. At the sight of Ariel, she had dragged in a deep breath. "*Damn it, Ariel!*"

Ariel had flinched. Her totally proper mother cursing, her mother who always said anyone who cursed was white trash. Of course, now it turned out that Mom had grown up eating out of tin cans instead of with silver spoons.

Back then she'd been confused by her mother's anger. But now, Ariel thought about her mom growing up in the Amsterdam Houses, and wondered if the outburst had been from guilt. She'd probably been hiding that box . . . or whatever it was.

Ariel tucked her hair behind her ears, then rummaged around inside the chest, but found nothing. Not that she had expected to find anything there. Her mother had been specific about Ariel finding something behind it.

She lowered the top, then grabbed the edge of the chest and pulled hard, tugging it away from the wall. There wasn't any box she could see. The wallpaper was just barely darker, not faded, but other than that, she didn't notice anything different. She dropped to her knees and ran her hand down the pattern of vines and roses, slowly, feeling. Her heart pounded. The wall felt normal.

She sat back on her heels, trying to figure out what she had gotten wrong. Her mother had said the memory chest, she was sure of it. Leaning forward, she ran her hand down the wall again, this time even slower. Then she felt it. A seam, a break in the wallpaper over a tiny door.

She broke out in a sweat. A burst of laughter from downstairs startled her. She glanced back, but the door to the study was still closed.

She ran her hand along the seams, but didn't find a handle. Frustrated, she banged and it popped open. She squeaked in surprise, then peered inside. Her heart squeezed again when she saw a box at the very back of the space.

"The box," her mother had said to her. It had just been the two of them in the car, blood all over, Ariel staring in shock.

She pulled the box out with shaking hands. Her fingers shook as her thumb pulled back the metal clasp. The lock was stiff, and at first the lid wouldn't give.

When Ariel finally pried it open, she found a big manila envelope. It wasn't sealed and inside she found a to-do list, a key, and two smaller envelopes, one with *Gabriel* scrawled across the front. The other was addressed to Mr. *Carter Davis.* Underneath that, her mom had written *Bell, Longo, Lynch and Smith, LLC.* Lawyers.

Do not read, Ariel told herself. None of it was addressed to her. Her mom had said to give it to her dad. And no question, just like everything else, she knew she totally didn't want to know what was written inside either one of these letters. But she also knew she couldn't hide anymore from the stuff she didn't want to know. If she turned the letters over without reading them herself, her father would never let her in on whatever secret her mother had hidden.

Wasn't learning the truth the whole reason for coming all the way out to Montclair in the first place? Hadn't Miranda coming out here for whatever stupid reason given her the courage to follow? To find out? It seemed like a sign that it was time.

She read the to-do list first.

1. Get copy of the will
2. Make copy of Anthony's document
3. Call C. Davis

Since it looked like everything was still here, and there was no sign of a will, Ariel assumed her mom hadn't finished whatever she had been doing. Swallowing, she opened the letter to the lawyer first.

Dear Mr. Davis,

I got your name from a friend I used to know when my father was still living. He said you were discreet, and could help me. This is something I have needed to deal with for some time now, but haven't had the first clue how to do it. I am getting a copy of my will. I would like you to add an addendum based on documents I'm supplying. I've also included a letter to my husband. Once everything is completed, I would like you to hold on to the entire package. If something happens to me before I can deal with this situation in a better way, please give the letter, documents, keys, and amended will to my husband.

Thank you,
Victoria Polanski Kane

Ariel took a deep breath and then slid her fingers under the flap of the second envelope, her chipped and half-painted nails taunting her as she

broke the seal. Her hands shook even more as she pulled out the letter
and started to read.

Gabriel,

Not Dear Gabriel, or Dearest Gabriel. Just his name. Short. Harsh.
Impersonal. She hated that.

> *If you're reading this, something has happened to me, which*
> *hardly seems possible as I write these words. But that's not the point.*
> *Will it surprise you if I said I was never brave enough? I never*
> *was, not really. I'm still not, as writing this letter instead of telling you*
> *to your face proves. But here's the truth: I never meant to hurt you or*
> *the girls. In my own way, with this key and letter, I'm trying to fix*
> *things. Believe it or not, I really do try to be a better person, even if*
> *you would swear that I rarely succeed.*

Ariel felt as if her mom's frustration and anger boiled from the page.
All that stuff, that emotion between her parents that she had never let
herself see.

> *I know as I write this that eventually I'll have to fix things in a*
> *better way than this letter I'm going to give to a lawyer. But I haven't*
> *been able to bring myself to tell you what I've done. I've worked*
> *hard for years to keep my secret.*
> *Frankly, I plan to live a long life, so with any luck you'll never*
> *know that I was a fool. I always said "Fake it 'til you make it." I*
> *wonder if that ever works, or if we end up spending our lives trying to*
> *be someone we're not. Who knows? But I do know that when it came*
> *to the Kane brothers, Anthony believed in me. Your brother loved*
> *me for the drama of me. You never believed. You hated the drama.*
> *Why couldn't I have just wanted Anthony?*

*The truth is, I wanted you all along, even though it was Anthony
who made me feel alive. Of course you never wanted me. I knew
that. But I wanted you anyway. I knew you'd give me the life
I wanted. So I got you the only way I knew how. I was young and
pretty, and had the sort of hunger that most hardscrabble, scared girls
have, which isn't so hard to understand, given where I came from.
I knew what I wanted and was determined to get it. That's all I could
see. I never considered who might get hurt in the process.*

*Of course you remember that drunken night when I seduced you
and ended up pregnant. You thought I was shallow, and you hated me
after that, but you married me anyway, as I was sure you would.
From the moment I met you, I knew you were a man who took his
responsibilities seriously. THAT is what I did love about you. And
I wanted that responsibility to be me. You would give me the life I
wanted. You would be my prince to my Cinderella. Foolish, I know.
But isn't that every poor girl's dream? Anthony would never be able to
do that for me. I thank my lucky stars every day for that night, for
Miranda. And I thank God you couldn't have loved Miranda more.
It's to your great credit that your resentment of me never spilled over
to our daughter.*

Proof that Miranda was Dad's real daughter.

Ariel's stomach lurched; she hated the truth, not that she really wanted
Miranda not to be legit. It was just that Miranda being legit proved that
Anthony hadn't lied about that part.

Her heart pounded, but she kept reading.

*That wasn't my only sin. I also knew you hated that Anthony
thought you seduced me to win me away from him. I'm still amazed
that you never told Anthony the truth: that I seduced you.*

If I'm really truthful, I loved that he was madly jealous that we

married. Do you understand the draw for a girl like me to have two
men seeming to fight for me, even if one of the men wasn't really
fighting for me, but for his unborn child? And when you never forgave
me—always made it clear that I had tricked you, even if it was
through your stoic silence—is it really a surprise that I would seek out
the only man who did make me feel beautiful and loved? When you
married me, I swore that I would never sleep with Anthony again,
and I swear I wouldn't have if you had ever tried to love me. Do you
get that part of this is your fault?

In the end, yes, I went back to your brother. Does it matter that it
wasn't right away? Does it matter that we both knew by then that
our marriage was falling apart?

Of course it doesn't. But even then, I was given a gift. This time,
it was Ariel.

Ariel moaned out loud, her fingers curling into the paper. She squeezed
her eyes closed, every inch of her growing hot and sick and hurting. But
she couldn't stop now.

Just as with Miranda, you loved Ariel from the moment she came
into the world. I saw the love in your eyes as you held Ariel for the
first time. I never had the heart to tell you Anthony was her father,
not even as a way to hurt you more when I still couldn't find a way to
make you want me. But Anthony knew, and I've paid dearly to keep
him quiet.

But that's the past.

Anthony Kane might love me in his own equally selfish way, but
he cares more about himself and money than anything else. Do not,
I repeat, do not ever let him convince you otherwise. If you are
reading this, then I'm no longer in a position to continue funneling
money to Anthony in order to keep Ariel safe. Please don't let him
hurt her. Please don't let him use her to hurt you. Hopefully by

*the time you read this, I will have been able to pull it all together so
that you have everything you need to make sure he can't.*

*I have done a lot of things I'm ashamed of. Despite how I got
them, the best thing I have produced in my life is our daughters. Ours.
Yours, Gabriel. Both of them. I can only hope my sins won't get in the
way of you keeping both of them safe.*

Victoria

Ariel couldn't breathe. What did it mean? How could Anthony hurt
her? A scream pounded inside her, wanting to get out. Panic licked at her
as her greatest fear was realized, the one that she had been too afraid to
say out loud: Anthony really was her father, and Gabriel Kane didn't
know. Yet.

After he read this, would he turn her over to Anthony?

"No," she whispered.

Her fingers closed around the small key, deciding she should figure out
what the key opened before she told anyone about it. Inch by inch, she
went through her mom's study, biting her lip hard to keep the tears away.
Maybe her mom had a safe somewhere with money to pay off Anthony.
She picked up decorative boxes and frames filled with photos—photos
of her, Miranda, Dad—looking for something that needed a key.

There was nothing. Her mom would never have hidden the box or
whatever it was in the bedroom, not the one she shared with Dad. Ariel
stuffed the envelopes in her backpack and left the study. She peered
down the stairs. Most of the kids were in the living room playing weird
dare games. She could just make out a girl shoving marshmallows into her
mouth, one by one, the kids egging her on and then laughing when she
spit them out. Seriously, idiots. But there was no sign of Miranda or Dustin.

She ran down the stairs, through the dining room, through the swinging door into the kitchen, then into the den. A bunch of kids were in
there now, but still no Miranda. Ariel kept going to the stairway leading
to the basement.

Nerves made her slip and clatter down the thin wooden staircase, catching herself on the banister, stumbling into the dark space, but she managed to find the tiny chain that worked the lightbulb. The bulb cast a weak light, not much, but she managed to find a flashlight, then went through the basement. She was hardly breathing as she went through old metal lockers with no locks, cabinets, boxes. Nothing that needed a key.

"Damn, damn, *damn!*" she cried, slamming the lid on a trunk, dust puffing up in the dank air.

Crashing down onto a low work stool, she dropped her head into her hands. She was covered in dust and grime, her wild hair tangled, her clothes filthy. But she still didn't have what she needed.

She sat up all of a sudden. Would their mom have told Miranda something? Was that why Miranda had said they would talk later?

Ariel hurtled up the stairs from the basement, her backpack banging side to side on her shoulders like a pendulum as she ran. In the den, two kids were now making out on the couch, the TV blaring, beer cans lying about the tables like crumpled tin soldiers. She raced through the swinging door from the den to the kitchen and then to the dining room and found a girl crying at the table, a friend trying to console her. She didn't stop. In the foyer, another girl stood on the stairs sipping a beer, a guy leaning up against the banister, probably trying to convince her to go upstairs to one of the bedrooms.

Ariel ran past them. Her shoulders had started to ache, so she pulled off her backpack as she entered the living room. Just then a cheer erupted, startling her. Two boys were stuffing the fireplace with old newspapers and flicking burning matches onto the paper. Every time they got a leap of flames, they cheered.

These dopes were still trying to make s'mores. "You can't do that! You'll catch something on fire!"

They didn't even look at her.

Two girls sat on the hearth, pulling out the graham crackers and chocolate, shoving marshmallows onto a couple of pens. The fire was messy, ash getting everywhere. Just the sight of the chocolate made Ariel desperately wish she was back in New York, sitting at the counter island in Portia's kitchen, watching her work her magic with food. If only she'd never come out here.

If only she'd never gotten in the car with her mother.

Tears beat behind her eyes like prisoners trying to escape. Someone started retching and she jerked around. A kid was vomiting into one of her mom's decorative brass pots. Three boys circled around him, laughing hysterically. "Lightweight! Lightweight!"

One of them held a bottle of vodka. Probably her dad's. Already empty.

Just then, one of her mom's tasseled pillows flew by her head. "Who the fuck are you, little girl?" a boy shouted, from where he slouched on the sofa, beer can in hand. Another boy, somehow looking older, sat there, his brow furrowed.

She dropped her backpack and picked up the pillow, hugging it tight. "None of your business. Where's Miranda?"

A bunch of them whipped around to face her.

"Freakin' A. It's Miranda's sister."

Ariel hardly recognized Miranda's new friend Becky. She had on a ton of makeup. "What the hell are you doing here?" Becky demanded. "You're supposed to be in the city."

"Becks," another girl said. "Cool it." Then she smiled at Ariel, sweet, too sweet. "You want to play with us, Miranda's sister?"

"No. And you better get out of my house before I call the police."

The girl just laughed. "Seriously, you're not that uncool, are you? Come on, do shots with us."

Her face felt hot and sweaty, her heart pounding even harder. "Where's Miranda?"

"What a baby!" Becky said, turning away. She saw Ariel's backpack and yanked it up. "Do you have any money in here?"

Ariel grabbed for it, but Becky leaped out of the way and started pawing inside. Journal, pens, multicolored socks spilled out. "That's mine!" Ariel yelled.

"We need money for booze," Becky said, staying out of reach. "Your dad's a freaking millionaire, everyone knows that. But all he had in this place was a few stinking bottles of Ketel One."

Ariel grabbed for the pack again, but Becky smirked and tossed it to another girl.

Ariel pivoted and leaped for the other girl, who only laughed and threw the pack over her head to one of the guys, who tossed it to another kid in the foyer.

It was like a game playing out in slow motion, until she realized that Becky was laughing even harder. She turned around to find the girl was holding her journal.

"'Musings of a Freak,'" Becky read, giggling madly. "You *are* a freak."

The music swirled through Ariel's head like notes swimming through melting marshmallow. It took a moment to figure out that this awful girl was reading her thoughts out loud—her frustrations, her hopes, her fears—for everyone to hear. Part of her was mortified, and some other part pulsed with fury. But something else clawed at her and stung her nose.

Smoke still puffed out into the room instead of going up the chimney. The boys making s'mores didn't seem to care. One of them threw back a shot, then tossed his plastic cup into the fire, making the smoke smell so bitter she could taste it on her tongue.

"Hey, moron—" she heard someone say, but then a big *pop* sounded and the fire flared up, and still none of the smoke went up the chimney.

"Shit," one of the boys said, falling back a step.

"Yeah," another said. "Son of a bitch, you're a moron."

Somebody threw a glass of beer on the fire, but it didn't go out.

"Oh, no," Ariel cried, swiping her nose with her sleeve, as it only got worse. She grabbed a beer can from the table and ran forward, too, but the can was empty. The fire popped, a flying ember hitting her sleeve. She stared in shock as her shirt started to burn.

"Damn." The cool boy from the sofa pushed up, tore off his jacket, and wrapped her arm with his coat. Then he grabbed a full water bottle from his pack and threw the contents onto the flames, and the fire sizzled and hissed as it went out. "Seriously, morons," the guy muttered.

Ariel dropped the empty can, and still, she couldn't do anything but stare, her mouth open.

The guy leaned down and looked her in the eye. "You're okay, kid. Got it? Now go home. Get out of here. You're too young to get involved with this crazy shit."

Her lip trembled.

"You're fine, kid, really." He straightened and shook his head. "I'm out of here. If you want a ride, this is your chance."

She couldn't move. She wasn't fine. Nothing was fine.

He shrugged and headed for the door. "I'm out of here."

She lost it then. She started crying in big, gasping sobs as she staggered back from the hearth. She dashed at her eyes, swiping away soot and tears and a year of holding on by a thread.

She didn't care what any of them thought of her. She couldn't stop crying. It was all of it, the one tiny gesture of kindness from a stranger who walked out the door, the forgotten house, her mom, the dad who wasn't really her dad, the lies she hadn't known about, the life she didn't know how to fix.

Somebody put a hand on her shoulder and she twisted away, facing the fireplace, her body racked by tears, gasping as she tried to catch her breath. But all she managed to suck in was smoke.

With a gasp of surprise, she felt her lungs squeeze, her throat going tight. Her eyes burned, and she felt them start to bug out. She told herself not to panic. She wheeled back around, looking for her backpack. Looking for Einstein. But he wasn't there. Her backpack was gone.

She opened her mouth to cough, but it wouldn't come, just more smoke filled her mouth and nose.

The kids started to murmur, their faces distorting. But she couldn't move. Her legs felt wobbly, sounds overloud in her ears.

"What's wrong with her?" she barely heard.

"Stop being a freak!" Becky shouted.

"I think she's having some sort of fit. Crap."

"She's probably epileptic. She's gonna froth!"

"Damn, get me out of here."

The voices swelled in her head before growing distant. Then all of the sudden she saw Miranda run into the room. Ariel wanted to weep in relief when she felt her sister's hands grabbing for her, hands circling her arms, rough and frantic. But a second later she realized that it was too late. Her head swam, the prisoners behind her eyes finally going quiet, the world going black.

And she disappeared.

Forty-one

⁘

As soon as Gabriel turned the Mercedes onto the narrow residential street, Portia knew for certain something was wrong. She felt it in the vibration of her thoughts, violets and watermelon flashing through her mind in a kaleidoscope of dread.

Gabriel must have felt it, too. He cursed beneath his breath and hit the gas, every ounce of civilized man falling away.

Portia had never been to New Jersey, much less to Montclair. The full moon cast silver light on the giant old houses that were set back from the road, built far apart, a gracious lawn rolling up to a sprawling Victorian with brilliant white latticework, followed by a stately redbrick Colonial, and finally a beautiful old Tudor, its slate roof shining like blue-black water in the bright night. The opposite side of the imposing street dropped off in a gentle cliff to even larger houses in the distance below.

Outside the Tudor, cars lined the road, lights blazing inside.

"The party," Gabriel bit out, slamming on the brake in front of the house.

Portia saw the teenagers coming and going. Gabriel double-parked in front of what she assumed was the Kanes' New Jersey house. Cars filled the long, narrow driveway that disappeared around back. Gabriel raced to the front door.

Portia was right behind him, unease filling her like hot water rising in a pan. It wasn't the idea that someone was throwing a party at Gabriel's house that concerned her. Something else quickened her pulse, a kind of horror that she couldn't name.

They were halfway across the lawn when kids started barreling out the front door, running and yelling at each other.

Gabriel pushed past them like a beast possessed, Portia at his heels. At some level the opulence of the house registered along with the dread, the sure knowledge that she didn't belong to this world, to this family. Robert's sprawling home was nothing compared to this stately mansion, her family's double-wide as foreign to this world as a mud hut on a Burmese hillside.

"Dad!"

Portia's heart stood still when she ran into the living room. Miranda was a mess of tears and wrecked hair, mascara streaming down her face, looking like a crying child playing dress-up.

"She's dead!"

Gabriel fell to his knees. When he did, Portia saw Ariel on the floor.

His roar filled the entire house as he pulled the girl into his arms. "What have you done?" he demanded.

"I didn't do anything!" Miranda cried, hugging herself.

Portia felt an odd calm come over her. She pulled out her cell phone. "Has anyone called 9-1-1?"

"I already did," Miranda managed, dropping down next to the girl and their father. "You have to fix her, Dad. Oh, God, it's my fault! Ariel! Wake up!"

Gabriel started CPR.

Kids were still running, a boy pounding down the stairs, towing a half-dressed girl. The music was nearly deafening, so Portia turned it off.

Then there was silence except for Miranda's sobs and Gabriel's measured counting as he blew air into Ariel's lungs and compressed her chest.

Portia sank onto her knees beside them. She took in the room, smelled the air. She turned back to Ariel. "Her lips are blue around the edges. It's an asthma attack. Where's her backpack?"

Gabriel and Miranda went stiff at the same time. Miranda leaped up. "It's got to be here somewhere!"

But the kids had evaporated. Ariel's backpack was nowhere in sight.

Gabriel raised his head, his hands compressing Ariel's chest with gentle force. "The yard," he ordered. "Someone dropped something in the yard."

Portia flew back out of the house and spotted Ariel's backpack lying in a forgotten heap in the dark. She careened back inside, ripping through its contents as she went until she found what she was looking for. She dropped down next to Gabriel, who grabbed the inhaler and put it into his daughter's mouth. He shot it once, then twice, then clamped his mouth over hers and resumed CPR.

Forty-two

❖

ARIEL SWAM in a murky place, where sound was muffled and light seemed overbright. But the worry, all the worry she had felt since the accident, was gone. She still felt the buzzing, but she was no longer a bee stuck in a jar.

She felt at peace.

This was where she wanted to be, a place where things were easier. This was what she had been moving toward ever since the accident, with all those horrible feelings slowly disappearing.

She had been right. She had disappeared, just like Mom.

For so long she had been afraid, but had refused to admit it. With the fear and worry suddenly gone, she felt herself expanding, as if she were flinging her arms wide and taking a deep breath.

But on the heels of that peace, she felt a tinge of panic trying to pry its way through the calm. Could she really leave her dad? Miranda? Even Portia? Would they be fine without her? Would they care?

"Ariel!"

The roar echoed in the quiet that surrounded her.

"No!"

She felt the vibration of the words against her body more than she heard them.

Dad?

"Ariel! Damn it, come back!"

For long seconds she felt the words, felt the way they surrounded her and pushed away the quiet. She felt torn between the peace and the wish to stop the pain she felt coming at her in a wave. The push, then the pull. The need to stay gone, the pull to go back.

Then all of a sudden, she saw her dad's face in her mind with that look he had at Mom's funeral when his mouth distorted and she knew he could have cried but wouldn't. Of Dad sitting at the breakfast table reading *The Wall Street Journal*, the way he had lowered the paper and raised a brow when she inquired if he was interested in having cocktails that evening, only to go back to reading without a word. Her dad, who didn't get ruffled by anything. Her dad, who she felt certain hovered over her now. Crying.

The world flooded back into her a startling gasp of breath, and she cried out in surprise. Air burned as it rushed into her lungs.

"Dad?" she managed, her tongue thick, her head light. She felt hot and cold all at once, and like she was going to be sick to her stomach.

Her father was leaning over her. "Ariel."

Not a question. A statement. But with the world coming back into focus, she remembered everything that was wrong, the peace gone.

He wasn't her dad at all.

Misery ripped through her as all the pieces jarred back into place. First her mom had been taken away. Now her dad. She wanted to go back to the quiet. She wanted to scream that it was all unfair. She wanted to tell him she would be the greatest daughter ever, that she'd do better this time at being perfect, that he'd be better off keeping her rather than giving her away.

But what if he didn't want her? What if he didn't want to deal with the trouble of always paying Anthony? How she wished he would never learn the truth.

She struggled to open her eyes. The minute she succeeded, her dad hugged her tight. "Oh, God," he whispered, making her feel safe for the first time since the accident.

"Dad?"

"God, Ariel," he said into her hair. "As soon as I get over the relief I feel right now, you're going to be in a mountain of trouble for running away."

"So you'll ground me?" she managed, wanting nothing more than her dad's infamous go-to form of punishment, anything to make her feel that their lives could be normal again.

He half laughed, half cursed, and held her tight.

Then Miranda came into view next to Dad's shoulder. "Ariel, I'm sorry!" she said, her voice warped by a sob. "I was so stupid to come out here. And it was stupid that I didn't come find you the minute I heard you were in the house. I—I almost killed you!"

Ariel shook her head, the effort making her senses spin. "No, you didn't."

Ambulance guys rushed in then, moving Miranda and her dad back.

That's when she saw Portia just looking at her, a strange mix of relief and sadness on her face. "Hey, kiddo. Welcome back."

As if Portia actually understood that she had gone, might not have returned.

Ariel smiled at her, feeling sort of shy, wanting to reach out, realizing that the one person she could have talked to all this time was Portia. She would have understood. Portia got all those things that weren't ordinary, like food that meant stuff, and how people could disappear.

But then her thoughts circled back to what she had found. As much as she didn't want to tell her dad about it, she couldn't be like her mother. No more secrets.

She pushed at the ambulance guy. "Dad?"

"What is it, Ariel?"

"I found a box Mom hid. It had a key and some letters in it."

Dad didn't seem to care. "Sweetheart, let the paramedics finish checking you over. We can talk about it later."

They started in on her—blood pressure, checking her eyes, temperature—then had her hooked up to an IV in record time.

"Quick onset, quick recovery. But to be on the safe side," one of them said, "she should be observed for twenty-four hours. We'll take her to Overlook."

"What?" Ariel said, her throat still burning. "Overlook, like the hospital? I can't go there. I have bigger problems. I found letters from Mom. And a key," she repeated.

The paramedics and Dad looked at one an other, and the paramedics fell back.

"What letters, Ariel? What key?"

"So," she began, hesitant, nervous, though her voice was getting stronger, the itch less intense, "you see, Mom told me I had to find the box."

Her dad got an even weirder look on his face.

"I don't mean she told me anything *after* she died. In the car, after we wrecked, before the police got there, she told me to find the box in her study."

"Why didn't you tell me?" he asked, his voice pained.

"I didn't want to know." Ariel tried to feel less stupid than she did right then. "But mostly, I guess, I didn't want Mom to be dead, and not finding the box made it less real."

"Who are the letters for, Ariel?"

She bit her lip, trying to push herself up to sit cross-legged, but her dad didn't let her.

"Fine," she exhaled. "Technically, one's for you. The other's for a lawyer." Then she rushed out the rest with a heave of breath. "But she told *me* to find the box, so I figured—"

"Ariel," he said, cutting her off, "let me have the letters."

As reluctantly as she had done anything in her life, she told him they were in her backpack. Once the pack was retrieved, he pulled the folded envelopes out. He read all of it. He swallowed hard, his throat working. Then he read the one to him again, and looked at her.

She told herself to have a little pride. Raising her chin, she said, "I guess I should call you Mr. Kane." She choked on the words, her voice clogged and raspy. "Too formal? How about Uncle Gabriel?"

"Oh, God," he whispered, pulling her back to him before setting her just far enough way that he could look her in the eye. "I'm your *dad*, Ariel. Always your dad."

Tears burned even hotter. "But the letter—"

"No buts. I raised you. I loved you from the second you were born."

"But Uncle Anthony—"

"Forget my brother, Ariel. You're my daughter, in every way that matters. And I keep what is mine. Always."

The words were fierce. "Really?"

"Really." He pulled her close. "You're mine, A."

It was sick possessive, but she had never liked her dad's whack-job bossy thing more than she did right then. She would have done her best to throw herself at him, despite the IV tube, but she couldn't. Not until the whole truth was out there. She couldn't leave it half done.

"Dad," Ariel whispered, not wanting to tell him the even bigger secret that she had tried to tuck away and forget, the last bit of poison she had refused to tell the Shrink, had refused to write in her journal. "Mom wrecked because of me."

His whole body went stiff. "What are you talking about, Ariel?"

She glanced over to where Portia was talking to Miranda, who was still crying. "I found Mom with, um, Anthony."

Her dad went completely still, and she felt the panic creep up again.

"Please explain." Short, clipped words, but her words spilled out in a rush.

"Miranda had gone into the city on a school trip. Mom forgot I only had a half day at school, then a Mathlete competition, so I walked home. And I, um, saw them, together."

His eyes narrowed. "I'm going to kill him."

"I waited outside for him to leave, so he wouldn't see me. When he left, I told Mom I knew. That I saw. That I was going to tell you."

Tears started streaming down her cheeks before she realized she was crying. "I was mad. I gave her the car keys and said—" The words stuck in her throat.

"What did you say, sweetheart?"

He looked at her with his craggy face, so fierce, but in that way he had that made her feel like he could do anything in the whole world.

"I told her if she was finished screwing Uncle Anthony"—she shuddered at the words—"that maybe she could find a few minutes to take me to the Mathlete competition." Ariel did her best to keep her voice steady, truthful. "Mom slammed into the car, mad."

Ariel had gotten in the backseat, just as angry. But her mom had acted like she wasn't even in the car, like she was invisible. Mom hadn't said a word about Anthony. No explanation, no promise that Ariel shouldn't worry, or that they would talk about it later. "She was really mad, her hands clenching on the wheel." She hesitated. "I might have been sort of mad, so . . . I asked her if she wanted me to tell you before I competed or after. Mom jerked her head back to look at me then. She turned away from the road, Dad, and started to say something to me." Ariel drew in a deep breath. "You know the rest."

Her dad's jaw worked, it seemed, like for a century. Finally he said, "Ariel, listen to me, and listen good. None of this, I mean none of it, is your fault. It's my fault, and your mother's fault. And Anthony's fault. But never yours. Do you understand me?"

Her eyes burned, relief washing through her, and she managed a nod, even if she wasn't entirely sure she believed it.

Portia must have thought they were finished talking, and she walked over. "You go with Ariel to the hospital," she said. "I'll drive Miranda back to the city and stay with her until you and Ariel are done."

Dad looked up. "Portia—"

"Gabriel, give me the keys," she said, stepping back.

Ariel watched as he stared at Portia, then nodded. "You're right. You and Miranda should go back. As soon as Ariel and I finish at the hospital, I'll call a car service."

He glanced at Miranda with a ferocious look, but at the same moment he stood and extended his arm. Miranda ran to him, and he pulled her into his chest.

"This isn't over," he said. "But we'll fix it. We'll fix whatever's wrong. Okay?"

Miranda hiccupped another sob, and nodded against his shirt.

Dad looked over her head at Portia and started to say something.

But Portia turned away, and Ariel saw a bunch of emotions race across his face. Anger? Frustration? Whatever it was, he definitely wasn't happy.

"Come on, Miranda," Portia said. "We'd better hurry." She took Dad's keys, then leaned over to Ariel. "Glad you're okay, kiddo."

Then she was out the door, Miranda in tow, Dad staring after her and looking like he wanted to punch the wall.

⁘

It took hours, but after another IV solution of some kind, and getting checked on every five seconds, eventually Ariel got the okay from the emergency room doctors to leave. But once they did, she and her dad didn't go home. It was somewhere around four in the morning. They went to a hotel near the hospital, just in case she had to go back in.

Which she wouldn't, but it made her feel better to have her dad fussing over her so much. Maybe he really did mean to keep her.

She took a long bath in a tub that was like a small pool while Dad went downstairs and managed to get someone to find them something to eat.

Finally, clean and fed, wrapped in one of the hotel's giant robes, Ariel curled into her dad's arms and looked up at him. He was sitting on the bed, his head back against the headboard. He seemed really tired, and it made her worry.

"Dad," she whispered.

He didn't open his eyes. "Hmmm?"

"I'm sorry I was the one who told you about the Uncle Anthony thing."

He didn't answer at first. "I already knew."

She jerked in his arms. "You already knew? For how long?"

"He told me six months after the funeral."

Exactly when they'd moved into the city. She took the information in, processing. "Is that why we left Montclair?"

"Yes. I wanted to be closer to you and Miranda."

"So he couldn't show up and take me while you were working in Manhattan?"

"Ariel, nothing like that is going to happen."

"But what if . . . what if Uncle Anthony fights for me? You know, because of money, or something."

He looked at her then, and that ferocious power thing he did so well was back. It didn't scare her at all, only made her feel weak with relief.

"There is no amount of money that will get in the way of you always being my daughter, Ariel."

"Is that what you two keep talking about? Is that what you want him to sign? Something that says I'm . . . not his?"

He pulled her closer. "Like I said, no matter what, you are my daughter. Don't ever forget that, Ariel. But, yes, I intend to make it legal."

"And that's how Uncle Anthony keeps getting money out of you? Like blackmail? Like he was doing to Mom?"

She felt him tense. "Let me worry about my brother. I will always take care of you. Can you trust me? Will you stop running around town trying to solve mysteries and let me do it for you?"

She blinked.

"Yep, I know all about your adventures."

"Are you mad?"

"I'm only angry at myself for not having gotten this dealt with sooner."

Ariel felt the vise around her chest ease. And just like the night she had fallen asleep in his study back in Manhattan, Ariel tucked herself even closer. She felt so tired, like all the energy she had used to keep things together had seeped out of her, in a good way, and she thought that finally she would really sleep.

"I bet you're going to rethink the whole no–cell phone thing now," she whispered as she drifted off.

She was almost sure she heard him laugh.

⁘

They headed out of the hotel in the morning and a car was waiting in the front drive. But instead of giving their address in Manhattan, her dad gave an address in Montclair.

"Where are we going?" she asked.

"To the bank." He held up the key she had found. "It's for a lockbox."

"How can you tell?"

"I used to have one just like it at a bank here in town. I never knew your mother had her own."

They walked into the bank and were ushered into a private area, a box pulled out and waiting on a table.

"Are you ready?" her dad asked.

Biting her lip, Ariel nodded.

Her dad took the key and opened the box. Ariel let out her breath in a rush.

"It's just papers!"

"Documents," he said as he began to read. When he finally set them down, he looked sort of angry, but also relieved.

"Your uncle Anthony signed over guardianship to me years ago. Though it cost Victoria to keep him quiet. She obviously intended to get it all to a lawyer so that if anything happened to her, there wouldn't be any confusion, but she didn't get it done in time." For half a second, intense anger flushed out everything else on her dad's face, but he swallowed it back. "After Victoria died, Anthony must have realized that no one knew about the documents, including me, so he started on me." He cut himself off after he seemed to remember Ariel was sitting there.

He leaned over and cupped her face. "All that matters," he stated, "is your mother made sure that legally, I'm still your dad."

Forty-three

⟐

PORTIA HEARD A CAR pull up out front, then the outer door of the town house opened, and her heart surged into her throat.

Neither she nor Miranda had slept much in the hours since they'd returned to the city. Even though she was sure they would have said yes, Portia hadn't wanted to impose even further on Stanley and Marcus by asking that they put up both her and Miranda. Plus, Miranda would want to be at home so she could see that Ariel was okay the minute she returned. So Portia had stopped by next door to say good night, and then returned to the town house. She felt surrounded by memories in the house, the memory of her great-aunt and the memory of what she had thought she shared with Gabriel.

Miranda had fallen asleep on the sofa. Portia had hunkered down in an overstuffed chair, reminding herself that this house wasn't a home, not the kind where she belonged, with its perfect, expensive fabrics, sterile of emotion despite the rich materials and heavy silk.

After a few hours, she had realized she wasn't going to sleep at all, so she had gotten up and gone to the kitchen. Eventually Miranda had followed, and the two of them sat there, not saying much, until the front door opened.

Miranda leaped up and flew down the hall. Portia drew a deep breath, then followed.

When she came out into the hallway it was just in time to see Miranda throw herself at her dad and sister. "I'm sorry!" the teen cried.

Looking on, Portia's heart twisted. She loved the girls and would miss them. But after everything that had happened, she knew she had no future in this house.

As if sensing her thoughts, Gabriel glanced up. His eyes drifted over her, dark, assessing, as if trying to understand what she was thinking.

"Dad," Miranda said, drawing his attention.

Portia didn't wait to hear what the girl had to say. She used the distraction to make her escape.

She slipped past the three of them, heading for the front door.

"Portia," Gabriel stated, hard and clipped, like a demand he expected to be obeyed.

She went faster.

"Portia." This time softer, mixed with a sigh.

Portia didn't care. She raced out the front door, literally running over to Stanley and Marcus's.

Stanley raised a brow from his place by the window when she walked in, and Marcus bustled her over to the sofa, plopped down beside her, and said, "Tell me everything!"

Portia caught her breath. "Marcus!"

"You can't hold out on me, not after all the Little Debbie cakes I gave you! I am dying of curiosity. You didn't give us one single detail last night! Granted, it was late, but now, out with it!"

She sank back against the cushions, suddenly exhausted. "Miranda went to New Jersey. Ariel followed, had a bad asthma attack, and ended up in the hospital overnight. She's fine now. There."

"Glad to hear it, but now I want the good stuff," he demanded. "What happened with Gabriel? Tell me he groveled at your feet, apologizing up and down for not bothering to mention he owned your apartment!"

"No, no apology." She pursed her lips. "Not that an apology solves anything."

The words were barely out of her mouth when her cell phone rang.

Kane, Gabriel.

She pressed ignore with relish. When she glanced up from the phone, Stanley and Marcus were looking at her. "What?" she said.

"You'll have to talk to him sometime."

"No, Marcus, I won't."

Marcus cringed.

Not two minutes later, someone was at the front door.

Stanley glanced out the window, then exchanged a glance with Marcus. This time it was Stanley who struggled up from the chair while Marcus gathered their coats.

"Where are you going?" she squeaked.

"No more hiding, Portia. Gabriel's a good man." Marcus paused and gave her one of the very few frowns she'd ever seen on his face. "True, he should have told you about owning the apartment. But he's still a good man. Deep down, you know that."

They hurried out the door, letting Gabriel in, but not before she heard Stanley growl, "You hurt her again, and you'll answer to us."

Once the door shut, Gabriel stepped forward. There was nothing soft and approachable about him. "We are going to talk, Portia."

"There's no point." She started to turn away, but he strode forward and took her arm. Not hard, not bruising; unrelenting, but oddly gentle. "You will listen to me. You owe me that."

All her careful calm evaporated. "I don't owe you anything! I'm not the one who lied and betrayed you."

"Damn it, I'm trying to apologize!"

She gasped her disbelief. "Last I heard, apologies don't start with barked-out orders!"

He visibly reined himself in, and let her go. With a few quick steps, she moved away.

He raked his hands through his hair. "I'm trying, Portia. I don't know the first thing about nice or simple. Charm. That's my brother's domain. I've always been hard." As if that made it better. "I know I've messed up at every turn. With you. With my daughters. Christ, I nearly lost one." The entire frame of his tall, hard-chiseled body shuddered, every bit of searing anger draining out of him. She felt his pain. She thought of the way he was when he made love to her, the control she knew he didn't believe he could afford to lose.

She wanted to reach out, but kept her hand at her side.

He stepped forward. She stepped back until she hit the wall. He didn't stop until he was inches from her. He took her in, assessing in that way he had, this time as if to determine if she was safe, as if he couldn't afford for someone else in his life to be hurt.

"Move away, Gabriel."

"That's not going to happen," he said softly. "We are going to talk. I am going to apologize. You need to stop running away from me and listen."

She met his gaze defiantly. "I don't *need* to do anything other than tell you to leave, because, apology or not, we're over."

He flinched, but didn't relent. "We haven't even begun, sweetheart."

"Don't 'sweetheart' me!" She tried to step sideways, but again he blocked her.

Then, as if he was giving in to something he fought, he ran one hand up her neck, his palm cupping her face, his thumb brushing over her cheek. She felt the tremor rush through his body, the heat that hit her. "If I could do it all over again," he said, his fingers sliding into her hair, "I would."

"But you can't," she snapped, forcing herself not to look at his mouth.

"I know that. I screwed up. I get that, too. And now I'm trying to explain. Something I haven't done a lot of in a long time."

"Ah, so the great Gabriel Kane, who doesn't answer to anyone, will deign to explain. And I'm supposed to be all excited about this big emotional breakthrough?"

His dark eyes went hard. "That isn't what I meant, Portia."

He looked at her, his jaw cemented before his eyes drifted to her lips. She knew he wanted to kiss her. Her heart sped up.

"I meant that it's not easy to explain because I hardly understand myself. I don't spend a lot of time thinking about what I feel, or why I couldn't bring myself to tell you I already owned the apartment. Not any of it. But from the first time I saw you sitting on the front steps, wearing those flowered shoes, something about you . . . spoke to me. Hell, I'd been dead for years, long before my wife died." He hesitated, as if searching for words, but clearly believing he had to. "Seeing you sitting there, I felt something . . . intense. Not long after, I recognized that if I let it happen, I would come to need you." His gaze hardened. "I don't *do* need."

"That's great," Portia said with a scoff, refusing to let up, unable to let up. She couldn't afford to. "You're just what every woman wants."

"Don't, Portia. Don't keep throwing this back at me." His face was ravaged. "I'm doing the best I can. I'm trying. At least give me that." He waited a breath, and when she remained silent, he continued. "I denied what you made me feel. Hell, I fought it tooth and nail. But every time I told myself to just tell you that I owned the apartment and kick you out, I couldn't. And that infuriated me. How had I become so weak? It's only been by not being weak that I've succeeded in life. Who the hell am I if I wasn't the strong guy? Look at this face, Portia."

Her breath caught in surprise.

"Is this the face of a man who can afford to be weak?" he demanded. "No, it's not. I learned that as a boy. But that's the thing: The minute you saw me, without having any idea who I was, or that I had money, you looked at me in a way I had never experienced before. You couldn't have been drawn to my money, because you had no idea who I was when you first saw me. You saw me walking toward you, I saw you see me. I saw the way you looked at me. Drawn in. You wanted *me*, Portia. I felt it. I saw it. And when you learned I had money, real money, the kind you needed, you wanted nothing to do with it. Do you know how amazing it was to me that you *didn't* want my money? Hell, you wouldn't even cash the check that I had to force you to take. Anyone else in your position would have snapped up my offer of financing—"

"Offered without believing in me," she interjected, holding on to her anger, hating that her heart was melting.

"But I gave you a check. It doesn't matter how it was offered, because you didn't want a penny of it anyway. Every day I have people who want a piece of me, but only for my money. Even my mother, my brother." He hesitated. "Even my wife. All they want or wanted from me was my money."

She swallowed back the ache she felt for him. She wanted to tell him there was beauty in every strong and harsh plane of his face. It got harder to hold out. Her fingers itched, not to bake, but to touch him. But on the heels of that thought came another. The reality of Gabriel's Meal, a reality that she wanted to run from, but couldn't. How could she after she had watched her grandmother being struck down by lightning based on a meal, the scar on her shoulder a reminder if she was ever inclined to forget?

Her heart slowed at the thought, a deep settling of resolve. As much as she loved him—and she knew she did—as much as she ached for him right then, despite what he had done to her, her grandmother's entry proved all the more that Cuthcart meals spoke truths.

The meal she had prepared for Gabriel had been followed by a very different kind of storm. Gabriel's Meal had been the beginning of a total unraveling of both their lives, starting with the fight between Gabriel and Anthony and ending with Ariel nearly dying, the arrival of the inspector squashing her dream sandwiched in between. Gabriel's Meal had spelled disaster.

"It's too late for us, Gabriel. You betrayed me. You lied to me." Emotion and pain swelled, pushing her on. "But the fact is," she stated, "you said I was ridiculous. Crazy."

"What are you talking about?"

"When I told you that Ariel was in New Jersey. You said, 'That's crazy. Hell, you are crazy. Ridiculous.'"

She could see by his expression that he remembered.

"And you didn't say it in some flip way. You looked me in the eye and I saw that you believed it. Admit it, Gabriel, you think I'm odd. Different. Ridiculous. Deep down, you don't believe in me. That makes you no different from my ex-husband. You both want me to be someone I'm not, someone who fits into a normal box, someone who doesn't know things because of food. My husband said I wasn't normal. You used different words, but you said the same thing." She had never felt so sad. "So no, despite the fact that all you have to do is touch me and I melt, despite the fact that I fell in love with you, madly, deeply, in a let-you-eat-crackers-in-my-bed, shouting-Stella-from-the-courtyard sort of way, there is no future for us." Her voice broke. "I deserve better than men who think of me as lesser than them, when they bother to think of me at all."

"Portia—"

She saw the pain in his eyes, but she didn't let up. "I deserve better than men who want me to fit whatever they think suits their particular life."

He stared at her hard, and she could see the truth sink in. And still, she didn't let up. "I thought you were a different kind of man, Gabriel."

He flinched.

She sucked in her breath, hating this, but held his gaze. "I fell in love with you, Gabriel. But you only thought of yourself. I deserve someone who will love me just the way I am. Now, please, move away. I want you to leave."

She saw the moment he realized she was serious, that she wasn't going to be convinced. After a long furious, aching second, he nodded.

He left her then, without looking back. And her heart broke a little bit more.

Forty-four

❖

"ROBERT BALEAU, please," Portia said into the phone, Stanley and Marcus standing on either side of her.

The woman who answered hesitated, then asked, "Who may I say is calling?"

Portia grimaced, glanced at Stanley, who scowled at her, then raised her chin. "His ex-wife."

The woman gasped. "Portia, is that you?"

Portia's stiffened. "Rayna?"

"I knew it! Portia, darlin', how are you?"

"I'm fine, how are you? What are you doing answering the phones?"

"Well, you know how you had to stay on top of everyone around here to get them to do their jobs. Now you're gone and that Sissy—" She cut herself off. "Let's just say that things aren't running too smoothly around here."

Portia had heard just that after a woman who used to work for Robert had tracked her down and offered her a bit of good fortune.

Rayna sighed over the phone. "He has me doing everything from answering the phones to dealing with the press. Lordy, do I miss you. And not just because without you things are a mess. Are you really okay?"

Portia searched for a cheerful voice to answer. "I'm great." She glanced at Stanley and Marcus. "And I'm about to be even better. Is Robert there?"

"Let me see—"

Suddenly Portia heard Rayna cover the receiver with her hand, but not before she heard Robert's familiar bark in the background.

Rayna came back, this time as proper as when she had first answered. "Yes, Mr. Baleau is in. I'll put you through." But just before she transferred the call, Rayna whispered into the phone, "Miss you."

Then the clicks before Robert bellowed into the phone. "Portia! It's about time you returned my calls."

As if she were a child reprimanded by an adult. It sank in that it had always been that way between the two of them, more so the longer they were married. She felt the sting of embarrassment.

Stanley must have sensed something, because he leaned forward and rasped, "We didn't spend the last twenty-four hours teaching you how to *not be* a nice girl to have you fall apart the minute you get on the phone with that guy!"

She squeezed her eyes closed. Their lessons didn't have one bit in common with the "ladylike behavior" her mother had drummed into her head. But even she had figured out that her mother's pilfered etiquette book was for the birds.

Every ounce of embarrassment and fury rose up, pushing every trace of devastation she felt over the loss of Gabriel aside. Never in her life had she wanted to kick someone's tail.

"It's time you pay what you owe me, Robert."

Stanley nodded.

Robert scoffed into the phone. "What are you talking about, Portia?"

"You owe me for the apartment!"

A surprised pause before, "Portia, you're upset—"

Stanley and Marcus waved their hands, shaking their heads. "Do not get upset!" they hissed.

"Me? Upset? Why would that be, Robert? You divorced me. Then you married the only friend I had in Willow Creek. Fine, that's your prerogative. But it's not your prerogative to withhold the money you owe me, both from our marriage settlement and the proceeds from the sale of *my* apartment—and let's not even discuss my forged signature."

"Portia, you need to calm down."

"Robert, I am calm, calm enough to tell you that I want the money you owe me wire-transferred into my bank account before the end of the day. I know exactly how much you got for my apartment, and I want every dime from the sale, as well as interest from the date of closing. *Capisce?*"

Stanley rolled his eyes. Marcus snickered. Sure, it was a little much. But she was on a roll.

Robert must have sensed that she was serious. Ever the consummate politician, he reined in the moral outrage and replaced it with something that had served him well in the past.

"Portia," he said, his tone aggrieved. "I feel terrible that you and I have come to this. But there is no reason for you to be going on so."

"Let me repeat myself: You must deposit every dollar you owe me in my bank account by the end of the day."

She could all but see him, nearly two thousand miles away, formulating yet another new move, a master playing chess. She was half certain he was enjoying himself.

"I don't have that kind of money readily available."

"Then you'd better find a way to get it. If you don't, I'll make sure your constituency learns you're a lying, cheating manipulator. I'm not so sure those same voters you say love you are going to be thrilled to reelect a man who swears he supports the sanctity of traditional marriage but got one of his employees—his wife's best friend, at that—pregnant while he was still married."

"I know you, Portia," he snapped, his patience spent. "You didn't fight me before. You won't fight me now. Nothing's changed. At heart, you're still a poor girl from a trailer park, raised by a crazy grandmother."

She laughed, which she knew he hadn't expected. "Maybe so. But what *has* changed is that I'm dead serious. Mark my words, I will tell the media about Sissy, but I'll tell the police about how you managed to sell my apartment. In case they don't teach basic law in that fancy law school you graduated from, forgery is illegal, Robert."

There was a moment of silence. "You wouldn't do that."

"Why on earth wouldn't I?"

She heard him draw a sharp breath. "You have no way to prove I spent a second alone with Sissy before I divorced you. Or how do you think you're going to prove I forged your signature. It's a perfect match."

"But that's the thing. Someone always knows the truth. You know that staffer you got to notarize my signature on the real estate documents? F. Don Whitting?"

The phone line crackled with a tense silence.

"Do you think for a second that if the district attorney's office starts poking around and asking questions, F. Don isn't going to cave and admit that you made him do it? I know you, Robert. I know how you operate. Plus, I just so happen to have all the proof I need to make a believer out of your constituency about Sissy."

She had obtained that proof of his infidelity from the fired employee.

"You can't do this!"

She nodded to Marcus, who pressed send on an ancient fax machine they still had attached to a second phone line, sending through a photograph showing a very naked Robert and Sissy, with a date stamp in the lower right corner.

"If I were you, Robert, I'd race to your fax machine and snag the proof before someone else sees it."

Robert cursed before the phone clattered on his desk. Portia waited,

Stanley looking smug, Marcus delighted, until her ex-husband came back on the line.

"You can't do this!" he railed.

"Granted, it's a little low-tech in this day and age of sex videos, but I'm guessing it will do the trick. Call your lawyer, Robert. Tell him to release my money or I'll start making some calls of my own. Police first, the Texas press second. You have until the end of the business day."

She hung up before he could respond, and Marcus and Portia danced. Even Stanley smiled.

Forty-five

·⟡·

As far as Ariel could tell, her dad had really messed things up. And the guy was supposed to be smart.

Once they got back from New Jersey, instead of solving things, her dad had gone over to see Portia and obviously made things worse. He had stormed back into the house and started ripping apart the basement apartment like a man obsessed with erasing every little bit of the woman who used to live there.

On top of that, he was erasing even more of their past by putting the New Jersey house up for sale. She ached a little bit at the idea, because it was like her mom had finally been put to rest. But she also didn't think she would ever be able to walk back into that house anyway. So why not sell it?

Now, three days after the whole asthma debacle, she came home from school to find piles of old linoleum on the front curb, waiting for the garbage truck. One more piece of Portia ripped away.

She dropped her backpack in the vestibule, then found her dad in Portia's apartment, the place a wreck. He wore a dust mask and seemed to be taking the walls apart with a crowbar.

"What is it, Ariel?"

She stood there in the dust and wrecked surroundings, trying to decide the best way to proceed. "How's it going?"

She couldn't read his expression because of the mask, so she just shrugged and walked around the place, just like how she had walked around looking at things the first time she snuck in while Portia and her sisters were sitting around eating.

"Ariel? What do you need? Rosalie made some cake and left it out for you."

Rosalie had started yesterday, replacing Portia. Not to be mean or anything, but nobody could cook like Portia, and they all knew it.

"I'm fine." She shrugged again.

He jammed the crowbar into the top of a piece of molding.

"You know, I was wondering," she said, proud at how casual the words sounded.

He stopped what he was doing and shot her a narrow-eyed look. She refused to let it get to her. This was too important.

"How did you find me? In New Jersey?"

He got that odd look he was getting a lot lately. Ferocious mixed with determination.

"I mean, who would have guessed. New Jersey? Seriously? You found me in New Jersey all by yourself? Ha-ha."

"What are you getting at, Ariel?"

"Me? Getting at something?"

"Spit it out."

And she did. "It just seems to me that you must have had some help."

"Portia told me where to find you." He turned around and gave the molding another sharp jerk. Nails squealed.

Of course she knew that, or at least suspected it, and hadn't she proven she was a majorly great sleuth?

"Really?" She pretended surprise. "How'd she know where I was?"

"She said she knew because of food. And flowers."

He sounded weird, which was super insane since Portia had been doing bizarre things with food ever since she'd landed in their town house,
just as she herself had already told him.

"Portia's good at that, you know, doing uncanny stuff with food," she
reminded him.

He just grunted, attacking the wall again.

"You remember that, right?" Ariel said.

He just gave her a look and told her to go upstairs before he slammed
the crowbar back into another innocent-looking piece of molding.

"Men," she grumbled, marching out the door.

❖

The weather started getting cold, and it looked like pretty soon it would
start snowing. Her dad just kept ripping away at the garden apartment.
While he'd had a whole crowd of people slaving away on their part of the
town house months earlier, he was using his own two hands to rip apart
the downstairs. Every day he worked down there, and every night he sat
at the kitchen table after she and Miranda had cleared away the food he
had cooked.

Yep, he was cooking again. Rosalie had lasted barely a week before
she had called them impossible and had departed. Ariel and Miranda
had made plans, or colluded, as a good detective would say, to run the
woman off. Sure, both of them felt bad about it, but someone had to do
something to make their dad see the light.

Instead of seeing the light, however, and clattering off to Portia and
convincing her to come back to them, he just added cooking back to his
list of duties. It was insanity, really, since even he admitted he was a horrible cook and they'd probably all keel over with food poisoning any day.
That, or starve.

Even more insane, Miranda had started helping him renovate the garden apartment. No sooner did Miranda get home from school than she
changed and headed downstairs like a regular Mini Me Construction Girl.

Ariel told herself it was ridiculous to be jealous. Dad had *chosen* her to be his daughter, even when he didn't have to.

The other surprise? Uncle Anthony.

"You know I love you, kid, right?" he said to her when he appeared one day in their kitchen, Dad looking like a ferocious, overprotective bear despite the apron he wore, since he was in the middle of making another awful dinner.

Ariel wasn't sure what to say to that. She looked at Anthony closely, trying to decide if he was the kind of guy who wanted the truth or a platitude. The thing was, she didn't have any idea what was in his mind.

"Sure, I know."

He gave her a wry look. "You're just saying that."

"Isn't that what you want to hear?"

"Nope. The fact is, I do love you, kid. Ariel." He glanced over at Dad, then bent down in front of her. "But I make a better uncle than a father. Do you understand that?"

Actually, she did, and she couldn't have agreed more. The tiny knot that had stayed inside her after having read one too many online articles about birth fathers wanting their kids back even after having signed them away eased.

She threw her arms around the guy's shoulders. "Thank you for letting me go, Uncle Anthony."

He held on tight for a long second, nodded at her dad, and left.

Later she had overheard her dad tell Nana that he'd given Anthony the money he wanted, even though all the new and better documents were already signed. Which made her heart buzz even more because her dad wanted her that much. Granted, it was not so buzzworthy that she obviously had a blackmailer's blood sloshing around in her veins. But she figured she was smart enough to beat it back if the need to con money out of people suddenly started rearing its ugly head.

After hanging up with Nana, her dad walked back into the study. He looked surprised to find her there. But she'd finally had it. He had fixed the Anthony thing. He was nearly done fixing the garden apartment. But, hello, why wasn't he taking all of her hints and fixing what was really wrong?

"You know, we've discussed how incredibly smart you are," she said without preamble.

"Why do I suspect I'm not going to like where this is going?" he said cautiously.

"I think you're stressed."

Up shot one of those eyebrows of his.

She hurried on. "Maybe with all that construction stress you're under downstairs, you haven't been totally able to figure out on your own that you need to do whatever it takes to get Portia back. Maybe it'd help if I made a suggestion."

"What kind of suggestion?"

"Groveling."

He skewered her with his eyes. "Groveling?"

"Yep, groveling, to Portia. And don't bother saying you don't grovel, Dad, because really, like I said, you've got to do whatever it takes. We need Portia. I do. Miranda sure as heck does. And, well"—she scrunched her shoulders—"I hate to break it to you, but you need her most of all."

Forty-six

◈

PORTIA STOOD ON Columbus Avenue, arms raised to the gently falling snow, reveling in the mounting signs that her life was falling in place.

After growing up in Central Texas, she had virtually no experience with snow. She tilted her head back, feeling the brush of snowflakes against her skin.

Straightening, she looked into the windows of what used to be Cutie's Cupcakes. The awful pastries had finally taken their toll, and when they did, the place had closed down and the space had gone up for rent. Yet another sign.

First, Robert had actually paid her the money he owed her. Then, just when she was ready to make a move, this perfect space came up for rent.

The minute she saw it, Portia had pulled out her cell phone right there on the street and called Cordelia and Olivia.

Since that day, the three Cuthcart sisters had worked tirelessly around the clock getting The Glass Kitchen ready—the real one, not the illegal one in a residential building. They'd taken on not one but two investors, using Portia's money to hire a financial planner who made everything legal and set up an agreement that made sure Portia's money would be repaid out of the first profits. She planned to buy an apartment of her own as soon as she could.

They were starting out small, mostly baked goods and a few entrées. Hopefully, with a combination of Portia's knowing, Cordelia's chatty advice giving and constant supply of helpful books, and Olivia's ability to fill the space with the perfect assortment of flowers, not to mention network, they would soon be able to expand.

For the moment, Portia was living in a small rented apartment of her own, pretty close to The Glass Kitchen. Everything was going better than expected.

But still, she felt empty, even standing around in falling snow in front of a dream that had finally come true.

Of course, she knew why.

She hadn't heard a single word from Gabriel since he'd walked out of Stanley and Marcus's door a month ago. She should have been relieved. But all she felt was miserable.

Pulling her coat tight, she locked the doors of The Glass Kitchen and hurried the few blocks to her new apartment. Taking off her mittens, she checked her voice mail. The first message surprised her.

"Portia, hi," the recording announced. "It's Miranda. Miranda Kane."

As if Portia could forget.

"I just thought you should know that Dad is using the kitchen. As in, he's cooking. I talked to Ariel about it, but she's being totally weird. She might have said something about how you, as a self-respecting adult, should be, like, trying to save me and her from Dad's cooking. Or something. All I know is that we are starving over here."

Portia heard the sound of Miranda unwrapping a piece of candy, as if her world was moving on and she needed to disconnect but didn't know how to break the tenuous connection. The thought tugged at Portia.

"*I'm totally not into missing anyone, but Ariel misses you. I can tell. Whatever. I just thought you should know.*"

Portia didn't call back. What could she say? The girls had lost so much, and she felt guilty to be part of it. But calling them only prolonged the inevitable. She wouldn't ever be a part of their lives.

The next day she worked all day. The Glass Kitchen was packed. She should have felt joy, but by closing time, she felt a strange sensation, like she was getting sick. Worse, all she could think about was food. More specifically, Gabriel's Meal kept circling back into her head, like some cruel reminder of what she could never have.

The kitchen staff had already left, and Olivia and Cordelia had departed early, though not before Olivia had shaken her by the shoulders.

"Portia, you know I love you, but you have to stop moping around."

Portia could hardly argue, so she just gave her a lopsided smile.

"Yes, you do," Cordelia had added, gathering her things. "And may I point out that while the store is crowded, it's crowded with *widows*, Portia."

"What?"

Olivia bustled close. "You didn't notice? It's not just widows. There was that poor woman whose son just died after a heart operation."

Portia did remember—how could she not, when the woman had burst into tears at the sight of the cupcakes with little trains on them that she had made. They had both cried before the woman took away six cupcakes so her family could celebrate her little boy's favorite treat.

"What are you saying?" Portia asked carefully.

"It's like all your buckets of sadness are bringing lines of mourners to The Glass Kitchen," Cordelia explained. "It's not bad, Portia. Lord knows, you're making them feel better. But I kind of miss a smile now and then, you know?"

Her sisters left her standing there speechless, until she finally turned around and started cleaning an already clean counter. A week's worth of customers started marching through her head—the eighty-year-old man with the exhausted eyes, the two women whose mother had just passed away . . .

"Crap," she said when she realized her sisters were mostly right. But the customers had all been grieving for someone they had lost. There was that man whose wife left him with a devastated five-year-old son, and that teenager who . . .

She snapped to attention when the bell rang and the door opened.

"We're not open—"

As she spoke, she turned and froze. Her hair was wild from a day of cooking and baking, and now cleaning. She looked awful and she knew it.

"Gabriel." She hated the breathy sound of her voice, the way her heart kicked up.

Of course he was still beautiful in that way she loved. Hard, craggy. Strong, as if with him she would always be safe. That was what had drawn her to him, right from the beginning. A beast would never let anyone hurt her.

Until he had.

"We're closed."

"Good," he said.

He made the point by turning over the little sign tacked to the door with yarn. "Now you really are closed."

"Which means you should be on the outside of the door. Not inside."

He flipped the lock.

Portia watched him, her eyes narrowing. "What do you think you're doing?"

"What I should have done weeks ago."

He had that way of seeming to catalog each part of her, as if reassuring himself that she was fine, that no harm had come to her in the weeks they had been apart. Portia stayed behind the counter, telling herself that she was above bolting for the side exit. She would deal with him as the adult she was.

"Gabriel," she said as he walked toward her, stopping on the opposite side of the narrow counter. "I really don't want to have another argument. Please."

"I messed up, Portia."

He'd already told her that, but this time, there was no anger in the words, only a commitment to truth.

"You said I didn't believe in you, that I didn't want you to be who you really are. I am going to prove that you're wrong. I do believe in you. I love you, Portia. I love you for every streak of frosting on your face. . . ." He bent over the gaily painted counter tiles and reached out to wipe her cheek, his thumb coming away with frosting. She was mortified until he licked the buttercream away, and her pulse leaped.

"I love you for each of the times you pushed me to see some truth I didn't want to face. For loving me just as I am. For taking care of my girls. For helping me save both of them."

His hand slid back into her hair and he leaned closer, his mouth hovering over hers. "I am going to prove to you that I listen. I am going to prove that I love you in that madly, deeply, let-you-eat-crackers-in-my-bed, shouting-Stella-from-the-courtyard sort of way."

Tears burned at the proof he had listened, at least to that.

"I love you for who you are. But I can't prove it to you here. Come to the town house, then I will prove it."

She managed to dash away the threat of tears. "You can't come in here and ask me to go to your house at the snap of your fingers." She raised her chin. "We are no longer friends with benefits, Gabriel. I'm sorry."

His features cemented, but not with anger. "We were never friends with benefits, Portia."

"Oh, that's right. We were fu—"

"Enough."

He said the word quietly, but with a strength that resonated through the café. "I love you, and the only thing that's *crazy* is if you think I'm going to let the best thing that ever happened to me walk out of my life."

He bent to her again and his hands ran down her arms. "Come home with me. Let me prove how much you mean to me."

When she started to resist, he shrugged. With one swift movement he lifted her over the counter as if she weighed nothing, putting her on her feet before him.

She shrieked with the surprise of it. At the same time, visions of the meal, Gabriel's Meal, danced through her head, taunting her.

"I can't," she breathed.

"Wrong answer," he told her, and actually smiled.

He bent down and had her over his shoulder before she realized what was happening.

"Put me down!"

"Sorry. Can't. If you won't walk on your own, I'll have to carry you."

"You can't carry me to your house like this," she snapped, bracing herself against his back and flailing her legs, trying to get down. "You'll get arrested!"

"If a cop stops me, I'll tell them what you've put me through and they'll drag you to the house for me."

"Ha-ha. If I tell them what you've put me through, they'd arrest *you and* throw away the key."

"Portia. I'm serious. One way or another, you're coming with me."

She made all sorts of outraged noises, but his grip only tightened, like a vise around her legs, and she realized she wasn't going to win this one.

"Are you going to walk?" he asked. "Or do I carry you?"

"Has anyone ever told you cavemen aren't attractive?"

"As a matter of fact, Ariel says pretty much the same thing all the time."

Instantly, she softened, her body easing on his shoulder. "How is she?"

"Missing you."

"Playing the guilt card?"

"Just telling the truth. Now, can I put you down so you can get your bag or whatever else you need? Or am I going to carry you home?"

He barely gave her a minute to get her coat and handbag.

"Front door's already locked," he said. "We'll go out the side door."

She glowered at him, but he remained unfazed, and all too soon they were walking up Columbus Avenue. He took her hand. She yanked it away, only to have him take it again.

"The caveman thing. Unattractive. Remember?"

He just laughed, pulled her hand up to his mouth, and kissed it. She hated that it felt good.

When they arrived on Seventy-third Street, the lights in the town house reminded her of how much she loved the place, standing tall like a wedding cake stacked up into the night sky, snow beginning to accumulate like icing on the window panes and eves.

Gabriel pulled her around to face him, his hand slipping into her hair and tugging her head back so he could see her eyes. "This is your home, Portia. You belong here. With me. With us."

She thought he was going to kiss her, but at the last minute, he pulled back. "First things first," he whispered.

They took the steps to the outer vestibule. She was surprised when he led her down to the garden apartment instead of straight inside to his apartment. The smell of fresh paint hit her first. Then she noticed the refinished hardwood floor on the stairs, the quaint welcome mat outside the open front door. Then she heard the sound of people.

"What's going on?" she demanded, her hand flying to her hair.

"You'll see."

"I'm a wreck!" she moaned, hanging back.

"Am I going to have to put you over my shoulder again?"

"You wouldn't dare."

He went for her, but she scampered back up a step. "Bossy."

"Stubborn."

It took a second for her mind to register all the people inside. Ariel, Miranda. Cordelia and Olivia. Even Stanley and Marcus.

Abruptly, the others became aware of her.

"Portia!"

She blinked, trying to take it in. Her friends and family were standing in the garden apartment . . . which had been completely redone.

"Don't you love it?" Ariel cried, flinging herself forward and winding her arms around Portia's waist. "Dad did it all himself."

Miranda nodded. "With his own hands."

Ariel stepped back. "Same thing, Mir."

"It's beautiful," Portia said, awed.

"It's your dream," Ariel explained, hands on her hips, looking bossy and worried, at the same time. "Not all perfect and professional like those people did upstairs. Dad took everything out, did it just like you wanted, then brought all the old junk back in, fixed up, cleaned up."

"Just as you described," Gabriel said, his voice deep with emotion. "I listened, Portia."

He had, that time they had lain together after making love, talking about her vision for the apartment.

"Oh, Gabriel, I don't know what to say."

Gabriel stepped forward and took her hands. "Portia, this is your home. The people here, we are your family. And in this town house, you have cooked or baked or done something for each person here. So I asked everyone to make something for you to show their thanks."

It was then that she noticed the table, set with the pitted silverware and mismatched dishes.

Stanley straightened, after placing a dish on the table. He took one look at her and grimaced. "Good Lord, woman, is that frosting in your hair?"

"Mind your manners, old man." This from Marcus, who was making room on the table for a platter.

"I can't tell you the last time I did anything in a kitchen," Stanley said, jutting out his chin. "But I did, for you. Because you're a dear," he added. "So I decided that I would make the one recipe I know. Sweet jalapeño mustard."

A jolt went through Portia.

"Can you believe it?" Marcus said. "A New Yorker who makes anything with jalapeños?"

"As you well know, I was born and raised in Texas. I might be old, but I still remember my mother's sweet jalapeño mustard."

Marcus wrapped a lanky arm around his partner's stooped shoulders. "Yes, once upon a time you were a good ol' boy from south of the Mason-Dixon Line. I made my fried chicken for you, Portia, to go with my beloved's mustard."

A chill ran down her spine.

"Miranda and I made biscuits!" Ariel cheered.

Portia couldn't move. She felt Olivia looking at her for a long beat, her brow furrowing. Then Olivia laughed and came forward, taking her hands, pulling her close, pressing her forehead to Portia's. "Some things are true whether you believe them or not," Olivia whispered just for her.

Portia's breath let out in a rush; then she threw her arms around her sister.

She then pivoted to face Gabriel. "But how did you know?"

His brow furrowed. "Know what?"

"The meal. You—this is the meal. It's *your* meal."

"What are you talking about? I just asked everyone to bring something for you, something they could make, something that meant something to them."

Portia swept her gaze over the table. The slaw was there, the buttery mashed potatoes. Each item from Gabriel's Meal sat on the table, just as she had seen it in her mind—this menu, in this garden apartment that she had loved since she was a child.

She didn't realize Gabriel had gone to the kitchen until she turned and found him reappearing. Before she could say anything, he held out a dish. "Strawberry pie—"

"With fresh whipped cream," Portia breathed.

"I made it," he said. "Can't swear to how good it is, but I know you love strawberries, and the girls say it's the only thing I've made in a month that was half edible."

"I can't believe it," Portia whispered. "*You* were the ones who were supposed to make the meal. Not me. That's why mine didn't work."

She looked at each person in turn, and then finally at Gabriel. "This is the meal that came to me when I first saw you on the steps. The meal I tried to make, but ruined."

She didn't wait another second. She ran to Gabriel, throwing her arms around him. "We're meant to be."

He tipped her head back. "It's the meal, the food, that's what convinced you?"

"Yes." Portia hesitated, holding her breath. "Do you understand?"

He looked into her eyes, really looked. Then he smiled. "What I understand is that the rest of my life will be filled with food, food that answers questions that haven't been asked yet, food that you know we need before we know why." He lowered his voice. "You're mine, Portia, and have been since the day I found you on the steps in your flowered shoes."

There was a universal groan, and Gabriel glanced over, as if he'd forgotten anyone else was there.

"What?" he demanded.

Ariel spoke up first. "Maybe think about asking her if she *wants* to be yours."

Portia only laughed. "The way I look at it," she said, "*he's* mine. The truth of a meal never lies. Seems only fair that I give back as good as I get."

Gabriel wrapped her in his arms then and kissed her, a deep claim mixed with an even deeper love and respect.

"Get a room," Olivia demanded with an amused smile.

"Seriously?" Miranda added.

"Sheez," Ariel chimed in.

"Come, sit, Portia," Cordelia said, taking charge. "Let's eat before it gets cold."

They gathered around the table and ate the meal, every last bite.

Later that night, Portia didn't return to the tiny rented apartment on Columbus Avenue. She stayed in the garden apartment and crawled into the old bed Gabriel had restored for her. Joy filled her for the first time in weeks when the man she was meant to be with climbed down the fire escape and into her room.

"Girls in bed?" she asked, sitting up.

He nodded and lay down next to her, pulling her to him. "I'm never letting you leave again," he whispered.

"No more secrets?"

"No more secrets."

"Can you really live with me knowing things are needed before we know why?"

He rolled on top of her, his hands framing her face. "I wouldn't have it any other way."

Then he kissed her, long and deep, and Portia knew she had truly found her home.

Sixth Course

❖

Dessert

Mountains of Wildly Sweet Watermelon
with Fresh Violet Garnish

Forty-seven

✦

THE GLASS DOOR OPENED, ringing the old-fashioned bell over the entrance to The Glass Kitchen. But the café was closed, and the customer was told to come back the next day.

Miranda was doing homework, Portia frosting a cake. Cordelia was setting one of the long tables with old silver and mismatched earthenware, while Olivia was arranging flowers and playing around with some sort of new software.

Ariel sat hidden in a small area in the back that had yet to be organized. No one in The Glass Kitchen knew she was there. She hadn't meant to stay out of sight. But when she came in through the side door, everyone was so busy that no one noticed her.

She sighed at the thought, hating the possibility that she would always be disappearing, an adjunct to these people, not ever completely a part of them.

But the minute the thought flitted through her head, she realized what the cake Portia was frosting was for. Her birthday. Today she was thirteen.

Linda Francis Lee

Ariel had sat down on an overturned plastic bucket, shocked. All these people were throwing a surprise party for her. So she stayed out of sight while they finished preparing, even though the brand-new cell phone her dad had gotten her kept vibrating because Miranda was texting her over and over, wondering where she was. Ariel watched and listened as they talked about making all of her favorite things.

Her life had changed so much in the last few months. As the *New York Times* food critic had written, "The Glass Kitchen, owned and operated by three Texas sisters who create magical food in a world that sometimes spins too fast, is a must for demanding New Yorkers."

The original Glass Kitchen cookbooks were kept in a country cupboard near the old-fashioned register, and were going to be published next year. Portia might have hidden them away in a closet for the first months she was here, but now Ariel found her poring over them almost every day.

The bigger change had come when Portia married her dad and moved in with them. Slowly Portia was turning the whole place into what even Ariel could see was going to be a real home.

When she saw everything was ready, Ariel nearly chirped with excitement, pulling out her phone and finally answering one of her sister's texts.

"Ariel will be here any minute," Miranda shouted, excited in a way that was still hard to believe.

But Portia had pulled Miranda into her circle, which made Ariel wonder if all along Miranda hadn't felt a little bit invisible, too.

"Is everyone ready?" Portia asked. She was rubbing her stomach again, the way she'd started to now that she was carrying around a baby in there.

At first, Ariel had been jealous, afraid her dad and Portia having a baby would crowd her out. But watching everyone talk about Ariel's favorite things made her realize she wasn't being as incredibly smart as she really was to think that.

She saw her dad walk over and pull Portia close, putting his big hand over hers. "Ready," he said.

Ariel knew that was her cue.

She slipped out the side and started to run the short distance to the front door, but forced herself to calm down. Then, taking a deep breath, she walked the last few feet to the front of The Glass Kitchen and stepped inside.

The bell rang overhead. She watched as Dad and Portia, Cordelia and Olivia, Miranda, and Marcus and Stan, whipped around. Even her grandmother Helen was there, still sad that Uncle Anthony had moved to Spain, but sort of resigned. Dad, with Portia's help, or maybe her insistence, had been trying to include Nana in more of their family dinners. Good luck with that, Ariel had swallowed back more than once.

At the sight of her, the whole crew's eyes lit up.

"Surprise!" they cheered.

Ariel slapped her hand to her chest and gasped. "Oh, my gosh! For me?"

Portia raised an eyebrow, and Ariel knew that her new stepmom saw right through her. Ariel just smiled as everyone crowded around her, bellowing the Happy Birthday song, Marcus and Olivia doing a good job of hamming it up. As soon as they were done, Ariel's dad came over and picked her up, twirling her around. "Happy Birthday, sweetheart. You're now officially thirteen."

She held on tight, relishing the fact that he was her dad. No one could take her away from him. They had legal papers to prove it.

He set her down and guided her to the table. All of her favorite foods marched down the center like an ordered list of prime numbers. Or maybe not, she amended. Maybe the dishes were lined up like grilled cheese sandwiches and tomato soup, cupcakes, banana pudding. And watermelon. Mountains of wildly sweet watermelon littered with violet petals, and even a centerpiece made from those same purple flowers.

Watermelon and violets.

She felt her eyes get hot, because it was like Portia had made sure her mom was there, too. And then, proving the point, Portia's arms went around her from behind and she said, "I'm so happy that she led me to you, sweetie."

Ariel leaned back into her, holding on to her hands.

The day Portia and Dad got married, Portia told her that they were one big family now.

"We're like a big pot of vegetable stew," Portia told her that day. "All the better for the mix of different flavors, even if it's messy."

Everyone started talking to her at once then, asking her questions, handing her presents. In one way or another, all these people here in The Glass Kitchen, all of them mixed together, big and messy, looked at her, saw her. She realized then that Portia was right. This had been the solution to her problem all along, because a big, messy mix of family like this would never let her disappear.

THE GLASS KITCHEN MENU

❖

First Course
Appetizer
Chile Cheese and Bacon-Stuffed
Cherry Tomatoes

Second Course
Soup
Crab and Sweet Corn Chowder

Third Course
Salad
Grapefruit and Avocado Salad with
Poppy Seed Dressing

Fourth Course
Palate Cleanser
Blood Orange Ice

Fifth Course
The Entrée
Fried Chicken with Sweet Jalapeño Mustard

Sixth Course
Dessert
Mountains of Wildly Sweet Watermelon with
Fresh Violet Garnish

❖ *First Course* ❖

Appetizer

Chile Cheese and Bacon-Stuffed Cherry Tomatoes

INGREDIENTS

20 cherry tomatoes

½ lb. bacon, cooked and crumbled

⅓ cup chopped green chilies (Old El Paso canned works well)

½ cup grated mix of Asadero or Monterey Jack cheese with
Cheddar cheese

DIRECTIONS

Preheat oven to 350°F. Carefully cut off a thin slice from the top of each tomato. Hollow out the pulp, leaving a thin layer inside, and discard the extra pulp. Turn the tomatoes upside down on a paper towel to drain. In a bowl, combine all the remaining ingredients. Mix well. Spoon the mixture into the tomatoes. Spray a cookie sheet with nonstick vegetable spray. Place the tomatoes on the cookie sheet. Bake approximately 15 minutes, or until the cheese is melty.

❖ *Second Course* ❖

Soup

Crab and Sweet Corn Chowder

INGREDIENTS

4 strips of bacon

2 tbsp. butter

½ cup yellow onion, chopped

½ cup carrot, chopped

½ cup celery, chopped

4 cups frozen yellow corn kernels, thawed

4 cups whole milk

3 cups low-salt chicken broth

1 medium potato, peeled and diced

Pinch of cayenne pepper

1 bay leaf

Salt and pepper to taste

6 tbsp. sour cream

½ lb. freshly cooked crab meat, cut into bite-sized pieces

DIRECTIONS

In a large saucepan, sauté the bacon until crisp. Place the bacon on a paper towel to drain. Pour off all but one tablespoon of bacon renderings. Add 1 tablespoon. butter, melt. Sauté the onion until soft. Add the carrots and celery; cook for 5 minutes. Set aside. Purée two cups of corn. Now, add all the corn to the onion, carrots, and celery. Mix thoroughly. Add the milk, broth, potatoes, cayenne pepper, and bay leaf, plus half of the crumbled, crisp bacon. Bring to a boil. Reduce the heat, cover, and simmer for 20 minutes. Remove the bay leaf. Add salt and pepper to taste.

Continue to simmer for an additional 10 minutes. Set the pan aside and let cool slightly. Stir in the sour cream.

Melt 1 tablespoon of butter in skillet. Sauté crab meat until heated.

Spoon the crab into bowls. Pour soup gently on top. Garnish with crumbled bacon.

Serves 6

Note: For a real Texas kick, season to taste with hot red pepper sauce.

❖ *Third Course* ❖

Salad

Grapefruit and Avocado Salad with Poppy Seed Dressing

INGREDIENTS

3 ripe, sweet grapefruits
3 ripe avocados
6 leaves butter lettuce

DIRECTIONS

Cut the grapefruits in half crosswise. Use a knife to cut grapefruit sections from the membrane. Cut the avocados in half. Remove the seed. Peel off the skin. Slice avocados into long slices.

Poppy Seed Dressing

INGREDIENTS

⅓ cup sugar

½ cup vinegar

1 tsp. salt

1 tsp. ground dry mustard

1 cup olive oil

1 tbsp. poppy seeds

DIRECTIONS

Vigorously blend sugar, vinegar, salt, and mustard until the sugar dissolves. While still blending, slowly add the oil. When mixed, gently stir in the poppy seeds.

Makes approximately 1½ cups.

Place one butter lettuce leaf on individual plates. Place grapefruit sections and avocado slices on each lettuce leaf. Drizzle the poppy seeding dressing on top.

Serves 6

❖ *Fourth Course* ❖

Palate Cleanser

Blood Orange Ice

INGREDIENTS

3 cups freshly squeezed blood orange juice (or use tangerines or oranges)

½ cup sugar

Juice of 2 large limes—adjust based on sweetness of oranges—the
  sweeter the orange the more lime needed

2 tbsp. orange liqueur

1 tbsp. kirsch

Vodka (optional).

DIRECTIONS

In a mixing bowl, stir together 1 cup blood orange juice and the sugar until they are thoroughly dissolved. Stir in the remaining blood orange juice, lime juice, orange liqueur, and kirsch. Mix thoroughly.

Pour the mixture into gallon-size plastic zip bags. Before zipping closed, squeeze out as much air as possible. Freeze overnight.

Take the bags out of the freezer; manipulate the bags with your hands just a bit to loosen up the ice. With a fork, break up then ice into small chunks. (The consistency should be icy slush.) Spoon into glasses. Top with splash of vodka if desired.

Serves 6

❖ *Fifth Course* ❖

The Entrée

Fried Chicken with Sweet Jalapeño Mustard

INGREDIENTS

    2 cups panko
    2 cups bread crumbs
    Seasoned salt, salt and pepper to taste
    2 to 3 eggs, scrambled (can use yogurt or buttermilk instead)
    6 boneless, skinless chicken breasts (use kitchen mallet to pound
        into flat, even pieces)
    6 boneless, skinless chicken thighs (use kitchen mallet to pound
        into flat, even pieces)
    Vegetable oil for pan frying